She felt his arms come around her . . .

Suddenly she was surrounded in warmth and strength. His arms felt reassuringly powerful.

She felt his muscles tense as he gathered her close. Crowded against his jacket, she inhaled the scent of the thick fabric. It reminded her of the smell of the dock at their place in Marin County. A little bit of tar, a little bit of diesel. The smell of a working man.

"Here we go," he murmured, and slid her off the seat.

The white glare of camera lights made Rachel burrow her head against Fred's chest. She felt him adjust her hair so it covered her face. His glove brushed against her cheek in the process, an oddly gentle gesture.

In the safe darkness, nestled against his chest, she took deep breaths. One of the firemen dropped a tool, and the sharp clang triggered one of the memories she'd been keeping at bay while trapped in the limo. Her kidnapper had brought her food in a dented tin dish. For the first few days of her captivity, she'd flung it against the bars.

She began to tremble, and felt the fireman tighten his grip. *Forget those horrible memories.* It was history, long ago and far away. It had nothing to do with the bizarre freak event of a crane landing on their limo. *Focus on the handsome firefighter.*

Romances by Jennifer Bernard

THE NIGHT BELONGS TO FIREMAN
FOUR WEDDINGS AND A FIREMAN
HOW TO TAME A WILD FIREMAN
SEX AND THE SINGLE FIREMAN
HOT FOR FIREMAN
THE FIREMAN WHO LOVED ME

An E-Book Original from Avon Impulse

ONE FINE FIREMAN: A NOVELLA

the NIGHT BELONGS *to* FIREMAN

A BACHELOR FIREMEN NOVEL

Jennifer Bernard

A V O N

An Imprint of HarperCollins*Publishers*

This book is a work of fiction. References to real people, events, establishments, organizations, or locales are intended only to provide a sense of authenticity, and are used fictitiously. All other characters, and all incidents and dialogue, are drawn from the author's imagination and are not to be construed as real.

AVON BOOKS
An Imprint of HarperCollins*Publishers*
195 Broadway
New York, New York 10007

Copyright © 2014 by Jennifer Bernard
ISBN 978-0-06-227369-7
www.avonromance.com

First Avon Books mass market printing: October 2014

Avon Trademark Reg. U.S. Pat. Off. and in Other Countries, Marca Registrada, Hecho en U.S.A.
HarperCollins® is a registered trademark of HarperCollins Publishers.

Printed in the U.S.A.

10 9 8 7 6 5 4 3 2 1

I owe thanks to several highly skilled professionals who helped me with this book. First, as always, my gratitude to Fire Captain Rick Godinez for sharing his firefighting expertise. Captain Mike Mac Innes and Los Angeles Fire Station 88 "A" Platoon showed me the ropes of USAR techniques. K9 search specialist Deresa Kenney and Huck were kind enough to demonstrate how rescue dogs do their amazing work. Any mistakes are mine, not theirs. Thanks also to members of my Facebook page who gave invaluable feedback about the challenges of being married to a firefighter. Thank you to Lizbeth Selvig and Tam Linsey for being such wonderful beta readers. I'm so fortunate to work with Tessa Woodward, who is both brilliant and kind. Alexandra Machinist, I'm so grateful to have you in my corner.

Most of all, this is for Scott, who makes everything magic.

The
Night Belongs *to* Fireman

Chapter 1

*N*o woman could help but notice the two men who strode into the City Lights Grill just after midnight. Not with that amount of pure, knockout maleness walking through the door. One had the broken-nose look of a boxer, the other a more fresh-faced appeal, along with a slight limp. Both moved as if they knew exactly what to do with their bodies at all times.

The two, who happened to be off-duty firefighters, didn't register the influx of feminine attention, maybe because they were used to it. Or maybe because the rougher of the two firemen was too busy lecturing the other.

"The problem with you, Fred," said Mulligan, "is that you're too—"

"If you say 'nice,' you'll be on your ass in two seconds." Fred Breen was at the tail end of a rough night. "And you know I can do it."

"Yeah, *now* I know, since you finally let me in on

your big secret. But check it out." He reached for the trophy Fred dangled from one finger, as if he didn't even care about it. "Second place, it says here. You know who second place is for? Nice guys. Guys who don't have the killer instinct. Guys who give kittens CPR—"

"Don't start with the kittens again. They lived, didn't they?" Fred flung himself into a chair at a table in the corner, then winced. He'd just spent the evening getting the crap beat out of him at the Southern California Muay Thai Championships. Every bone in his body ached, and his muscles had gone into some sort of traumatic shock. "And did you happen to notice the guy who took first? Jet Li couldn't have beaten that guy. He's like a sixth-generation master."

"Excuses, excuses. My point is, I've noticed a theme in your life, Freddie-boy. Take Courtney—"

"Don't finish that sentence, Mulligan."

Even Mulligan, instigator that he was, backed off from the feral glare Fred aimed at him. "Pitcher?" he asked innocently.

"Yeah, sure." Beer or a full-body transplant, either would do.

Mulligan headed for the bar while Fred, nearly comatose, slumped further into his chair. He knew that no one at the firehouse liked his ex-girlfriend Courtney, which was *exactly* why he hadn't told anyone they'd broken up. He was tired of everyone's opinions on his life. Including Courtney's. She insisted on calling their current breakup a "trial separation." Getting beat up by Muay Thai masters was easier than ending things with Courtney.

He flexed his left elbow gingerly. It seemed to still function, and apart from the bruises on his rib cage, he'd gotten off pretty easily. His face showed nothing worse than exhaustion. He didn't ever notice the pain during a bout. But afterward . . . that was a different story. That was why he trained only during his four days off from his firefighting duties. It took time to recover.

Why, he asked himself for the thousandth time, did he insist on throwing himself into that ring? What did he get out of it besides bruises and stiffness? Well, and the secret knowledge that he could disable every guy in the San Gabriel Fire Department. After all his training, he could probably even beat his brothers, who were all in various branches of the military.

He planted the trophy, a brass-plated karate figure mounted on a square base, in the middle of the table and glared at it. *Second place.* Never mind that second place was the highest he'd ever ranked. Never mind that Namsaknoi Yudthagarngam was essentially unbeatable. Never mind that his brothers wouldn't take him seriously even if he had won. Was Mulligan right, and he was doomed to second place because of his—

His thoughts were interrupted by the sudden whisking away of the trophy. He looked up to see a girl in a bridal veil brandishing it in the air. Under the veil she had masses of wild dark hair and looked like big trouble.

"Cindy Barstow is hereby awarded the title of Most Bodacious Bride!" She mimicked a trumpet call to the women crowding around her, one of whom, a curvy blonde, raised her arms in a victory gesture and made a "gimme" gesture at the trophy. The dark-haired girl in the veil then bent to whisper in Fred's ear. "Sorry, it was a dare. You can't deny a bride during her bachelorette party."

Temporarily stunned by the sudden onslaught

of femininity—and the clean, rosewater fragrance of the girl's hair—Fred warily surveyed the women surrounding him. Four of them, all dressed in skimpy party dresses and sparkly tiaras. All seemed seriously buzzed.

With perfect timing, Mulligan reappeared with a foaming pitcher of beer. "Ladies," he said in greeting. "If you're here to celebrate, welcome aboard."

"What are we celebrating?" an Asian girl in a hot-pink tube dress asked. "I mean, besides the tragic loss of an exceptional single lady to the enslavement known as matrimony?"

"I like your style, babe." Mulligan gave her a once-over. "You busy later?"

"Oh, I plan to get busy later." She flipped her hair. "But probably not with you."

"Ouch." Mulligan mimed a shot to the heart. Then he plucked the trophy from the dark-haired girl's hands and transferred it to the Asian girl. "There you go. Prize for best putdown."

"Hey!" The girl in the veil squawked and dove after the trophy. "I stole that fair and square."

The girl in hot pink held on tight to it. "Back off, Rachel. I earned it with my outstanding bitchiness."

Laughing, the two girls pretended to tussle over the silly prize. *Rachel*, thought Fred. *Her name is Rachel*. The other two girls took sides, raucously rooting them on. *Oh yes. Seriously buzzed.*

Fred, watching their antics, heaved a sigh, which hurt his ribs. He was too sore for this. But he'd been carrying that trophy and he knew how cheaply it was constructed. He knew what would happen next. He rose to his feet, wincing all the way, and stationed himself strategically behind the girl in the veil. Sure enough, the thing flew apart, the statuette in the hands of Hot Pink, its base in the hands of Bridal Veil.

Rachel stumbled backward, right into Fred's arms. He absorbed the impact of her petite body and sputtered against a mouthful of bridal veil.

"Oops! I'm so sorry!" The girl righted herself, pushing away from him. Suddenly his arms held no silky, warm presence. He swiped the veil out of his vision and found himself looking into wide, concerned eyes of an unusual deep indigo color. Two spots of pink burned in her cheeks. "Are you okay?" she asked him. "Did I hurt you? You look like you're in pain."

"I'm fine," croaked Fred, whose ribs were throbbing. "Are you okay?"

"Just embarrassed." She leaned toward him intimately, a little wobbly. He caught that fresh fragrance again, like morning rain in a rose garden. "I really shouldn't ever, ever drink. And usually I don't. But it's a special occasion, you know. And Cindy made me wear the veil, which means I have to do what she says. According to her rules. 'Cuz she's the bride."

Mulligan came over and clapped a hand on Fred's shoulder, harder than he had to. "Freddie can take it. He's a stud. That's what we call him, actually. Stud. Not just any guy can win this." He hoisted the trophy high in the air. "Champion in the Betty Crocker Bake-off."

Fred shot him a baleful look.

"That doesn't look like someone baking," pointed out the curvy blond girl, Cindy the bride. "Unless that's a rolling pin in his pants."

"Fred," Mulligan whispered loudly in his ear, "I'm in love. Can we party with these girls for a while?"

Rachel overheard. "No," she said. "Absolutely not. Right, girls? Bachelorette parties aren't supposed to have *boys*."

"Unless they're strippers," said the fourth girl,

whose short hair looked like a spiky red dandelion. "Are you guys strippers?"

"Something could probably be arranged," said Mulligan. "Wouldn't be the first time." He jerked his head meaningfully in Fred's direction. "You should get him to tell you about it."

True, Fred had once taken part in a bachelorette party strip show. Never to be repeated, he'd vowed. "Mulligan, sit down and shut the fuck up," he told the other firefighter.

"Ooh," said Hot Pink. "Are you going to let him talk to you that way, big guy?"

Fred shot Mulligan a warning look. He was nearing the end of his tether. Sore, bruised, and he hadn't even had a sip of that beer yet. Plus he was hungry. True, the dark-haired girl, Rachel, had felt wonderful falling into his arms. If it were just the two of them, alone, maybe with a hot tub and a bottle of ibuprofen . . . some Tiger Balm . . . massage oil . . . Not that he was thinking *that*, no way, not with Courtney still calling every few days. He wanted out, but he didn't want to hurt Courtney.

"Yes, I am," said Mulligan, dropping into a chair. "He's more of a badass than he looks. Nice seeing you, girls. Best wishes on your upcoming nuptials."

"Nuptials!" the redhead shouted. "Someone said 'nuptials.' You know what that means. Everyone do a shot!"

The other girls groaned and they all fluttered away toward the bar.

As she left, Rachel flipped her veil over her shoulder, catching Fred in the corner of his eye. He clapped his hand over it, while she muttered a horrified apology, then fled.

Fred sank into his seat.

"You owe me big-time," said Mulligan grimly. "Those girls are hot."

"Just pass me the beer." But even as he drank, Fred couldn't help watching the girl in the bridal veil choke down her shot. She really shouldn't be drinking. With a tiny frame like hers, she probably couldn't handle more than a teaspoon of tequila. Maybe he should keep an eye on her. Which would be easier if his eye weren't throbbing from getting nicked by her damn veil.

"Here's what we're going to do," Mulligan was saying. "We're going to organize a firehouse fight club, and take bets. I'll put all my money on you and say I'm rooting for the underdog, and . . ."

Fred tuned out the other firefighter as Rachel slid off her stool, steadied herself, then set off across the bar. She seemed to be headed for the door in the far corner, the one with the red exit sign. Maybe she'd decided to go home. Not a bad idea, in his opinion, except the path to the exit took her right through a game of darts, to which she seemed completely oblivious.

Abandoning Mulligan, he dashed across the room and whirled the girl out of range of the flying darts.

"I . . . I was going to the bathroom," she stammered, looking bewildered.

"Bathroom's this way." He spun her around so she faced the other direction. "Darts are the other way. Can you manage it or do you need an escort?"

She bristled. "I'm not going to the bathroom with some strange guy I don't even—"

"Not me. One of your friends."

"Oh." Her face flamed. "You must think I'm a total ditz."

"Not at all," he said politely, which made her face

turn even more crimson. She tore her arm from his grasp and headed for the bathroom, indignantly muttering something about overprotective men.

Well, if that was the thanks he was going to get . . .

Shrugging, he returned to Mulligan, who drained his mug and eyed him with amusement. "At least she didn't whack you this time. So back to fight club. It's not a bad way to prove up. Show the crew you're more than a kitten lover. Let that pretty face of yours fool them, then bring down the hammer. If I hadn't seen you in that ring, I wouldn't have believed it, Fred." His cell phone rang. As Mulligan muttered into his phone, Fred watched the dart players finish a game, then start another, then finish that one.

Mulligan ended his call. "I might have to hedge my bets, though, in case you decide to pull your punches. It's that nice guy thing again. How do I know you aren't going to wuss out and . . ."

"Hang on."

Rachel had been gone too long. He just knew it. Leaving Mulligan in mid-sentence, he hurried to the dark hallway where the men's and women's bathrooms were located. Sure enough, there she was, a silvery sprite in the dim fluorescents, bending over a guy who knelt on the gritty, sawdust-covered floor. His chinos and stained crewneck sweater screamed vomiting frat boy.

"Are you all right?" Rachel was asking him in a concerned voice, seemingly oblivious to the fact that she was alone in a dark hallway with a drunk.

"Awesome." The guy swiped a hand across his face. "Hey, you're pretty. Gimme a kiss."

"Uh . . . no thanks." She started to straighten up, but the guy latched on to her arm.

"Come on, baby." He sang, "You can leave your

veil on . . ." and tugged her so she lost her balance and started to fall on top of him.

Fred didn't wait another second. He strode to her side, swooped her out of the drunk guy's reach, and whisked her down the hallway. Her rosewater scent teased his nostrils; he resisted the urge to bend closer to sniff her hair, a move that might shift him from rescuer to stalker.

With her dark curls falling back over his arm, she tilted her head back to glare at him. "I had the situation handled."

"You're welcome," he said grimly.

She seemed to puzzle over that for a second. "I guess I was supposed to thank you."

"Some people would at least consider it."

Her quick shimmer of a smile cast sparks of light into their grungy surroundings. "Who are you, anyway? Why do you keep"—she gestured wildly, bonking him on the chin—"popping up like this? Did my father hire you?"

"What?" The throb in his chin distracted Fred from her odd question.

"He insisted on hiring the limo driver, but he didn't tell me about hiring anyone else."

He had no idea what she was talking about, but she seemed to forget about the subject anyway. He headed down the hall, toward the bar. Surprisingly, she didn't ask to be put down, and he didn't offer. She needed to be with her friends. And for some reason, he needed to make sure she was safe. Besides, it felt good, holding her in his arms, so good he sort of lost track of time. The hallway seemed to go on forever, and yet end too soon.

When they stepped back into the bar, the blonde, Cindy, spotted them and came hurtling over, shrieking bloody murder.

"What happened? Are you okay, Rachel?"

"I'm fine," she grumbled, as Fred set her on her feet. "Someone threw up in the hallway and tried to come on to me. Apparently this guy"—she jerked a thumb over her shoulder, jabbing him in the chest, making him wince—"thought it was a federal crime."

The spiky redhead appeared at Cindy's shoulder. "The most important question is, how's the veil? It's my turn to wear it."

Rachel whipped the veil off her head, dragging long strands of her hair along with it. "No, the important question is why this complete stranger thinks I can't take care of myself."

Now that was just too much. Fred threw up his hands. "Really? The important thing isn't nearly walking into a game of darts? Or worse?"

Rachel, struggling to free her hair from the veil, turned to her friends. "Don't I have enough people watching every little thing I do? Why *him*?"

Exasperated, Fred reached over and untangled her veil from her hair. "You are the strangest girl I've ever met."

"What kind of thing is that to say—"

"All right, all right." Cindy grabbed her hand. "Let's go. Limo's waiting." She bundled Rachel behind her and addressed Fred. "Thanks for everything, attractive stranger. She's usually such a sweet girl, believe it or not. Devotes her life to helping animals, will do anything for a friend, even drink too much champagne during her friend's last night of freedom . . . okay, we're going now."

They all waved good-bye and flocked to the door. After they left, the entire room seemed to go dim.

Back at the table, Mulligan tossed some money down and pushed back his chair. "Nice move, bro.

You scared away the only girls worth talking to in this whole joint."

"I didn't scare anyone away. I rescued her from being slobbered on by a vomit-covered idiot." Fred worked at a knot in his neck, trying to understand how the night had begun with a mauling in the fight ring and somehow gone downhill from there.

"Details, details," said Mulligan. "Come on, let's ghost. I want to see what's rolling at Firefly."

"Nah, man. I'm done. If that bout wasn't enough to do me in, that girl was. She got in more hits than Namsaknoi." He tenderly felt his jawbone, where she'd bonked him in the hallway.

Mulligan cackled. "You should date her. I can see you with a girl like that. She'd keep things hopping."

"*Not* going to happen. The girl I go for is going to be nothing like her."

"I wouldn't say *nothing* like her," mused Mulligan as they headed for the exit. "She'll probably wear a veil at the wedding."

"Nothing like her," said Fred firmly. "What kind of woman nearly walks into a game of darts?"

"Someone fun, someone who lets loose once in a while. Someone who's not Courtney. Someone who doesn't think she's superior to everyone else in the damn world."

Mulligan's lip curled. The guys really didn't like Courtney. Sometimes Fred thought he would have called it off much sooner if he hadn't wanted to prove them wrong. Dumb, since they *weren't* exactly wrong. "Courtney," he pointed out, "is proud of my fight trophies. She wouldn't rip them apart." He gave a mournful glance at the dismantled statuette in his hand.

"Right. She'd probably polish them every day in

their little glass case," said Mulligan. "Because she's a control freak."

"And Courtney wouldn't be caught dead alone in a dark hallway with a drunk. What was that girl thinking?" He followed Mulligan through the door into the cool of midnight. The loud music from the bar chased them, the wail of U2's "Mysterious Ways" suddenly stifled as the door slammed shut.

"Seems like you were watching every move she made."

"Someone had to," he grumbled, trying to remember where he'd parked.

"Holy shit," Mulligan breathed.

Fred was still scanning the street for his truck. He remembered parking next to a construction barricade. The City Lights Grill squatted in the shadow of the old City Hall, which had partially burned a couple of years ago. They were finally starting to rebuild, and during the day this entire area was a construction zone mess. At night, it was a ghost town of earth movers, backhoes, and cranes.

"There it is," Fred said, finally spotting his Toyota pickup and moving toward it. But Mulligan snaked out a hand and stopped him cold. The big guy's phone was at his ear.

"Look," he said, and pointed up the street, to the end of the block.

The sight made Fred's blood run cold. Illuminated by the chill light of a streetlamp, a white stretch limousine was stopped in the middle of the street. Its roof was crushed by the arm of a crane, awkward and ungainly, like a metallic giraffe that had toppled over. Steam hissed from the engine. If the crane had hit the gas tank, it could explode at any moment.

"Calling 911?" he asked Mulligan.

"Yup."

The door opened, spilling a blast of music and a handful of people. "Keep everyone back. I'm going in." Fred ran toward the limo.

Chapter 2

As the fire department's newest Urban Search and Rescue member, Fred would have gotten the call if he'd been on duty. Of course he would have been in Truck 1, with all his gear, not to mention the Jaws of Life, air bags, and other tools to extract people from wrecked cars. But there wasn't time to worry about that. He had to do what he could right here, right now.

As he got closer, he saw that the telescoping steel structure of the crane arm had struck toward the rear of the limo, pinning the passenger doors. The truck to which it was mounted lay on its side, its bed abandoned. Whatever idiot had been operating a crane truck at night had fled. A pallet of something, possibly shingles, had spilled across the sidewalk on the other side of the street.

The driver's side door of the limo hung open and a man in a dark suit and cap knelt on the pavement.

Blood ran down the side of his face. Fred ran to meet him.

"Did you turn off the engine?"

When the driver just stared at him blankly, Fred crawled into the driver's seat and turned the key in the ignition. If there was a gas leak, the smallest spark from the engine could send the limo sky-high.

When the world didn't explode, Fred let out a breath and extracted himself from the vehicle. The driver was still staring at him with a look of confusion. Fred gave him a quick assessment. Dazed, disoriented, thready pulse. Very possible head injury.

"In the back. Party," he told Fred. "Girls."

"I know. I'm a firefighter, and so's my friend back there. We'll take care of it. Can you make it to the sidewalk?"

The driver shook his head. "I can help."

Absolutely not. Fred didn't need an injured civilian getting in the way. "No need. The fire department's been called, they'll be here any minute. The paramedics will want to take a look at you." He took off his sweater, balled it up, and pressed it against the cut on the man's head. "Keep pressure on that wound." He lifted the man's hand to take the place of his own, and shifted to the firm, matter-of-fact tone that he always used at fire calls. "Sir, please sit down right away so we can do our job."

The driver toddled off, slumping onto the sidewalk with a moan.

Fred did a thorough check under the vehicle, searching for signs of a fuel leak. When he found none, he turned his attention to the best way to get the girls out of the mangled limousine. He could grab a tire iron from his truck and knock out a window, or maybe pop open a door.

Oddly enough, the front of the vehicle didn't look so bad. The rear looked like a crushed eggshell, but luckily, it was an extra-long limo and the middle didn't seem too severely impacted. As he'd been trained, he did a quick assessment of the crane's stability. If it was going to shift again, he needed to be prepared. But the long, gray metal struts of the crane seemed rock-solid, as if the piece of machinery would never budge from its new resting place.

Now for the passengers.

He crouched next to the passenger side rear window. It was halfway open, which was lucky because he'd be surprised if anything worked in this car anymore. Inside, the four girls from the bachelorette party were squished together in the long, leather-covered seat, bent slightly forward, the crushed roof pressing against their heads. Rachel, crammed against the driver's side door, was the only one still conscious. Maybe her small size had kept her from getting knocked out. She was hyperventilating, her breath coming in quick, wheezing gasps. She turned her head from its awkward position and fixed him with enormous eyes, purple in the pale illumination from the streetlights outside.

"Can you . . . we have to get . . . help," she gasped.

"I'm going to get you out," he said, sticking with the fire scene voice that always worked magic with panicking accident victims. "But I'm going to need your help, okay? I need you to take a good long breath."

He held her gaze until she gulped some air, and saw the most extreme edge of her panic subside.

"That's good. That's very good. The best thing you can do is keep calm. What's your name? We were never formally introduced," he added with a smile.

She managed a whisper of a smile in response. "R . . . Rachel."

Thankfully, she seemed to be alert and not disoriented. His guess would be that her severely dilated pupils were due to panic, not a head injury. But panic could lead to injury, so keeping her calm was all-important. A glance at the door behind her told him it was much more damaged than the one on the passenger side. He'd have to work from this side, leaving her extraction for last. He hoped she was okay with that.

"Rachel. That's a pretty name."

A quick flash of incredulity crossed her face. *Idiot.* She wasn't a four-year-old. She didn't need her name complimented. Still, any expression besides hysteria was a plus, so he considered it a win.

He shifted his attention to the interior of the limo, assessing the conditions for extraction. The air reeked of alcohol. Nope, a four-year-old, she definitely wasn't. They must have been having quite a party.

"Don't judge. It's just champagne," Rachel said, sounding annoyed. Good. Annoyance was a lot better than panic. "Cindy's wedding's in two days, so you have to get her out of here. She's okay, isn't she?"

"One thing at a time. Are you injured, Rachel? Does anything hurt?"

"Oh." She examined her left arm, which looked as if the limo door had nearly squashed it. "Barely bruised. I was watching out the window and saw this truck tipping over and this huge construction thing falling. I tried to warn the driver, but . . . I'd know if anything major was broken, right?"

"Possibly." He didn't want to explain that adrenaline masked the pain of a trauma.

She glanced at him sharply, then dragged in a long, deep breath. He noticed that her hands were clenched so tightly on her seat belt that her finger-nails were white. "Really, I'm okay. I don't think I'm hurt."

"Good. Then let's get you guys out of here. My name's Fred, by the way. I'm a firefighter with special training in situations like these."

Of all things, she let out a burst of laughter. Slightly hysterical laughter, he noticed, as if she were clinging desperately to her control. "You're Fred the Fireman?"

"Yes." Though he wasn't sure why that was so funny.

"Do you know Thomas the Tank?"

Oh. Now he saw what had set her off. "I'm familiar with his work, yes."

Her pale lips curved into a smile, or probably the closest thing she could manage at the moment. "And you have special training in smushed limos?"

He gave her a rueful smile. Maybe a little entertainment would help her deal with the situation. "Among other things, sure."

"What exactly is your training? Because from where I'm sitting, things are looking a little sketchy. How many situations like this have you been in? I mean, kind of like this?"

Fred, reaching an arm inside the half-open window to feel for the redhead's pulse, clamped down on his irritation. "I'm certified in Rescue Systems, stuff like high-angle and low-angle rescues, trench rescues, confined space rescues, swiftwater, personal water craft, structural collapse, rope rescue, GPS awareness, and Instructor 1A and 1B, all of which qualifies me for Urban Search and Rescue, which is handy in an earthquake zone. But do you think we could discuss my career later? Right now I'd really like to get you out of here."

"Oh. Right. Obviously you're highly qualified. I'm sorry, I'm a little . . ." She took another deep breath. "I have a problem with small spaces. A big problem."

The tension in her voice made him look at her more closely. He hoped she wasn't going to start panicking again.

"Keep looking out the window, Rachel. That might help. We're going to do this as quickly as possible."

She turned her head, fixing her gaze on the world outside the window, and seemed to calm down. "I'm fine. I promise."

Fred nodded, and stood up. He stepped away from the limo to consult with Mulligan, who had run up behind him.

"I'd feel better if we could shore up the crane, just in case," he told the other firefighter.

"Good thing it's a construction zone," Mulligan said.

"Exactly what I was thinking. I have a tire iron in my truck. I'll see if I can pop the doors. You go look for some two-by-fours or something." He spotted a couple leaving the bar. They gaped at the scene, the woman whipping out her phone to take pictures. "Go. I'll see if I can keep the area clear."

Mulligan ran off, hurdling over one of the construction barricades. Fred spotted some orange cones and, at a fast jog, planted one at the head of the street and one at the end. The couple backed off. On the way past his truck, he grabbed a tire iron.

When he came back to the limo, at first he thought Rachel had fallen into unconsciousness. But her head swung around as soon as she heard him. The sight of her deep purple eyes made him blink. She looked so fierce, teeth gritted, the tendons of her neck wire-tight.

Normally he'd try to get the more seriously injured victims out first, but he didn't want a panic attack on his hands. He'd better get her out first, before she lost it completely.

"I'm going to try popping your door with a tire iron," he told her. "I think I can get it open enough to pull you out."

"What about my friends?"

"I'll get them from the other side."

She frowned. "But they're more badly hurt. You should get them out first. I'm fine. I got this. Maybe I can even help from here."

He felt a sudden shot of admiration for her. Her mouth was still white around the edges, but she was holding herself together with a steely will. Maybe she wasn't the airhead he'd taken her for. Almost unconsciously, he found himself checking out the rest of her. Her wavy black hair was drenched with sweat and clung to her forehead in dramatically thick strands.

"Think hard before you offer that," he told her. "It means you'll be stuck in here longer, and you mentioned not liking small spaces. I don't know how long the extraction will take."

Cindy moaned, and opened her eyes. "Rach? What happened?"

"Shhh," Rachel murmured. "There was an accident. But the firemen are here and they're going to get us out."

"Accident? There can't be an accident. I'm about to get married!"

Rachel met Fred's eyes over Cindy's head. "I can handle it," she told him, her face set with determination. "Get the others out. I can help."

Fred made the decision instantly. Some accident

victims made the process more complicated, but Rachel seemed strong enough to be an asset.

Sirens sounded. He'd never been so glad to hear them in his life. Lights flashing, Engine 1 pulled up at the curb a short distance away, a paramedic van close behind. Firefighters in turnouts jumped out of the rig. The C shift was on duty, which meant Captain Jeb Stone, heading up the engine company, would be the incident commander. Paramedics ran to help the limo driver.

Fred quickly briefed Captain Stone. "I suggest attempting extraction from the passenger side, after we get some air bags going under the crane. We have four females trapped, two are unconscious, injuries unknown. Tell the paramedics to set up for C-spine."

Captain Stone nodded, then relayed the instructions on the tactical channel. "You want to stay with the victims?" he asked Fred, who nodded firmly. Technically, he wasn't on shift, but the hell with that. "Good," Stone said. "Keep them calm and see if you can assess their condition a little better."

Fred turned back to the window of the limo and spoke to Cindy. "Cindy, I need you to tell me where it hurts."

She rolled her head to the side and, still clearly disoriented, peered at him. "Hey, you're the one with the trophy."

"*Was* the one with the trophy." Come to think of it, he had no idea where the thing had gone. He'd flung it away when he'd gone running toward the limo. "Can you move your limbs freely?"

"Limbs? Rachel, why's he asking about my limbs? Who are you, anyway?"

Trying not to laugh, he pulled out his best reassuring smile. "Just call me Fred the Fireman."

Rachel's snort of laughter made his heart give a silly little jolt.

Rachel managed to keep it together by the skin of her teeth. Pressed between Cindy and the limo door, her trembling body drenched with the sweat of fear, she forced herself to shift her focus from her trapped state. Every time she felt the walls of the limo close in and the panic rise, she looked at Fred the Fireman. Something about him made her feel better, as if everything would—or at least might—be okay. After all, he'd intervened on her behalf a couple times already. She'd thought he was attractive back in the City Lights, but now, using him as an anchor against the tug of terror, she gave him much closer attention.

His eyes were the kind of deep, velvety brown that always seemed to reflect some kind of light. Shining eyes, she thought vaguely. No bad guy can fake *shining* eyes. She figured he was maybe a few years older than she was. Lines crinkled at the corners of his eyes when he smiled. And he smiled so easily. It gave her a warm feeling—he wouldn't be smiling so readily if things were really bad. He'd lost the brown Henley he'd worn earlier, which left him in nothing but a white T-shirt, now streaked with grease and dirt.

And he seemed so capable. Not show-offy, just smart and skillful. The other firefighters, who were all a blur behind him, seemed to defer to him and respect what he said. One of them brought him a bulky firefighter's jacket with reflective stripes and some gloves. He pulled them on.

"All right, then," he told her and Cindy. "The trick here is to get you out without hurting you worse.

Just so you guys know, the crane is being shored up to keep it from shifting once we start the extraction. We're going to open the door now."

Rachel just had time to wonder how on earth he was going to open a door that had been partially flattened when another firefighter heaved into view a giant tool that looked like a claw. After some loud, horrible mechanical screeching, the door was lifted away and Fred the Fireman was crouching next to Feather. An intense desire to flee the stifling, stinking deathtrap of a limo grabbed hold of her. If she could just get out, fight free, run and run until no one could catch her . . .

She yanked herself back to reality. She was here, now, not in that other bad, horrible place. And her friends needed her. If there was one thing she would never, ever do, it would be to leave behind someone who was trapped, or someone who needed help. She'd die first.

Focusing carefully, she unclenched her fists, where her nails had dug gouges into her palms. She took hold of Cindy's hand in both of hers, looked into Fred the Fireman's kind eyes, and said something she rarely, if ever, said to anyone.

"Tell us what to do."

Rachel made it through the next half hour on a combination of sheer willpower and random babbling. Every nerve in her body screamed to get out of that limousine, but she refused to give in to the panic. Cindy passed out again, but Rachel managed to stay alert while Fred, with the help of another firefighter, maneuvered Liza and Feather out of the car. As soon as each girl was freed, Fred handed her off to a team of paramedics who whisked her away on a gurney. As each moment passed, the desire to be free of the space grew stronger. If she gave in to her deepest primal instincts, she'd be clawing her way past her best friend, broken bones be damned.

But she didn't. When it was Cindy's turn, she tried to help, though she had almost no room to move. Fred had to come halfway into the limo to operate, and this close she saw sweat beading his face and tension in his jaw. He looked so young for such a big responsibility as saving four people's lives.

"How old are you?" she asked him without thinking.

He ignored her, rightfully so, focusing his entire attention on maneuvering Cindy's limp form into his grip. She liked his face, with its square jaw and nicely shaped mouth. *Nicely shaped mouth?* Was this really the right moment for that kind of observation? Hell, she had to distract herself somehow.

"I'm sorry. That wasn't an appropriate question. Clearly you know what you're doing. And I hate it when people jump to conclusions when they don't really know you. Don't you?"

His jaw tightened.

"And now I'm making it worse. I'm really sorry. I'm not myself at the moment. Although you probably wouldn't like me when I am myself either. My father says I'm headstrong. But that's just because I don't do whatever he tells me. Don't get me wrong. I do some things he tells me. Most things, actually. And that's probably what's wrong with my life, right there. Do you think you could give me something to make me stop babbling?"

A smile pulled at the corner of his mouth, and when he looked up, Cindy securely in his arms, the light in his eyes made her momentarily breathless.

"Don't worry. Nothing you say during an emergency counts. It's like Vegas."

"What happens in the car crash stays in the car crash?"

"Exactly. I'm ready to take Cindy out now."

Rachel felt cool air against her side as Fred bore Cindy toward the door. She could practically smell the freedom. Once Cindy was out, she could scramble out of here and run, run, run . . .

Too bad she couldn't explain so Fred the Fireman could understand. *See, when I was eight, I was kidnapped and held for ransom in a cage the size of a cereal box, and ever since then I've been a little sketched out by tight spaces.*

"One more thing," Fred added as he neared the door. "You'll probably be tempted to get the hell out of here once Cindy's gone. Please don't do that. You might have injuries you don't realize. The safest course is to take it nice and slow and controlled. And let me do all the work."

She nodded. And she certainly intended to do as he asked. Fred, unlike many people in her life, had proven himself to be completely trustworthy up to this point. But when Cindy's warm, suffocating weight had been lifted off her, giddy relief flooded through her in a hot rush. Suddenly all her carefully maintained control shattered. She crawled across the seat toward the gaping hole torn in the side of the limo.

Fred was still blocking the door—or the space where the door had been—with his bulky fireman's jacket. He was saying something to someone but everything was just a buzzing in her ears. She had to get out, *out*. She aimed a shove at his back but her hand landed on the rear of his jeans. He turned, looking down at her with an exasperated expression.

"What are you doing?"

"I have to . . . I need to . . . get me out . . ." The air felt like cement moving in and out of her lungs.

"I told you to wait."

The censure in his voice was exactly the right thing to bring her to her senses. "Right. And I did. Now I'm ready to leave," she announced, clinging to her dignity with all her might.

Her efforts didn't seem to impress him at all. He looked amused by her declaration. "You can leave. I promise. I'm not aiming to keep you in a wrecked limo all night. I was trying to deal with these reporters out here. I don't know how they got this close, but they did. I blame Ella Joy; that woman could talk her way into a mama bear's den. Anyway, come on out, but you'd better be ready to be famous." He shifted to the side, and she saw something even worse than being trapped in a small space.

Camera crews.

She shrank back in the limo, chills racing up her spine. "No," she told Fred. "I'm not getting out until they leave."

He did a double take. "Excuse me? A second ago you were practically mauling me to get out."

She tried to answer but couldn't, emotions seesawing through her.

"I'm confused," he said. "What's going on?"

Digging deep, she dredged up enough control to answer. "I won't go on camera. Either make them go away or I'm staying in here." She gave him her most mulish look, the one that made her father practically lose his mind. But in this case, her father would agree with her one hundred percent. She couldn't let the cameras get a shot of her.

"I have a better idea. Let me handle this." Fred crouched down and beckoned to her, opening both his arms. "If you turn your head against my chest, no one will be able to see your face. I'll put you right in the ambulance, and you'll be off to the hospital before anyone's the wiser. Okay?"

She stared at him, feeling as if he were the only solid thing in the swirling fog of panic. She took in the warmth of his dark eyes, the firmness of his jaw. If she didn't get out of this limo soon, she might seriously lose it. If she could trust anyone, surely it would be this kindhearted, if slightly annoyed, firefighter.

She nodded, then felt his arms come around her. It happened so swiftly it took her breath away. Suddenly she was surrounded in warmth and strength. His arms, under the padded jacket, felt reassuringly powerful. The guy was strong, she realized. He didn't look like a huge, muscular guy, but he didn't blink at carrying her weight. She felt his muscles tense as he gathered her close. Crowded against his jacket, she inhaled the scent of the thick fabric. It reminded her of the smell of the dock at their place in Marin County. A little bit of tar, a little bit of diesel. The smell of a working man.

"Here we go," he murmured, and slid her off the seat.

Chapter 3

The white glare of camera lights made Rachel burrow her head against Fred's chest. She felt him adjust her hair so it covered her face. His glove brushed against her cheek in the process, an oddly gentle touch.

In the safe darkness, nestled against his chest, she took deep breaths of the night air, saturated with the comforting scent of Fred's jacket. Thank God, thank God she was out of there. She couldn't go through that again, couldn't *ever* go through that again.

One of the firemen dropped a tool, and the sharp clang triggered one of the memories she'd been keeping at bay while trapped in the limo. Her kidnapper had brought her food in a dented tin dish. For the first few days of her captivity, she'd flung it against the bars. Headstrong even at eight years old. Later, she'd given in and eaten his food.

She began to tremble, and felt the fireman tighten his grip. The gentle up-and-down bounce of his stride was surprisingly soothing. *Forget those horrible memories.* It was history, long ago and far away. It had nothing to do with the bizarre freak event of a crane landing on their limo. *Focus on the handsome firefighter.*

Outside the safe circle of Fred the Fireman's arms, reporters were shouting questions.

"How long were you trapped inside? What's your name? Is it true you were on your way to a bachelorette party? Did you ever expect something like that to happen? It's a miracle everyone survived the crash, do you have anything to say to the heroes who rescued you?"

"Keep back," she heard Fred say in a commanding tone. "She doesn't want to talk. If she changes her mind, she'll contact you."

"Can you at least tell us her name?"

"You know I don't have clearance to talk to the media. We have a PIO for that. Contact him if you have any more questions."

"Come on, Stud," came a sultry female voice. "You gotta give us something here. This is the biggest story we've had in months. We're calling it the Miracle on Main."

"You're a genius, Ella Joy. How do you do it? Year after year after year after—"

"Very cute, Stud. You're going to pay for that one." But from the way the reporter teased him, Rachel had the feeling she liked him. And why not? He'd just rescued four damsels in distress, practically single-handedly. Now he was going above and beyond the call of duty by shielding her from the cameras. And Lord, he was strong. He didn't even seem to be breathing hard after everything he'd done.

She heard the sound of a car door open, then found herself peering inside another confined space, this one packed with medical equipment, IVs, a gurney, a paramedic. Suddenly the craving for freedom overwhelmed her. *No. No. Absolutely no. I can't go in there.* Like a wild animal, barely aware of what she was doing, she pushed against Fred's hard chest and wrenched herself out of his hold.

"What the hell?" he exclaimed, but her feet were already on the ground. One of her strappy sandals slipped under her foot, and she staggered. Fred reached for her, but she yanked her arm away so he couldn't grab it. Her flying hand accidentally slammed against his nose, and he jerked back.

"What are you doing?" He sounded more shocked than angry about his nose.

He grabbed for her, but she backed away from him. Even in her runaway panic, she remembered to keep her face turned away from the cameras, and her hair loose across her features. The reporters might think she was a madwoman, but at least they wouldn't get a shot of her face. She launched herself away from the cameras, away from Fred, dodging other firefighters who tried to stop her, scrambling past the orange cones that marked the perimeter of the accident.

She ran and ran, just as she had when she'd scrambled out of that warehouse prison. When she reached the next street, out of sight of the nosy media and the well-meaning firefighters, she slowed to a fast walk, taking big gulps of the night air. Her heart was still racing with the aftereffects of her terror. Her skin felt clammy with sweat, not exercise sweat but the fight-or-flight kind.

Fight or flight—or *both*, in her case. Looking down at herself, she heaved a giant sigh. Flecks of blood dotted her silver mesh party dress. One of her sandal straps had broken, making her drag her left foot. She probably looked like a runaway from a home for deranged debutantes.

She wondered what time it was. The occasional car rumbled past her, but the street was mostly deserted, the streetlamps granting pools of amber light to the sidewalk. Even though San Gabriel was generally safe, she had no business walking alone out here.

She should call Marsden for a pickup. The security guard was on call until the limo brought her home, which wasn't going to happen now. Luckily, her little chain purse still dangled against her hip. She'd call in a minute, once she'd gotten hold of herself. Once she could face getting into another vehicle.

Tremors kept traveling through her body. Had she really punched Fred the Fireman in the nose before taking off as if the flying monkeys of Oz were after her? Now he probably thought she was bipolar *and* paranoid. She winced, remembering the shock on his face as her hand connected with his nose. It hadn't been a hard strike, more of a glancing blow, surely not enough to actually break his nose. *Sorry, Fred the Fireman. Sorry about the nose. Sorry I won't ever see you again.*

Reaching Vista Street, she turned right, toward her apartment building. It was only a few miles away. Surely she could face a short ride with Marsden at the wheel. She'd open all the windows and keep her head halfway out the window, like a dog enjoying the rush of wind against her face.

Okay, she could admit it. Her behavior wasn't always what most people would call normal. But she'd learned over the years not to judge her occasionally weird reactions. Her only real regret was punching Fred, who'd been extremely cute and kind and strong and someone she could absolutely develop an enormous crush on given the opportunity. Which she wouldn't have, thanks to her temporary return to Crazytown.

She wondered why the reporter had called him Stud. Most likely because she wasn't the only one who'd noticed his thoroughly obvious hotness. *Put him out of your mind*, she advised herself. Punching someone who's trying to rescue you, then fleeing with no explanation isn't the recommended method for attracting a guy.

With a big sigh, she dug out her cell phone and called Marsden. "The limo had an accident," she started to explain, her voice wobbling, the shakes starting again.

"Stay right where you are. I'm on my way." His gruff, worried voice nearly made her cry.

"I'm at—"

"I have your location." He ended the call. Of course he had her location. All Kessler employees were equipped with the most cutting-edge technology, as befitted members of the Kessler Tech empire.

She put her cell back in her purse, and rubbed her arms against the slight night chill she hadn't noticed in the throes of her adrenaline rush. As soon as Marsden got her home, she'd feed Greta, her border collie; take a shower; change out of her blood-speckled party clothes; and go to the hospital to check on Cindy, Liza, and Feather. She'd overheard one of the paramedics say that everyone was alive and responsive.

But as she knew all too well, some injuries couldn't be seen from the outside.

The next morning, Fred's nose still ached and had turned purple. He considered blaming it on his epic bout with a Muay Thai master, but unfortunately, he was pretty sure the whole incident with Rachel had been caught on camera. As he padded gingerly through his sunny, tract-style house toward the kitchen, he vowed not to turn on the TV today. He did not want to know what that embarrassing moment looked like on Channel Six.

He also had no intention of setting foot inside his favorite spot, his garage–turned–martial arts studio. He'd started studying jujitsu, then gotten into Muay Thai, and become so dedicated he'd banished his truck to the street so he could use the garage to work out. Unfortunately, he wasn't the only one who liked to work out there.

Barely eight o'clock in the morning, and already the three bright-eyed Sinclair kids from across the street were sitting on his front porch. As soon as they caught sight of him through the front picture window, they banged on the door until he opened it.

"You locked your door," said ten-year-old Tremaine indignantly. "How we supposed to get in if you do that?"

"You're not supposed to get in unless I want you to," explained Fred. Not that he'd ever turn them away. He got a huge kick out of the kids, and they were nearly as obsessed with martial arts as he was.

"Aw, man. That's cold," complained Tremaine's twin, Jackson, as they all bounded into his house, as if propelled by a slingshot. "Dude, whazzup with your face?"

"Accident," said Fred shortly. He didn't want to think about his damn nose. Every time he remembered last night, it throbbed. "Where's your mom?"

"She's studying."

"No, she's in the shower," said little Kip, who was

two years younger and very literal-minded. "*Then* she's studying."

With three rambunctious boys, their mother, Jasmine, had her hands full. Fred didn't mind helping her out, but at the moment he could use some peace and quiet.

"Why don't you boys come back later and I'll teach you some new moves?"

"What about breakfast?" Kip, who was going through a growth spurt, asked.

"You haven't eaten yet?" Fred winced as he bent to pick up the newspaper off the front porch. Maybe he'd go to the gym later for a sauna.

"Mama said she'd pay you back if you give us some Froot Loops or something. While she's studying."

"Froot Loops are not a healthy breakfast."

"She said you'd say that, and that she'd pay you double for a healthy breakfast."

Fred unrolled the newspaper. Usually he did a quick scan for news from the various parts of the world where his brothers were deployed. But today the crane accident dominated the front page. Crap. He rolled the paper back up. Maybe he'd give it to Stan, the firehouse dog, as a chew toy. "Your mom drives a hard bargain."

Kip took his thumb out of his mouth again. "If that's too 'spensive, we'll take the Froot Loops. We won't tell."

Fred had to laugh at that. The kids were so cute. Their father, a member of the Army Rangers, had been killed in Afghanistan. They'd told him that they'd only seen their father for short bits of time. Jasmine got some money from the government, but her real challenge was time. She was trying to finish her real estate training so she could bring in some extra cash.

"Tell you what. I'll pour you boys some cereal and you can eat it—quietly—while I take a hot shower. If you're quiet enough, I'll let you spar."

Tremaine jumped to his feet. "How quiet do you mean?"

"Like is this okay?" Jackson mimicked chomping cereal as if he were a warthog gnawing on a bone.

"No."

"What about this?" Tremaine moved his jaw up and down with a high-pitched whining sound.

"No."

"What about this?" Kip joined the fun, chewing while jumping up and down so hard the windows clattered.

"You guys are hilarious. I think you should join a comedy club, I really do. Maybe go on tour and buy your own breakfasts. Now do you want cereal or not?"

"Sir, yes, sir!" They all performed admirable salutes. There was something to be said for the military, Fred thought as he led them into the tidy kitchen. In fact, sometimes the Sinclairs reminded him of an African-American version of his own family—a bunch of boys destined for the armed forces.

The kids crowded around the bar he'd built to separate the kitchen from the living room while he barked orders.

"Tremaine, bowls. Jackson, spoons. Kip, milk."

They hopped to it, and in under a minute they were each perched on a stool and had a bowl in front of them. He poured the raisin bran—Jasmine knew perfectly well he didn't keep Froot Loops in the house—and ignored the groans of complaint.

"Eat quietly, or no lesson," he warned.

They all instantly went silent. As a threat, it worked every time. They loved their jujitsu lessons.

In the silence, his phone rang. He took it into the living room and lowered himself carefully onto his couch.

"Hello?"

A brisk female voice answered, "Hi Poochie. It's me."

Fred nearly groaned out loud at the horrible nickname. Where had Courtney gotten Poochie? And why had she never asked if he minded? And why was she calling him? "Hi, Courtney. How did your exam go?" Courtney was getting her business degree. After that, she wanted to get married. On their third date, she'd told him that he fit all her criteria for a husband. He hadn't felt complimented; he'd felt cornered.

"Killed it."

He pictured her aiming a shotgun at her exam book. Courtney almost always got what she went after, as she was fond of boasting. The only thing she hadn't gotten yet was a commitment from Fred. No matter what Fred told her, she couldn't quite believe that he didn't want to link his future with hers.

But he didn't. He wasn't in love with her and was never going to be. As soon as he'd figured that out, he'd begun the breaking-up process.

"I saw you on TV. You're a superstar."

"Nah, just another day at the office."

"They didn't make it sound that way. And they kept referring to you as a Bachelor Fireman." She sniffed, which evoked a vivid picture of her. That sniff usually went with a curl of her lip and a twitch of her perfectly highlighted blond ponytail.

"That's just a stupid media thing, Court. Sells papers, or ad spots, or whatever."

"I'm not complaining about it. It's a good business opportunity. You're famous, and we should be profiting from it. I have some ideas for us."

Ideas for us. As if they were still together. Would always be together. What part of "I want to break up" had she blocked out? All of it?

An image flashed through his mind—the crushed interior of the limo, and Rachel's wide eyes alive in the darkness, like the petals of a violet. Even though she'd fought him like a wildcat and bloodied his nose, he could still feel the supple weight of her in his arms. He'd felt more captivated in those few short moments than he ever had with Courtney.

Bad, Fred, *bad*. Why was he thinking of some girl he'd never see again while on the phone with the woman he'd been dating up until two weeks ago? He dragged his attention back to the phone call.

"Courtney, we broke up, remember? There is no—"

"Let's not have this conversation right now," she interrupted. "Are you trying to upset me?"

He clenched the phone in his fist, resisting the urge to slam it against the counter. How did she always manage to make him feel like the bad guy, no matter what he did or said?

In a huge stroke of luck, his other line beeped. For a wild moment, he wondered if it was Rachel. Maybe she was calling him with an apology for the nosebleed. "Gotta go, Court. I have another call coming in."

"Call me back, okay? We're not done."

Oh yes, we are, he thought. *And one of these days you'll get it.* He clicked over to the other call.

"Well, hello, hero." His little sister, Lizzie, greeted him. "Did you know that you're all over the news?"

"Yeah, I'm starting to figure that out. Please don't tell me they showed that girl ditching me." Just what he needed: the most humiliating rescue operation in San Gabriel history. The hero fireman dumped by his rescuee. He remembered Ella Joy's threat. *You'll pay for that, Stud*. She certainly had the ammunition for it.

"What are you talking about? All I know is that my friends are calling me and asking for your number."

Um . . . what? Fred frowned, wincing as the skin of his nose pulled tight.

He rubbed his forehead, wondering if that blow to his nose had knocked him into the Twilight Zone. "I'd better check this out. I'll call you back, Lizzie."

He got up and returned to the kitchen, where he'd left the newspaper on the kitchen island. The boys barely looked up from their voracious consumption of raisin bran as he shook open the paper.

"Dude," said Tremaine, impressed. "Is that you?"

The full-color photo splashed across the front page showed Fred striding toward the camera, smiling at the blond girl, Cindy, as he carried her away from the mangled limousine. Her arms were around his neck. Since he didn't have his proper gear, his whole face was visible, including his smile. The headline read: "Hero in Action." The caption read: "Local firefighter saves bride after a freak crane accident."

At least the picture didn't show him getting punched out by Rachel. But why was the newspaper making such a big deal out of the extraction? He wouldn't mind being called a hero if he'd done something heroic. But he was just doing his job. And in the photo, he was just walking, really. Walking while carrying a pretty girl. Not exactly hard work.

"It wasn't all me," he told the boys. "Mulligan was there, and then the whole crew showed up. It wasn't just me."

"You're the one carrying the girl," pointed out Jackson. "Nice moves."

"It wasn't a move. It's my job."

"You must like your job. Look at you smiling. I can see your teeth. You ought to floss more."

"Hey, maybe you're on TV!" Tremaine jumped up and ran to grab the remote from the coffee table. He clicked it at the flat-screen on the wall, then punched around the channels until he found one showing the local news.

Channel Six's Ella Joy filled the screen. Despite his vow to avoid the news, Fred drew close to see what she had to say.

She was introducing a story about the accident, with a huge graphic trumpeting the "Miracle on Main." With a sense of the inevitable, Fred lifted his head to watch. Ella had made her threat, and now she was going to deliver on it. He braced himself for a shot of a wild-haired girl in a silvery dress punching him in the face. Cue the embarrassing public humiliation of Fred Breen, Bachelor Fireman.

But that's not what came next. Instead, they ran a shot of him crouched next to the limo. As the camera rolled, he extracted the first girl from the limo, handed her over to the paramedics, then stuck his head back in the limo.

Nothing spectacular, but the way they shot and edited the footage, it looked as if he was single-handedly saving the day.

"We've gotten used to the heroics of our favorite fire department," recited Ella Joy dramatically. "But yesterday, the Bachelor Firemen outdid themselves. With a bride's life at stake, Firefighter Fred Breen, one of the few remaining *single* Bachelor Firemen, put his own safety on the line to rescue not only Cindy Barstow, but her three bridesmaids. One by one, he pulled them to safety. One by one, he delivered them into the hands of paramedics. One by one, he brought joy into a dire situation."

Here they cut to a shot of him cradling Rachel against his chest. It brought the entire experience back to him. He'd been so distracted by how good she felt that he'd forgotten she didn't tolerate small spaces well. No wonder she'd panicked at the sight of the ambulance. He just wished she'd said something instead of punching him out.

Ella Joy continued. "Today, the survivors of that terrifying accident are speaking out."

The blonde, Cindy, appeared on the screen. Pale but composed, with a small bandage on her head, she sat holding hands with her fiancé. "That fireman is a hero," she said, shakily. "We have to postpone our wedding a little, but we're going to dedicate it to him. Without him, it wouldn't even be happening. And if it's true that he's one of the Bachelor Firemen, well"—she managed a smile—"my bet is he won't be for long. Single girls out there, what are you waiting for?"

"That's it." With a gesture of defeat, Fred tossed the newspaper over his shoulder. Instead of making him look bad, Ella Joy had made him look good. *Too* good. First a kitten lover, now this. "I'm doomed."

Chapter 4

Rachel dreamed she was jumping off the tip of a construction crane, but instead of crashing to the ground, she was captured by a soap bubble, like the good witch in *The Wizard of Oz*. It tickled her skin, which made her giggle and shiver. Then the bubble popped, thanks to the annoying sound of a tinny voice. She woke up instantly. Greta was licking her chin and her phone was playing the ring tone she'd assigned to her father: Madonna's "Papa Don't Preach," her own private joke.

She rubbed Greta's head as she swung her feet over the edge of her four-poster bed, onto the plush pile carpet. When she'd insisted on staying in San Gabriel after college, her father had insisted on buying her the top floor apartment in the most secure building in town. He'd then wired the entire place with motion sensors and hidden cameras. And he'd bought one of the bottom floor apartments for Marsden.

Yup, that was life as the overprotected only daughter of America's third wealthiest man.

Gathering herself together, she plucked her phone off her nightstand. "Yeah, Dad. I'm up."

"Why didn't you call me?" Rob Kessler's intense, rat-a-tat voice pulsed through her iPhone as if it was impatient with such a flimsy physical tool. It was like being woken by a jackhammer.

Right away her hackles rose. "Because I'm *fine*. My friends are fine too. Cindy has two broken ribs and Liza has a concussion and . . ."

"And Feather has multiple abrasions, I know. I have my sources at the hospital."

"So much for patient confidentiality."

Her father let out his trademark harsh bark of a laugh, as if a real laugh would take too much time. Rachel wouldn't be surprised if her father had hacked into the patient records. When he wanted information, nothing stopped him. As one of the world's foremost experts on computer security, he knew all the tricks. And he didn't hesitate to use them when it came to his only child.

"I figured Marsden would fill you in on every-thing, so why take up your time with a redundant phone call?"

"He did. But that's no excuse for not calling me. An agreement's an agreement."

Ever since her kidnapping—which was basically since she could remember—her father had been almost unbearably hyperprotective. She couldn't blame him. To be helpless in the face of anonymous kidnappers must have been maddening. And then there was the unsettling fact that Rachel's kidnap-per had never been caught or even identified. It was like living with the proverbial other shoe hanging over your head. She tried to remember that at moments like this.

"I'm sorry, I should have called. I was with my friends at the hospital and then I came home and conked out. I was going to call you first thing." She slid out of bed and padded into the living room, which was dominated by floor-to-ceiling windows. They didn't open, of course, being made of special reinforced glass. The heavy drapes were actually bulletproof.

She drew one open and looked down at the rest of San Gabriel's charming suburban landscape. In her opinion, spring was the most beautiful time of year here, when the jacarandas bloomed and the hills held a tender shade of green instead of their usual parched brown. Greta stood next to her, as if enjoying the view along with her. She held her favorite toy in her jaws, a simple length of rope that she loved to chase around the apartment. As a puppy, Greta had been abandoned in a concrete sewer. It was hard to believe she was the same traumatized pup.

Smiling fondly at her dog, Rachel tugged the rope from her clenched jaws and tossed it across the room. Greta went bounding after it.

"We might have another problem," Rob Kessler said. She pictured her father, sitting tailor-style at the special desk where he kept his array of computers. He detested chairs, and always insisted that everyone sit on cushions on the floor.

"The reporters," she guessed. "But I was careful to hide my face. That fireman helped me."

"Frederick Lancaster Breen from San Gabriel Fire Station 1."

She lifted her eyes to the ceiling. "Fred," she corrected, to prove she knew something her father didn't. Besides, she'd developed a real fondness for the name. It was so unpretentious and straightforward. It would always make her think of a helping hand reaching out in comfort.

"Also known as Stud."

So much for knowing more than Rob Kessler. He probably even knew *why* Fred was called Stud, but she wasn't about to ask that. "Okay, so you've already found out everything there is to know about the poor random firefighter who happened to stumble onto the scene. What's the big problem?"

"One of Channel Six's cameras managed to get a shot of your profile while Breen was carrying you to the ambulance. Somehow I missed that one. I managed to keep everything else off the air."

Everything else. He must be referring to her freak-out.

Greta panted next to her, her moist brown eyes begging for another toss. "You're insatiable," Rachel whispered to her.

"I've put in a call to Dr. Stacy."

Rachel gave a silent, horrified *Noooo* that made Greta back away. She'd had enough sessions with Dr. Stacy to last her two lifetimes. Sure, the therapist had probably saved her sanity. But she wasn't that fragile anymore, no matter what her dad thought.

"It wouldn't hurt to talk this over with her. It must have brought back . . . well, you shouldn't have been stuck in that vehicle." His voice deepened to a fierce growl. "Someone ought to be fired. Starting with that drunken construction worker."

"Dad! Don't you dare fire anyone." After her kidnapping, Rob Kessler had fired his entire security staff, and he'd been a little trigger-happy ever since. "It was probably just an accident. Do they know what happened?"

"Untrained asshole downed too many six-packs, then decided to prove he could move a load of shingles. Charges are being filed, not by me but by his boss. I'm not happy with the limo driver either. He was supposed to keep you safe, that's why I hired him."

Rachel had caught a quick glimpse of the driver's bloody face after the crash. The poor guy didn't need her father on his case too.

"Dad, stop trying to blame someone. It was just an accident. They happen. You can't control everything. And it turned out okay, didn't it? None of us are hurt."

"But a shot of you might have slipped through. I don't like it, Rachel. My gut says this is trouble. It's a sensitive time right now. My congressional testimony is scheduled for later this month and we'll be beating off the media with a club. I'm sending an extra bodyguard down there."

Rachel gripped her phone, feeling another primal scream coming on. She couldn't let all her efforts to carve out her own life slip away. "No, Dad. No, no, no. I don't need another bodyguard." She didn't mind security, but she hated being shadowed. "You already have Marsden reporting in twice a day. Why don't you just implant some kind of chip in me so you always know where I am?"

A short silence followed. Horror washed through her.

"Dad. Please tell me I don't have a chip."

"You don't have a chip."

"Don't lie to me."

"Rachel. I would never do something like that without your permission. But it would give me some peace of mind."

"Oh my God." She clutched at her head, feeling a thudding ache coming on. "I'm going to forget you ever said that. And *no* bodyguard."

Deciding that a large amount of coffee was needed to deal with this conversation, she crossed to the expansive, state-of-the-art kitchen. The coffee-maker was already set, which meant the cleaning crew had been in yesterday. She pressed the button, suddenly longing to be at work, where she actually *did* things.

"All right. No extra bodyguard for now. But you have to keep your eyes open. If anyone recognizes you from the news, you call me. I sent you some links to the footage that aired. You might be hard to identify, but then again, we don't know who's watching. Remember what happened your fresh-man year?"

"Of course I remember." A rave at a San Gabriel College frat house, an accidental hit of Ecstasy, and she'd let her real identity slip. Luckily, the guy had accepted her father's hush money. The experience had put her off partying for good. Except for last night, of course. A wistful smile crossed her face as memories from the City Lights Grill came back. For a short time, she'd actually felt lighthearted and carefree.

What had ever happened to Fred's trophy, anyway?

"I'll be careful, Dad. I promise. I mean, I already live like a nun, but I'll try to kick it up a notch to saint."

"That's my girl."

Rachel ground her teeth.

"Whatever you do, stay away from Channel Six. They'll probably be trying to figure out who the crazy missing bridesmaid is."

"Good to know I've made my mark."

"Last resort, we hire another bodyguard." He hung up before she could protest.

"Grrrrr." Conversations with her father often left her in this state of mind, frustration in a tug of war with love. She knew her father would do anything for her, and anything to keep her safe. He'd failed once, and he'd never recovered from it. Neither of them had.

Standing at the huge picture window with its panoramic, bulletproof view, she stretched her arms overhead. A quick inventory of her various aches and twinges told her nothing was too injured.

A discreet knock on the door signaled Marsden's arrival. "Come in."

As her longtime security guard walked into the apartment, she realized with a pang that he was showing signs of age. His tight-curled, close-cropped brown hair was dappled with gray, he was getting a little jowly, and he moved with his usual morning stiffness. The man didn't say much, and he didn't try to boss her around, which made him the only bodyguard she'd ever felt comfortable with. He was from the South Side of Chicago, his wife had died a few years ago, and his two sons were grown. Other than that, he didn't say much about himself.

"Thanks for filling in my father," she told him as she poured him a cup of coffee. She added a dollop of cream and a healthy scoop of sugar, just the way he liked it.

He shrugged. "Seemed like he already knew."

"Sometimes I think he has spy satellites on a direct feed to his brain."

Marsden hmphed, sitting on one of the bar stools at her kitchen island and taking a long swallow of his coffee. "Nice brew. Thanks."

She eyed him carefully, debating her next question. Marsden had been in the Marines for a long time before her father had hired him. He'd raised a family. He knew much more about the real world than she did.

"What do firefighters like?" she blurted. It had occurred to her that she ought to thank Fred the Fireman in some way.

Marsden barely raised an eyebrow. "Depends on the firefighter, I'd say."

"Okay, well, a young firefighter." *A very attractive one.* "Very . . . um . . . good at his job." She pondered for a moment. "I was thinking maybe a fruit basket, like the ones Kessler Tech sends to clients."

Marsden seemed to choke a little on his coffee.

"Or a spa basket," she added quickly. "Mineral salts and so forth. Enzyme masks."

Marsden put his mug down carefully. He definitely seemed to be trying not to laugh. Her face heated. Was it her fault that she'd never met a firefighter before? She had no idea what sort of person became a fireman and what they might like. Signing up for a job that made you run toward danger instead of away from it made no sense to her.

"You could bake something," he suggested.

She cast her eyes toward the intimidating six-burner Viking stove that dominated the kitchen. It scared her and, quite frankly, the last time she'd used it, it had seemed to be mocking her. "Like a cake?"

"Cookies. Brownies. Something they can pop in their mouth without dirtying a dish."

She grinned, delighted. "That's clever, Marsden. I wouldn't have thought of that. Thank you."

He stood up. "Better go check the perimeter." That was code for toss the ball with Greta in the park around the corner. Rachel whistled for the dog, who came running, her leash already in her mouth.

"Take your time. I don't have any clients until later. I'll text you."

Marsden nodded and headed out the door, Greta practically running circles around him as he went.

Rachel thought for a moment about his suggestion of baked goods, then carried her cup of coffee to her desk and turned on her computer. She was a Kessler, after all. Why not use the Internet to figure out what kind of gift to get for a kind, heroic fireman to whom you were sort of attracted?

More than "sort of," she had to admit. "Extremely" would be closer to the mark. Was he really as good-looking as she remembered? She recalled a dimple in his cheek, or maybe not so much a dimple as a dent that appeared whenever he smiled. But maybe she'd imagined it. If she watched the links her father had sent, she could find out how much of Fred's sexiness was real, how much she'd imagined.

She opened her e-mail and clicked the first link, gasping at the horrifying sight of the crane sprawled atop the limousine. How the hell had anyone survived? Let alone all of them?

And then there was Fred, addressing someone holding a microphone to his face. His hair was tousled with sweat. She hadn't taken much note of its color before. It was a luxurious brown, the color of a sable coat. He spoke with a charming sort of humility, coming across as cheerfully down-to-earth and not at all accustomed to speaking to the media. "Sometimes you just get lucky, and this is one of those times. Not to say that it's lucky to have a crane fall on top of you. That part was unlucky. But it could have been so much worse. Maybe God has a romantic streak and didn't want to ruin the wedding."

From off camera, the reporter laughed. "Don't

you think you had something to do with saving all those lives? They're calling you the Bachelor Hero of San Gabriel."

"Excuse me?"

"We know you're a modest man, so maybe you don't—"

"You don't understand. *I was just doing my job.*"

The camera shifted to aim at the reporter, who turned out to be the glamorous anchorwoman, Ella Joy. "And so the legend grows. Don't let Fred Breen's humble manner fool you. He's a hero, through and through. You might remember him from the *Cooking with Heat* project, a cookbook which he spearheaded, with all proceeds donated to the 9/11 fund."

Here they showed a shot of a slightly younger Fred eagerly displaying a cookbook for the camera. Lord, he was adorable. Since Rachel's father owned an animation studio, among many other things, she'd met her share of movie stars and celebrities over the years. But none of them had come close to Fred's unselfconscious appeal.

"We'll have a lot more on Firefighter Breen and the new Urban Search and Rescue Squad in our special hour-long report tonight, *Heart of a Hero.*"

Off screen, she heard Fred spluttering. "Heart of bullsh—" before the sound was cut off.

Rachel took a long swallow of her coffee. This was bad. Very bad. While she appreciated Fred's reluctance to grab the spotlight, the truth was he didn't have much choice in the matter. If the media decided to turn him into a story, he'd be a story. And if he was the story, she couldn't go anywhere near him.

The thought made her unexpectedly sad, as if she were passing by a warmly lit house she'd never be able to enter. Instead of taking a present to the firehouse, she'd have to order something to be delivered.

She clicked on the next link, and this time she saw Fred heaving her into his arms and settling her against his chest. A shiver passed through her, a visceral memory of what it had felt like to be nestled so close to him. And then she saw it. The way she'd shaken the hair away from her face, so it didn't get caught in the fasteners of his jacket, left her profile momentarily exposed. The camera didn't zoom in on her or linger on her face in any way, but that didn't matter. Anyone with any sort of technical knowledge at all would be able to zoom in on the shot and get a pretty good image of her.

Well, there was nothing to do about it now. Once it was online, there was no scrubbing it out of existence. She just had to hope it didn't go viral, that the kidnapper never saw it, that the kidnapper had moved on to other concerns or maybe that he wasn't even alive anymore.

The threat still hung over her head, the way it had since she was eight years old. She was only twenty-five, too young to have her life ruled by some maniac with a grudge against her father. But what choice did she really have?

Sighing, she turned back to her Internet search and Googled "gifts for hot firemen."

"Sweet heavens," she whispered, as images populated her screen. Weren't firemen supposed to wear shirts?

When Fred arrived for his next shift, it didn't take long for the teasing to set in.

"Bachelor Hero, coming through," said Mulligan.

"Trying to get lucky with a bridesmaid?" teased

Vader, who was now Captain Brown. Making captain hadn't put a dent in his exuberant sense of humor.

"I'm dedicating my divorce to you, hot shot," growled Double D. "Except my wife won't give me one."

Only Sabina showed him any sympathy. She shepherded him toward the kitchen, growling at anyone who tried to stop them. Ace the rookie, whose time at the station was nearly up, gave him a salute.

"Nice story. Uh, my sister told me to ask for your number," he added in a mumble.

"Give her Courtney's. They can duke it out," said Fred, grinding his teeth.

Sabina shoved Ace out of the room and shut the door. "Stud, I know what you're going through. If you need any help dealing with the media, come to me, all right? I'll beat them up for you. Only metaphorically, of course." Sabina had been a child star before she'd joined the fire department. For a long time she'd actually managed to keep it a secret.

"It's not a problem, Two. They'll forget about me in no time. I'm boring. I'm not a legend like Brody, or photogenic like Vader. I'm just me. They'll move on."

Sabina gave him an odd look. "Don't sell yourself short, Stud. We gave you that nickname for a reason."

"Yeah, because I'm not one. It's known as irony. Or sarcasm."

"If you ask me, it's neither one. It's a self-fulfilling prophecy. We called you Stud, now you *are* a stud. And the Bachelor Hero."

He couldn't help laughing at the absurdity. "Come on. I'm just a regular guy."

"We'll see. Anyway, this came for you."

She held out an envelope addressed to him. "Do

you know what I went through to keep the guys from opening this?"

"It's probably nothing interesting."

"I'm interested."

And as soon as Fred saw the feminine, careful handwriting inside, so was he. Intensely interested. In fact, the little hairs on his arms prickled. He had no doubt in his mind who had sent the note, even before he started reading. "Dear Fred the Fireman: I will be forever grateful for your heroic actions in the wake of the crane incident. Please forgive me for hitting your nose. It was entirely accidental and thoroughly regrettable. As a token of my gratitude, a donation has been made to the San Gabriel Urban Search and Rescue Squad. Also, you will find that your next umpteen coffees at the Lazy Daisy Cafe have been paid for. With warm appreciation, Rachel Allen."

Fred stared at the envelope, which, now that he noticed, was made of the sort of extra-thick ivory paper you didn't find at Staples. "Umpteen coffees? Who the hell is this girl?"

Sabina was quickly scanning over his shoulder. "Your newest fan, Stud. If you're going to have a groupie, why not a rich one?"

"But how did she know about the Lazy Daisy? That's just eerie."

"Everyone in town knows the crew goes there." Sabina peered at the scrawled signature. "Wait a second. Does that say Rachel Allen?"

"I think so."

"Then I know who she is."

Chapter 5

"Vader, I need to borrow Stan for a few hours," Fred announced a few days later, as their shift was ending. The firehouse dog, hearing his name, raised his head. Vader, who was scowling at the desktop computer, transferred that scowl to Fred.

"What for?"

"Personal business."

An array of expressions crossed Vader's face, curiosity vying with the urge to tease. "Do I want to ask why you need the firehouse dog for your personal business?"

"Look, it might even be good for him. It's like a field trip."

"What kind of field trip?" Vader might be big and ripped, but he was very far from dumb.

"The kind . . ." Fred hesitated, then finished at lightning speed. "Where you take your dog to get therapy."

"Huh?"

"Dog therapy," Fred repeated. Sabina's revelation that Rachel was a respected dog therapist had inspired this crazy plan. "Stan could probably use it. What else is he going to do today, nap?"

Stan cocked his head, then rested his chin back on his paws.

"See?" Fred said triumphantly. "It's not like I'm interrupting his magnum opus on the trade policies of third world countries." Which happened to be Courtney's current project.

Vader stared at him. "I know you're speaking English, but nothing's making sense. Back to the part about dog therapy. Does this have anything to do with a girl?"

Yup, Vader definitely didn't miss a trick. Fred nodded cautiously.

"Is the girl Courtney?"

Fred shook his head.

"Then go. Have fun. Stan, be a good wingman, just like I taught you."

Stan reluctantly got to his feet and padded over to Fred. "Thanks, Vader. I'll have him back in no time."

Vader waved him away. "Just make sure to feed him a lot. You know he gets cranky without regular snacks."

"You'd make a great dad, you know that?"

Vader shot him a sharp glance. "Why do you say that? Do you know something I don't know? Cherie tell you something? Did she take the test yet?"

Fred backed away, flinging his hands in the air. "Why would she tell me anything? I was just making an observation."

"Girls tell you shit. They can't help it. It's that magic nice-guy—"

"*Don't say it.*"

"Fine. You're an asshole. Get the fuck out of my

office," said Vader good-naturedly as he turned back to the computer. Fred went, Stan trotting dutifully at his side.

They drove to the far edge of town, where Sabina had said Rachel's dog therapy practice was located. He'd debated long and hard about making this visit, but he couldn't seem to get her out of his mind. And shouldn't he thank her for the generous gift? It was only polite. By bringing Stan, he figured the whole thing would look more natural, as if he'd just happened to run into her while trying to do something for his dog.

He found himself at a wooded park surrounded by a concrete wall with loops of barbed wire on top. A discreet sign announced it to be the San Gabriel Refuge for Injured Wildlife. An ironwork gate barred the entrance, which was watched over by two security cameras. Sure seemed like a lot of security for a wildlife refuge. He leaned out of his truck and pressed a button on the small intercom.

"Yes?"

"I'm here to see Rachel Allen. I was referred to her for my dog. He's been having some issues." That's what you were supposed to say, right? A mounted video camera angled toward the car, and he indicated Stan, who sat next to him in the front seat, not looking one bit traumatized the way Fred had asked him to.

"Park in the north lot," said the disembodied voice. The gate opened and he drove past, down a long, curving drive lined with eucalyptus trees. He gave a slow whistle. A lot of money must have gone into this place. Some wealthy donor's vanity project, no doubt.

He reached a collection of beige stuccoed buildings with a Spanish hacienda feel. A more modern barn and aviary looked as if they'd been added later, along with a fenced-in corral. Fred spotted a llama and some goats munching grass inside the corral. The place had the atmosphere of a spa or some sort of meditation center, but it smelled and sounded more like a zoo. He located the north lot and discovered that it sat next to a cute little guesthouse with the word "Therapy" painted on a sign over the door.

"You ready for some therapy, boy?" Fred asked Stan. "You must have something wrong with you. That time you swallowed the gel pack still giving you nightmares?"

Stan merely cocked an ear at him.

"Seriously, do you have to look so well-adjusted?" Fred grumbled. "You're going to blow my cover."

As he opened the front door of the little building, Stan scampered between his feet. The beagle had a thing about entering a room first; come to think of it, maybe he needed therapy for that. The space, which was set up like a waiting room, was empty and simply furnished. A jewel-toned Turkish rug, a large mahogany desk the size of a small ship, a comfortable-looking armchair arrangement, and that was about it. A closed door led to the rest of the guesthouse; that must be where the actual work got done.

"Hello?" he called.

"One minute!" A little thrill ran through him at the sound of Rachel's voice. Uh oh. Thrills weren't good. He hadn't come here for thrills. *Then what did you come here for?*

The door opened and there was his answer. She immediately filled his vision as if nothing else was present. Her thick, curly hair was held back at her neck with a clip, and she wore simple black pants and a tunic top with an embroidered neckline. He made a quick check. Yes, her eyes were exactly as he'd remembered, that deep, velvety purple like the heart of a pansy. Or was it a petunia. Anyway, it was the spark in her eyes that really got to him, and beyond that, the shadow of something sad.

"Fred the Fireman?" She looked astonished. "What are you doing here?"

Good question. He shouldn't be here. He should be sparring. Painting his sister's apartment. Anywhere but here, pretending to need therapy for a dog that wasn't even his.

"It's Stan," he said, tugging on Stan's leash. "He's been having some problems."

Her expression instantly transformed into one of concern. She came forward, crouched in front of Stan, and murmured, "Well, aren't you a fine-looking dog? Will you let me pet you? Do you mind?"

Since Stan was already enthusiastically butting his head against Rachel's hand, the answer seemed clear. She looked surprised as Stan welcomed her caress. Fred took note of the small size of her hand, and the sure way she handled Stan. "He seems pretty happy to me. What sort of behavior is he exhibiting? And what's his name again?"

"Stan."

"Interesting name for a dog."

"Long story, but Stan is short for Constancia. We couldn't let him have a girl's name, so we call him Stan."

"That's thoughtful, but dogs don't have our ideas of gender-based nomenclature," she said absently.

Gender-based nomenclature. Huh. Fred found himself even more fascinated by her than he'd been at the accident scene. She was such an odd mixture of things, courageous and clearly intelligent on the one hand, but a little . . . flaky on the other.

"So what behaviors have you worried?"

On the spot, Fred searched for something plausible. Clearly he hadn't thought this through. Showing up with Stan was one thing; lying about him was another. "Well, he sleeps a lot. I'm worried that he might be depressed."

"How's his appetite?"

"Voracious." For some reason, the word, hanging between them, took on a sexual undertone. Fred hurried past it. "I thought maybe it's a psychological thing. You know, childhood issues. I mean, puppyhood."

Narrowing her eyes at him, she offered Stan a treat, which he gulped down with his usual eagerness. "Have you noticed any limpness in his tail?"

"Limpness?" Somehow, that sounded sexual too. "Um, no," he answered in a slightly choked voice. "His tail is . . ." *don't say stiff . . .* "not limp. He wags it a lot."

"Is he still interested in playing, chasing balls, that sort of thing?"

Fred couldn't answer. He needed to give his dirty mind a damn timeout.

She rose to her feet and planted her hands on her slim hips. She had to be one of the most petite girls he'd ever met. "Are you making fun of me?"

"No."

"Stan doesn't have any issues, does he? What's going on here? Is there a reporter outside? Is this some kind of camera crew ambush, the fireman hero reunited with the girl he rescued?"

"What? No!"

"I've seen all the stories on TV. They're calling you the Bachelor Hero."

He groaned and rubbed the back of his neck. "Ella Joy's playing some sort of game, trying to make me into a superhero. Believe me, I'm doing everything I can to avoid her and her cameras." An idea came to him. "Maybe that's what has Stan so upset."

"Oh please." She took a step toward him, looking so furious he feared for his nose. "Leave poor Stan out of this."

"You aren't going to punch me again, are you?" he asked, standing his ground.

She stopped dead, looking completely taken aback, then crossed her arms over her chest. "I didn't mean to punch you. It was an accident. And I apologized. Is that why you're here, for another apology?"

Stan pawed at her pants leg, clearly hoping for more petting. Fred watched in amazement, since Stan usually kept his distance from strangers. Rachel must really have a way with dogs.

"No. *I* wanted to apologize. I shouldn't have tried to put you in the ambulance right away. I knew you were having trouble with your claustrophobia. I owe you an apology for that."

She examined him closely. The thoroughness of her inspection gave him a disembodied sensation, as if the two of them were floating together a few feet off the ground. He stood still and let the moment play out.

"You don't owe me any apology," she finally said, a wide smile breaking across her face. That grin gave her an entirely different look, sort of mischievous and pixie-faced. "I assume you got my note?"

"I did. And I'm afraid department regulations prohibit me from accepting personal gifts."

Her smile vanished. "Really? But I looked online and read that many firefighters drink coffee, so that seemed like a good choice, and then I read that the Lazy Daisy is popular with the . . ."

Fred could have kicked himself. Rachel clearly

wasn't used to being teased. She wouldn't last two minutes at the firehouse. "I'm kidding," he interrupted her. "It was going to be a clumsy attempt to ask if you'd like to take a drive to the Lazy Daisy with me and cash in one of those coffees."

Her mouth dropped open, then a slow flush drifted across her cheeks. "Oh."

"Very clumsy," he added. "If you laugh me out of your office, I wouldn't blame you."

A notch appeared between her eyebrows. "So your dog is fine."

"As fine as a dog surrounded by firefighters can be. Sorry for dragging him in here."

She knelt next to Stan and ruffled his ears again. "That's okay. It's nice to see Stan."

He noticed that she didn't say anything about it being nice to see *him*. Maybe she was still worried about the Bachelor Hero crap.

"The truth is that I shamelessly used him as an excuse to check on you. I wanted to make sure you were okay, and the news hasn't said anything about you."

"They've been too focused on you, I think." Still occupied with Stan, she glanced up at him. The black fringe of her eyelashes was astonishingly long.

"Flavor of the week," he said.

"I don't know. The media can be like a dog with a bone. Sorry, Stan." She patted his sleek brown and white head. "I don't mean to compare you with those vultures. The thing is"—she rose to her feet—"I don't like cameras."

"I remember."

"And you're on every news show lately, so I don't think—"

"My fifteen minutes will be over before you know it." Fred smiled. "I think Snooki's making an appearance at the mall. I'm old news, Rachel. Believe me."

She eyed him warily. "I don't think you are. And I know they're curious about the disappearing bridesmaid. I'm sorry, I just can't take a chance."

The look on Fred the Fireman's face made Rachel feel about as low as the carpet under her feet. And the thing was, she didn't want to turn him down. Everything about him appealed to her. She'd never been drawn to huge, muscular men; perhaps because the man who had abducted her had been brutally strong. Fred, to her mind, had just the right balance of muscle and agility. His presence, and his brilliant brown-eyed gaze, made her office foyer several degrees brighter.

He shoved his hands in his pockets and angled his head briefly toward the floor, before looking up and giving her a quick nod. "I understand. Offer's open in case you change your mind."

He turned to go, giving Stan a soft whistle. The dog didn't hesitate, but jumped to his feet to follow Fred, whom he clearly adored. Rachel saw so many wounded and traumatized animals that she'd nearly forgotten what a happy dog looked like. Stan was a very contented canine.

At that moment, as had happened so many times in her life, a dog helped her make a decision.

When Fred was halfway through the door, she called after him. "Would you like a tour of the place, since you're here?" He paused, giving her the opportunity to appreciate the muscular shape of his rear. She used to tease her college roommates for obsessing over men's butts, but at the moment she completely understood why. Because a fine male rear end made you think of the way he'd use those muscles to control his thrusts, to grind . . .

She shook her head to clear the sudden swarm of hot images. Where the heck had that come from? She didn't normally lust after virtual strangers.

Fred stepped back into the room. She managed to lift her gaze just in time to innocently meet his eyes, even though her face felt hot.

"Sure, I'd appreciate a tour. I never even knew this place was out here," he said.

She made a show of checking her schedule, though she knew her next appointment was in an hour. "Fine, then. Just give me a second, okay?"

He nodded and snagged his thumbs in his back pockets. She backed away a few feet, then hurried through the back door and swung a right into the bathroom. Hair: totally boring in her work ponytail. Face: no makeup. Outfit: dull as dirt. Normally she dressed for her clients, who happened to be dogs, and none of them cared what she wore. But for time spent with a cute guy, it simply wouldn't do.

She whipped out her cell phone and called Cindy, who'd been released from the hospital the day before and probably needed some distraction.

"Girl emergency," she hissed into the phone when Cindy answered.

"What's up?"

"Remember the fireman from the limo?"

"The totally hot one who saved our lives? Well, duh. I might name our first kid after him."

"He's here. I'm going to show him the Refuge."

Cindy let out a long whistle. "Hoo boy. Let me guess. You smell like dog pee."

"Oh my God, I didn't even think of that." She sniffed at her blouse, then grabbed an atomizer from her purse and drenched herself in the outrageously expensive House of Chanel custom perfume her father had ordered for her eighteenth birthday.

For sure, when her father had given that gift, he hadn't meant it to cover up dog pee.

"Get rid of your hair tie," directed Cindy. "Men love loose hair."

Rachel yanked her hair from its ponytail and shook it out. "Done. What else?"

"What are you wearing? Is it sexy? Or at least stain-free?"

She shot an agonized glance at her top, which was about as sexy as a maternity blouse. She ran to the bathroom, where she kept a laundry hamper, since plenty of her clothes had gotten soiled in the line of duty. Rummaging through it, she didn't spot anything in better shape than what she was already wearing.

"This is a disaster," she moaned to Cindy.

"Forget it. Men don't care about clothes, except when it comes to taking them off. Just don't forget to smile. Don't pull that hands-off-or-my-bodyguard-will-stomp-you thing you usually do."

"I don't do that!" Did she?

"I'm just saying. Be friendly. He's earned it."

"Friendly. Right. How are you feeling?"

"A thousand percent better. This is so much more fun than *Teen Mom* reruns. Call me after, okay?"

Rachel hung up and stared at herself in the mirror. She looked too pale, and not so much friendly as . . . alarmed. If only she'd gone to a normal high school and had slumber parties and done makeovers and gone to proms. If only she'd casually dated, fallen in love, gotten her heart broken, all the usual teenage rites of passage. But she'd done none of those things. She'd alternated between pricey, private Everwood School for Girls and home tutoring. In college, for the first time, she'd made real friends, not fake whose-family-has-more-money friends. But she still hadn't gotten the hang of casually dating. Face it, doing anything casually was pretty impossible for her.

But none of that meant she couldn't give a nice, cute fireman a tour without looking like Wednesday Addams. She pinched her cheeks, trying to give them some color.

"Ow." That hurt. But it did make two distinct dots of pink appear on each side of her face. She rubbed at them, trying to make the color spread. Would a slap in the face work better, give more of an all-over flush? Then again, it might be hard to look friendly if her cheeks were in pain.

She poked at her hair one more time, then made a face at the mirror. *Who do you think you are, Scarlett O'Hara?* With a roll of her eyes, she abandoned her reflection and went back to the foyer.

As it turned out, her ridiculous efforts paid off. She experienced the thrill of seeing Fred's eyes widen and an appreciative grin spread across his face. "Your hair looks pretty like that," he said. Such a simple compliment, and yet it kindled a trickle of warmth in her heart. Maybe because he said it so sincerely. He obviously meant it. Compliments usually made her suspicious, especially when they came from men back home trying to suck up to her father.

But Fred had no idea she had anything to do with America's third wealthiest man.

"Thanks," she said, then stuffed her purse behind her desk. It was safe here. Everyone who worked at the Refuge had been extensively vetted by her father's security team.

She led the way onto the gracious grounds of her favorite spot on earth. She'd worked so hard to create the Refuge for Injured Wildlife. No one knew how hard, and she couldn't tell Fred without revealing her true identity. She wasn't ready for that. "Is Stan pretty well behaved around other animals?"

"If you have any rescued squirrels, I'd tell them to hide," he said lightly. "And your sheep will be herded so fast they won't know what hit them. On the other hand, if anyone's trapped, he'll let you know. He used to be a rescue dog."

She led the way down the main path that wound through the grounds. "I've thought about training my border collie to be a rescue dog. She has an amazing prey drive."

"Stan has an amazing sleep drive, but I'm sure he used to be great. Right, Stan?"

The beagle gave Fred a world-weary sort of look. Rachel smiled to herself. Whether he intended to or not, Stan was telling her a lot about her visitor. All good, so far.

"What would you like to see first? Do you like birds? Camelids? Foxes? Goats? Someone just brought in a wounded short-eared owl."

"Do you take in every sort of animal?"

"Yes," she said proudly. "At least temporarily, until we can figure out the best place for them. We don't turn any animal away. We only have a small staff, about six people, plus security, but we manage to do a lot."

"I've got this bruised nose," Fred mused, running his hand across it. "Is there a space for me?"

Again, she laughed. Fred had a way of drawing the laughter from her. "I hope the other guy looks worse."

"Nope. The other guy looks pretty good." He cast her a sidelong glance that made her face heat.

"Well," she said tartly. "If it's any comfort, no one

watching me walk home that night thought I looked good. I had blood speckles everywhere. People probably thought I had chicken pox."

He stopped, turning her to face him. "Yeah, I've been meaning to ask how you got home. I was worried but didn't know how to find you."

"I was fine." She waved a hand dismissively. "Honestly, after being penned up in that limo, it felt good to walk for a while. I went home and then to the hospital."

"You know, I've been at a lot of accident scenes, and I've seen some strange things."

Rachel dreaded what was coming next. People often thought she was odd. It came from spending too much time with animals and a taciturn security guard. "Let me guess. I take the cake?"

"Well, it's true that I've never been punched in the nose during a rescue before. But that's not what I was going to say. I was going to say you're one of the toughest accident survivors I've ever seen."

"Oh." The way he was looking at her, so closely, his dark eyes taking in everything about her, made her feel very exposed. "Really?"

"It made me curious. I was hoping I'd run into you again. And then you sent that note."

Shivers were traveling down her arms. This whole conversation felt unexpectedly intimate. "I felt bad. You didn't deserve the way I acted."

"I didn't take it personally. But"—he gave her a sidelong look—"there might be a way to make it up to me."

"I can't go on a date with you," she said quickly.

"Go on a date?" An expression she couldn't interpret crossed his face—maybe shock? "Not like that. That's not what I mean."

"What do you mean, then?"

For a moment he simply stood, hands in his pockets, as if utterly perplexed. "I'm trained in urban search and rescue," he finally said. "I volunteered in Japan after their last big earthquake."

That certainly came out of the blue. "Okay."

"I've worked with both rescue and salvage dogs. I know someone who trains them. I could . . . help you train your dog."

She had the feeling he was making it up as he went. But why? If he wanted to see her again, why didn't he just ask her? He was really confusing her. "You're offering to train Greta?"

"Yes."

Adding rescue dog training to the Refuge's repertoire would be wonderful. Starting with Greta made sense, and it was something she'd been thinking about for a while. His offer was tempting, if only there were a place she wouldn't worry about news cameras. Her apartment was safe, but she never invited anyone there other than Cindy, Liza, and Feather, who already knew her story. Then the perfect solution came to her.

"Fine, I'll bring Greta to your house. Friday at eight." She grinned at his obvious surprise. "I'll bring the ice cream."

Chapter 6

What the hell was he thinking? He shouldn't be offering to train another girl's dog. If Courtney caught wind of this, she'd be furious, no matter how broken up they were. Once again, he'd feel like the bad guy. He should take back his offer, right now. He couldn't have Rachel coming over, even if it was just a friendly dog-training session. Which was exactly what it would be, nothing more.

True, he liked walking beside her, liked being able to glance over at frequent intervals and take in her wildly curling black hair and her enthusiastic gestures as she pointed out features of the Refuge. He liked listening to her grow more and more passionate in her descriptions of things like feeding schedules and the effect of oil spills on wildlife.

He liked watching her with the animals. Never in his life had he seen anyone with such an affinity for injured creatures. Even the owl, who'd just been brought in, seemed comfortable with her presence and allowed her to gently test the splint on its broken wing.

"Are you a vet?" he asked as she adjusted the towel keeping the owl warm.

"No. I completed most of a vet tech program, but I don't need a degree to do what I do. We have a couple of actual vets here who perform surgery and work with the wildlife. My work is with dogs. I'm just . . . a dabbler, I suppose."

"My friend Sabina said you helped a search dog who'd been injured in a mudslide and traumatized."

"Yes. Dog therapy. Laugh if you want."

"I'm not laughing." He wasn't. Now that he'd seen her with Stan, he didn't think it was at all ridiculous.

She rewarded him with a quick smile, like a crystal catching the sun. "People bring their dogs to me when they're exhibiting strange behavior, and I try to figure out what's going on and how to help the dog."

"How do you do it?"

"I can't really explain. Ever since . . . well, something bad happened to me when I was young, and a German shepherd saved my life. Ever since then, I feel as if I can understand them. Dogs have all sorts of ways to communicate with us, if we pay attention. The tilt of their ears, how they hold their tails, if they bare their teeth. Even an air snap has a purpose; it doesn't necessarily mean they're going to attack. When I work with dogs and their owners, I work mostly on communication. Dogs are very intelligent, but if their owners are confusing them or not providing good leadership, they can develop bad habits."

"Sabina said you have an amazing record of success."

"Thanks," she said, shrugging. "Mostly, I just

want to help the dogs. I've never forgotten how one helped me."

Fred was finding it hard to tear his gaze away from her. While she might not be the most typically pretty girl, she was fascinating to watch. Her face held lots of opposing angles that somehow managed to balance perfectly. Her eyebrows tilted up while the corners of her mouth slanted down. Her high cheekbones gave her an almost exotic look, as if she had a dose of Gypsy in her. He caught a faint whiff of her fragrance, light and fresh, like a walk through a rose garden after a morning rain.

She seemed different here. Calmer, maybe. Less skittish. Happier. As he watched her crouch to check on a tortoise with a bandage on its little leg, he got a flash of the way she'd bent over the drunken kid at the City Lights Grill. Now that he knew her better, he saw that she'd been trying to help the guy the same way she tried to help wild animals.

That realization brought a surge of protectiveness. Someone that softhearted could get into big trouble.

As they headed back toward her office, he asked, "How are your friends?" The last he'd heard, everyone had been released from the hospital and the wedding postponed for a month so everyone's bruises could heal.

"They're all getting sick of telling the story over and over again. And Cindy really wants to invite you to the wedding."

Embarrassment crept over him at the memory of how Cindy had announced on TV that she was dedicating her wedding to him.

"Tell her there's no need for that."

"Oh come on. They'd really appreciate it. She's going to send an invitation to the firehouse."

"I'm a little wedding-ed out. I've been to three in the past year."

"Yes, but how many of those were people whose lives you'd saved?"

He thought about it. "Actually, all of them, in a way. Although Psycho would never admit it."

"Psycho?"

"Another fireman. He moved to Nevada, so I don't have to save his ass anymore. But if you pinned him down, he'd tell you I had his back a bunch of times. Sabina too, and definitely Vader. I saved Vader's mom when their house burned down."

"You just go around saving people's lives?"

He shrugged. "Well, sometimes. If it works out. It's the nature of the job."

"I've never met a firefighter before." She paused to wait for Stan to take a leak on the base of a tree. He hadn't even noticed that Stan had to pee; she really did have superior dog communication skills. "You're not exactly what I would have expected."

"What'd you expect?"

She eyed him up and down, giving him that tingling sensation again. "I didn't really think about it, I suppose. Maybe more . . . swaggering?" She put her thumbs in the belt loops of her pants and mimicked a boastful stance, lowering her voice to a macho growl. "I can put out fires with nothing more than my bare hands and a mouthful of spit."

He gave a surprised hoot of laughter. "Have you met my captain, Vader? Dead-on. Nah, I'm just kidding. Firefighters have a pretty healthy respect for fire. If we ever swagger, it's just to keep our confidence up."

"You don't seem to swagger much. You must be really confident."

Taken aback, he paused outside the closed door of

her office bungalow. "I don't know. My brothers are confident—you don't want to mess with them. Me, I'm confident in my training and my crew. When I go out on a call I feel like I know what to do. What's that add up to?"

"Sounds like confidence to me. I'm not just good with animals, you know," she added. "I'm pretty perceptive when it comes to people too."

"Oh really?" He knew he shouldn't ask the next question, but he just couldn't help it. "So what have you picked up about me so far?"

"You really want to know?"

He angled his head to look down at her. In the world of San Gabriel firefighters, he was on the short side at roughly six feet. Rachel stood nearly a head below him, so if he leaned forward, he'd be able to press his lips to the dark curls framing her forehead. Not that he would, of course. He barely knew her, and then there was Courtney.

Courtney, who would make someone a power-house wife, and didn't understand why he wasn't that "someone." Courtney, who usually got what she wanted and didn't like to lose.

Rachel, despite obvious signs of wealth, didn't look like someone who always got what she wanted. She looked like someone who knew life could knock you over the head sometimes.

He realized they were staring at each other. If she was really good at figuring people out, she'd probably already determined that he wasn't the star of the firehouse, or the star of anything, despite Ella Joy's new crusade. He was just . . . Fred. Fred the Fireman. He put out fires and got people out of trouble.

While she was . . . well, whatever else, she was clearly something special.

"Sure," he said, his voice gruffer than he intended.

He cleared his throat. "Lay it on me. What have you picked up about me?"

"This," she said in a dreamy voice. Then, under his astonished gaze, she tilted her body toward him, rose onto the tips of her toes, and brushed her lips against his. He froze as a wash of electricity sizzled across his nerve endings. The touch was so slight, so brief, like a butterfly coming to a rest. Her breath was warm and sweet; he wanted to soak it in through every pore.

And just like that, every thought that didn't involve Rachel Allen fled his mind.

He felt as if every cell of his body had turned into one of those satellite arrays, rotating toward a newly detected signal. *Who's this? Where did she come from?* Electric desire raced through him. He wanted to know her, body and soul, on a raw, primal level. He wanted Rachel Allen in a way he'd never wanted anyone—or anything—before in his life. Urgently. Compulsively. Impossibly.

Sanity returned in a cold wash of horror. He backed off, putting his hands on her shoulders to set her away from him. That was a mistake, since the feel of her made him instantly hard. "I have to go," he said, releasing her and taking a big step backward.

"I'm sorry," she said, putting a hand to her lips, astonished. "I didn't mean to—"

"That's okay. I didn't mean to either—" He broke off, completely unsure of what he wanted to say. "I mean, it was me. It was both of us." He should cancel Friday night. Bad, bad idea. No way could he have her in his house and not try to kiss her again. And kissing couldn't happen again.

He opened his mouth to call it off, but instead uttered the words, "I'll see you Friday at eight."

Holy fuck. That wasn't calling it off. That was the opposite. *What was wrong with him?*

She bit her lower lip, looking troubled. Good. If she was going to back out, he should let her. It would be better for both of them.

Courtney's angry face filled his mind's eye. She'd be furious, even if he hadn't initiated the kiss. She'd grill him about it, then explain why a "trial separation" didn't include kissing other people. He'd be expected to buy her something, or go get mani-pedis with her, or go to one of her business school keggers. God, he'd probably get back together with her out of sheer guilt.

Everything in him rebelled, and he knew right then, with complete certainty, that he'd had enough. One way or another, he had to make Courtney understand they were through.

A little whimper from Stan brought him back to the moment.

"Friday at eight," he said in a slightly choked voice, then wheeled around, Stan at his heels. He quickly gave her his address before she could say anything else. "I just have to take care of something first."

Rachel closed her office door behind her and leaned against it. What on earth had possessed her to *kiss* Fred? She never initiated kisses, and usually waited a long time before letting anyone kiss her. When other girls complained about men wanting them for sex, Rachel felt the opposite. In her case, sex was way down on the list of what guys wanted from her. Most of the men she dated came from her father's world and thought of her as Rob Kessler's daughter, with all the connections and advantages that brought. In San Gabriel, as Rachel Allen, she didn't date much; it felt dishonest.

This kiss was totally different. For a moment, it had been sheer magic, as if some sort of enchanted spell had sprung to life around them. Then he'd ended it so abruptly.

Maybe he'd been as shocked as she was. She hadn't intended anything like that. The kiss had been meant as a thank-you for saving her, for saving her friends. Really, she'd been aiming for his cheek. She wasn't sure what had happened along the way. The closer she'd gotten, the more aware she'd become of his hard body, the smell of his skin, the strong tendons that stretched from his neck to his shoulders, the sturdy health he exuded, the firm curves of his mouth . . .

Yes, that's where the problem had started. His mouth.

Once she'd been leaning against him, her lips on his, nothing had triggered the panicked desire to run that often flooded her when she got close to someone. The opposite, in fact. She'd had a very strong urge to climb his body like a monkey. It was a good thing he'd stepped back in such a hurry, or he might have found himself playing jungle tree.

On her desk, her phone made the little buzz that meant someone had called while she'd been out. Strange, she never forgot her phone. She always had it with her, for her father's peace of mind. If Fred the Fireman had made her forget her phone, he'd accomplished one more astonishing first.

It wasn't a call, but a text message from Bradford Maddox IV, one of the Refuge's board members and a friend of her father. *Saw you on TV. Glad everyone's okay. Please advise regarding new wedding date. Looking forward to escorting you to the happy event.*

Ugh. In all the drama of the accident, she'd forgotten that Bradford was taking her to Cindy's wedding. But the worst part was that he'd seen her on TV. Did she have to tell her father about that? If she did, he'd insist she get an extra bodyguard, and there would go her freedom. Such as it was.

Good Lord, couldn't she just have one tiny sliver of a normal life? Maybe a sliver the size of one evening at a cute fireman's house? Cute didn't really cover it, she was beginning to realize. Outrageously attractive was better.

Yes, she'd wait until after her dinner at Fred's. Then she'd let her father know about Bradford's text.

Chapter 7

Rachel kept a close eye on the news over the next couple of days. Everyone seemed to have forgotten about the runaway bridesmaid, but the stories about Fred just kept on coming. Every other day, it seemed, another dire situation occurred and Fred the Bachelor Hero saved the day.

First came a surprise May storm, which sent rain lashing across Rachel's picture windows and caused flash flooding on the highway that led to the desert. An elderly woman who was heading out to view the wildflowers got trapped in her car by quickly rising floodwaters. The entire rescue was caught by a camera in a hovering helicopter.

"Once again, firefighters from San Gabriel Station 1 were first on the scene. While some firefighters secured the car, to keep it from being swept downstream by the raging floodwaters, our favorite Bachelor Hero, Firefighter Fred Breen, fought the current and was able to pull Alison Barnstable out of her watery trap. The grandmother of three was overwhelmed with emotion as Breen carried her across the flooded highway."

Then came a shot of the elderly woman alternately sobbing and laughing as she clung to Fred. He slogged his way through the water, talking to her the entire time, clearly putting her at ease. He was so *good* at what he did. And yet he didn't seem to think it was anything special.

"All credit goes to Mrs. Barnstable for her quick thinking," he told the anchor, Ella Joy, when she stuck the microphone in his face after the rescue. His drenched hair was plastered to his head, which somehow made him look even more attractive. "If she hadn't called 911 right away, we might not have gotten to her in time. She kept her head and did all the right things."

"What are the right things to do? Can you explain to our viewers?"

"The most important thing is not to panic. Pay attention to flash flood warnings and if you see standing water on the road, don't try to drive through it. Every situation is different, depending on how submerged the car is and what the situation is. Sometimes you want to close the windows to equalize the pressure, but in other situations the window can be an escape route. That's why keeping your head is so important. Getting trapped in a car under water is terrifying, but it is often a survivable situation."

Rachel couldn't take her eyes off the TV. Who knew a fireman giving safety instructions would be so sexy?

"This sounds like a subject for a news special," said Ella Joy.

Fred gave a tired smile. "It would be a real service to your viewers. San Gabriel doesn't get a lot of flooding, but when it happens, it's frightening and dangerous."

"Thank you for talking to us." Fred nodded and hurried off to join the other firefighters.

Ella Joy turned to the camera. "Stay tuned for more on these freak floods and what you can do to stay safe. I just got word from our producer that we'll be airing a special on survival situations. And for those who want to hear more from our favorite Bachelor Hero, we've been promised that Firefighter Breen of the Urban Search and Rescue Squad will share some tips with us."

Cindy, Liza, and Feather came over and the four of them, cozy in her top floor apartment, with the rain running in blurry streaks down the windows, watched every second of that news special. Aside from flood and earthquake survival tips, the special also mentioned a new Facebook page dedicated to Fred the Bachelor Hero. It already had over a thousand members, and was growing fast. Not only that, but T-shirts proclaiming "Fred's My Hero" were showing up all over town. Like it or not, Fred was becoming a star.

Feather immediately went online and ordered them each a T-shirt.

Rachel didn't tell them about her plans to see Fred on Friday. It felt like a delicious, private secret. Time and again she told herself she should back out of their dog-training session, now that he was such a media draw. But that infamous, headstrong side of her refused to do it. The fact was, she wanted to see him again. It was as simple as that.

Besides, she didn't want to disappoint Greta.

Everywhere Fred went, someone was sticking a camera in his face. He'd actually started getting recognized *on the street*. In line at the Lazy Daisy, girls wanted to talk to him. He got requests for autographs on inappropriate body parts and fan mail with invitations to dinner.

Everyone wanted to talk to the Bachelor Hero. Fred had never been one of the attention-grabbing members of the department. He'd always wondered what that would be like, and now that the limelight had hit, he wasn't sure he liked it. He didn't like people looking at him differently. Even Mrs. Gund, the crusty owner of the Lazy Daisy, acted starstruck and mixed up his muffin order. His barber asked him to sign a copy of the newspaper article about the crane accident. His dry cleaner made him brownies. It was all so strange.

The firehouse crew teased him about his new fame, of course. Mulligan left lipstick kisses on his locker, and someone mocked up a photo with his face over Justin Bieber's body as he was mobbed with fans.

He tried to take it in stride, since he was facing an even bigger problem.

Courtney really, *really* didn't want to get the message that they were through.

"Fred, just because a girl kissed you doesn't have to mean the end of our relationship," she said with an impatient sigh as he walked her to the San Gabriel College parking lot after class. "Couples get through this sort of thing. Sometimes it makes them closer. It's not like you cheated."

"But it's not fair to you. You deserve more." So much for his hope that the kiss would make her give up on him.

"I forgive you, okay? It's not like you initiated it. Let's just forget it and move on."

"I can't. I don't want to."

"Why is it all about what *you* want? I'm the injured party and I'm fine with it." They reached her older-model BMW, the one she intended to trade in for a brand-new version as soon as she got her first job. She took out her keys and clicked the unlock button.

"But Court—"

Suddenly he had an armful of books and she was opening her car door. "Be a nice guy and put my books in the car, would you?"

Desperate, Fred saw his chance slipping away. A horrible vision of life as Courtney's husband flashed through his mind. Always trying to get her to listen. Always backing down because he didn't want to hurt her. Because he was a "nice guy."

The words "nice guy" echoed through his brain. Being a nice guy was one thing. Being a pushover was another. And what Courtney didn't understand about him was that he had never been a pushover.

He loaded her books into the car, shut the door, and stepped back. She beckoned him toward the passenger seat. Even in the twilit parking lot he could make out the impatient curl of her lip. He turned to go.

"Good-bye, Courtney."

"*No.* We decided. You are not doing this."

"I *am* doing this. We're done. It's not going to work out." Her mouth popped open to argue some more. "When you look at me, do you see anything besides a Bachelor Fireman? *Any* Bachelor Fireman?" Her mouth snapped shut with a click of molars. Boom. So that was it. It sure had taken a long time to figure out. "Courtney, listen close. I'm *never* going to marry you. That's not ever going to happen." A sudden stroke of inspiration made him add, "Don't you think it's better if you start looking for someone else right away rather than dragging it out?"

She twitched her ponytail behind her back. "But I've invested six *months* in you."

"Better six months than a year. Or two years."

He watched that one sink in. "Is this because the other firefighters don't like me? You shouldn't listen to them. They're jerks, and they're sexist too. I didn't want to say this before, but they have a problem with successful women."

Hell, no. Going after his firehouse crew was not a smart move.

"Stop it right there, Court. Those guys are like my brothers and sisters, and if you paid any attention, you'd know they're not like that. Brody's wife is a journalist. Captain Stone's is a press secretary. Cherie's starting a movement therapy program for kids." Courtney opened her mouth but he kept on going. "Katie Blake just finished her degree in elder care. Psycho's wife, Lara, is a doctor with her own clinic. Maribel up in Alaska just won a huge award for her photography. No one at the station has a problem with successful women. And have you forgotten about Sabina and One? They're both badass. We're breaking up because I don't love you, I don't want to marry you, and you should be with someone who does. End of story. Good-bye." He spun away and headed across the lot toward his truck.

"That's . . . You're . . . I was wrong!" she yelled after him. "You're not a nice guy!"

He probably shouldn't be pleased by those last words, but he just couldn't help it.

Eight o'clock on Friday night found Fred making spaghetti sauce and trying to get the Sinclair boys to go home.

"Your mother wanted you home at seven-thirty. What are you still doing here?" he called from the kitchen.

"We're practicing," squeaked Jackson. For the past hour, he and Tremaine had been working on a new hold Fred had taught them. Right now he was probably facedown on the living room carpet. "You told us we gotta practice harder. Mama said so too."

"If you go home now, I'll spar with you tomorrow." Bribery usually worked with the kids. "I have someone coming over."

"Oooh, dude's got a date," Tremaine yelled. "He's going to get some tonight."

Fred cringed, glancing at the clock timer on his stove. She was three minutes late. That probably meant she wasn't coming. "It's not a date, Tremaine. I don't want you talking like that here. This is like your dojo. Respect your dojo."

"Sorry, Mr. Fred." Tremaine led the other boys into the kitchen. "You should let us stay so we can help out."

"Oh, really, I should? How would you help out?"

"Bring the food and shit. Get her some water if she wants water. Or if she wants a soda we can do that too."

"We do that for Mama," Kip piped up.

Jackson added, "We can make you look good too. Act like we really like you and say good things about you."

"I thought you did really like me."

"We like you better when you're not kicking us out of your house," he explained.

"Nice try, but I got this," he told them. "I'll be lucky if she shows up at all, and I don't want to scare her off."

"Why would we scare her? She afraid of kids?"

"I don't know. The only thing I know for sure is that she likes dogs."

Tremaine immediately dropped to his hands and knees and began howling. Kip laughed hysterically and started hopping around, yipping like a Chihuahua.

"Okay, that's it. Everybody out. If you're not gone in the next two minutes, no lessons this weekend."

The boys raced out of the kitchen. Fred looked down at the splash of tomato puree on his T-shirt. Very suave. Rachel probably always hung out with men who had food all over their clothes. He left the pan on a low simmer, checked to make sure the pasta water wasn't boiling yet, and dashed into his bedroom, stripping off his stained T-shirt on the way.

When the doorbell rang, he called, "Be there in a second," and grabbed a loose black long-sleeved shirt, with a T-shirt already nested inside, off the back of his chair. The arms were still inside out. He'd worn it for only an hour yesterday; it should be clean enough. The best he could do at the last minute. Hurrying back to the living room, he tried to put the shirt to rights as he went. He was still trying to get the sleeves untangled when a laughing voice surprised him.

"I wasn't sure I had the right house at first. I wasn't really expecting a doorman."

He glanced up sharply. Rachel stood just inside the still-open door, a sleek border collie at her side. Kip was standing proudly next to her, his hand on the doorknob. He kept sweeping deep bows as if Rachel were visiting royalty.

"That's enough, Kip. You can stop now," he told the boy. "And you can close the door."

Kip enthusiastically shut the door.

"With you on the *outside*," Fred said through gritted teeth. He transferred his gaze to Rachel. She looked mouthwatering in a deep burgundy, clingy kind of top, with her hair loose to her shoulders. One hand held her dog's leash, the other a grocery bag.

"Hi," he said, realizing at that moment that he wasn't wearing a shirt. Because, of course, his shirt was still bunched up in his hands.

"Wardrobe assistance!" called Jackson, striding in from the living room. "You said you didn't need help, dude. Looks to me like you need lots of help."

"I don't need help," he ground out. "You guys are supposed to be gone. Neighbor kids," he told Rachel. "They, uh . . ."

Just then something came flying through the air with an inhuman shriek. Fred tossed his shirt over his shoulder and raised his hands to deal with the unknown threat.

In a blur of black sweat suit, Tremaine was sailing through the air, one foot aimed squarely at Fred's jaw. He must have jumped from the coffee table or something, because usually he couldn't reach higher than mid-chest. Fred quickly assumed a fighting stance. "Nice move, terrible timing," he told the kid as he deflected, flipped and set him on his feet. Tremaine stood, dazed, as if he didn't know what had hit him. He feinted another attack move, but Fred got him in a headlock so he couldn't do any more damage.

At the same time, he put out a hand to stop Jackson's somersaulting approach, catching him with a firm palm to the forehead. "Let me guess. You guys are helping me impress Rachel with my martial arts prowess. Have you forgotten you're only ten? You're making me look bad, not good."

He released them both. They hung their heads and scuffed their feet on the floor.

"But I appreciate the effort," he added, since he couldn't bear to see them look so downcast.

Tremaine, rubbing his shoulder, revived. "He can beat grown-ups too," he told Rachel eagerly. "We watched him beat up a guy at the gym, it was sick."

"That's, uh . . ." Rachel seemed at a loss for words. He couldn't say for sure how she was reacting, because he was afraid to look at her. In fact, he wouldn't be at all surprised if she ran out the door the second it was cleared of blockading kids.

Instead, he looked around for his shirt. Jackson gathered it up, neatly separated the T-shirt from the outer shirt, and presented them with a bow.

"Thank you." He pulled on his T-shirt, which made him feel more in command of the situation. "Now can you guys please go? Remember what I said before."

"That you didn't need help. That's okay. You didn't mean it," said Tremaine confidently. "Ma'am, you tell him."

"Um . . ." she said, looking completely at sea.

"Out," said Fred firmly, and corralled the boys out the front door. Rachel stepped aside so they could pass.

"Is that ice cream?" Kip yelled. He had an unerring nose for sweets.

"New York Super Fudge Chunk, Chubby Hubby, and Cherry Garcia," Rachel answered. She looked relieved to finally be on familiar ground. "And I promise that we'll leave you some leftovers, since you've been such good butlers and doormen."

If anything was guaranteed to cement their approval, that was it. They skipped out the front door, hooting and hollering, and shot across the street to their own house. The last thing Fred heard was "He's going to get some, for sure!"

Cringing, Fred shut the door firmly, then locked it. Then slid the deadbolt, which he normally never used, into place. "I'm really sorry about that." He turned to face her, expecting either shock or horror, or some combination. Courtney had been appalled by the Sinclair boys and their nonstop energy.

But Rachel's face brimmed with amusement. "Don't be sorry. They're so much fun. Do they really come over here all the time?"

"All. The time. Their mother says they need a male role model and I'm the closest they've got. Want me to take that off your hands?"

"Sure." She handed over the ice cream, which made him relax a little. Contributing ice cream seemed like a commitment to stay for the entire dinner. Which reminded him . . .

"Uh oh," he said with dread. "Something tells me the boys didn't get around to checking the pasta. Come on in, make yourself at home." He hurried into the kitchen, where the pasta water was at a full boil, making the lid bounce up and down with a clatter. "I hope you like spaghetti, because it's the only thing I make well," he called to Rachel. "Usually," he muttered.

The pasta sauce had thickened around the edges of the pan and made sluggish gurgling sounds. He turned it off, jabbed violently at it, then went hunting through his cabinets for a package of spaghetti. How could this be such a disaster already?

"I love spaghetti," Rachel said, making him jump. He hadn't realized she'd followed him into the kitchen. "Do you mind if I put the ice cream in your freezer? It's starting to melt out here."

Oops. He'd left her ice cream on the counter while

he dealt with the looming spaghetti crisis. "Yeah, yeah, go ahead. I promise no neighbor kids will jump out at you. Reminds me of the time we got a call from a woman during a blackout. She was freaking out because she'd put her dead cat in the freezer and it was starting to thaw out."

Spaghetti package in hand, he pulled his head from inside the cupboard, horror dawning as he replayed his words. "Did I really just mention a dead, frozen cat? To a pet therapist who works at an animal refuge?"

Rachel closed the freezer door and faced him. Her face was the same deep red as her top, making him wonder if she'd gotten freezer burn in there. As a trained paramedic, should he do something about that? What was the treatment for freezer burn? What about the treatment for full-on, maximum strength humiliation?

Their eyes met. Dry sticks of spaghetti slid through his fingers and bounced onto the floor like pickup sticks. Rachel burst into laughter.

Chapter 8

Rachel felt all the worries of the last few days float away on a cloud of laughter. The accident, her friends' injuries, the news cameras, the text from Bradford, and of course, always, the kidnapper, it all vanished at the comically mortified expression on Fred's face.

"It's . . . it's okay," she managed when she finally managed to stop the waves of giggles. "You didn't have to make dinner for me anyway. We can go straight to ice cream. Or straight to Greta."

Her dog was sniffing at the dry spaghetti and pushing it with her nose, trying to determine if it was edible. Fred bent down to give her a pat on the head. The motion pulled his T-shirt snug against his chest muscles, which made her remember the sight of him without his T-shirt. Which made her mouth go dry.

That image wasn't likely to leave her any time soon. At first glance, Fred didn't look like a muscleman, but the guy was rock-solid. His torso was a spectacular landscape of rippling muscles. With his shirt on, he looked like a cute, nice guy. Without his shirt, he looked like someone you didn't want to mess with. A badass. The easy way he'd lifted her out of the limo made complete sense now.

"Is there any way we could start this evening over from the beginning?" Fred was still crouched next to Greta, staring in dismay at the spaghetti littering the blue-and-white kitchen floor.

And that was the other thing. Fred's home was so . . . homey. The windows had ruffled curtains, not reinforced bulletproof glass. Instead of state-of-the-art stainless steel, the kitchen featured worn wooden butcher blocks and counters the color of speckled sunshine. She tried to imagine what would have happened if three exuberant boys had tried karate kicks in her apartment without previously notifying Marsden. There probably would have been lawsuits involved at some point. The thought of the kids made her smile.

"No way," she told him emphatically. "So far I've been treated like a queen. I had the door opened for me and got my own personal martial arts exhibition. I wouldn't change a minute of it."

The dimple that appeared in Fred's cheek when he smiled made her a little weak in the knees. "You're a good sport. I like that in a guest."

She smiled back. Something hummed between them, and again the memory of his bare, tautly muscled chest flashed into her mind. No one would guess he had so much hidden power under that shirt. It was as if he was masking his true identity beneath a regular-guy exterior.

He broke the moment by clearing his throat. "Unfortunately, I'm pretty sure that was my last package of spaghetti. But . . ." He whipped a piece of paper off his refrigerator, which was cluttered with photos and magnets shaped like fire engines and Betty Boop. "My sister, who visits a lot, made this list of takeout places. Anything look interesting?"

He handed her the sheet of paper. At the top, its title, written in round handwriting, read, "In Case of Emergency, Call These Numbers. Aka How Not to Starve at Freddie's House." A list of restaurants and phone numbers followed, with short descriptions such as "killer egg rolls" and "chicken salad = eww." One of the notations caught her eye.

"'For a hot date, try the fudge cake'?" she read aloud.

He snatched the list away. "My sister likes to ruin my life on at least a biweekly basis. How's pizza?"

"Perfect." They settled on ingredients, finding themselves perfectly in harmony on the issues of green peppers—only if they were the last vegetable on earth—and pepperoni—it couldn't be considered pizza without some. He opened the fridge and retrieved two bottles of beer, while she tried very hard not to notice his butt. And failed.

"Like a glass?" he offered as he dialed the number of the pizza place. She shook her head. "I'll order. Go ahead into the living room and I'll be there in a second."

She, Greta, and her bottle of microbrewed beer wandered into the living room. She sank onto Fred's comfortable couch and surveyed his decor. Clearly he'd spent little on his furniture and a lot on the big plasma screen TV mounted on the wall. The house definitely felt like a bachelor pad, although the neighbor kids had left their mark with a few abandoned Transformer toys. He had no security whatsoever; in fact, one of his windows was open, letting in the evening air. No screen, she noticed. Someone could climb right in.

Oddly, it didn't make her nervous. The house felt safe to her. Or maybe Fred's presence made it feel safe. After all, he'd practically made a second career out of rescuing her.

As Fred came into the room with a tray filled with wooden bowls of chips and salsa, she gave him a big smile. "That looks perfect. Chips, pizza, and ice cream, my favorite kind of meal."

Fred sat on the armchair kitty-corner to the couch. Greta trotted next to him and fixed a determined gaze on his face.

"Ignore her," she told him. "Greta, stop begging." She gave her dog a subtle hand signal.

Greta gave her a reproachful look and dragged herself dramatically to a corner.

"She's such a drama queen," said Rachel. "I don't know if that makes for a good rescue dog or not. I figure she might like all the applause."

"Hmm, I don't know. How does she handle physical discomfort?" Fred offered her a torn-off paper towel. She thought of the linen napkins at Cranesbill, and the housekeeper's likely look of horror at the thought of eating off a paper towel.

"She spent a week starving in a sewer pipe before I got her."

An appalled look widened Fred's eyes. "Poor girl. But that might be a problem because rescue dogs need to be able to work around rubble."

"Yeah, I should test her on that."

"We could take her to a fire station where they do USAR training, for earthquakes and so forth. They have big piles of concrete and an overturned train set up. We could see how she takes to it."

"Maybe." Depending on how safe it was from

prying media eyes. She carefully brought a chip to her mouth, holding the paper towel underneath it to avoid spills. He noticed her caution.

"Don't worry about dripping on the floor. The . . . uh . . . the kids do it all the time. Any stains are entirely their fault." He gave her a ghost of a wink, and she relaxed a bit. If this was her one tiny sliver of "normal life," she wanted to take full advantage and find out all about him.

"How old is your sister?"

"Twenty-three. But she's been hopelessly spoiled by having four older brothers, so she's more like twenty, on a good day."

She stared. "There are five kids in your family? Are you the oldest?"

"Oh no." Fred scooped up salsa with a chip. "I'm the second youngest. All my brothers are older. They're all in the military. Two in the Army, one in the Marines. I'm the only one who stayed around, so I get to walk Lizzie through her heartbreaks. I have a stash of chick flicks and extra pints of ice cream in the freezer."

"That's a bit of a cliché, don't you think?"

She thought he'd be offended by her comment, but he wasn't. He tilted his head and thought about it. "Maybe it is, but it seems to work for Lizzie. She spends the night and rants about clueless guys, we eat ice cream and watch a movie and that seems to do the job. Whatever works."

Rachel thought Fred's sympathetic company was probably all Lizzie really needed, but she didn't point that out.

"How about you?" Fred asked. "Brothers or sisters?"

"None. Well, I had a stepbrother and sister for a short time, but that marriage didn't last. I never saw them after my father and their mother divorced. It was nice while it lasted, though." She'd never told her father, not wanting to make him feel bad, but she'd cried herself to sleep for weeks after that particular divorce. Her stepsiblings had wanted nothing to do with her anymore, which had hurt her terribly.

"So you lived with your father?"

"Yes." His name hovered on her lips. She pressed them close together to stop it from leaking out. That bit of information could ruin everything. "My mother died when I was seven and it broke my father's heart. He married two more times, but it's never been the same. At least according to . . ." *The household staff.* Again, she caught herself. "People who knew him back then."

Fred took a swallow of his beer. "Do you remember your mother?"

People didn't ask about her mother much. Maybe because once they knew about Rob Kessler, everything else faded away. He was the sun, blotting out every other celestial body. "I mostly remember the feeling of being with her. You know what I mean?"

"What was the feeling?"

Again, something no one had asked. Not even Dr. Stacy, who'd always focused on her time as a hostage. "Lightness. Laughter. Safety." Three things she hadn't felt much since her mother's death.

"My mother's more of a tough cookie," said Fred. "She had to be, raising a rabble like us. She's from the drill sergeant school of parenting."

"What about your dad?"

"Same, except he was often deployed too. I broke the family tradition by going into firefighting. They never let me hear the end of it, believe me."

She found the whole picture fascinating. A bunch

of big, loud soldiers tromping around the house being ordered around by their mother. "Why didn't you join up too?"

Looking embarrassed, he ran a hand across the back of his head. "My brother Jack says I'm too much of a . . . softy. Well, that's not the word he used, but you get the point."

She frowned, trying to understand. "Softy" didn't exactly describe the man who had dragged them all out of the limo. "It's not like you went into hairstyling or something."

The groove in his cheek deepened as he gave a laugh. "Believe it or not, Trent, my oldest brother, actually does a mean buzz cut. He used to trim the whole family's hair. Thing is, my brothers have a point. I'm better suited to the fire service. I guess I wanted to protect people without having to shoot anyone. I look up to my brothers, they're heroes, all of them. But I'll never be like them."

She puzzled over the picture he was painting. It seemed as though Fred thought more highly of his brothers than of himself. Which, considering that he'd saved her life, she didn't really agree with. "Are you close?"

Fred shrugged. "Sure. Family, you know. I worry about them when they're deployed."

"They must worry about you too. Firefighting's a dangerous job, from what I've heard." No need to tell she'd been researching the topic online.

He munched on a chip with an abstracted frown. "Lizzie might worry. And my mom. But my brothers have enough on their minds without bothering with San Gabriel Station 1. Except . . ." He hesitated.

"What?" She nudged his leg with her foot, which gave her a little thrill even through her flats and his jeans.

"Except for lately. They caught wind of this media crap and they're all over it. I wish they'd go back to forgetting the firehouse exists." He looked so glum that she had to laugh.

"Maybe they're jealous."

He shot her an incredulous look. "Believe me, each of my brothers has a couple inches, a lot of pounds, and a few medals on me. No one's jealous of Fred the Fireman."

"Really?" She crinkled her forehead skeptically. "The Bachelor Hero? The one all the girls are going crazy over? I picked up a button the other day, you know. It says 'Fred's My Hero.'"

He carefully put down his paper towel, made a show of dusting off his hands, and leveled a threatening glare at her. "I'm afraid I'm going to need that button, miss. You have five minutes to hand it over."

She picked up her purse and shoved it behind her, so it was wedged between her back and the couch. "I don't think so, Officer. I paid good money for that button. Ninety-nine cents, I think it was."

"I'll give you five bucks for it. Five times the asking price. A hundred times its actual value."

"It's not about the money," she said virtuously. "I can't be bought."

He left the armchair, took a step toward her, and leaned over, bracing his hands on the back of the couch behind her. A sharp thrill raced across her skin. "Everyone has their price. I'll get you another bottle of beer."

"No, thanks. I'm not a big drinker, as you probably figured out the first night we met."

"Good point. An extra slice of pizza, when it finally gets here."

He leaned closer. She noticed amber glints in his velvet-brown eyes, the smell of tomato sauce and . . .

that mouth again. "Not a chance. I'm trying to cut down on cheese."

"First crack at the New York Super Fudge Chunk."

"All forms of dairy, in fact." With each shake of her head, each denial, giggles bubbled to the surface. By now she was plastered against the couch, her purse a hard lump against the small of her back and Fred so close she felt the warmth of his breath fanning her face.

"Maybe I'll have to find some other way to persuade you," he said, low in his throat, his voice a good octave deeper than usual.

She squeaked out an answer that was little more than a surprised grunt, before he was kissing her, hot and deep. Not like the kiss she'd given him, which had barely qualified for the name. This kiss sent lust streaking through her like a freight train. She forgot about the purse, forgot about her squished position. Arching her body against his hard, eager weight, she kissed him back, just as fiercely as he was kissing her. He made a funny sound and, with one knee on the couch, took her face into his hands and devoured her mouth. His fingers fanned across her jaw, his thumbs stroked along her cheekbones. Her heart raced about a mile a minute.

When the doorbell rang, they pulled apart with a sharp gasp. Had she made that sound, or had he? Or both? She took in a long, ragged inhale. A few inches away from her face, Fred fought for breath, his eyes dark as midnight.

"Holy Bomb Squad," he muttered. "I thought it might have been a fluke, but it wasn't."

That was more words than she could manage. She struggled to sit up, still mute, while he backed away, adjusting his jeans. Her eyes flew to the impressively large bulge at his groin. The thought came to her that she'd done that. She'd turned him on and gotten him all hot and bothered, with nothing but a kiss. Heat flashed through her all over again.

"Must be the pizza guy. Let's hope he's near-sighted," he said, wincing as he swung off the couch. "Lamb chops," he chanted under his breath. "Cod liver oil. Creamed spinach. Bugs in my cereal milk."

She giggled, which she seemed to do a lot around Fred, when she wasn't kissing the bejeezus out of him.

"Just warning you," he said over his shoulder as he loped uncomfortably toward the door, "if I look at you I'll lose it again. So don't take it personally if I avoid looking your way until my . . . um . . . tent pole goes away."

She was already thinking of ways to get the tent pole back when she caught sight of the very last person she wanted to see at Fred's door.

The person who'd rung the doorbell wasn't carrying a pizza box. She was carrying a bottle of wine.

"Hi, Stud," purred Ella Joy as she prowled toward him. He held up a hand to stop her.

"This isn't a good time."

"Not yet, it isn't. If you play your cards right, it could be."

"Ella, I'm serious. Whatever you're up to, I'm not interested."

Fred looked nervously over his shoulder, but couldn't see Rachel or Greta. Maybe she'd found her way to the bathroom. He devoutly hoped that she had. He didn't want Rachel to get the wrong idea. Ella Joy was a man-eating anaconda, and sure, he'd been bowled over by her the first time she'd had dinner at the firehouse. But that was a long time ago, and he was no longer susceptible to her brand of sleazy ambition.

She was staring at his crotch. "My, my. Have you been thinking about me?"

"*No*. Except to wish you'd leave me alone. You're taking this too far, Ella."

Her gaze was still fixed on his erection. It was starting to go down, thanks to the shock of her appearance, but it had a long way to go. He'd never felt anything like the urgency that had overwhelmed him while kissing Rachel.

"I'm starting to see the reason for your nickname," mused Ella. "You never struck me as a 'stud' before now. But my, my, my. Little Freddie's packing some heat."

She advanced toward him, handing him the bottle of wine. He backed away in horror. The last thing he wanted was to have Ella touch him, or to accidentally touch her. He was sure it would be like touching a snake.

"What are you doing here, Ella? I'm busy."

"You don't look busy."

"I'm about to meet someone." If Ella hadn't seen Rachel, he didn't want to give away her presence.

"Someone better than me?" She pouted.

So much better. It would be like comparing ice cream to a frozen lump of coal. "I didn't invite you here." He put some steel into his voice. "You're one step away from trespassing."

"Rawr." She mimicked a tiger claw. "Oh fine. How about we cut the crap?"

"Since you're the only one dishing out the crap, go right ahead."

"Tired of your fifteen minutes already, Freddie?"

Again she tried to move past him, but he barred her way. He couldn't, absolutely *could not*, let Ella see

Rachel. Rachel was trying to avoid the news cameras, for some reason.

"If it was just fifteen minutes, I wouldn't mind. But we're past a week now, and enough is enough."

"Never enough, Stud. Never enough. But don't worry your pretty little"—again she glanced down his body—"head about it. I'm willing to negotiate."

"What are you talking about?"

"I'd planned to simply seduce you, but you clearly want to make my life difficult. So I'll make you an offer instead. I'll lay off the Bachelor Hero stuff, even though it's great for ratings and my news director will complain, if you do one thing for me."

"What?"

"The missing bridesmaid. I happen to know that you received a thank-you note from her. I've been hitting one dead end after another. None of the other bridesmaids will tell me anything." She pouted. "Women can be so difficult to work with. The limo driver is useless. None of my usual sources will give me anything. My investigative instincts are telling me there's something interesting going on here. And now you, dearest sweetest Fred, have the only hint of a clue. So, let's deal."

He stared at her. Maybe calling her an anaconda was too kind. "Why do you care about finding someone whose only claim to fame is getting rescued from a crushed limo? You interviewed everyone else, why isn't that enough?"

"Because, since you seem to forget, I am a reporter. Something tells me there's more to this story. Why did she run away? Why is she so hard to identify? Why did my killer footage of her punching you disappear from our news archives? It doesn't make sense. Think of it this way. If she's perfectly innocent and has nothing to hide, then it won't matter if I talk to her. If she isn't, well . . ." She shrugged. "Then you've done nothing wrong by telling me where she is."

A niggling seed of doubt entered Fred's mind. Ella was right. There was something odd going on. Rachel was very secretive and she had run away for no good reason. Something was going on. Something she hadn't told him.

But right now, none of that mattered. With a lightning-quick move, he flipped Ella off her feet and over his shoulder in the classic fireman's carry. Then, as she pounded her fists on his back, he marched her down his front walkway. He deposited her next to her BMW and pointed to the sidewalk.

"See that line?" He indicated the seam where the sidewalk met his front lawn. "You step one foot over it and I'm calling the police. I'll file charges of trespassing and invasion of privacy. Not to mention being a total B word."

Ella flounced toward the driver's seat of her little convertible. "You're in for it now, Stud."

"Bring it," he growled, hands planted on his hips. "Just don't try any crap like this again."

The convertible peeled off in a plume of expensive German exhaust. That made twice in a week that he'd pissed off a woman in a BMW. Hopefully they wouldn't all form a gang or something. Fred took a moment to catch his breath, then jogged back inside his house.

Rachel and Greta were gone.

Chapter 9

Rachel slipped out the side door and paused at the edge of the lawn long enough to see Fred man-handle Ella Joy into her sports car. She and Greta hopped into her dark blue Saab with its tinted, bulletproof windows. Then she drove home, refusing to think about what she'd witnessed until she was safely inside the cocoon of her own apartment.

Marsden, of course, was waiting in the foyer of the building. He frowned when he saw her and lumbered to his feet. Greta trotted happily toward him for some cuddling. "Home early, eh?"

"A reporter showed up at his house," she said glumly. She'd sworn Marsden to secrecy about her dinner at Fred's. "Greta and I had to make a quick escape behind his back. Now he probably thinks I'm even weirder than before."

Marsden grunted, then fell silent as he walked her to the private elevator that serviced her floor. He turned the key and the cherrywood doors opened silently. All three of them got in. Rachel steeled herself as the doors slid shut, enclosing them in claustrophobic, luxurious privacy, as if preserving them in amber for some future generation.

A sense of defeat gathered in the pit of Rachel's stomach as the elevator lifted them upward, away from Fred's world, into her private, lonely sanctuary. So much for a nice, normal evening with a cute fireman. Why had she even bothered to try? It was impossible. Every time she tried to step out of her own little bubble, something happened to drive her back in. The only saving grace was that her father didn't know about Fred.

"You could tell him the truth," Marsden commented.

"Tell my dad? There's no need. I won't ever see Fred again."

"Not your dad. Fred."

She whipped her head around, shocked down to her toes. "Tell Fred the truth about what?"

"Who you are. Why you left."

For a moment she was too stunned to say anything. "How can I do that? My father would freak out."

"It's possible," Marsden acknowledged. The elevator came to a gliding halt at the top floor and the doors whispered open. Rachel stepped out quickly, with her usual sense of relief at being released from a small space.

Marsden did his routine check of the apartment and the security system while she opened a can of dog food for Greta. The only other people in San Gabriel who knew her real name were her roommates at San Gabriel College. And her father had insisted on vetting them, interrogating them, and asking them to sign confidentiality agreements. It had been humiliating. Sometimes she suspected that the staff members at the Refuge might know, though none of them had ever said so.

She didn't want to put Fred through anything like that. But what if she just told him on her own, without bringing her father into it? The thought made her slightly dizzy, as if she'd stepped onto the edge of a cliff.

If she were smart, she would avoid Fred completely. He was a link to that reporter, Ella Joy. But the truth was, she didn't want to avoid him. The mulish, headstrong side of her rose up in revolt. Why should she have to avoid someone so great— and such a good kisser—because of something that had happened nearly twenty years ago? It wasn't fair.

Marsden entered the kitchen. "All clear."

As always. Sometimes she thought he had the most boring job in the world. "He could have sold me out, you know."

Marsden just listened, in that stolid, calm way of his.

"The reporter was looking for the missing bridesmaid, and I was right there. She even tried to bribe him. But he didn't give an inch. He threatened to charge her with trespassing." She smiled at the memory. "I don't think he likes to be pushed around."

"Sounds solid."

"He's a good guy." Somehow, that seemed like an understatement. In the short time she'd known him, Fred the Fireman had rescued her, protected her, and put himself on the line for her. Without any idea of who she was.

Didn't she owe him the truth?

Her stomach growled. She thought of the pizza

that had probably been delivered to Fred's house by now. "Want to order a pizza?" she asked Marsden, who nodded.

"I could eat."

Vader fed the length of four-inch hose toward Fred, who stood on a platform atop the hose tower. "You're saying she skipped out on you again? Stud, you're losing your touch."

"I thought I didn't have a touch."

"Oh, you have a touch, all right. You've got your own fan club now. I saw a story on it."

Fred pulled the hose over the top of the tower and straightened it. They'd just finished washing it and now it had to dry. "Let me guess. Ella Joy."

"Yeah, dude. I think she's obsessed with you."

Fred groaned. "She's trying to pressure me. But I'm not giving in. If I ever seem like I might give her an interview, I want you to tie me to this hose tower and stuff a rag in my mouth."

"Kinky," said Vader approvingly. "Didn't know you had it in you."

"What?" Fred shook his head. "What is wrong with you?"

"The question is what is right with me. Ask Cherie, she'll tell you."

Fred finished adjusting the hose and climbed down from the tower. "No thanks. I don't need another lecture on the wonders of Vader Brown."

Vader sighed happily, his rugged face going soft around the mouth. "I gotta tell you, Freddie, I never thought marriage would be such a good time. You should try it. Not with Courtney," he added quickly.

Fred tightened his jaw. Courtney had left three messages on his phone over the past two weeks. He had no interest in calling her back. They hadn't even dated that long, and they'd never had the kind of sparks he had with Rachel Allen.

But at least Courtney wasn't mysterious, like Rachel. The doubts sown by Ella Joy had multiplied in his mind. He'd Googled the name "Rachel Allen" and found about a billion, none of whom seemed to be the Rachel Allen he knew. Or didn't know.

"I broke it off with Courtney," he told Vader. "But she's pissed."

Vader threw an arm across Fred's shoulders. "Stay strong, bud. Stay strong. You know she's not right for you. Want some advice?"

Fred wanted to refuse, but Vader barreled forward without a pause.

"Now that you're a superstar, you're going to have to grow some balls. I'm not finished." He tightened his grip as Fred tried to pull away. "I know what a stand-up guy you are. Hell, you saved my mother's life. I'm not calling you a pussy here. I'm saying that you bend over backwards for the ladies, and sometimes that's a good thing, sometimes it isn't. Sometimes they don't want you to bend over backwards. They want you to bend *them* over while they beg you for—"

"Okay, okay," said Fred hastily. "You're a captain now, remember?"

"Right. You get the point. Standing up to Ella's a good start. Breaking up with Courtney is good, even if it was a long time coming. Now you have to carry that same attitude into finding the right girl. Go after what you want. Don't take no. But say no when you mean no. Get it?"

Before Fred could tell Vader what to do with his idiotic advice, the audio alarm interrupted them with a USAR call for Truck 1. Man stuck in a ravine—

that meant a high-angle rescue. Fred ran to the apparatus bay, pulled on his jumpsuit and steel-toed boots, grabbed his bag of gear, and hauled himself onto Truck 1. On the way to the location he fastened himself into his harness and put on his helmet, then stuck his radio into a pocket of his jumpsuit.

Five minutes later Fred peered down from an overpass into a ravine, where a man had been stuck in a tree since four in the morning. The IC ordered a two-line rappel system set up, and told Fred, the best paramedic on scene, to lower himself down to the victim. As they worked, the victim, whose name was Diego Montoya, told them in a mix of Spanish and English about how he'd been running from his ex-girlfriend, who was coming after him with a knife. He'd climbed over the guardrail, then tumbled headlong into the upper branches of a eucalyptus tree. He was very anxious to know if there was a blond woman with a knife nearby.

"Have you and your girlfriend ever considered counseling?" Fred asked once he'd lowered himself into the tree. He did a quick assessment of Diego's condition, but didn't see anything beyond scrapes and a cut over his eye. "I'm going to fasten this harness around you. Keep holding on to the tree," he instructed.

"You think that would help, sir? *Mi madre* says Kelly is just crazy. But you know what they say, crazy in the head, crazy in bed."

"Sure, but is that the kind of relationship you want?" He secured the harness around Diego, then pulled the line as a signal to the others to pull him up.

"Very good question, *señor*. I ask myself this, as I sit in this tree, one inch from certain death. Is she worth my life? Maybe I shouldn't have flirted with her sister."

"Really, you think so? All right, you're going to get hoisted up to the overpass now. Hang on. I'll be right behind you."

Diego kept getting caught in the branches, and Fred had to do some impromptu chopping with his knife. Sweat was pouring down his face by the time Diego swung free from the branches. The crew pulled Fred up next. As soon as he stepped over the guardrail, Diego grabbed him in a bear hug.

"*Gracias, gracias,*" he kept saying, tears rushing down his cheeks.

"*De nada.*" Fred shook his hand, trying to put things on a more professional footing. "Don't forget the counseling."

"*Sí, señor.* Whatever you say."

Fred turned to find himself face to face with a camera and a smug Ella Joy. "The Bachelor Hero strikes again," she said into her mic. "Fred Breen, what can you tell us about this life-or-death situation? Witnesses say you saved this poor man from plunging to a gruesome death."

"*No hablo inglés,*" he said as he brushed past her.

Some of the other crew members cracked up. He heard Ella address the victim. "What do you have to say to your rescuer?"

"I want to say, Kelly, baby, I love you and I'm sorry, *mi amor.*"

Fred smiled as he stowed his lines and harness into his bag. *Take that, Ella Joy.*

When he got back to the station, he found out that several people had called. The messages included the usual flirtatious invitations, a call from Courtney, and one from Rachel. She had, miracle of miracles, actually left her phone number.

He hesitated a moment before calling her back. On the one hand there was that urgent attraction and even fascination. Even the sight of her name on the slip of paper made his blood run hot. On the other hand, he didn't need any more drama. He'd reached his quota with Courtney.

In the end, there wasn't really any question. He dialed the number.

"Can you come to my place?" she asked without much preamble. "I really need to talk to you."

"Is everything okay?"

"It's fine. I . . . I'll explain when you get here."

"I'm working until tomorrow morning."

"I'll have breakfast waiting. Pepperoni pizza okay?"

"Cute, very cute. Fine, I'll swing by after work." She gave him the address. He stuffed it in his pocket and refused to think about it until the next morning.

Unfortunately, by the next morning he was a sleep-deprived zombie. The crew had kept busy with call after call. And when he wasn't out on a call, he was receiving platters of baked goods from the residents of San Gabriel. Oddly, they all seemed to be female.

So when he strode to the front door of 100 Vista Drive, it didn't register at first that he was looking at a building more suitable for Los Angeles or New York than humble San Gabriel. It was all glass and steel. It even had a doorman, a grizzled African-American fellow who seemed to be expecting him. The doorman guided him to the elevator and pushed a button. The elevator whisked him up on silent, whizzing pulleys, then whispered to a stop at the top floor.

The elevator button panel called it the penthouse. Fred had never been in a penthouse before.

Rachel was waiting for him at the open door of the

only apartment on the floor. Even in this state of advanced fatigue, he appreciated the sight of her forest-green leggings, loose yoga-type top, and bare feet.

"Thanks for coming," she said, her gaze darting behind him. Was she nervous? What did she have to be nervous about? She lived in a mansion, or the apartment building equivalent of one.

"You mentioned breakfast," Fred said. "I hope that includes coffee, because I'm wiped."

"Of course. Rough night? I saw you on TV."

He held up a hand. "Don't tell me. I don't want to know."

"It wasn't that bad. They only called you Bachelor Hero twice."

He smiled, and she beckoned him inside.

For a surreal moment, he wondered if he was still asleep and having some kind of very weird dream. Everything inside her apartment was pristine and perfect and looked like it cost a million dollars. The coffee table seemed to be formed of some rare metallic substance with speckles of glitter embedded in it. The rug was so soft and plush, it was probably hand-woven cashmere from wild goats roaming the Himalayas. Everywhere he looked, something impossibly expensive and luxurious stared back.

And the worst of it was, Rachel looked as if she belonged here. With this backdrop, she looked rare and expensive herself. The thought of his spaghetti sauce and eight-year-old doorman named Kip made his face prickle with mortification.

"I'll get the coffee. Sit down and rest." Rachel pointed to a couch upholstered in buttery soft rust-colored suede. A woven throw was artfully draped over the back.

"If I sit down on that I won't wake up until tomorrow," he told her.

"Do you want to talk later? We can reschedule. I'm not due in at work until later this afternoon."

"No, thanks. I don't have a lot of time. A guy's coming over to fix the toilet and . . ." He felt like an idiot talking about plumbing in this immaculate space, with this beautiful girl looking at him expectantly. "Never mind. What did you want to talk about?"

She bit her lip. "There's a very uncomfortable chair in the corner. Guaranteed to keep you awake. I'll be back in one second."

Uncomfortable though it was—the fabric seemed to be made of recycled scrub brushes—he still nearly drifted off. He should have gone straight home for some shut-eye before coming here. He started when she appeared with a tray that held a silver coffee-pot and two large mugs. A basket covered with a napkin released an amazing, buttery, sugary, life-is-good fragrance. Mingled with the aroma of rich, dark coffee, it was enough to make him decide the place wasn't so bad after all.

She pulled another armchair across the soft carpet. "Do you want to sit here now? Have you had enough?"

"Nope. I'm good. My butt is used to it now." He took a gulp of coffee and downed the pecan raspberry muffin she offered him. Moaning in appreciation, he barely remembered his original reason for being there. But he couldn't delay forever. "So what's up, Rachel? If it's about the media, I'm doing what I can to keep it under control. But there's not a whole hell of a lot I can do. I'm sorry about Ella Joy showing up the other—"

"My real name is Rachel Kessler," she interrupted. "Allen was my mother's name, so it's not a lie. But my real last name is Kessler."

"Oooo-kay." This didn't seem like groundbreaking news. So she used a different last name. Maybe she liked it better. He looked at her blankly, noticing the tension in her posture and the way she was watching him, as if cringing internally. "Cool," he offered.

Man, he was tired. He swiped a hand across his eyes, trying to focus.

"That name doesn't mean anything to you, does it?" The realization seemed to stun her.

He frowned. *Rachel Kessler.* Maybe it did have a certain ring to it. If only he weren't so exhausted. "I suppose I've heard the name before, but I can't put my finger on it. Rachel Kessler," he repeated.

"Try Rob Kessler."

Now that did strike a chord. A big one. How had he missed *that*? He shook his head to clear it. "The computer genius billionaire. That Rob Kessler?"

"Yes. He's my father."

Her father was Rob Kessler? Fred's thoughts went on a dizzying carnival ride, the kind that spins you upside down and makes you throw up on your date. Rob Kessler was one of the richest men in the world. He'd invited the daughter of one of the richest men in the world to his house for spaghetti. Then he'd dropped the spaghetti on the floor and ordered pizza. Not only that—horror filtered through him. He'd *kissed* her. *Twice.*

Oh God. Did Rachel invite him here to warn him that Rob Kessler didn't want Fred the Fireman touching his daughter ever again?

"I . . . I didn't know," he managed to get out.

"I know you didn't know. That's why I'm telling you," Rachel said, a bit impatiently. "I felt you deserved to know why I'm so camera-shy, and why I had to leave that night at your house. Very few people in San Gabriel know who I am, and I definitely don't want the local news to find out. Now you understand, right?"

Did he? He was so confused. So tired and jumbled up. So Rachel had a rich computer genius father, which somehow explained why she didn't like the media. Yeah, he supposed that made sense. But it's not like she herself was famous. Reporters didn't bother with the adult children of billionaires unless they got a DUI or partied with Lindsay Lohan or did something else newsworthy . . .

And then some long-forgotten fact niggled at his memory. *Rachel Kessler*. A tech legend's child kidnapped . . . held hostage . . . it had been on all the news channels. He'd been thirteen, and caught up in his own crap, but the story had been so chilling and dramatic, everyone had been talking about it. She'd been held in a tiny cage for weeks. It suddenly clicked.

"Small spaces."

She gave a tiny, wistful nod, as if the world was closing in once again.

Chapter 10

In the time she'd known Fred, Rachel had never had any trouble interpreting his feelings. Exasperation, concern, the intent to kiss . . . it was all written right on his face with no attempt at disguise. But now, something had changed. He sat sprawled in her grandmother's horsehide armchair, peering blankly up at her through bloodshot eyes. Rachel had no idea what he was thinking. Maybe her revelation was no big deal after all. He'd probably seen all kinds of things in his line of work. Maybe he was angry and didn't want to tell her. Maybe . . . maybe . . .

Rachel clenched her hands around her mug of coffee. It smelled acrid to her, and the muffins she'd ordered from Cindy's parents' bakery clogged in her throat. This was a mistake, a huge mistake. What if he told someone else her secret? She'd have to leave San Gabriel and the Refuge and her only real friends and . . .

She made to stand up, but he snaked out an arm and stopped her. "Do I get to ask questions?"

She sat back down, jerky as a marionette. "Possibly," she said, not wanting to promise too much. "What kind of questions?"

"Are you okay now?"

For a moment she went blank. "You mean since the kidnapping," she said slowly as his meaning sank in.

"Well, yeah."

Was she okay? Interesting question with no simple answer. "You're looking right at me. What do you think?"

He narrowed his reddened eyes at her. "I think you're avoiding the question. That's okay, it's probably a dumb question anyway." He stopped, and scratched the back of his head, leaving a swath of mink-dark hair standing straight up. Staring into his coffee cup, he seemed to draw in a deep breath. "So you're, what's the word, the thing celebrities do when they don't want anyone to spot them . . . incognito?"

She crossed one leg over the other, not liking the tone of his question.

"First of all, I'm not a celebrity. I'm just a person who happens to be the daughter of Rob Kessler, who happened to make a lot of money and a lot of enemies. Can you blame me for not wanting to walk around announcing my identity?"

He set down his mug with an ominous click. "I didn't say I blamed you. I just asked."

She hated the way he was looking at her, as if he was disappointed or maybe annoyed. *Annoyed?* What right did he have to be annoyed? She shot to her feet. "I'm damned if I do, damned if I don't. If I used my real name, people would assume I'm trying to win special favors. If I don't, then I'm 'incognito,' like some spoiled movie star. *Incognito.* Do I look like I'm incognito?" Even she knew she wasn't making sense, but the unfairness of the situation made her blood boil. She hadn't asked for any of this.

"Hang on a damn second." Fred leaped to his feet too, brushing against his coffee cup, which wobbled dangerously close to the edge of the table. "You insist I come over here after the longest fucking shift in history, throw your fancy apartment in my face, and announce you're a billionaire. Then I ask one simple question and you jump all over me."

The shock of his reaction reverberated through her system. No one talked to her like that. *No one.* Not even her best friends. Definitely not the Refuge staff or Marsden or her father or any of her father's household staff. "I didn't throw my apartment in your face. It's my apartment. That's all. How do you throw an apartment anyway? I'm not Thor."

He ignored her feeble attempt at a joke. "You could have met me at a coffee shop, or a park, or at my house. You wanted me to see your place."

"So you could understand."

"Understand what? That you're wealthy? Point taken."

Their gazes locked. Steam was practically coming out of Fred's ears. She thought of the panic buttons installed throughout the apartment. One click and Marsden would be up here in a flash. He was probably waiting right outside the door.

She pictured Fred being dragged out of her apartment. That would teach him to be nicer to her. She'd shared her deepest secret; why was he focusing on her apartment? Who cared about that?

She tried one last attempt at an explanation. "I don't want people to know me as Rachel Kessler, famous kidnapped kid. I want them to know me as Rachel Allen, dog therapist. Is that a crime?"

Fred struck the heel of his hand against his forehead as if a light bulb had just turned on. "The Refuge for Injured Wildlife. You own that place. That's why there's so much security. I thought you just worked there."

"I never said that."

"You can probably hire every dog trainer in California. I bet you were laughing your ass off at my pathetic little offer of help."

"No, of course not," she said hotly.

He didn't seem to hear—or care. "Is that why you decided to come to my place? You were slumming it?"

"No! That's ridiculous."

"Ridiculous. Right." Again he passed his hand across his eyes. "My God, and then I kissed you. I was one step away from boning you right there on the couch. You must have been thanking your lucky stars Ella Joy showed up when she did."

The blood drained from her face. How dare he say something like that? Before he could say any more cruel things, she said loudly, "Three-two-seven," the code numbers for the voice-activated panic button.

"Three-two-seven? What are you talking about?" Again, Fred scrubbed a hand through his hair. "Rachel, look, I'm sorry. I shouldn't have said that. That was way over the line. You threw me for a loop and I'm trying to get my bearings, that's all." He gave her an exhausted-looking smile. "Ask any firefighter's family. End of a shift is no time for a serious conversation."

At the sound of Marsden at the door, she turned her back on Fred. Even though fury still raced through her veins like acid, it turned out that she didn't want to actually *witness* Fred being dragged from her apartment.

"Time to go, kid," she heard Marsden say.

"Rachel!" Fred said in an urgent tone. "What the hell's going on?"

The sound of a scuffle followed, but since Marsden was a highly decorated former Marine she had no doubt how it would turn out.

She was wrong.

"The least you could do is tell me you want me to leave," came Fred's furious voice. She spun around. Astonishingly, he had Marsden in a headlock, and didn't even seem to be breathing hard. "You invited me here, Rachel *Kessler*. Don't you think it's a little rude to throw me out?"

She clutched her hands together. "Stop it! You're hurting him."

"I'm not hurting him." He released Marsden, who stumbled forward, his hand at his throat. Rachel rushed to help him.

"I'll be leaving now," Fred announced to them both, then glanced around the room. "I'm leaving now," he repeated, more loudly. "In case anyone at the other end of a hidden camera wants to know."

And he stalked out of her apartment.

Rachel helped Marsden onto the suede loveseat, where he sat, taking in deep, wheezing breaths. "Are you okay?"

"Humiliated. But okay."

"Oh, that jerk! I can't believe he did that to you!"

Marsden gave a dry chuckle. "Child, I started it. Took him about half a second to get the best of me. Kid's got some moves."

"Well, it seems very rude to me. Stay right here, let me get you some water." *Moves*, she thought indignantly as she hurried to the kitchen. He had moves all right. *I was one step from boning you right there on the couch.* Shivers raced through her at the memory of that statement. Is that really what would have happened if Ella Joy hadn't appeared? Spontaneous, hot sex—that was the kind of thing Liza did. And hadn't Cindy had sex in the kitchen the first time she and Bean had gotten together?

As she filled a glass from the filtered water spigot on the front of the fridge, another thought struck her. Fred hadn't coddled her the way many did. He'd shown her his honest reaction, whether she liked it or not. For better or worse, he hadn't held back. A secret sense of astonishment curled through her. Whatever else that exchange had been— surprising, distressing—it was real. So few things in her life, aside from the dogs she worked with, ever felt real. Even the Refuge was a carefully guarded bubble.

And in thanks, she'd kicked him out of her apartment. Well, tried to kick him out. Even in that, Fred the Fireman had surprised her.

Fred was halfway down the street, completely caught up in his fury at Rachel's actions, when he noticed the black sedan cruising next to him. It had black-tinted windows and a German name he didn't recognize. It looked like the sort of car the CIA might use, or some international assassin. When the rear passenger side window rolled down, he half expected a revolver with a silencer to come next. Except that this was sunny San Gabriel, California, not some spy movie. Instead of a gun, two very intense dark eyes aimed virtual bullets at him.

"Frederick Lancaster Breen. Let's talk." The man in the sedan had a deep voice, and sounded like he was in a big hurry.

Fred kept walking. "I don't talk to strangers. Especially anonymous ones who know my middle name."

After a brief silence, the man said, "I'm Rob Kessler. Please, this won't take long. I'll drive you home."

"That would be counterproductive, since my truck's right over there."

"Then we'll take a short drive. We'll be done in fifteen minutes. That's all I can spare."

Now that made Fred want to laugh. God forbid he take up too much time during a conversation he hadn't asked for. After amusement came curiosity. Given how he'd just left things with Rachel, he couldn't imagine many fond feelings would be coming his way from her father. But maybe he didn't know about the scene in her apartment. Or maybe he did, and wanted to yell at him about it. Since there was only one way to find out, he got in the car, circling around to slide onto the rear driver side seat.

The black leather interior welcomed him like some kind of exclusive men's club. He caught the scent of smoky green tea. Steam curled from the stainless steel mug in Rob Kessler's gloved hand. The man was long and lean, almost emaciated, and sat tailor-style on the backseat. He had dark slanting eyebrows—much like Rachel's—and a chin studded with dark stubble. He wore a black turtleneck and wire-rimmed glasses.

Fred had read a few things about Rob Kessler over the years, but in his advanced state of exhaustion, he couldn't remember any of them. Not that it really mattered at the moment.

"What do you want?" he asked bluntly. "I'm late for my nap."

"I don't sleep much myself," said Kessler, taking

a sip from his mug. "Rarely more than two hours at a time."

"Then you'd make a good firefighter."

"Not a career I ever considered," he said dryly.

Fred gave an unwilling laugh. "Yeah, well, only a certain kind of lunatic does."

"Have you ever thought of a different career?" At some unseen signal, the driver began coasting forward. "Around the block, that's all," Kessler told them both. "We should be able to finish our business by then."

"Probably, since I can't imagine what business we might have." Fred was truly bewildered, and he didn't think it was due to sleep deprivation. Something strange was going on here. "As for your question, I considered the military. Air force, most likely. But I ended up with the fire service."

"You have an excellent record."

He shifted uncomfortably on the sleek leather. "You checked? Why?"

"I'm an information addict. I can't ever know enough."

"But why would you want information about me? I barely know your daughter. And after this morning, I'm sure I'll never see her again." That statement made him suddenly miserable. He'd behaved horribly to her, he knew it. Finding out she was Rachel Kessler was like finding out she was Beyoncé—completely and terminally out of reach. "You can stop collecting information on me."

"Not true," said Kessler sharply. "You will see her again. I want to hire you."

"*What?*" He shook his head, certain he'd misheard. "What the hell for?"

"Protection."

"She has a security guard. The dude who kicked me out of her apartment."

"That's not what the tape shows."

"I knew there were hidden cameras!" Fred's triumph shifted to disgust. "You spy on your own daughter?"

"Only when necessary. An unknown man coming to her apartment made it necessary. The video camera activated when she gave the alarm code."

Fred remembered all the things he'd said to Rachel. Hadn't he mentioned boning her on his couch? Was Kessler going to murder him now? Was that what this was all about? But no . . . she'd said the code after that part of the conversation. After he'd been so rude.

"What I saw was the second-place winner of the Southern California Muay Thai Championships kicking my security guard's ass. I want to add you on as a second bodyguard."

"What . . . no . . . *what*?" He'd officially stepped down the rabbit hole and landed in a train wreck. "I'm not a bodyguard. I'm a firefighter."

Kessler ignored him, continuing in his intense, vibrating voice. "I have congressional testimony coming up. That means extra, undesirable media attention. I need someone with my daughter twenty-four hours a day. I need someone living in her apartment with her. Someone quick and smart and strong. Someone she's comfortable with."

"That is not me," Fred said firmly. "She just booted me out."

"Yes, but you were there because she invited you. She's never invited anyone inside before. Except her friends, and none of them are bodyguard material.

She trusts you, or she never would have told you who she was. I've forbidden it."

Fred swallowed hard. Rachel had broken her father's rules in order to share her secret with him. In return, he'd tossed it back in her face. He'd acted like a jackass. "I . . . I'm not the right guy. I already have a job. And I only won second place in that tournament. I don't have the skills."

"You as good as won first. No one could beat Namsaknoi Yudthagarngam. He's been trained from birth."

"Right?" Fred said eagerly, clapping his hands on his thighs. Sweet vindication. "No one believed me about that."

"Believe it, it's true. You're even better than you thought." Kessler gave him a funny half smile. "So are you in?"

"No. I don't know anything about being a bodyguard."

"You're skilled with weapons." It wasn't a question. Obviously, Kessler had done his research.

"Of course, everyone in my family is. Military, you know. But I don't like to use guns."

"That's good. I don't want some trigger-happy jarhead around my daughter. I want someone smart, competent, skilled, courageous, and trustworthy. You're it. Driver, head back."

Oh no. This was all moving too fast for Fred. Especially at this hour of the morning. "Mr. Kessler, I have a job already. I can't just leave the firehouse."

"Two weeks. That's all I'm asking. Until my testimony's done. You can take a two-week leave, right? I checked your departmental regulations."

Fred nodded dumbly. Yes, he could take a leave.

"I'll sweeten the deal. Something you can't resist."

Kessler probably thought he could buy everyone

under the sun. "I don't need any money," he started to say, but Kessler cut him off.

"I know you don't. You do okay, and you're single with no dependents. I know money's not a big issue for you."

Of course he knew. Was there anything he didn't know? Again, Fred thought uncomfortably of the way he'd kissed Rachel.

"But you do need to get the news media off your back. Two weeks out of the spotlight would help. And I can pull some strings at Channel Six. The news director owes me some favors. I can get Ella Joy to drop the Bachelor Hero stories."

Fred stared. Could this man really do all that? Eyeing his emphatic, bony profile, Fred didn't really doubt it. "I would definitely appreciate some peace and quiet on that front."

"I can't hypnotize the female population of San Gabriel, sadly," added Kessler with a hint of dry humor. "But I can buy up all the fan club buttons." He turned his head sideways, narrowing his penetrating gaze at Fred. "You aren't yet convinced, are you?"

Fred hesitated. "The thing is, I just passed all the training for USAR—Urban Search and Rescue. The crew needs me. There's only six of us in the whole city. I don't feel right walking away, even if it's just for two weeks. I worked my ass off for that gig. And I love it. I finally have a chance to prove myself, and—"

"How much did Rachel tell you?" Kessler interrupted again.

"Um . . ." Fred fumbled to remember. "Just who she was, and then I remembered that she was kidnapped, and—"

"Did she tell you that she escaped the bastard?

On her own, except for the help of a stray dog? Did she tell you that he probably would have killed her if she hadn't? Did she tell you that the kidnapper was never identified, let alone arrested?"

The questions were coming fast as bullets. Fred froze, unable to move, even to shake his head yes or no.

"Here's something I'm certain she didn't tell you, because she doesn't know. I've never told her. Every few years, the kidnapper sends me a message. Know what that message is? Same thing he told her every time he put her back in that cage." The rage vibrating through the man's body seemed to shake the car. "*To be continued.* That's what he says, taunting me like the sadistic demon he is. To be continued. So." The car jerked to a stop next to Fred's truck. Kessler drilled Fred with eyes of midnight steel. "I'm going to ask you again, since I know what really drives you. I know you can't resist someone who needs help. *Are you in?*"

Chapter 11

"**N**o!" Rachel, doing a fair imitation of a violet-eyed Tasmanian devil, glared at her father, then Fred, then at Marsden for good measure. "I refuse."

"There you go," Fred told Kessler. "I told you she wouldn't go for it."

"She'll go for it," Kessler said grimly.

"Now you're talking about me right in front of me. That's even worse than trying to hire a bodyguard behind my back."

"Two weeks, honey. That's all it's going to be. Until my testimony's done."

"It's going to be zero weeks." Rachel looked truly furious, and Fred couldn't blame her. The way Kessler treated her must make her feel like a child. "One bodyguard is more than enough, right, Marsden? You're being paranoid."

"There are worse things than being paranoid." Kessler scraped out the words.

Rachel flinched, then turned desperately to her

security guard. "Tell him, Marsden. We're fine the way we are."

"Truth is, I recommended him." Marsden jerked his head toward Fred. "We could use him."

Fred glanced at the older man in surprise. Not more than half an hour ago, he'd had the guy in a headlock. Now he was advocating for him?

"Been feeling some aches and pains lately," Marsden added, though it clearly cost him to admit it. "Wouldn't want you to pay for that."

Rachel looked stricken by that news. She bit her lip then whirled around, turning her back on them all. She had changed into work clothes, a light gray sweater and khaki pants. A clip held her hair in a knot, so Fred could make out the delicate tendons of her neck. Greta trotted to her side and rubbed her head against her leg.

"But why him?" she tossed over her shoulder. "He's a fireman, not a bodyguard."

"I'm confident he's got the right skills," said Kessler. "And you seem more comfortable with him than—"

Before he could continue, and before Rachel could erupt into a full-scale rejection of him, Fred interrupted. "Can I have a second to talk this over with Rachel?" And before she could get mad that he was excluding her, added quickly, "Is that okay with you, Rachel?"

Kessler gave him a long, intense scrutiny, then nodded once. "You have ten minutes. Marsden, come with me."

The two men left, the door quietly sliding shut behind them. Fred wondered if they were going to watch the conversation on the hidden cameras. "Do you know how to disable the video system?" He asked Rachel.

Wordlessly, she walked to an Impressionist painting on the wall—he wondered if it was the real thing—flipped it up to reveal a console, and pushed a few buttons. She didn't meet his eyes, and a slight flush lingered on her cheeks. It occurred to him that she probably felt embarrassed.

"I didn't like the idea at first either," he said matter-of-factly. "I flat-out said no, in fact."

Anger flared in her eyes, which she finally raised to meet his. "Is that supposed to make me feel better? Why would you want to play bodyguard to some incognito spoiled rich girl?"

"Come on now. I never said anything like that."

"I can read between the lines."

He tried a smile. "I overreacted, I was exhausted, but I never called you spoiled. I might have called you rich."

Her lips twitched in a brief smile, which she quickly tamped down. She leaned one hip against the arm of her couch. Greta draped her chin across Rachel's thigh, begging for some petting. Rachel absently obliged.

"My father is very good at getting his way. He must have offered you something really big to get you to change your mind. Lots of money, of course. But it would probably take more than that. Does the fire department need something? A new engine or ladder or whatever?"

Fred held on to his temper. "We didn't even discuss payment."

"Then what? What would make you leave your action-packed Bachelor Hero job to babysit a dog therapist for two weeks? How did my dad talk you into it?"

"I said yes on one condition." It hadn't been easy extracting that concession from Kessler, but since it was a deal breaker for Fred, eventually he'd given in.

"What's the condition?" Rachel must have been rubbing Greta's head a little too roughly, because the dog gave a slight whimper.

"That he lets me tell you everything. So you know *why* he wants you to have more protection."

Rachel froze, her hand still on Greta's warm, silky head. She knew her father kept things from her. That was his nature. He consumed information like a crack addict, but he gave it out like Scrooge. It had always driven her crazy, but why would Fred care about that?

She eyed him closely, noticing the deep shadows under his eyes and the exhaustion sketched across his face in creases. The poor guy probably regretted ever walking into the City Lights Grill, into the Kessler vortex. But she couldn't let her softhearted side, which wanted to tuck him into a bed and let him sleep, distract her.

"All right. Tell me."

Fred didn't dance around it. "The most recent message your father got from your kidnapper was about six months ago. It came to his private e-mail."

Chills shot through her. She'd known the kidnapper made a periodic reappearance. Her father and Marsden gave her reports that she knew were carefully edited, but she always sensed when something had happened. Maybe it was time to hear the full truth, with no censoring. "And it said?"

"Like all the others." He hesitated. "'To be continued.'"

Nausea clutched her by the throat, darkness crowded the edges of her vision. She'd never forget those words, hissed in that man's sadistic, mocking voice. She jumped to her feet, dislodging Greta, and stalked into the kitchen. She was not, absolutely not, going to lose it in front of Fred.

She went to the coffeemaker and poured herself another cup, her hands shaking. No wonder her father was freaked out. His private e-mail—that meant that the kidnapper was still lurking around Dad's territory. She took a deep breath, then another. Okay, so the kidnapper was still tormenting her father. The fact remained he'd made no more attempts on her life or safety. Maybe he didn't know where she was. Maybe he intended to get to her father some other way.

Or . . . maybe he was just biding his time.

"I suggested that one of my brothers might be a better choice." Fred's voice behind her made her jump. "I think Jack has some leave coming up."

Rachel had a sudden panicked vision of a big military guy with a brush cut storming through her apartment. "No thanks."

Face it, she was going to have to give in on the bodyguard thing. This new piece of information made it official. She hated the intrusion on her privacy, but she wasn't stupid. Would it be so bad having Fred around? Even at this moment, when she was still trembling from anger and shock, the presence of his strong body and square-jawed face made her feel safe.

For a moment, she thought about how things had been at his house, fun and normal and relaxed. So much for that. The Kessler curse had struck again.

She took another mug from the cupboard, poured coffee into it, and offered it to Fred.

"You'd be bored out of your mind shadowing me for two weeks."

"I don't think so." His firm, quiet statement made her flush. "I figure I'll focus on training Greta. Maybe learn how to splint an owl's wing or bandage a rabbit's foot. Would it be so bad, Rachel?"

His phrasing echoed her own thoughts. "We kissed," she pointed out.

"I remember. I almost mentioned it to your father. Should I have?"

"No!" she snapped, then realized he was teasing. She tilted her head to the ceiling, praying for strength. Oh, this was turning out to be complicated. "We should pretend it never happened. You probably kiss people all the time. I know I do."

Now *that* was a blatant lie. Getting involved with men held so many land mines that she rarely attempted it. And none of the sexual encounters she'd experienced held a candle to Fred's kisses. From under her lashes, she stole a glance at him. He was toying with his coffee mug, staring into the depths as if it held all the answers.

And suddenly she felt horrible.

"Actually, I don't kiss people all the time," she corrected herself softly. His gaze flew to meet hers, and suddenly it felt as if a pathway had opened up between them, a river of connection, swollen and tumbling with confused emotion. If she dipped a toe into it, it would sweep her away.

"Besides, my father doesn't have to know everything," she added.

"Does he know that?" Fred's dry question, delivered over the rim of the porcelain coffee mug, made her laugh. Clearly, Fred had already gotten the hang of the mighty Rob Kessler. It made her feel a little less alone, actually.

He put down his mug and ran his thumb up and down the handle. His thumb was large and sturdy, just like the rest of his hand. Her stomach clenched in a sort of electric shock. The force of it astonished her; she actually put one hand to her midriff. Never, ever in her life had she reacted to a man the way she responded to Fred.

If he was here, with her, around the clock, would she be walking around tingling all the time?

This was a bad idea. A really bad idea. She was crazy to even be contemplating it.

Greta trotted over to Fred, sniffed his pants leg, then curled up next to him, her chin on his shoe.

And suddenly she was back in that place, that lonely cage, where the only friendly face was that of a stray German shepherd. She used to watch him for hour after hour, soaking in his every twitch and growl, learning his moods. She called him Inga after her doll at home, even though she figured he was probably a boy dog. He was hungry all the time, so she tossed him food through the bars of the cage they kept her in. Then one day, when one of the hired guards had opened the cage door, Inga sank her teeth into his leg and wouldn't let go. In her mind, Rachel clearly heard the dog telling her to run. She scrambled out of the cage. The guard kicked her in the head with his free leg, but she kept going, out of the old warehouse. Gunshots rang out. She never knew if Inga got shot, or if the guard was shooting at her. If so, he missed. She kept running and running, into the desert, until she passed out. The next thing she remembered, she was in a hospital and her father was there.

Ever since Inga, she'd never gone wrong following the guidance of a dog.

"What are you thinking?" Fred's soft voice brought her back to the moment.

She took a long, bracing swallow of her coffee.

"I guess . . . I guess I was thinking that we should do this."

"You're right. We should."

"But I still don't understand why you *want* to."

He met her eyes, his expression so determined that she started. This must be the "badass" Fred his friend had mentioned at the City Lights Grill. "Believe me, as soon as your father filled me in on the situation, there was nothing on earth that could have kept me from taking the job."

She screwed up her face in genuine puzzlement. "Is this a man thing? Do you *like* danger? Or wait, maybe it's a crazy firefighter thing?"

She didn't understand why that made him laugh so hard. "Don't think being my bodyguard gives you license to tease me," she told him. That just made him laugh all the harder.

"A little teasing never hurt anyone," he said with the ghost of a wink. "Take it from me."

Vader scowled at Fred from behind his desk. Station 1's newest captain had always been the most fitness-obsessed in the crew. Thick ridges of muscle bulged against his uniform shirt. Powerful tendons flexed in his forearms. Fred couldn't help thinking that Vader would be a much better choice as a personal bodyguard. No one would dare mess with Rachel if Captain Brown was on the job.

On the other hand, he might be inclined to pick a fight just for the recreational benefit.

"How long of a leave of absence?" Vader asked.

"Two weeks. Maybe three." Kessler's testimony was supposed to happen in two weeks, but Fred thought it wise to leave his options open.

"And what is this special project? Something to do with USAR?"

Well, it was a sort of rescue situation taking place in an urban area. "Something like that," Fred murmured. "I can't say too much about it."

"Military? Something to do with your brothers?"

"Nah, nothing like that."

Vader narrowed his eyes at him. Fred wouldn't mind filling him in; it might help to have backup. But Rachel had asked him not to tell anyone at the station, in case word got back to Ella Joy.

"It's personal," Fred finally said. "I can't say any more."

"Is it about that girl? The one from the limo?"

How the hell did Vader guess? Fred didn't answer.

"I recognize trouble when I see it," said Vader. "And that girl is five-alarm trouble."

Well, yes, that was definitely true. Rachel had already upended his life in any number of ways. He could only imagine the challenges of guarding her. But Vader didn't need to know any of that.

"I'll take the time without pay. But this is something I have to do."

Vader looked like he wanted to say more, and maybe in earlier days he would have. He would have found some way to tease Fred or coerce the information out of him. Instead, he offered him a nod of agreement. "All right. If you need anything, let me know."

He stood, and they shook hands. It felt weirdly formal.

"Stud, I don't know what's going on with you," Vader added, tilting his head to squint at him, "but you seem different. You all right? You're not into anything dangerous, are you?"

That might be understating it. "Everything's cool."

After taking what he needed from his locker, he drove home. On the way, he dialed Lizzie. "Remember how you keep saying you owe me?"

"Yep," she said cheerfully. "I probably owe you about fifty gallons of ice cream by now."

"I don't want ice cream. I want a favor. You know the kids across the street? The ones with the single mom who always needs help?"

"You mean the little ninja speed demons? Oh no."

"Oh yes. You offered, Liz."

"I never offered babysitting!"

"It's not babysitting. It's . . . ninja sitting."

"Can I actually sit *on* them? Because that would be a different story." She giggled. "Fine. What night are we talking about?"

"Well, that's the thing." He explained the situation in terms as vague as possible. A two-week special project that required his USAR and martial arts training. But Lizzie wasn't buying it; she had a sixth sense for anything related to personal drama.

"This involves a girl, doesn't it?"

"Does it matter?"

"If it's Courtney, count me out."

"It's not Courtney. I told you we broke up."

"Yes, but I know her, and I know she wouldn't put up with someone breaking up with her."

"Believe me, it's over."

"So it's someone different. Someone you like? A lot?"

Fred let his silence do the talking, and it seemed to work.

"So if I agree to help you, your love life might improve?"

Again, he let Lizzie think whatever she liked. But once he started working for Rachel, any personal involvement would be completely unacceptable.

"I'm taking your silence as a desperate plea for help in the romance department. And so I consent to your request," Lizzie said graciously.

"You're a saint."

"As long as you let me meet her."

"You're a saint *and* a blackmailer."

He had a much harder time explaining the situation to the Sinclair kids.

"Someone needs my help," he told them seriously, after he'd gathered them into his practice studio. "When someone needs your help, you can't just walk away. At least, I can't."

"But you help people all the time," whined Kip. "And what about us?"

"You'll be fine. I'll be back before you know it."

They all stared at him stonily. "That's one of those bullshit things grown-ups say," said Tremaine bitterly.

"Hey," said Fred gently. "I know it's tough." Maybe their father had said the same thing, right before shipping out for the last time. "But I'm not going off to war. I'm just going to help a friend for a few weeks. My sister's going to house-sit and she'll hang out with you. She knows a few self-defense moves, so you can spar with her. Maybe even teach her a few things. And I'll call your mom every few days so you know I'm okay. How's that?"

When he threw in ice cream sundaes, they finally seemed to forgive him.

He collected enough clothes for a few weeks and took care of some bills. Before he left the house, he did a quick Google search to refresh his memories of Rachel's kidnapping. At that time in his life, when he was thirteen, he'd just gotten his first girlfriend and had been preoccupied with finding time to make out with her behind the half-pipe in the park.

Rachel had been going through a very different experience. She'd been snatched on her way home from a neighbor's house. Her bike was found later, mangled in the bushes. She'd been held for almost a month. The kidnapper had taunted Kessler by sending the local media distorted video clips in which he wore a Freddy Krueger mask. One of them had shown Rachel tied to a chair, blindfolded. In the video, the masked man had brandished a pair of scissors near her face. She didn't make a sound, not one. In the end, all he did with the scissors was cut her hair, thick black locks falling to the dirty floor.

How an eight-year-old had found the courage and daring to escape was pretty much a miracle, the reporters kept emphasizing. One article interviewed people close to the family about a year after her escape. Everyone agreed that Rachel wasn't the same girl anymore. She didn't talk for months after her escape, and when she did, she spoke slowly and cautiously. One doctor, who admitted he hadn't treated her, speculated that she might have trauma-induced brain damage. The stories painted a picture of a previously boisterous tomboy who was now afraid to go outside. The fact that the kidnapper had never been caught haunted the family.

No one knew how it affected little Rachel.

The story tore at Fred's heart and made him want to rip that evil man limb from limb. Rachel shouldn't have to live with that sort of fear hanging over her. No one should.

And if he could do something about it, even something as minor as hanging out with her until her father testified, he would.

Chapter 12

Rachel's guest suite had its own bathroom, Jacuzzi jets in the bathtub, and a remote control for the curtains. Everything was decorated in shades of sage green and ivory, like a photo spread in one of the magazines Fred's mother kept in the bathroom. A plush carpet cushioned the bedroom floor, and the bed itself was covered in a silk comforter as light as mist.

He'd never experienced anything like the luxury Rachel took for granted. The Breen household had been chaotic and loud, and the brothers had been hard on the battered furniture. He'd shared a room with his brother Zee until his senior year. At the firehouse he slept on something little better than a cot. And he'd never given much thought to his own home decor.

What must Rachel have thought of his utterly ordinary living quarters? Then again, who cared? He'd never aspired to be Martha Stewart.

"I've been thinking about how to make this work." Rachel appeared at his side with a pile of freshly washed towels. He jumped.

"You know, I think this carpet's a security risk," he told her. "It's too damn quiet."

"Want me to wear a bell?"

Sure. And nothing else. Damn. He really had to do something about this crazy attraction. "Not you, silly. Anyone who tries to sneak in."

She laughed. "Wait until I show you the multilayered security system. You won't be worried about the carpet. Besides, knowing my father, this carpet is programmed to recognize people's body weight and set off an alarm if it doesn't match someone on the approved list."

He eyed the ivory pile beneath his feet. "Remind me not to gain any weight."

"Anyway, about the ground rules."

"Right. Ground rules." He took the towels from her.

"First of all, I was thinking we should wipe the slate clean, so we're starting over on a professional basis."

"Makes sense."

Her shoulders lost some of their tension. He wondered if it would be "professional" to offer her a neck rub. Probably not.

She went on. "Neither of us wanted this arrangement, but if we're very clear about our respective needs, we should get along okay."

Needs. Did she have to mention needs? Especially while she was wearing black yoga pants that showed off every curve of her legs?

"I don't have needs," he said firmly, trying to convince himself. "I'm here to do a job, that's all."

"Yes, but if you think about it, we're going to be

living together for at least two weeks. Like room-mates," she added. "When I roomed with Liza, Cindy, and Feather, we had a weekly meeting to air any issues we had."

"I'm not going to have issues." He tried not to laugh at the idea. "I have brothers and I work at a firehouse. We never air any issues. Except after Double D's meatballs. We have to air the whole place out then."

"That's gross." At the look of horror on her face, he gave in to his urge to laugh.

"You have no idea." He looked at the pile of towels she'd given him. "What's all this for, anyway?"

"Hand towel, bath towel, bathrobe, washcloth, just the basics."

He scowled down at the pile. "Do I have to use them all? I'm more of a single-towel kind of guy."

"You don't have hand towels? What do you dry your hands on?"

He shrugged, walking into the sunny tiled bath-room to deposit the towels on top of the toilet tank. Apparently that was the wrong place for them. She immediately hung a smallish towel and a washcloth on the rod next to the sink. The urge to tease her again came over him. "I dry my hands on whatev-er's available. If nothing else, the bath mat."

"The *bath mat*?" In the midst of hanging the bath mat on the side of the tub, she clutched it in horror.

"Of course, I don't always have a bath mat around. So sometimes I use my own hair. Or my ass cheeks."

"*What?*"

He lost it, breaking into laughter. "We've really got to work on your gullibility while I'm here. Maybe I should charge your father extra for that."

She pinned him with wide, suspicious violet eyes. "So you don't dry your hands on the bath mat?"

"No, that part was true."

He kept his face deadpan, giving nothing away. She took a step closer, and the hair on his arms prickled. He tried really hard not to think about getting her naked in that Jacuzzi tub.

"Well." She gave him a sly smile. "Please don't dry your hands on the living room carpet. The housekeeper would have a fit."

He laughed out loud. So Rachel could give as well as she got. Oh yes, this was going to be more fun that he'd thought.

"We'll put it in the ground rules. What about the bedspread?"

"Definitely not, but I'll consider the sheets."

Oh damn. Did she have to mention the sheets? The atmosphere in the bathroom tightened, as if someone had sucked some of the air out of the room. He felt a little light-headed. She must feel it too; her cheeks flushed and she ran her tongue across her lips.

He took a quick step backward and bumped against the sink. *Keep it professional.* He wasn't here to flirt, he was here to work. "How about you show me the security now?

Rachel shook herself out of her trance and practically ran out of the bathroom. She was going to have to work on her immunity to Fred. Something about his sunny sense of humor really got under her skin. No one ever teased her. People tended to tiptoe around her, not joke around with her. Joking around with Fred felt good. Really, really good.

She reminded herself that he was working for her father, and only for a couple of weeks, and that she'd been the one to declare their relationship purely "professional."

Regaining her cool, she showed him around the rest of her apartment, the spacious living room, the tricked-out office, the entertainment room, the kitchen. It took quite some time to demonstrate all the security measures her father had instituted.

Fred paid close attention as she showed him the hidden alarms, the reinforced glass in all the windows, the bullet-proof drapes, the motion sensors.

"Every time I leave the apartment, I set the alarm that activates the motion sensors. It would be highly unlikely that anyone could come in here undetected."

"Is it hooked up to a monitoring system?"

"Yes. There are cameras all through here." She waved at the upper corner of the living room, where a discreet wall sconce disguised one of the cameras. "They deactivate when I turn off the alarm system, but any panic button or a voice code will reactivate them. Marsden has access to the video feed and so does the security team at Cranesbill. That's my father's place in Marin."

He waved his hand in front of the wall sconce, which was cast from imported Italian bronze. "How do you know someone isn't watching right now?"

"Because I turned off the alarm. All the cameras are dead."

"Do you know that for sure?"

Rachel shrugged uncomfortably. She'd made her father promise not to ever invade her privacy by activating the cameras himself. She chose to believe he'd honor that vow, but did she know for sure? "I've never put it to the test, put it that way. But my dad promised and I believe him. Anyway, he's a busy man. He has better things to do than spy on his daughter. He just wants to know that all measures are being taken."

Fred didn't look convinced. "Maybe it's time we put it to the test." He put his hands to the top button of his jeans.

"What are you doing?" Alarmed, Rachel grabbed at his arm.

"Stand back," he said with mock seriousness. "This is man's work."

"What . . ."

Turning his back to the camera, he unbuttoned his jeans. From where she stood, a step or two to his right, she caught only a side view, but enough to be struck dumb, like one of those nightmares in which everything moves in slow motion. By the time she gathered the words to protest, he'd already pulled down the top of his jeans, revealing the upper half of his muscular rear.

Fred was mooning the million-dollar Kessler security system.

Rachel squeezed her eyes shut, waiting for the sky to cave in. Her father would never tolerate a gesture of disrespect like that. If any of the security team saw it, not a second would pass before they'd be pinging their boss, shooting him a still shot of his daughter's new bodyguard's ass.

But nothing happened.

"How long would it take?" Fred asked cheerfully.

She pried one eye open to see that he'd refastened his jeans, and was settling them back into their comfortably butt-hugging position. "What?"

"For your father to be notified, and for you to get a call. What else would you be waiting for? You look like a bomb's about to drop."

"It wouldn't take long," she admitted. "By now you'd be fired."

"First of all, I doubt that. Your father got the message. Second, now you know."

"Know what, that you have a cute butt?" she shot back.

He raised an eyebrow at her. "Is that a fact?"

Fizzy energy shot through her. Joking around with Fred was better than playing Ping-Pong while sipping Bellinis on a cruise to Mexico. "What I saw of it was all right." She sniffed. "I didn't get the full view."

"I'm not getting paid enough for the full view." He winked. "Though I did dance at a bachelorette party once. Just think, if you and your friends had hired some fireman strippers instead of renting a limo, we might never have met."

She pretended to consider that. "There's always next time. Liza's getting pretty serious with her boyfriend. Anyway, even though what you did was completely inappropriate, I'm glad you did it. You proved my dad isn't spying on me."

"Not really. Just that he's not spying on you at the moment." Fred made a circuit of the room, peering at all the electronics nestled in corners and potted plants. "It must be a strange feeling to think you're being watched all the time."

"You get used to it, I suppose. I knew the bathroom was safe, because my father wouldn't be that invasive. I tend to take long baths."

A sudden stillness made his shoulders rigid, as if she'd said something disturbing. *Long baths.* Did the mention of her taking a bath make him tense up?

"And I spend a lot of time naked in bed," she added innocently. "Same situation there."

Fred cleared his throat as he inspected a small statue of a shepherdess. "That's cool."

She smiled privately. Fred wasn't the only one who could put something to the test. Their chemistry was still there, and not only on her side. Even though so much had changed between them, at least their attraction hadn't disappeared.

"Do you have any guns in the apartment?" Fred was all business again.

"Yes, I have a .357 Magnum and a concealed weapons permit. But I don't like carrying it with me, so it's usually in that drawer there." She showed him the ornate little vanity with the hidden drawer where she kept her weapon. "I have an identical one at work."

"Why don't you carry it with you?"

"Because I'm a horrible shot. Marsden tried to teach me and I did get better after a while. But not nearly good enough. It would be more likely that someone would grab the gun away from me before I could get off a shot." Learning to shoot had been a nightmare. She didn't like the pistol's violent jerk and the deafening retort gave her terrible anxiety that lasted for days. And that was with ear pro- tection. If she had trouble with the gun under the controlled circumstances of a shooting range, how would she manage in a crisis situation? Even her father had eventually agreed they were better off not relying on her skill with her revolver.

"Have you had any training in self-defense?" Fred was asking.

"Are you kidding? Of course, starting from the age of about twelve, from a former Mossad agent. Mr. Eli gave me Krav Maga lessons for years. I can handle myself pretty well, but I've gotten rusty since I went off to college."

"I could work with you on that while I'm here," Fred offered with a studied sort of casualness. She imagined the close contact a martial arts lesson would require. Pictured his hard body next to hers, adjusting her stance. He'd have to put his hands on her, probably, so she could practice a counterattack. She swallowed hard.

"I don't know if we'll have time," she said awkwardly. "I have a lot of appointments this week. And then there's Greta."

"Right. Of course."

A few days of living in close proximity to the most distracting, fascinating girl Fred had ever known forced him to develop a few survival techniques. He knew she liked to start the coffee so it perked while she showered. As soon as he heard her stirring, and knew she'd be emerging from her bedroom dressed in those silk pajamas designed to drive a man insane, he zipped out of the apartment to walk Greta. He spent the entire walk trying not to imagine her preparing for her shower. Sliding the silky fabric over her taut, ivory-skinned torso. Leaning in to test the water, like a naked nymph. What color would her nipples be? Pale pink, and tasting like rose petals? Or a deep, erotic brown? Usually, by the time he reached the little park where Greta relieved herself, he'd gotten a grip on himself.

But being with Greta reminded him of the way Rachel lavished kisses and cuddles on her dog. He'd never envied a canine before. Not that Rachel wasn't kind to Fred as well. His favorite brands of Pop-Tarts and microwaveable dinners had mysteriously appeared in the cupboards. When she discovered his weakness for survival reality shows like *Man vs. Wild* and *Naked and Afraid*, she'd ordered them all on Netflix. That's the way she was. Reserved on the surface, but with a hidden vein of thoughtfulness that could really get to you.

Three days into the job, he headed out for a sparring session with his Muay Thai teacher. He went through the usual security routine, leaving Rachel immersed in research on a three-toed sloth someone had brought into the Refuge. As he walked through the elegant lobby, which was adorned with gilt-framed mirrors and an orchid arrangement, Marsden intercepted him.

"How are things going?"

"Fine, sir."

The man nodded with an air of satisfaction. "Had a feeling it would work out."

Since Marsden seemed to be in a talkative mood, which had never happened before, Fred jumped at the chance to ask a question that had been bugging him since that first day.

"Mr. Marsden, I've been wondering why you recommended that Mr. Kessler hire me. You know I'm not any kind of trained security specialist."

"You do all right." Ruefully, the man rubbed his throat, where Fred had gotten him into a headlock.

"She should have the damn FBI protecting her," said Fred. "Not some fireman with a black belt."

Marsden pulled him to the side, out of earshot of anyone exiting from an elevator. Fred's gym bag swung against his thigh.

"I've been working for the Kesslers for a long time, son. Rachel's one in a million. Brave as hell, and kind. She'd rather die than see someone get hurt. But in all my time, I've never known anyone as lonely as that girl. Rips your heart out."

Fred's heart gave a weird little clench. The picture Marsden painted was so sad. "Are you saying she needs company?"

"She needs more than a dog and an old marine. But she won't do anything to upset Mr. Kessler, and he keeps a tight eye on her. Thought I'd maybe found a way to kill two birds with one stone."

"You mean get her a guard and . . ."

"A friend."

A friend. Marsden had recommended him to Kessler for *that*? It seemed like an elaborate way to find someone to keep Rachel company. It wasn't exactly a hardship, after all. Fred eyed him closely, but the guard's face revealed nothing but innocent intentions.

A friend. Was that really his true purpose here? In that case, it was too bad the fantasies keeping him up every night weren't at all friendly. He had to think this over in private. "Well, thanks for thinking of me."

He nodded at Marsden and prepared to head out the door, but the man held him back with a hand on his arm. "Another thing, son."

"Yeah?"

"If anyone heard me, Kessler'd have my ass." He leaned closer. "Don't pay attention to him. He likes to believe he rules the world, and he's got his ideas of how people should treat his daughter. They're not always on the mark, if you ask me. Don't let him intimidate you."

Fred cocked his head. "Just because he's a billionaire genius and I'm a firefighter? Why would that intimidate me?"

Marsden laughed. "He shits on a crapper like the rest of us."

"I'm hoping I can take your word for that."

The guard clapped him on the shoulder. "I knew this would work out."

After a week of guarding Rachel, Fred knew there were two things about this arrangement that he hadn't considered. He adapted to her luxurious surroundings well enough, though he felt like a dickhead trying to figure out her high-tech appliances. Things like titanium, voice-activated toasters and a refrigerator that told you when you were low on eggs. He was pretty good with technology, with all his firefighter training. But computer voices rubbed him the wrong way.

The second thing—maybe not so unexpected—was how hard it was to be around her without revealing his raging lust for her. Being around her was so much more exciting than being around anyone else. Even though she was mostly reserved, when she did come out with one of her quick-as-a-flick responses or wide grins, the pleasure of it nearly knocked him off his feet. He wondered what she would have been like if her life hadn't been torn apart by a sadistic kidnapper. Would she be relaxed and giggly and carefree, more like Lizzie?

It was impossible to say, and he didn't need to know the answer anyway. He liked her just as she was. It was hard to remember that when he'd first seen her at the City Lights Grill he'd considered her a bit of an airhead. Now that he knew her better, he wished she'd let that goofy side of herself show more. She was too serious, too careful. She poured all her softhearted impulses into the animals at the Refuge. He'd like to see that carefree, laughing side of Rachel again someday. Where was that Rachel hiding?

Chapter 13

"He's just providing extra security until the congressional hearings are over," Rachel told Cindy in her private office. Cindy was worried that her ungainly young golden retriever, Sir Giggles, was getting too hyperactive and uncontrollable. At the moment, the dog was roaming the training room, investigating the various toys piled in the corners.

"Oh, I see. 'Extra security.' Is that what they're calling it these days?"

Rachel turned red. "It wasn't my idea. Or his."

"I think you should put the moves on him," Cindy said in a loud whisper, crossing one leg over the other. She wore bright red shorts and a gold tank top. She lit up the little office like a torch. "He's coming to the wedding, right?"

"Yes, he has to come now—as my bodyguard. I have a date for the wedding."

"Don't tell me it's that horrid Bradford."

"He's not horrid. He's on the board of directors for the Refuge."

"Yeah, because he's trying to get into your pants." She pushed her sunglasses on top of her head.

"Cindy, I'm not like you. Guys don't act like that with me. They want . . . something different."

Ebullient and gleefully, unabashedly plump, Cindy had been one of the most fun-loving girls in their year at San Gabriel College. She always came back from her wild parties with stories about the boys pining for her. Until she lost her heart to Bean. "You are so naïve. You're gorgeous, Rachel. Just because you don't play it up doesn't mean it ain't so."

"Back to Sir Giggles. You said he's been almost biting? Grabbing your arms in his mouth?"

"Yes. Bean's worried that he's too aggressive." Rachel glanced at the lively, curious dog nosing around the room. He didn't look aggressive in the least. "Now back to Bradford. When did I give you permission to bring that stuck-up stick to my wedding?"

"You knew I was going to bring him!"

"That was *before* you had a sexy bodyguard with a killer ass. Oooh, have you seen him naked yet? Like, when you're waiting for the shower, and he just happens to forget his towel when he comes out of the bathroom?"

"He has his own bathroom."

"Judge, please direct the witness to answer the question." Cindy lifted a gold, sparkly-tipped finger, as if signaling a judge.

"I haven't seen him naked."

"Half naked?" Cindy asked hopefully. "Throw me a bone, here. Not you, Sir Giggles." At the sound of his name, Sir Giggles trotted over to the table where they were sitting. "What degree of sexy fireman nakedness have you witnessed?"

Rachel always did have a hard time lying. "Okay. I saw him without his shirt once, and then another time I brought in his clean laundry while he was changing." Even though she'd backed out right away, the image of his muscular butt in that dark blue underwear was seared permanently into her brain. He looked like some kind of model with his arms overhead, his back muscles rippling, his head caught in his white T-shirt.

It wasn't easy sharing living quarters with someone you were wildly attracted to.

"And?" Cindy asked impatiently.

"And nothing. A lady doesn't spy and tell."

"Then who'd want to be friends with a lady?" Cindy looked genuinely outraged. Rachel couldn't help laughing.

"Okay, I will say that . . . as good as you might imagine he looks . . . multiply that by . . ."

Cindy leaned closer, her mouth, red as her pedal pushers, open in anticipation.

"Mmmm . . . maybe a thousand."

Cindy sat back, surveying Rachel as if she'd just handed her a box of chocolates. "What was that you said once about a hidden camera system at your place?"

Just then, Sir Giggles apparently decided he wanted in on the party. He rose onto his hind legs and put one paw on the table.

Cindy turned to him, scolding in a playful voice. "Down, you goofy boy, you know better than that."

Ears twitching eagerly, he put a paw on her arm. She gently pushed it off, then went for his collar. "Down, boy, don't you remember anything those trainers taught you? Honestly, I think it was all a big waste of money. Down, you, down!"

Sir Giggles's tail wagged madly back and forth. He put both his paws on her arms, as if they were about to dance, then mouthed her right forearm. Finally, with a constant, breathless running commentary, Cindy wrestled him to the floor. She sat back, exasperated. "See what I mean? He's impossible."

Rachel nearly burst out laughing. "He thinks it's a game. He's not being aggressive at all."

"A game? But I keep telling him to get down and he won't listen!"

"But you're interacting with him the way a dog at play would. If you want him to stop playing, you need to be very still. And your voice has to be serious, not fun. I know that's hard for you, because you're a fun person. Watch me. And don't say or do anything."

The next time Sir Giggles put his paws on the table, Rachel gave a stern, no-nonsense gasp and kept her body ominously still. Surprised, he dropped back down to the floor.

"Good dog, very good dog," she told him, and offered him a liver treat, which he gobbled up.

They went through the same routine again, a few times, until Sir Giggles finally got the point. Staying feet-to-the-floor meant a reward. Jumping on the table brought no fun. Cindy watched, mouth ajar, as Sir Giggles settled quietly and happily next to her chair.

"I don't get it. What have I been doing wrong?"

"Dogs pay attention to your body language even more than your words, so you have to make sure you're communicating what you intend to. Be careful about rewarding him for bad behavior with something that looks like pure fun to him. Sir Giggles is very smart, so he'll get it. He just wanted to play."

"So he's not just a big rascal trying to get away with something?" Cindy bent and patted Sir Giggles on his side.

"There's nothing wrong with wanting to play, that's what dogs do. Dogs don't have hidden agendas, and they don't hide what they want. They're always truthful. The problem is, we don't always understand what they're saying. Dogs aren't like people. They don't know how to lie or manipulate, the way people do."

Cindy's hand stilled, and she gave Rachel an uncharacteristically grave look. "Oh honey. You're breaking my heart."

Rachel bit her lip. Had she revealed too much about her take on the world?

Cindy stood up and hooked Sir Giggles's leash onto his collar. "Thanks for your tip, Rachel. You're amazing. Here's a tip for you, because I love you. Ditch Bradford and bring Fred to my wedding."

While Rachel was busy doing whatever she did with her "clients," Fred used the time to explore the Refuge. More specifically, to scope out the security. The place had ten staff members, four of whom were security guards. Two were veterinarians, and the rest were called "techs," but their jobs seemed to be mostly feeding animals and tending to the structures and grounds.

A small stuccoed bungalow from the pre-earthquake safety era served as the headquarters of the Refuge's security team. Fred thought about introducing himself, but he didn't know if the guards knew they were responsible for the daughter of

America's third richest man. Instead, he avoided that building and wandered through the compound, noticing hidden cameras scattered throughout.

In the medical wing, he joined a small group watching the newly arrived three-toed sloth. The creature huddled in the corner of its cage, ignoring the pile of leaves collected for it.

"We can't keep it," one of the techs was saying. "It belongs in the rain forest. It's not warm enough here."

"Rachel won't send it away until it's feeling better," said another.

"It's feeling bad because it's cold. We need to put it on a plane to Costa Rica."

"You tell the princess."

Someone cleared his throat, and Fred caught an embarrassed look from the tech. "Didn't see you there," the guy said resentfully. He had long hair held back in a ponytail with a leather thong.

"Don't mind me. I've never seen a three-toed sloth before. Just came to check it out." Fred wasn't surprised at the tech's comment; everyone at the Refuge treated Rachel as if she was one step away from royalty. Conversations in the kitchenette stopped when she walked in. No one cracked a single joke about the skunk with the scent gland disorder. It seemed strange to him. He didn't find her intimidating; why should they?

But the incident made him wonder how much she knew about the staff. When Rachel finished with her appointments for the day, he broached the subject while she locked up her office.

"Does the staff have to go through a security check?"

"Is the pope Catholic?"

"Hey. I'm just trying to be thorough."

Rachel closed the front door, locked it, and went around back to the little fenced-in yard where Greta played during working hours. At the sight of them, Greta bounded across the grass in great leaps.

Fred persisted. "Kessler Tech owns this place, right?"

"Wrong. It's a private nonprofit. Kessler Tech helps fund it. There's a big difference."

He flung up his hands. "Sorry. Didn't mean to offend you." After a pause, "What's the difference?"

Rachel opened the gate and Greta rubbed against her legs with nearly orgasmic joy. "The Refuge was my idea. I had to fight for it. My father thought it was too risky. But I had some money left from my mother, and I lined up a board of directors, so Dad didn't really have a choice." She shot him a gleam of a smile as she lavished caresses on Greta's head. "I'm a lot more stubborn than I look."

Fred knew she was stubborn; he'd seen it in the limo. But he probably would have called it something else. Determined, or brave.

Rachel continued. "Dad eventually got on board, but he doesn't really understand why animals mean so much to me. As long I leave the security to him, he leaves me alone."

"So everyone gets vetted?"

She let out a huge sigh. "Up the ying-yang, yes."

"And you trust them all? You've worked with them enough to be sure they're safe?"

"What are you getting at?" She closed the latch of the gate and swung to face him.

"Well, I've been shadowing you for almost a week now. Your apartment building is more secure than the Pentagon. The only other residents are two elderly couples and a widow, all extensively vetted by the Kessler security team. Your car has bulletproof windows and a double-reinforced body. The big weak spot I see is this place."

"It's surrounded by an electrified fence and has twenty-four hidden cameras." She waved her arms at their surroundings. A slight breeze made the leaves of the aspens quiver. A small olive-drab bird rose into the air, then landed with a flick of its tail on a fencepost. Fred had to admit that the Refuge seemed too peaceful to harbor any danger. "You're being paranoid. Maybe Dad's insanity is catching."

She stalked away from him, followed by the capering Greta. He hurried after her. His intention wasn't to tick her off, but he'd been hired to protect her, after all. These questions seemed important.

"What about when people bring in their pets, or injured animals? Do those people get checked out?"

"Yes! The security guards don't let anyone in here unless they've gone through a weapons check."

"But what about the staff? How well do you really know them?"

"Fred! I trust my staff. I don't hire anyone who isn't a hundred percent committed to helping animals. Now will you stop this?"

"I'm just trying to—"

"I know what you're trying to do. Stop it . . . just stop it." She reached the small gravel parking lot and started scrabbling through her purse. "*Damn it.*"

"Hey. Hey." Fred gently took the purse from her and held it open so she could search inside. "Why are you so upset?"

"I'm not upset. Everything's fine. We've never had any problems here. It's a *refuge.* A safe place. Do you know what my father would do if you start making a fuss about the security?"

That brought him up short. He hadn't thought of

that. "I'm just asking for my own information. I'm not going to say anything to your dad."

"Aren't you? Don't you work for him? Do you have any idea what—" She broke off, grabbing her key out of her purse, then snatching back the bag. Before she could open the door, Fred blocked it with one hand.

"Finish your sentence. Do I have any idea what . . ."

She angled her head away from him, the dark strands catching amber light from the sinking sun. "Forget it," she choked.

"Let me guess. Do I have any idea how much this place means to you? Do I have any idea how crushed you'd be if your father shut it down?"

Her slim body went still. The breeze caught at her spring-green blouse, made the thin material press against her back, outlining the clasp of her bra. The little detail tugged at his heart. He noticed that a whisper-slight strand of hair had caught in the chain of her necklace. Rachel might be rich beyond his wildest dreams, but she was also painfully vulnerable.

He cleared his throat. "Listen, Rachel. Remember how I set that condition when your dad wanted to hire me?"

She sniffed, lifting her head a tiny bit. The delicate tendons of her neck shifted under her baby-soft skin. He wanted to taste her there. He wanted to taste her everywhere.

"I told him I wouldn't take the job unless you knew the whole story. I'm not sure I ever explained why that was so important to me."

She fiddled with her car keys. He really wished she'd look at him, but didn't press her.

"So here's the reason. It's *your* life. You deserve to

be completely informed about it. You're not a child."
Thank God she wasn't, or he'd have to have a long
talk with his lust-crazed body.

"No, I'm not a child," she said in a husky voice
that seemed to communicate directly with his hor-
mones. "But my dad worries, and I can't blame him."

"How about this. I'll make you a promise. I won't
say anything to your father until I say it to you first.
If I see something that alarms me, I'll tell you. Then
we can both consider what to do. But I won't do anything without you knowing about it. What do you
think?"

Slowly, ever so slowly, she turned. Leaning one
hip against the door of her specially altered Saab,
she raised her eyes to meet his. The wariness in
those violet depths nearly broke his heart. The wariness, and the longing to trust. "That sounds fair,"
she said cautiously. "Aren't you sending reports to
my dad, the way Marsden does?"

"Nope. I'm leaving that to Marsden. I wouldn't
want your father to suffer from information
overload."

A smile twitched at her lips. Her full, down-
turned lips. The lips he hadn't been able to get out of
his mind since their two sizzling kisses. "I wish you
could understand . . . what it feels like to have one
tiny bit of freedom, and to be constantly worried it
might get taken away."

He touched her cheek, very quickly and lightly,
because he just couldn't help it. "I'm on your side. I
promise."

He thought about that promise during the entire drive
home. His week of guarding her had made him
realize that he'd never choose her life, no matter

how much money it came with. Kessler was such a maniac about security that he insisted on vetting everyone who got close to Rachel—or even got close to getting close. No wonder she stuck with a very small, tight group of friends that she'd known since college. She was lucky to have *those* friends.

Rachel had confided that her father hadn't even wanted her to attend college. "You can get the same education or better online," he'd told her. But she'd stuck to her guns until her father agreed to San Gabriel College because it was so "small and dull."

As a native San Gabreleño, Fred didn't appreciate that description, but he could see Kessler's point.

With all those restrictions on her social life, Rachel didn't get out much, at least compared to most girls her age. Like Lizzie, for example, who had boys trailing after her like toilet paper on her shoe. But Rachel didn't seem to mind. The Refuge was her passion, and when she wasn't at work, she was reading books about animal behavior and training techniques. Twice a week she took a ballet class at Move Me Dance Studio, where Cherie worked. Marsden told Fred he'd discreetly done a check on every student in the class. Fred thought that was going overboard, unless some ballerina planned to take her out with a wayward pirouette.

Rachel might be content with her existence, but Fred kept thinking about the first time he'd seen her, that giddy, devil-may-care girl who'd waltzed up to his table and snatched his trophy. And he couldn't forget the look he'd seen in her eyes as she'd talked about her lack of freedom.

So that night, after they'd consumed a pepperoni mushroom pizza for dinner, and after Marsden had dropped in for his nightly check-in, Fred decided to spring a surprise on her.

"What are you doing tonight?"

"Um . . . the usual?"

"Studying up on three-toed sloths?"

"I think we can create an acceptable environment for it, if we just—"

"I have a better idea." He strode to the couch and swung her to her feet. "We're going out."

"Out . . . what? Where? I can't go out." She pulled her hand from his.

"Why not?"

"Because . . . work and . . . Dad wouldn't . . . Marsden already—"

He gave her a wicked smile. "But you'll have your bodyguard with you. You'll be perfectly safe. That's what they hired me for, right?"

She gazed at him with something dawning in her eyes. Something wild and hopeful, daring and gut-wrenching. "What are we going to do?"

"Whatever you want. Whatever you've always wanted to do, but never gotten the chance. Sky's the limit, baby." He threw open the drapes, revealing the star-spangled indigo sky and pulsating lights of a busy Friday night. He tilted his head back and pretended to howl at the golden sliver of moon. "The night belongs to us."

Chapter 14

The Kesslers hadn't always been rich. Rachel could just barely remember the deliriously manic time of Kessler Tech's IPO, when her father became an overnight billionaire. The next day her mother had taken her to a toy store and said she could buy anything in the place. She'd dashed from Barbies to toy pianos, to a miniature cotton candy maker, finally settling on a sparkly silver bike with blue fringe on the handlebars.

Now, with San Gabriel's nightlife spread before her like a buffet of fun, she remembered that kid-in-a-candy-store feeling. It started with her outfit. When she'd first gotten to college, she'd bought a bunch of crazy outfits, but she'd put them away after the frat house incident freshman year. She dove into her closet and came out with skin-tight black vinyl pants and a belly shirt with the words "She's So Vain" written in sequins. She added sparkly eyeliner and shook out her hair into a wild, fizzy black halo.

The expression on Fred's face made her want to turn pirouettes across the floor.

"It's a damn good thing you have a bodyguard," he grumbled as he set the security alarms.

"Seriously, I don't know why I ever resisted the idea," she said cheerfully, which made his face go dark.

"It's a good thing you have *me* as a bodyguard," he corrected.

The possessiveness in his voice made her shiver.

"What's the grungiest, nastiest dive bar in town?" she asked after they'd settled into her Saab.

Fred started up the car. He'd insisted on driving, so she could have a drink if she chose. "That's easy. Beer Goggles. Used to be Katie's bar, Hair of the Dog, but it burned down."

"*Beer Goggles?* Yes, let's go there. That sounds perfect."

"No."

"Why not? You said anywhere I want."

"Because it's . . . and you're . . ." He scrubbed a hand through his hair, stealing a sidelong glance at her outfit. "Should have kept my big mouth shut," he grumbled, turning the car around. "The minute I say we're out of there, we're out of there."

"Fine," she said meekly.

Inside Beer Goggles, it took crucial minutes for her smoke-induced coughing fit to subside and her vision to adjust to the murky darkness. By then she was seated in a booth, clutching a Sierra Nevada and shrinking under the weight of a bar-full of speculative male eyes.

"I thought smoking in bars was against the law." She barely managed to hack out the question before another coughing fit struck. She downed most of her beer as if it were water.

"Beer Goggles claims to be on tribal land," Fred explained. "There's a whole lawsuit going on. Here, have some bar snacks." He pushed a dirty dish of shriveled pea-like objects that might once have been pistachios. Or gallstones, for all she knew. Her stomach roiled. "Ready to go yet?"

"She just got here." A giant wearing a black leather jacket and a Cyclops-eye tattooed on his forehead loomed over them. He had the voice of an emphysema patient. "Trying to keep her to yourself, kid?"

"Just giving the lady what she wants." Fred didn't seem intimidated by the man's bulk, but Rachel sure was.

"We were just leaving," she said quickly. Fred rose to his feet and faced off with the giant.

"Can you step aside, please?" His manner might be pleasant, but Rachel could sense the tension radiating from him. The man stepped aside a mere half inch, enough so Fred could squeeze out of the booth. He did so, his back to Rachel, his entire focus on the Cyclops-man. The next thing happened so fast, Rachel barely saw it through the smoke. The man reached for Fred, as if aiming to pick him up by the back of his jacket. Fred ducked, used the man's momentum to flip him around, and toppled him to the floor. Then he twisted the giant's arm in such a way that the man couldn't budge without pain.

"Come on, Rachel. Step right over him."

Just to be safe, Rachel grabbed for the only thing that felt like a weapon, the dish of bar snacks. Gingerly she stepped over the spitting, cursing man.

"Stay close, Rachel," Fred warned her. "I don't want anyone else getting stupid ideas." He addressed his immobilized opponent. "Are you going to be good, or do I have to tear a rotator cuff before I let you go?"

"I'll sue."

"You attacked first. Right now there's no damage, but I can change that." He gave one more little twist, then released the man.

"You'd better stay away from this place," Cyclops threatened.

"I can live with that. Come on, Rachel." Fred took her arm and hustled her toward the door. Everyone was watching them, peering through the haze. It wasn't just cigarette smoke, she realized. Several customers were openly smoking weed. Maybe that's why no one seemed very motivated to get up and make a brawl out of it.

When they were almost out the door, she glanced back and saw the gigantic Cyclops-man stumbling after them. "Fred!" She cried, then did the only thing she could think of. She flung the dish of pistachio-peas across the floor, where they made a skittering sound like a hundred tiny marbles. "Run!"

They ran for the door, hand in hand, and the last thing she saw was the Cyclops slipping on the rolling bar snacks, helplessly windmilling his leather-clad arms.

She collapsed into the Saab. Hysterical laughter came bubbling out of her mouth. "Did you . . . see his . . . face?"

Fred, breathing hard, started up the car. "I'm glad those snacks were good for something. Now let's get the hell out of here."

She bounced up and down on the seat. "That was . . . I know it was dangerous and I hope he didn't hurt you, but that was *totally awesome*."

"So we can check grungy dive off your list? Please tell me yes." He pulled away from the curb.

"Oh, I suppose," she said, still flying from the

adrenaline rush. "I don't want to wear out my favorite bodyguard."

His smoldering glance made her fly even higher. "I don't wear out that easy." The promise in his voice sent shivers down her spine. "Where to now? Tattoo parlor? Cockfight? Gang war?"

"Is the carnival still in town? I always wanted to go, but my father got an eye twitch every time I brought it up."

"San Gabriel Fairgrounds, here we come."

The brightly lit streets sped past. One beer, and she was already entering that expansive, carefree, babbling state.

"You have no idea how sick I get of being Rachel Allen Kessler," she told Fred. "Sometimes I pretend I'm someone else. Someone who isn't guarded and hunted and watched. I've thought about wearing a disguise so there's no chance of anyone recognizing me."

"What would you do?"

"Nothing too radical. Go out dancing. Play pool. Play bocce ball with the old guys in the park. Talk to people. That probably sounds dub." She gave a hiccup. "I mean dumb."

Fred shot her a sidelong look as he downshifted around a corner. "You're a lightweight, aren't you?"

"Yup," she said cheerfully. "I really never, ever drink. Hey, do you think the carnival has bumper cars?"

Ten minutes later, Rachel was screaming with laughter as Fred slammed his car into hers. The guy was ruthless. And he liked to trash talk. "Bring it, rich girl," he taunted as he pinned her car against the wall. "My eight-year-old neighbor drives faster than you."

"You ain't seen nothing yet, Turbo." She fought back, ramming her car against his until she won a little breathing room. "They'll have to bring out the Jaws of Life when I'm done with you." She zoomed off and he chased after her.

"All talk, no action," he said as he nipped her bumper. "Better change your name to Rachel Roadkill."

"Freddie Fender Bender," she yelled over her shoulder. She yanked the wheel to the side and zipped around him, getting in a sneak sideswipe in the process.

"Prepare to surrender."

By the time she gave in, tears of laughter were streaming down her face. Fred might be kind-hearted, but he was viciously competitive when it came to bumper cars.

"You look so normal," she complained, as they walked across the fairgrounds, sharing a bag of roasted peanuts. "Then you turn out to have this vicious competitive streak. Do you take all games this seriously?"

He shrugged, his wide shoulders rising and falling under his black T-shirt. The bright glare from a cotton candy booth turned his hair shining mahogany. "I'm a guy, I'm a Breen, and I'm a firefighter. You do the math."

"Surrounded by testosterone," she guessed.

"More like raised on a diet of one hundred percent testosterone."

She peered at him as they sidestepped around a group of kids sporting face paint—a pirate, a ninja, a dragon. "Then how'd you end up with a sensitive side?"

"How do you know I have one?" He pulled her close as a teenager zoomed past on a skateboard.

The brush of his warm, solid frame made her throat go dry. His muscled thigh bumped against her hip. She heroically suppressed a whimper. Why'd Marsden have to pick such a cute body-guard? Was he trying to torture her? "I know you have a sensitive side because I see it every day. I see it with the animals at the Refuge, with your neigh-bor kids, everywhere except in a bumper car."

"You should see me on a basketball court."

"Really?"

"I'm not tall, but I play hard. I had to, growing up, or I would have been roadkill. Competitiveness kind of runs in the Breen family."

The silky hair on his arm whispered against hers as he stepped back to give her space. If that slight bit of contact felt that delicious, what would the rest of him feel like?

"And by the way, if you ever run into my broth-ers, don't mention anything about my alleged sensi-tive side. You have no idea what they would do with that shit."

"Oh, I won't mention a word," she assured him. "But I might compliment your oldest brother—Trent, right?—on his famous haircutting skills." She winked at him. Fred was so good at teasing her, and she loved how it made her feel, as if champagne bubbles floated through her veins. But it felt even better to tease him back.

He narrowed his eyes at her. "I see your evil plan. Trent won't be able to fight back, because you're a civil-ian, not to mention a woman. So he'll go after me for ratting him out. Is this revenge for the bumper cars?"

"Oh yes. Better watch your back, fireman."

"Bring it, rich girl. Ever gone bowling?"

She couldn't help squealing with delight. "Can we go, can we go?"

What kind of childhood didn't include bowling? It was practically un-American. Even though Fred was too caught up in Rachel to hit a single strike, it was worth it to see the joy on her pixie face, her sparkling smile, the delight in every line of her provocatively vinyl-clad body. Good thing she had no idea he was going through the evening with a constant semi-hard-on.

There were still at the bowling alley, and she'd just collapsed next to him, laughing over her latest gutter ball, when a snide voice cut into his pleasantly lustful thoughts.

"I suppose this is one of those 'successful women' the firehouse is so crazy about?" Courtney stood over them, holding hands with a guy from her business school program. She gave Rachel a pointed, disdainful look, taking in her belly shirt and black vinyl.

Fred went on full alert. "How you doing, Courtney?"

"Great. Very *successful*. I aced my finals. And did you get my phone messages about how I've moved on?" She pointedly squeezed her classmate's hand. Her gaze kept flickering to Rachel, but the hell if Fred was going to introduce them.

"Congratulations. I knew you would."

"Haven't seen you on TV lately. Did the press get tired of you?"

"Something like that."

Courtney dismissed him and turned to Rachel. "I'm in business school. What do you do?"

Rachel said promptly, "Dog groomer." Fred nearly spurted his Orange Crush all over Courtney's painted-on jeans. "I started with people, but I flunked out of beauty school and now I just do dogs."

Courtney's eyes narrowed, but Rachel stood her ground. "Do you have any dogs?"

"I'm too busy for pets."

"That figures."

"What's that supposed to mean?"

Fred jumped to his feet, blocking the line of sight between Rachel and Courtney. His bodyguard duties had better not include stopping a catfight. "We have to go. Nice running into you, Courtney."

"Are you serious, Fred? *Her?*" Courtney hissed. "She's the skankiest thing this side of the Sunset Strip. Look at that top. I mean, everyone else is."

"Hey!" Rachel yelled from behind him. "Are you dissing my outfit?" Apparently channeling a reality show contestant, Rachel was trying to claw her way from behind his back. He held her off like some kind of bouncer.

"OMG, she's crazy. You're really scraping the bottom of the tramp barrel, Freddie. So sad." Courtney rolled her eyes dramatically and sidled off, dragging her business-school boy toy like a pet on a leash.

As soon as she was out of sight, Rachel doubled over in laughter. "That was . . . She actually thought . . ." She could barely speak through her wheezes. "That was the most awesome thing ever."

"I suppose that was on your list?" Irritated, Fred crossed his arms over his chest. "Catfight in a bowling alley?"

"I just . . . No one ever sees me that way!"

"Let's go." Fred hadn't enjoyed the encounter nearly as much as Rachel clearly had. He grabbed her hand and pulled her to her feet. Whirling around, he headed for the shoe rental return. Rachel skipped after him.

"Is she an old girlfriend or something? She was

being so mean to you. I was trying to help you get rid of her."

"Yes," Fred answered shortly, unwilling to reveal anything more about Courtney. "We dated for bit, then we ended it."

"It sounded more like you ended it."

Fred didn't want to answer that. He didn't want to talk about Courtney at all. Desperately he turned the subject around to Rachel. "What about your exes? What sort of guys do you go out with?"

"Me? Oh, you know . . ."

They reached the benches at the shoe rental return. He plopped down and began unlacing his bowling shoes. "No idea. That's why I'm asking."

"Well," Rachel sat down next to him. "I don't go on many dates here in San Gabriel. Back home, I usually go out with people my father already knows. We might go to a fund-raiser or a charity event, things like that. He's less worried about that type of person."

"The rich type," Fred offered grimly.

"Not necessarily rich. Just . . . in the same world, I suppose."

"You don't have to explain." He understood perfectly well. Never in a million years would Rob Kessler consider plain old Fred Breen suitable dating material for his daughter. Bodyguard material, sure. But that's where it ended. The thought made him suddenly grumpy.

She folded her arms across her chest. "You have this look on your face like we're snobs."

"I didn't say anything."

"I can tell what you're thinking. You're not very good at hiding your thoughts."

"Better than you think," Fred muttered. If she had any idea how many of his thoughts involved her body parts, she'd be stunned. "Your father wants the best for you, that's all. I don't have a problem with that."

"I'm twenty-five years old. Don't you think I can decide for myself who's best for me?"

"Your father runs security checks on your dates," he pointed out. "What happens if he says no? That'd be the end of that, right?" He didn't know why he couldn't leave it alone. The thought of rich guys in tuxedos escorting her to fund-raisers made him crazy.

She yanked off her bowling shoes and glared at him. "You are so annoying."

He shrugged. "Just pointing out the obvious."

Surging to her feet, bowling shoes in hand, she rounded on him. "You know . . . up until now, this has been the best night of my life. And I was going to . . . to kiss you for it."

The way she said "kiss" made him think she meant something different. That thought kept him rooted to the bench while she continued her rant.

"But now you've ruined everything. And I'm not going to kiss you. I'm just going to . . ." She interrupted herself by bending down and pressing her lips onto his. Sweet fire crashed through his system. He went hard as a bowling pin, and his head spun. Images cascaded across his vision. Her legs in those black vinyl pants. The thin sliver of skin revealed by her belly shirt, and her vulnerable shadowed navel. Unable to stop himself, he shaped his hands to her waist, feeling the tender give of her skin and the slickness of the vinyl.

She yanked her head away from his, putting her hand to her lips as if she couldn't believe what she'd just done. Then she took a giant step back, so her body slipped from his hands.

"Okay, I guess I will kiss you. *Did* kiss you. Once. That's all. Because it was a really great night. Can we go now?"

He took in a deep, lung-clearing breath. "In a minute."

"I want to go now!"

"In a minute."

She flicked an indignant glance up and down his body, which didn't do his painful hard-on any favors. "Oh."

Chapter 15

Rachel had been all set to tell Bradford Maddox IV that she no longer needed an escort to Cindy's wedding. But then Fred had started in with his teasing, and his insinuations that she wasn't in charge of her own love life, and she changed her mind. He could take his opinions and his rude ex-girlfriend and shove it.

Sure, maybe he had a point. Her father did dictate certain aspects of her life. On the other hand, she'd fought so hard for every piece of her independence. If her father had his way, she'd be back at Cranesbill, attending charity events with millionaires. Instead she was living on her own in San Gabriel and running the Refuge. Didn't Fred understand what a miracle that was?

Still, the germ of truth in Fred's accusation got under her skin. It seemed even more accurate when Bradford picked her up in his red Porsche convertible. Dressed in a custom-tailored suit, his Bluetooth behind his ear, he looked the part of the picture-perfect Silicon Valley venture capitalist.

Come to think of it, she'd never seen him without his Bluetooth.

Bradford helped her into the Porsche with a glance back at Fred, who was just getting into his pickup. "You got yourself an official stalker?"

"That's one way to put it." She didn't want to talk about Fred. She wanted to get to the wedding, stand next to Cindy on her big day, then get straight to the champagne.

Bradford had been the first of her father's colleagues to back the Refuge, and she'd always been grateful for that. Anyone who cared about animals was okay in her book. On the other hand, the last time she'd seen him he'd talked about nothing but his financial dealings and never mentioned the Refuge. She was starting to wonder how deep his commitment to wildlife went. And if he rattled on about his investments again, she might start to zone out.

Well, at least it was a wedding, so there would be plenty of distractions.

Distraction Number One, a fireman named Fred, followed close behind them as they drove. Rachel kept stealing glances in the rearview mirror, which meant she kept missing Bradford's efforts at conversation. He didn't seem to notice as he related the current Silicon Valley rumors.

"So how are the creatures faring?" Bradford asked when he'd run out of tech business gossip.

"The Refuge is doing well, for the most part. There were quite a few mountain lions and coyotes injured in that brushfire last month. We've been busy patching them up."

"Coyotes." He shuddered. "Aren't they classified

as vermin? My neighborhood in the San Jose hills is infested with them."

"Maybe you're the ones doing the infesting," she pointed out, bristling. "Why should you have any more right to be there than they do?"

He gave her a patronizing smile. "Your passion for your work is praiseworthy."

The words might have been dipped in suntan oil, they were so smooth. Fred might tease her until she lost her temper, but at least he wouldn't spout fake flattery.

Forget Fred.

At the wedding chapel, she stood alongside Liza and Feather. Cindy being Cindy, she'd commanded them to wear their sexiest little black dresses and the most outrageous shoes in their closets. Rachel had chosen her favorite dress, the one with the heart-shaped neckline that revealed just a touch of cleavage. It flared in flirty folds just above her knees. Her shoes of choice were metallic stilettos.

Her gaze kept stealing to Fred, who stood at the side of the chapel in brown gabardine dress pants and a creamy sweater. She knew he was trying to look as inconspicuous as possible, but somehow she couldn't keep her gaze off him. Forcing herself to check in on Bradford, who sat midway down the aisle, she noticed that he was murmuring something into his Bluetooth. What kind of person took a phone call during a wedding?

The brief ceremony passed in a blur. When the minister proclaimed them man and wife, Bean kissed Cindy so hard her feet lifted off the floor. Rachel felt a shocking, profound moment of envy. Would she ever love and be loved like that? She'd put her heart and soul into the Refuge, because anything else was too complicated. But now something wild and wanting tugged at her heart. Why couldn't she . . . why shouldn't she have love, romantic love, like other people?

They all drove to a restaurant called Castles for the reception. As Bradford helped her out of the Porsche, she tried to catch Fred's eye. But he had his game face on and was scanning the area for . . . something. Something that wasn't her. Feeling out of sorts, she let Bradford guide her into the magnificent interior of the restaurant. She cast a grumpy glance at her surroundings. Strange how gilded columns and crystal chandeliers could feel like a prison when you were facing tedious conversation with a man who didn't interest you.

Luckily, Liza and Feather pulled her aside as soon as they walked in. With a smoothly social laugh that grated on Rachel's nerves, Bradford backed away to fetch drinks. Fred, channeling James Bond or someone, cruised the perimeter of the restaurant.

"We're dying to know why you brought two men to a wedding," Liza whispered. "We're not talking ménage here, are we?"

Rachel's face went so hot she pressed her hands against her cheeks. "That's disgusting."

"Which part of it's disgusting?" Feather looked sensational in a black tube dress, lace-up go-go boots, and a chunky crystal necklace. "The older-dude-with-Porsche part or the sexy-hot-fireman part? He's the one who saved us from the limo, right?"

Rachel nodded miserably. "Dad hired him to be my bodyguard, that's the only reason he's here. My date is Bradford. Fred's just doing his job."

Her two friends draped sympathetic arms around her. "And you like the fireman. Of course you like the fireman." Liza shook her head so her dangling chandelier earrings brushed her jawline. "But you can salvage the situation."

"How?"

"Three words. Make him jealous."

"Who?"

Liza sighed. "Rachel, you really need to spend less time with dogs and more time with men. Fred the Fireman, that's who. You're here with another man. That's a chance to make Fred jealous."

"That seems so mean."

"A little jealousy never killed anyone," said Feather blithely. "He's a big, strong fireman, he can take it. Sometimes guys need a little kick in the pants, that's all."

"But I don't even know if he's . . . if that's . . . what I want."

"Don't pull that with us. You and the fireman were flirting with each other back when he was Random Cute Guy with Trophy at the City Lights Grill."

"That's ridiculous. I had too much champagne and he kept getting me out of trouble. Besides, you guys made me steal that trophy. There was no flirting, that's for sure. I'm not even sure I know how to flirt."

"This is the perfect moment to learn. Go forth and flirt with Bradford and make Fred jealous." Ruthlessly, Liza gave her a little push toward Bradford, who was making his way across the room with two flutes of champagne. "Come on, make us proud."

The whole thing seemed like a horrible idea, but since Bradford was her date, she ought to at least be nice to him. They found Cindy and Bean and offered their congratulations.

Cindy leaned in to whisper in Rachel's ear. "You

ready for this?" Then she tapped a champagne bottle with a fork. "Attention, wedding people!"

Into the surprised silence, Bean spoke. "Thanks for coming, everyone. In case you never watch the news, the fact is that Cindy might not even be here today if it wasn't for *that man* right over there."

He pointed at Fred, who had propped himself against a wall across the room. Looking startled, Fred jerked to attention.

"That's right." Cindy spread her arms wide in an extravagant gesture. "Fred Breen, awesome San Gabriel firefighter, this is all thanks to you."

"We're grateful, man. Really grateful. We have a special gift for you."

Bean reached behind him to grab something from the banquet table. With a triumphant gesture, he thrust it into the air.

A trophy. Rachel gasped. *The* trophy. The one with the karate guy. It had been glued back together and a black plaque had been added to the base. Cindy must have gone back to the City Lights Grill and found it.

"It says 'First place in our thanks, Cindy and Bean Potter,'" Cindy said. "Let's hear it for Fred, everybody!"

Everyone cheered wildly as Fred made his way to collect the trophy. Even though his face was beet red, he was a good sport about it, bowing and hugging the pair, even doing a funny end-zone style dance. Why did he have to be so darn . . . *endearing*?

After the excitement had died down, Rachel, feeling thoroughly disgruntled, joined Bradford at a small table, along with plates of crab cakes and baked brie with asparagus. Bradford launched into an account of the leveraged buyout he'd just orchestrated.

As she'd feared, Rachel started to zone out. Fred took a table nearby. That was good, right? He would see her laughing and having fun with Bradford, and jealousy would ensue. Then he'd sweep her into his arms and kiss the breath out of her and . . .

One of the platter-bearing servers, a young blond woman, stopped to offer him steamed dumplings. When he looked up with one of his friendly smiles, she lit up. They began chatting away like new best friends.

Rachel ground her teeth. Who was supposed to be making who jealous? Or should there be a "whom" in that sentence? She pondered that grammatical question, then remembered that she had a job to do, and it didn't involve staring at Fred while he flirted with someone else. She forced herself to turn back to Bradford. Remembering Liza's orders, she offered Bradford her most dazzling smile.

Annoyingly, he barely noticed, since nothing could be more fascinating to him than his investments. Keeping her smile fixed on her face, she rested her elbows on the table and her chin in her hands, as if he was so riveting she couldn't even hold up her own head.

The drone of "debt to equity ratio" and "cash flow" made it impossible for her to overhear what Fred was saying to the waitress to make her laugh so much.

Forget Fred, she ordered herself. *Don't be rude. Focus on the man in front of you.*

But she couldn't. She just couldn't. Her thoughts kept drifting to the handsome fireman at the table behind her.

"I have to visit the ladies' room," she murmured as soon as Bradford paused for a breath.

He nodded absently and took a sip of his Grey

Goose martini. She wondered if he was calculating its cost-per-sip.

Fred was still deep in conversation with the waitress. The poor forgotten steamed dumplings were about to slide off the tray. Rachel tried for a sexy swish as she passed Fred's table, but it had no effect. He and the waitress seemed to be locked in some sort of instant love connection.

In the ladies' room, she finally let the smile drop from her face. Her cheeks ached from the effort of looking interested. She took a long time washing her hands, going after every little crevice that might hold a speck of dirt. This was a disaster. Liza's stupid plan had completely backfired on her. She was swimming in jealousy, a horrible feeling, like wading through a swamp. Her friends were absolutely wrong. She'd never wish this feeling on anyone, not even her worst enemy. And Fred wasn't close to her worst enemy. He was kind and sweet and brave, and he was probably going to fall in love with that waitress and in later years they'd laugh at how they met, when he was guarding that odd, freaky rich girl, the one who'd once been kidnapped.

Ugh, she hated feeling sorry for herself. Self-pity was even worse than pity. *Get over yourself. Go out there and dazzle someone. Anyone.*

She flung open the door and strode out, only to slam into a man's hard chest. Fear shafted through her. In a sudden blind panic, she flinched backward, but the man grabbed her by the upper arms.

"What happened? Rachel, is something wrong?"

Her swimming vision cleared, and she realized the man was Fred. Handsome, wonderful Fred, holding her steady, worry in his dark eyes. She shook her head. "Sorry. You surprised me. What are you doing here?"

"I looked up and you were gone. You're supposed to tell me when you're going somewhere. How can I protect you if you wander off on your own?"

Now that was just the icing on the cake. "You were occupied. I didn't want to ruin your moment."

"My moment?" A little crease appeared between his eyebrows. Her gaze drifted to his mouth. She hadn't been this close to him since the kiss at the bowling alley the day before. Her lips tingled just remembering that kiss.

But then jealousy lanced through her again. What if he was planning to kiss that waitress? Maybe they'd already made a date for later tonight. Or in a week, when he'd done his duty as her bodyguard.

Stop being such a child, she thought fiercely. But she couldn't help it. "You and the waitress were having a moment. I think she's into you."

He narrowed his eyes at her. "Really, is that what you think?"

"It was obvious from the way you were looking at her," she burst out. "As if you wanted to order her instead of the crab cakes."

He shook his head incredulously. "Are you jealous of Mindy?"

Mindy. Of course she would be named Mindy. Cute blondes were always named Mindy. Fred and Mindy. Perfect. It sounded like a frickin' sitcom. "Just because you look at her like you want to gobble her up, and you don't even notice when I leave the room, of course not, why would that make me jealous? Don't be ridiculous." She tried to shake him off, but he clamped his hands tighter. The heat of his grip ignited something deep inside her, some ferocious, primal urge.

She fought against it, her gaze clashing with his.

He looked as fierce as the wild bear that had once found its way to the Refuge.

"First of all, I went to high school with Mindy and she married a good friend of mine, who might complain if I gobbled her up. Second of all, aren't you the one looking at that dude like he's Brad Pitt and Bill Gates rolled into one? And if I didn't notice when you left the room, why would I be here right now?"

"You probably have to pee," said Rachel stubbornly, too miserable to give an inch.

He let out an incredulous snort. "Are you kidding me?"

His scent was taunting her, that freshly laundered, healthy man smell. Would he mind if she licked his neck? Because she really, really wanted to. She leaned in, just a hair, just so she could inhale a tiny bit of his essence.

Slam. Suddenly she was smack against his chest again, sealed against him, thigh to collarbone. All the breath fled from her body, chased by violent shivers of need. His arms clamped around her.

"Are you playing some kind of game with me?" he growled in her ear. "I knew you left the room because it felt empty. I knew because I couldn't smell the rose garden anymore. Because everything went flat without you. Is that what you want to hear? You want to hear how it's torture watching you with some other guy?"

She shuddered against his body, like a junkie who'd finally gotten a fix. Wrapping her arms around him, pulling him even closer, she stammered, stupidly. "R-rose garden?"

"Rose garden and rain." He nuzzled the tender spot below her ear. "Right here."

Shivers skittered from her frazzled nerve endings in a direct line to her nipples. She pushed her breasts against him, needing the hard pressure of his chest. In a daze, she caught his deep groan rising through his rib cage, through his sweater. "I want you," she said in a ragged voice. She wasn't even sure what it meant, since she'd never felt this way before. But no other words seemed to express the turmoil raging inside her.

"*Fuck*," he said with equal rawness. "I want you so much I can't see straight." With a strangled groan, he thrust her away from him. "But we shouldn't. I'm working for you."

She gave a helpless little whimper, which made his eyes darken. He caught her to him again. "Just tell me one thing. Do you like that guy?"

"No, I just wanted to make you jealous," she burst out. "And it didn't even work. All it did was make me crazy."

"Oh, it worked all right," he said grimly. "Too fucking well." And he claimed her mouth in a savage kiss.

Chapter 16

Yes, yes . . . this was what she'd wanted. Glorious
hardness against her, raw passion firing her from
the inside. They crashed against the wall of the little
restroom alcove, feeding on each other like wild
beasts. A potted ficus on a side table wobbled, about
to topple to the floor. Fred snaked out his arm to
rescue it, while Rachel clutched madly at his back,
where the slide and flex of his solid musculature
nearly made her swoon. *Losing her head* . . . The
phrase swam into her dazed brain. It had never
made sense to her before, but that's exactly what
she was doing. The feel of him, the smell of him, the
taste when she finally allowed herself to slide her
tongue along his neck.

"I have to say something," she gasped. But then
she couldn't remember what it was. The utter, overwhelming sweetness of Fred's hands on her drove
everything else from her mind.

"Can it wait?" His mouth was buried somewhere

in her hair so he could deliver maddening nibbles along the whorls of her ear. "Because I don't think I can stop."

His callused palms stroked heat along her exposed shoulder blades, then traced the dip of her sweetheart neckline, setting the sensitive skin of her chest ablaze. "You've been driving me crazy with this dress. I don't know how Bradford kept his hands off you."

The mention of Bradford finally brought her back to her senses. She pulled away, panting, then clutched at his shoulders to stabilize herself. The wallpapered alcove spun around her like a kaleidoscope of cream and gold. "Oh God. Bradford."

He yanked his hands off her and buried them in his hair. "I'm sorry. I'm so sorry, Rachel."

"Don't be." She shook her head fiercely as she adjusted her dress. "This was all my fault. Anyway, Bradford doesn't care about me. If my last name was Spurkel he wouldn't say boo to me."

"Spurkel?" Fred scratched at his head. His hair stood up in all directions. He was so adorable her knees shook.

"Generic silly last name."

Fred took a long step backward and shoved his hands in his pockets as if to keep them safely stowed away. A huge bulge protruded from the front of his pants. She covered her mouth as a little laugh escaped her.

"Laugh it up, Kessler," he said with mock grimness. "Enjoy yourself while I suffer."

Behind them, someone cleared his throat. Fred spun around, while Rachel peered over his shoulder, sure it was Bradford. Luckily, it was a stranger in a business suit, who muttered, "Get a room," before pushing his way into the men's room.

Fred turned back to Rachel, offering his hand. "You'd better get back to your date."

"It's not a date," she told him, suddenly horrified at the idea that she'd kissed one man while out with another. "I'd call it more of a business conference. All he wants to do is talk about his investments."

"Rich guy, huh?"

She shrugged. "I'm sure he'd show you his port-folio if you asked."

A shadow came over Fred's open, square-jawed face. "Come on. He must be wondering where you are."

Rachel managed to avoid both Fred and Bradford for the rest of the reception. She wasn't sure why Fred had changed gears, going from passionate kisser to blank-faced bodyguard. But it made her heart ache. Those few hot moments had made her long for him with an intensity she'd never experienced before. It felt as if they'd become neurologically connected in some mysterious way. Even when she was chat-ting with Cindy's parents, she knew exactly where he was. She knew when he was watching her, knew when he turned his attention elsewhere.

At the same time, she didn't think she could bear another car ride with Bradford. As soon as it seemed polite to leave the reception, she pulled him aside.

"I'm exhausted, Bradford," she said, hiding a yawn behind a discreet hand. "Would you mind if I drove home with Fred? It'll save you the trip."

"In what? That truck's one step removed from a mechanical bull. Surely you'd rather ride home in the Porsche." He took her arm possessively. She slid it out his grasp, trying to hide her instinctive revul-sion. She wanted only one man touching her, and it wasn't Bradford.

"No, thanks. Thank you for accompanying me,

Bradford. I'm glad we got a chance to catch up. I'll send your best to my father." She stuck out her hand, leaving him no choice but to take it. His blue eyes, pale as dawn, flickered between her and Fred, who'd just joined them.

"What's up with this guy?" Bradford asked nastily.

Rachel stiffened. Was it so obvious that she turned into a human torch the instant Fred got close? "I told you Fred's my temporary bodyguard. We're driving to the same place, I'm exhausted, and I'd rather just catch a ride with him."

Bradford toyed with the Bluetooth practically implanted in his ear. "I don't like what's going on here."

Fred, who'd been silent until now, stepped in. "Whether you like it or not, Rachel said she's tired and would prefer the evening to end here."

Slowly, reluctantly, Bradford directed his attention to Fred. The two men faced off with each other, Bradford's cool, moneyed sophistication versus Fred's forthright sturdiness. A little thrill went through her as she realized there was no contest, not really. Maybe it was Fred's experience with fires and rescues and other life-threatening situations, but he didn't back down one bit under Bradford's narrowed, condescending stare. The exact opposite, in fact. His solid strength made Bradford seem almost inconsequential.

Maybe Bradford realized it, because his lips tightened. "I hope you don't think anything's going to come of this," he told Fred, his lip curling in disdain. "I think I can speak for Kessler when I say—"

"*Bradford,*" Rachel hissed, balling her hands into fists. "You don't speak for my father, and he doesn't speak for me. How dare you? We're leaving now. And don't call me again, unless it's on board business."

The color came and went along his bladelike cheekbones, then he whirled around and stalked from the restaurant. Rachel, so furious she was shaking, clutched at Fred's arm. Without a word, he guided her along a path through the linen-draped tables. The low clinking of champagne glasses rang in her ears with a bell-like din, adding to the drumbeat of furious thoughts. Why did everyone think they had a say in her love life? Did Bradford really think she was so obedient to her father that she couldn't make her own choices?

Halfway home, she realized she was saying these things out loud. The restaurant sounds had been replaced by the rumble of Fred's truck. He was driving, focused on the road ahead, listening with a frown.

"Well?" she demanded. "Don't you think he was completely out of line?"

His hand tightened on the steering wheel. "I don't like the guy, but he probably has a point."

"A point? A *point*? What point?"

"Rachel Kessler and Fred Breen. Does that make sense to you? Wealthy heiress and ordinary fireman. Come on."

She turned on him in a passion. "Don't do that. Just don't, or I swear I'll . . . I'll . . . throw myself out of the truck."

He took a turn so tightly the tires squealed. "Don't even joke about that."

"Why should someone who saves people's lives be less important than anyone else?"

"It's not about importance . . ."

"What, then? Money? Sure, Bradford knows a lot about money. I thought he cared about animals too, but he doesn't. All he cares about is his portfolio. I bet the Refuge is nothing more than a tax write-off to him!" That, to her, was the worst sin of all. "My father might be rich, but he cares about things besides money. He loves computers and he wants everyone else to love them too. He'd probably be designing new systems for free. I should have known Bradford wasn't like that."

Fred drummed his thumbs on the steering wheel. "So Bradford isn't your favorite person."

"No. Or the fifty other men just like him who've asked me out."

"Fifty?"

"Fifty, a hundred, what does it matter? I'm not interested in men from my dad's world. And they're not really interested in *me*. They have no idea what my life is *really* like. I know what they want from me. The Kessler billions." That came out more bitter that she'd intended.

"Well, that's not what I would want."

For a moment, she lost her breath, desperate for Fred to continue that thought. He brought the truck to a jerking halt in front of her apartment building, then leaned toward her, his hand rising halfway between them. Her cheek tingled, waiting. She wanted, needed him to touch her. But then his gaze arrowed past her, and she swiveled to see Marsden waiting for them in the lobby.

His hand dropped away; she watched it with a sense of despair, as if it symbolized her entire life. Always separate, always apart.

"Go ahead upstairs," he told her. "I'll watch you until you're inside, then park the truck. Tell Marsden to do the security check with you."

She lingered on the sidewalk, seized by the feeling that as soon as she parted from Fred, he'd put her out of his mind forever. "You're coming up right away?"

"Yes." He hesitated. "But Rachel . . ."

"I'll see you upstairs." She hurried away from the truck before he could say anything else. Whatever he was about to say, she could already imagine. *It was a mistake. I'm not from your world. Your father would fire me.* Who could blame Fred if he said any of those things? What sane man would want to take on her and her father, not to mention a possibly vengeful kidnapper still on the loose?

Upstairs, Greta squirmed happily against her legs. Rachel kicked off her stilettos and knelt on the floor to hug her. Her warm doggy enthusiasm made the tight, fearful knot in Rachel's chest loosen. It was okay if she made a fool of herself in front of Greta. Dogs didn't care about things like that.

A tear dropped onto Greta's fur. "Oh Greta, I'm afraid I've ruined everything," she whispered to her dog.

A hot tongue licking her hand assured her that she hadn't. She swiped at her tears with the heel of her hand and padded into the kitchen, illuminated by nothing more than the light of the stove hood. She didn't want to turn on any more lights; the semi-darkness suited her mood. In the pantry, she took out a can of dog food and found the can opener.

If she could do nothing else in her life, she knew how to make dogs happy. Maybe that would be enough. It used to be enough. Until she met Fred.

"Rachel," came his voice from the other side of the kitchen.

She spun around, clutching the half-opened can, her stomach cratering with fear. Here it came. Rejection, withdrawal, abandonment. All of the things she'd been imagining. Instead, he opened his arms with an almost helpless gesture, as if to say, *Here I am, if you want me.*

The most undignified sound came out of her mouth, a sort of sniffling gulp. He seemed to know exactly what it meant. A grin spread across his face, creases tugging at the corners of his dark eyes. She tossed aside the can of dog food and launched herself into his open arms.

Fred would never forget the feeling of Rachel's full-throttle leap into his embrace. For that one moment, all her protective layers were ripped away, and he saw the beautifully warm spirit who lived inside. The way her face came alive, the way her feet actually left the ground on her way to him, as if she trusted him absolutely. The idea that this reserved, precious person would open herself up to him gave him a sense of awe.

While parking the truck, he'd come to a decision. Even though he couldn't imagine getting a thumbs-up from Rob Kessler, this wasn't about the man. This was about him and Rachel, and at the moment, she needed him. And if he didn't have her, he might lose his mind. So he'd go for the ride as long as it lasted, or until Kessler brought down the hammer. If—when—his heart got broken, well, Lizzie owed him plenty of Chunky Monkey.

"I thought you might be angry," she whispered. He saw the tracks of tears on her cheeks, and wiped them away with a thumb.

"Why would I be angry?"

"Because Dad dragged you away from your nice life and your firehouse and now I'm making things even more complicated."

"I had a say in the matter," he said dryly. "If I

didn't want to be here, I wouldn't be. I don't care what the Mighty Kessler offered."

She gazed at him wonderingly, her violet eyes scanning his face. "You wouldn't, would you? People don't make you do things. Not even my father. You do what you feel is right. You do what you want."

He brushed a gleaming strand of hair behind her ear. "Believe me, I don't always do what I want. If I did, I'd have had you in bed that first night."

She swallowed so hard he saw the shift of her throat muscles.

"What do you want, Rachel? You, not your father, not your friends—you?"

"I want you," she whispered. "But I know it's wrong. No, not because of Dad," she said quickly, when he started to speak. "Because you didn't come here for that. And I know we should keep things professional and you're working hard to protect me and I don't want to—"

He sealed his mouth against hers in a fast, hard kiss, as if stopping her breath would halt the flow of her thoughts. "Did anyone ever tell you that you worry too much?" he whispered against her mouth.

"It's been mentioned once or twice," she whispered back. "I have my reasons."

"I know you do." He ran his hands along her sides, along the sleek black curve of her waist, down to her ass, as he'd been wanting to do all night long. She shivered under his touch. "But do you think you could turn your brain off, just for now?"

She nodded. He hoisted her legs so they wrapped around his hips, and settled his hands under her rear. Her dress rode up to her thighs, where satiny skin gleamed in the glow of the stove light.

"I'm going to make love to you," he told her firmly. "If you have any objections to that, tell me now."

"Not a single one," she said fervently, peppering kisses onto his cheeks and jaw. "If you don't start soon, I might burst into tears."

"No more tears, unless it's because I make you feel so good." He nibbled on the delicate skin just below her ear.

"So confident," she teased, leaning in to follow the movements of his Adam's apple with her tongue. "You think you can bring me to tears?"

"If you can cry over dog food, you can cry over me."

Her laughter bubbled up like uncorked champagne. "I wasn't crying over dog food, silly."

Greta bumped against his leg. She was pushing the can around the kitchen with her nose, sniffing it, trying to figure out how to get inside. This struck both of them as hilarious and they burst out laughing. Greta started, then gave them an outraged look that sent them into more gales of laughter.

Fred let Rachel down so she could finish feeding Greta. He watched her empty the can, rinse it out, then wash her own hands. Each moment that ticked past made his desire ramp up even higher.

When she was finally done—it seemed to take an eternity—Fred whisked her out of the kitchen to the living room, where they tumbled together onto the suede couch. Fred pulled her on top of him and their laughter drowned under hot, drugging kisses. He unzipped the back of her dress and sat her up so he could draw it down her body. Her hair streamed in wild curls to her shoulders. Her skin gleamed like marble, a living marble that responded to his touch with floods of vibrant color. Even her breasts, as he unpeeled the dress from her body, were washed with pink, like icing on a birthday cake. He paused before going any further than the tops of her breasts.

"I've been trying to picture you naked for days," he whispered. "But I think my imagination needs work. You're even more beautiful now that you're real and you're right here on top of me."

"Really, you've been thinking about me that way?" She snuck her small, cool hands under his sweater. He thought his pounding heart might leap out like a fish. "Because I can't stop thinking about you lying over there in that bedroom. Stark naked."

He swallowed hard. "How do you know I sleep naked?"

"I don't." The pink in her cheeks deepened to the crimson of geraniums. "That was just wishful thinking."

"What else did you wish for?"

"This," she said simply. "You. To be close to you." She tugged at his sweater. "Do you think you could . . . ?"

He sat up against the arm of the couch, reached back, and yanked his creamy wool sweater over his head, dragging his T-shirt along with it. When he was bare-chested, she placed a hand over the center of his rib cage. "I remember this chest," she said in a husky voice. "I've never shown up for dinner at a half-naked man's house before."

"At least I had pants on."

"Yes, that was extremely disappointing," she said gravely, making him laugh. With her pixie features shining with delight, her wide grin nearly taking over her small face, he knew he'd never seen anything more beautiful in the world.

If he could make her happy, even if only for the span of time required to make passionate love to her, he would.

Chapter 17

The feel of Fred's bare skin against hers was enough to send Rachel into a stratospheric state of pleasure. It was as if she'd been starving, and was finally sitting at a sensual buffet where she could gorge herself without embarrassment. She ran her palms across the tight muscles of his torso and the light dusting of silky dark hair. Every muscle was firm and sharply defined, as if sketched by some master of anatomy.

"You're beautiful," she told him.

"Nah," he said, embarrassed. "I'm your basic guy. I can show you ten guys at the firehouse more ripped than me."

"To me, you're perfect." She slid her hands under the waistband of his pants and felt the tender skin of his lower belly quiver.

He groaned. "You can't say that yet. You haven't seen the whole picture."

"Very good point," she agreed, moving to unfasten his pants. When she reached the zipper, he stopped her with one hand. Once again, his strength took her breath away.

"Not yet. I've been waiting long enough to see you like this. I don't want to rush through it. Keep your hands still or I'll completely lose it."

The note of command in his voice gave her a little shock. She let her arms relax at her side, palms up, which gave her a delicious feeling of offering herself to him. He reached for her breasts, cupping them tenderly, stroking their soft under curves. Her nipples tightened visibly; inside, she felt a tugging ache. His gaze, latched onto her chest, went lazy and hot. As if they had all night, he explored the shape of her breasts with his thumbs, circling the exposed globes, drawing ever closer to her nipples, which began to throb.

She shifted restlessly so she could feel the hard ridge of his erection against her sex. The pressure made them both groan out loud.

"No rushing," Fred said sternly. "I've still barely gotten to touch you."

"What do you mean, barely? You're driving me crazy. Could you . . ." She leaned forward, shivering, needing more contact.

"My pleasure," he murmured, and dragged his thumbs across her pebble-hard nipples. A sharp streak of pleasure made her jump. Her vision blurred slightly, and she caught her lower lip between her teeth.

He spent an excruciating amount of time playing with her breasts, shifting between tender explorations and hard squeezes that overloaded her senses and made her want to scream. Even though shivers racked her body, he refused to be hurried. He gathered her close so he could run his tongue across the taut peaks. His deep suckles and gentle nibbles made her writhe on top of him, her thighs tightening around his hips.

Finally, finally, he lifted her up and worked her little black dress off her hips, leaving her in nothing but her black silk panties. She was trembling so hard she was no help at all in the process. Part of her resented him for being so in control while she was shaking with waves of hot want. But then he half tumbled off the couch, shoved off his wedding pants, and she caught an eyeful of what their make-out session had done to him. All other thoughts fled her mind. His thickly swollen penis stood straight out from his body, its heavy weight buoyed by the intensity of his arousal.

Rachel's breath stuttered in her throat. She didn't have a ton of experience, but none of what she did have prepared her for the sight of Fred. Were penises supposed to be this size? It was nearly as thick as her wrist. "That's . . . not normal," she said warily.

"Normal enough," he muttered, his hungry gaze still consuming her body. "I'm in the normal range."

"Maybe the outer limit," she said dubiously.

"Yeah, something like that. Don't worry, I've never had any complaints. I'd never hurt you."

"How can you be sure?"

He kicked his pants aside and returned to the couch. "Communication. If something doesn't feel good to you, we stop immediately."

She swallowed hard. Communication was not one of her strengths, at least when it came to people. Dogs were one thing, but people had so many contradictions and secret hidden agendas. She had secrets of her own, so she always watched her words very carefully. But Fred was great at communication. If she just followed his lead, maybe it would all be okay.

When he made to sit down next to her on the couch, she stopped him.

"My turn to look at you," she told him. She touched a tentative finger to the hot, velvety tip of his erection, then circled around the rigid flare of the head. Her finger seemed to take an insanely long time to travel its complete circumference. When she stole a glance at his face, she saw that he'd clamped his eyes shut. Knots of tension rippled his jaw muscles.

Pure female satisfaction made her want to purr. She'd never felt sexually powerful before, but the strained expression on his face made her confidence soar. "Does this feel good?"

"Yes," he choked out. "But I think you'd better stop."

"Not yet." First, she wanted to run her fingers down his full length, appreciating each hard ridge and soft vein she discovered. His shaft grew even harder under her exploring strokes. Bending down, she touched her tongue to the very tip, tasting tender skin and a drop of salt.

"Okay, that's it," growled Fred. "There's only so much I can take."

Suddenly she found herself on her back, sprawled across the couch, her legs lifted so he could slide off her panties, which were already soaking wet. He stilled for a moment, holding her legs apart with firm hands on both of her thighs. The position felt exposing, vulnerable and erotic.

"You are so dang beautiful." The rough edge in his voice was sweet music to her soul. He drew one finger down the center of the thatch of downy hair, right where the need crystallized into a throbbing point. It was as if he'd tugged on a string attached to her sex. Almost involuntarily, she pushed her hips against his finger, mutely begging for more. He gave it to her. Another finger. More pressure, more friction, more pleasure. He touched her with so much honest appreciation that tears sprang to her eyes. Under his strong hand, she felt beautiful and free.

Free to twist against him when he escalated the pace of his stroking. Free to moan and babble urgent things like "Faster, please, oh, don't stop, oh my God." Free to grab his erection and rub it against her mound. When he drew his hips away, she actually shouted at him. He just laughed, crawled between her legs, and lowered his mouth to her sex. She stopped shouting and started panting.

Her entire being homed in on the warm, fleshy tongue stroking intimately against her, dragging bursts of bright sensation from her core. His mouth covered the tender, slick tissues of her sex, delving, testing, savoring. And then . . . oh glory . . . he did something with his thumb, touched some spot that might as well have been the detonator on a bomb, because she exploded in shocking waves of bright heat. It went on and on, the spasms grabbing her body with brilliant cataclysms of pleasure. Bits of information filtered through the madness: her spine bent in a tight arch, her fists filled with couch upholstery, his hands a miracle from heaven.

And then, tragedy, his hands left her and he disappeared from the couch.

Panting, melting, she watched him move to the little pile of clothes on the floor and rummage for his pants. She stared at his young, tough body as he knelt. He moved with complete physical confidence, like one of the mountain lions at the Refuge. Quiet strength and smooth grace, each tendon and muscle flexing in perfect harmony with the others. He extracted his wallet from his back pocket, plucked out a condom, tore it open, and worked it over his massive hard-on.

Then he pounced on her, his knees on either side of her hips, surprising a laugh out of her.

She was so slippery, so drenched in satisfaction that his size barely registered. As he entered her she felt remade. Stretched and expanded, all hesitation and doubt chased from her body by his full-blooded, iron erection. He eased inside her, every new inch of progress making her more open and more wild. She reached down to put her hand on his powerful thigh, feeling the muscle flex as he fought to control his movements. He hung above her, breath ragged, steam practically rising off him.

"You feel so good," he muttered, his face set in fierce lines. "I might lose my mind here."

"So what?" She gasped as he claimed another inch. "I already lost mine, and I don't miss it at all."

He gave a ragged laugh. "Good point. Okay, then. You ready?"

"Bring it, fireman." She grinned up at him with an unfamiliar feeling of sassiness. She never felt relaxed during sex, the few times she'd tried it. There was too much to worry about—expectations, the tabloids, consequences. But this felt so different, as if she and Fred were creating their own perfect, steamy world one caress at a time.

"Brace yourself, sweetheart." He thrust his hips forward until he was seated entirely within her. She let out a squeak. She hadn't known that anyone could go so deep inside her. She hadn't known there was *space*. And who could have guessed it would feel so *good*? The slow friction of his shaft dragging across the hidden recesses of her flesh sent pleasure skipping through her system. She bent her legs so he could go even deeper. *Oh my God. How could anything on earth feel so amazing?*

Then he shifted from that long, slow spearing to

a steady in-and-out penetration that had her eyes crossing. She couldn't hold back her primal groan. He pulled out, his thigh muscles clenching, then thrust in again. Remembering the way she'd noticed his butt, and how she'd pictured it during sex, her face heated. She lost herself in the smooth flex, the hot clench, the thrust and rock and grind. Losing all control over her limbs, she surged against him, wanting more, harder, again. And then all she could think about was how incredible he felt inside her, the heat of his body against hers, the sweat on his straining face, the pulses of light flashing in her vision, the electric surge racing toward her, crashing onto her, breaking her into a million particles of shimmering ecstasy.

Buried inside Rachel's sweet, trembling body, Fred wondered if he'd blown a blood vessel. He'd never come so hard in his life.

"I didn't hurt you, did I?" He peeled a stray lock of tumbling dark hair off her cheek. "Please tell me I didn't. I kind of lost it for a second there." He'd been completely consumed by his need to have her, and now tenderness clawed at his insides. His duty was to protect this girl, not harm her.

"You didn't notice the cries for help?" she asked dryly. "No, you didn't hurt me. What about me? I think I might have punched you again." Lifting a hand to his face, she traced the outline of his nose. "Yup. It's a little red."

"I didn't notice. I was a little busy getting the top of my head blown off." He started to pull out of her body, but she stopped him.

"I don't want you to leave me yet," she said softly. Her violet eyes darkened, and her inky lashes fell over them. "We could sleep here, just like this. Never have to be alone."

Her melancholy tone made him uneasy. Rachel was full of fascinating opposites—tentative but wild, a little innocent but electrically responsive. And always, underneath, the suggestion of loneliness.

"You're not going to be alone. I live here remember? I'm your twenty-four-hour-a-day shadow."

"Right." Her lips, inflamed from his kisses, lifted at the corners. Then her eyes flew open. "Right!" She struggled to sit up, while he gripped his cock with one hand to keep it from getting too jostled in the process. He slipped from the hot clasp of her body into the cooler air. "Oh no! Is this going to make everything more awkward?"

"Everything?"

"Well . . ." She slid her tongue across her swollen lower lip. "You being my bodyguard and us having . . ."

"Sex," he prompted.

"Yes. Sex." Her cheeks flamed fuchsia. "Really, really good sex."

"I thought so. I'm glad you agree." Actually, it made him feel like Superman.

"We can't tell my father."

He didn't bother to point out that his parents weren't usually his first phone call after sex. Obviously she was experiencing a freak-out and he'd just have to roll with it. "Agreed."

"Not because he wouldn't approve. Not that. But I don't want him to think you can't do your job just as well as before we had sex."

The mention of Kessler put an end to his post-coital buzz. He stood up to track down his pants. "Rachel, are you sure you really need a bodyguard?

I haven't seen one thing out of the ordinary since I've been here." A thought had begun to form; maybe he could stop being her bodyguard and they could date, like normal people.

She scrambled to her knees on the cushions of the couch. Its dark rust shade set off the pearly paleness of her skin and the ruby-red points of her nipples, making her look positively erotic. "Are you quitting? Because if you are, you'd better tell me right this second."

"Quitting? How'd you get from 'Do you need a bodyguard?' to 'I'm quitting'? I committed to this job, and I'm not bailing on it. But your dad's testimony's coming up soon and we haven't seen one sign of anything suspicious. I just want to know that I'm doing something important. Something that matters."

"It matters to me." She curled her legs under her and clasped her hands together on her thighs. He wished he could take a picture of her, just like this, tumbled and flushed and honest. "What other bodyguard would ever take me out and play bumper cars with me? Or get in a bar brawl?"

He winced. "Definitely not a professional one."

"I'm serious. I want you to stay. But I *really* don't want things to be awkward between us. We need to have a serious discussion."

"Okay. Let's do it." Since their discussion needed some lightening up, he pulled on his boxers. A gift from Lizzie, they had little red fire hydrants scattered all over them.

Her eyes drifted to them, and he saw her try to control a smile. He went to the couch and sat next to her. He crossed one leg over the other, so she couldn't possibly miss the fire engines.

"Serious discussion time."

"Um . . ." she bit her lip. "I suppose we could not have sex again."

"Okay. Who votes for that? Anyone?"

Neither one raised a hand. He smiled smugly. At least they weren't pretending to like that plan. "I have another idea. We could just play it by ear. It's only another week."

She drew her legs up against her chest and wrapped her arms around them. "Play it by ear. You mean, no ground rules?"

"I can think of one. No more Bradford."

"No. Of course not." She looked appalled at the thought. "Okay, I have another. None of your fan club girls."

He raised an eyebrow at her. "Then we might have a problem. Reliable sources say you own a 'Fred's My Hero' button. You must be in my fan club."

She leaned against him, rubbing her head on his arm like a kitten. He wanted to eat her up. "Right at this moment, I'm the president of the Fred Breen fan club. Will you sign my boobs?"

"Sure. One catch. It has to be with my tongue." He pinned her, giggling, to the back of the couch, cupped her breasts in his hands, and traced his name across her chest with his tongue, wrapping the E around one nipple and landing the final N on the other. Then he went back and filled in some blank spots with little nibbles. By the time he was done, she was squirming and sighing, and he scooped her into his arms and headed for the hallway that led to the bedrooms.

"Your bedroom or mine? Bathtub? Linen closet? Entertainment room?"

"Um . . ." Her cheeks flushed, and her eyes glimmered like stars in the twilight. "All of the above?"

"You're on."

Chapter 18

*O*ver the next three days, the sun rose and set, San Gabriel residents commuted to and from work, took their kids to school, and complained about the early heat wave, while Rachel and Fred holed up in her apartment and immersed themselves in each other. They exited only for essential reasons such as Rachel's appointments at the Refuge. Other than that, they stayed inside and explored each other with an intimacy Rachel had never experienced.

Fred was a sensual man. He liked being naked. He liked her being naked. He liked exploring her body with every tool at his disposal: fingertips, tongue, lips, teeth. In this realm, between the sheets, he claimed complete authority, and she didn't argue one bit. For one thing, he was so much more knowledgeable and . . . carnal. She'd never indulged that side of herself before, at least not to this extent.

Everything he did felt good. She loved waking to the feel of his hands roaming her body, delving between her legs as she surfaced from sleep. A warm, rough palm massaged gentle circles around her clitoris, while hot breath fanned her cheek. Maybe inhibitions didn't work first thing in the morning, because she felt no shame when she ground her sex against the heel of his hand, or when he flipped her onto her knees and dragged her ass into the air. Heat flashed all the way to her toes as she buried her face in the covers. Her cheeks burned with it, her thighs trembled. He could see everything—everything!— and it didn't matter because he wanted her, and she wanted him. She wanted him in her, around her, on top of her, beneath her, anywhere at all, as long as they were skin to skin.

Every part of her, skin and flesh and spirit, brightened when he was near.

When she thought about how much she loved being with him, she got nervous. He would be her bodyguard only a short while, until her father's testimony, or maybe a little longer, until the media moved on. What would happen after that? What would it be like to go back to her more solitary, sheltered existence? Maybe it would be better to not get used to having Fred in her life, to not *enjoy* him so much. But she couldn't stop, didn't want to stop. Not when every moment they spent together felt so joyous and free.

Not that it was always perfect. He still teased her, and sometimes they squabbled over things like whether *Grease* was a better movie than *Rock 'n' Roll High School*. Fred didn't get her addiction to crossword puzzles and did his best to distract her. His best was very, very good; it involved tying her to the bedposts while he filled in the answers, on her skin, traced by his own personal writing tool.

They played naked Scrabble, with the loser required to do whatever the winner wanted. She won. To her surprise, what she wanted most at that moment was to explore his beautiful penis with her tongue. She made him lie still, stretched out on her bed, with his hands behind his head, while she pressed kisses onto his half-aroused member. After only a few kisses, it began growing and stretching toward her. His penis fascinated her, both soft and hard, sweet and salty, fierce and vulnerable, like a club wrapped in living velveteen. She loved the way it responded to her in its own language of twitches and jumps. She loved the way his thigh muscles strained and his hips bucked under the strokes of her tongue. His hands dug into the sheets as if she was dragging him off a cliff with her mouth. As if to keep himself from grabbing her head and pounding into her.

She wouldn't have minded, but he always kept a leash on himself, as if he was still watching out for her even while losing his mind. Which meant he didn't *really* lose his mind. And part of her wanted him to.

She did her best to obliterate his control, sucking him to a ruthless, shouting climax that would have woken the neighbors if she had any. Afterward, he lay, wrecked, in her antique four-poster bed, his elbow crooked over his face, his chest rising and falling with deep shudders. She rested her chin on his chest, squinting at the slight black hairs until they looked like tangled underbrush in a forest.

She ran her fingertips over the ridged muscles of his torso, feeling the warm stickiness of sweat. "Have you ever come so hard you forgot where you were?"

"No," he admitted, his voice still raspy. "I never want to lose that much control."

"Why not? You make me forget everything. Maybe control is overrated."

"Depends on the situation. When you have a big old crowbar sticking out of you, and it's inside another person, you don't want anyone to get hurt."

She let out a soft laugh, a puff of air that stirred the silky hairs. Sunlight slanted through the window, casting a bright rectangle across Fred's middle. "You make it sound like a weapon, like a tire iron or something."

"Of course it's a weapon. A weapon of loooove."

She snorted, and rubbed her cheek against his chest. Fred was so darn *cute*. She could barely stand it sometimes.

"But I'm a lover not a fighter," he continued. "Especially with that thing."

"I can't believe you call it a 'thing.' You're going to hurt its feelings."

"Then it's a good thing you're around to boost its self-esteem." He glanced down his body at his exhausted member, which rested against his leg in a dusky curl.

"I'm a dog therapist, not a penis therapist."

"You should branch out. We can call you the Penis Whisperer."

"How flattering. Maybe I'll put that on my résumé."

He wound his fingers through her hair and gently tugged, the way she liked. Tingles of pleasure danced across her scalp. "Does a girl like you need a résumé?"

"Not really," she admitted. "My clients don't ask for a résumé. It's all word of mouth. But when my college roommates were applying for jobs, I helped them write their résumés. And before I started the Refuge, I considered applying for a job at The Gap or something. Krispy Kreme. Dog walker. Something in the non-Kessler world."

How had she gotten onto that subject? That's how their conversations went. From goofy sexual puns to revelations about their pasts. No topic was off limits; maybe that's why talking to Fred was so addictive.

"So why didn't you get a job like that?"

"It didn't seem right. I don't need the money, and I'd be taking a job from someone who does. And wherever I worked, my employers would have to deal with my crazy security-obsessed dad. And just think about the stress Dad would go through. I couldn't do that to him. I caused him enough stress when I was . . . kidnapped."

She didn't usually use that word, but everything was different with Fred. She didn't want to hide anything from him.

Fred was looking at her so closely, she almost wished she hadn't mentioned her kidnapping. "You don't like to talk about that, do you?"

"No. I mean, I've been through plenty of therapy. I *can* talk about it, even though I couldn't at first. But I don't want that crazy man to dictate who I am. If I'm just the girl who got kidnapped, I might as well have stayed in that cage."

Gently, his hand slipped to the nape of her neck and found a knot of tension that had suddenly developed.

"What if you're the girl who escaped the cage?"

An image from her captivity flashed through her mind, the big man coming toward her with that horrible white mask. Her scrambling back against the bars, warm pee running down her leg because she was so scared. Escape. Could she ever *really* escape? She prayed he wouldn't ask more about the kidnapping. She didn't want to go back there anymore, didn't want her mind occupied by those memories.

He must have picked up on her silent plea because he changed the subject. "How did you start the Refuge for Injured Wildlife?"

She could have kissed him. "Well, I knew I wanted to work with animals. I used to bring rescues home to Cranesbill all the time. It was a hobby, basically, but since it didn't involve any ominous people, my dad was okay with it. So I figured an animal refuge would be a good choice. In college I took a few workshops with a dog trainer who uses more intuitive techniques, and loved it. He said I was a natural, and that it would be a crime for me not to use my talents. That fit well with the refuge idea, although I have to keep my dog therapy office away from the wildlife areas. I found an abandoned wilderness training camp and we converted the buildings into what we needed. Since we were starting the place from zero, my father was able set up the security the way he wanted. And I didn't take a single job away from anyone. We created jobs, in fact. We hired two vets and four techs. So everyone was happy."

He was quiet for a long moment. "So you built an animal refuge. Just like that."

"Well, it took almost a year to build it and hire the staff. It's still a work in progress. I'm really interested in the rescue dog project." She wondered why he was being so silent. "Does it seem strange to you? I wave my father's magic checkbook and ta-da! . . . instant animal refuge?"

"No," he said softly. "I mean, yes, I'm not used to that kind of power. But that's not what I was thinking. I was thinking that you have an incredible heart. You could do anything in the world, and you choose to help animals. I admire you."

She sat up and pushed the hair out of her eyes. "Are you teasing me?"

"Hell, no. I'm being sincere."

"If you look at it another way, I'm a spoiled rich girl who plays with animals because that's all her daddy will let her do. My biggest claim to fame is being kidnapped when I was little."

With a sudden move, he flipped her onto her back. "Why are you so hard on yourself? You're doing something you love and you're trying not to hurt the people you care about. I think you're amazing. And if there's any spoiling to be done"—he pinned her arms to the side—"I'll do it. With my weapon of looooove."

With that, he dragged his tongue across her nipples until she whimpered from the hot pleasure coursing through her.

"Do you have any idea how beautiful you are to me?" he murmured against her breasts. "In every respect. But especially your body."

"Excuse me?" She tried like hell to frown, but it was hard when her nipples were responding like spring shoots to sunshine. "Especially my body? What kind of thing is that to say?"

"Shallow but true. I mean, look at you. This skin." He nuzzled her chest, his hair tickling her nipples unbearably. "These perfect boobies."

"*Boobies?*" She gave a snorting laugh and tried to tug her hands free. A pointless effort, with his strong hands still binding her.

"Yes, I said boobies." He nipped at them gently, taking first one, then the other into his mouth. "Perfect," he mumbled. He inserted his thigh between hers. Firm muscles and hot skin pressed against her mound. She squirmed against the intrusion, then went all liquid inside.

He shifted to nudge the little knot of nerves that had been craving his attention. How did he know? The man was a magician. She yelped, then snapped her mouth shut.

"Don't keep it in," he murmured. "I like to hear your sounds."

"I don't make sounds."

"Yes, you do. I love your sounds. They turn me on. Especially when you don't even know you're making them. The more sounds, the merrier. Sounds, smells."

"Smells? Ew." She tried to close her legs, but he merely wedged his thigh closer.

"Your scent is one hundred percent pure erotic. Kind of spicy, like cinnamon or something. But also fresh, like morning rain. Rose bushes. One whiff and I go a little crazy. I just can't help it. And then there are the textures."

"Textures?" she said faintly. He was moving against her with a slow grind. The rhythm seemed to take over her entire being. Her heartbeat raced to catch up.

"Yes, textures. Is that weird, that I notice textures? Well, I do. For instance, the skin on your inner thigh is softer than anywhere else on your body. Guaranteed. I've cross-checked your entire body. The inner thigh wins." He nudged her legs open. They fell apart like sliced butter. "But it might be time for another inspection."

Then suddenly her hands were free, his strong ones were under her ass, her legs were draped over his shoulders, and his mouth was on her sex. He burrowed into her soft privacy, opening the outer lips like petals on a flower.

That was it for talking. No more banter, no more

soul-baring, nothing but moans and shrieks and pleas for mercy.

She didn't really want mercy, of course. She wanted more. More of what she seemed to experience only with Fred. When the rolling wave lifted her up toward the blinding sky, when it tossed her into the air and spun her around until gravity no longer applied . . . when she shrieked and sobbed, her only anchor his warm mouth latched to her sex, a shocking thought came to her.

All her life she'd craved freedom. In bed with Fred, she felt freer than she'd ever dreamed. Free to say whatever she wanted. Free to feast herself on his strong, eager body, free to have one screaming orgasm after another, free to tease and fight and laugh.

Free to forget all about the evil man who might still be hunting her.

Chapter 19

"I need to take a couple hours off this afternoon," Fred told Rachel one morning, after a few of the most deliriously sex-drenched days he'd ever experienced. Not that he was worn out; not at all. He'd be happy to continue indefinitely, but he'd gotten a phone call from the firehouse.

"What's up?" They were about to start Greta's training session in the park across the street. Rachel wore a grungy T-shirt with the words "Bite Me" emblazoned across the front, along with ratty sweatpants. God, she was adorable. He couldn't look at her without counting the minutes until they could go back to bed.

"Got a call from the firehouse. One of our guys, Double D, needs some help. He and his wife are moving, and he dropped a microwave on his leg. Classic Double D. Fractured it in two places. He's out of commission and they have to be out of their house by Friday. His wife is freaking out."

"They can't hire movers?"

Fred had to take a deep breath before he answered. Moments like this reminded him of the world Rachel inhabited, one in which money solved most problems.

Not all problems, he reminded himself, or she wouldn't be living like a refugee in her own apartment.

"They don't have that kind of money. Firefighting isn't exactly a high-paying profession, and they've got two kids in college. The kids are in the middle of exams, or they'd fly back and help. That's actually why Double D's moving, so they can lower their mortgage payments."

Rachel bent to let Greta sniff a piece of rawhide, letting her hair fall across her face. Through the dark tendrils of her curls, he saw a wave of crimson stain her skin. Damn, he hadn't meant to embarrass her. She'd revealed enough about her history that he knew she hated the ways in which her father's status isolated her. "Right. Of course. So you and your friends are going to help out?"

"We're making a work party out of it. I'm supposed to bring some beer. And some muscles. My assignment is to help Patty pack up the bedroom."

"Why you?"

He shrugged, embarrassed. "She says I'm the only one she trusts with her personal stuff."

"Really?" They reached a quiet section of the park. After a careful check, Rachel unfastened Greta's leash. "I should think she'd want another woman. Why not Sabina or One?"

"I can't believe you remember their names." He'd told her all about the various members of the firehouse crew, but he hadn't expected her to pay such close attention.

"Of course I remember. In my head, they're like characters in a movie. Especially Sabina, since she was actually *in* a movie. Why doesn't Patty want Sabina to help her?"

Fred took the training toy from Rachel. His role was that of "victim." He'd hide and Greta would have to find him. "Sabina intimidates her, and One's on vacation. I wasn't even going to go, since I'm on leave, but we always try to help each other out when stuff goes down. Especially when someone gets hurt, although usually injuries happen on the job, not from a kitchen appliance. Anyway, Double D called and begged me. He claimed he would have been on his knees if he weren't on crutches. Then he made me an offer I couldn't refuse."

She hung on his words, her eyes alive with merry laughter. He'd never seen anyone get so much entertainment from hearing about the firehouse. "I can't wait to hear. What's the offer?"

"First of all, Patty's making her special lasagna. But the big thing is that he promised to sing to me. 'Call Me Maybe.' You'd never guess it, but he's got a great voice. I would have made him dance too, but he's on crutches."

"Is he a good dancer?"

"Not at all." He gave an evil grin. He missed the firehouse, missed the teasing and the comradeship. He even missed Double D, salty old coot that he was.

"Well." Rachel cocked her head, tossing Greta's leash from one hand to the other. Greta panted excitedly, eyes shining. She loved the training sessions; they involved retrieving things and winning treats, after all. "I think I should come too."

"Excuse me?"

"It sounds like they need all the hands they can get. If I can be helpful, why not? Besides, I can meet the other firefighters. They won't be characters in a movie anymore."

"You sure you want that? You might enjoy them more from the safety of a movie theater."

"Don't be crazy. I'm sure I'll love them. We'll tell them I'm your cousin or something."

He looked at her dubiously. "Well, we both have dark hair. I suppose we could pass for cousins." When she offered him one of her wide, spectacular smiles, the ones that reached right into his gut and stirred him all up inside, he gave in to the constant urge and yanked her against him. "I'm pretty darn glad you're not my cousin." He nibbled her soft, sweet-smelling neck until she giggled and squirmed.

"None of that in front of the guys."

"Hell no. You'd never have any privacy ever again." He took a quick glance around, then snuck his hand under her T-shirt and stroked her silky skin until it warmed and her nipple rose against the worn fabric of her T-shirt. "I think something urgent has come up. Want to hide behind a tree and play 'victim' with me?"

"No, thank you," she said, flushing as he fondled her responsive nipple. "But if you do really well in this training session, I'll give you a treat."

"Oh boy!" Fred released her and bounded across the grass in great, Greta-like leaps, the sound of Rachel's merry laughter chasing him. Her laughter was all the reward he needed; throw in more between-the-sheets time, and he was a happy guy.

Double D lived in a sprawling Tudor-style house with a wide front lawn filled with packing boxes and brawny, attractive men. Rachel swallowed hard as they approached the intimidating group. She'd never seen so many flexing muscles and fine asses in one place. In her eyes, none of them compared to Fred, but she still couldn't help noticing how amazingly good-looking they all were.

A couple holding hands stopped to say hi on their way out. Fred introduced them as Captain Brody and his wife, Melissa. Rachel stiffened; she'd seen Melissa's news reports on TV, and even though they were always well done, she couldn't help her automatic wariness around reporters.

"We only stopped by for moral support," explained Melissa. "My dad is watching the baby, and my Lucian withdrawal kicks in at about half an hour."

"It's nice of you to come and help," Brody said, shaking Rachel's hand. "How do you know—"

"You can interrogate her some other time, Brody." Melissa tugged his hand, and Brody gave in. Rachel decided she liked the green-eyed reporter—as much as she could like any member of the media.

Fred introduced her next to his new captain, Vader Brown, who had a muscleman physique crammed into a ripped SGFD T-shirt, as if his pumping pectorals had burst right through the material. As soon as Fred said the word "cousin," Vader launched into a coughing fit. Fred glared at him until he straightened up and offered his hand to Rachel.

"Captain Brown, great to meet you. Any cousin of Freddie's is a cousin of . . . well, anyway, thanks for pitching in. Double D! Come meet Fred's *cousin*."

Rachel shot Fred a sidelong look of alarm from under her eyelashes. He shrugged. "Just ignore them and don't tell them a damn thing. That's how I do it."

A man in a full leg brace swung over to them on his crutches, his big belly hanging over his belt.

Okay, so not *all* the men here were magazine material. "Stud, you old sneak. You never told us you had a beauty in the family. Must be a distant cousin, is all I can say." He gave Fred a caustic grin and stuck out his hand for Rachel to shake.

"Pretty distant," Fred agreed.

Rachel shook Double D's hand, then decided to get Fred back for all the times he'd teased her over the past few days. "Double D, do you mind if I ask why you all call him Stud? Did that start because of the fan club?"

Out of the corner of her eye, she saw Fred stiffen.

"Fan club? Don't get me started on that fan club. They've been stopping by the station nonstop since you been gone, Freddie. Wanting to know where you are, when you're coming back, what color undies you wear. Ella Joy keeps coming by too."

Oh crap. Over the past few days, she'd forgotten all about that news anchor who had shown up at Fred's house.

"You didn't tell her anything, did you?" Fred asked.

"'Course not. Unless you want me to. Want me to tell her you're off to Borneo to count monkeys or somethin'?"

"We can handle Ella Joy," Vader said. "The more important question on the table is how Fred got his nickname." He shot Rachel a complicit grin. She decided she liked Vader, even if he did look as if he could pick up the moving van all by himself.

"Right," said Double D. "Not much to that story. He got it on his first day as a 1, when he—"

Fred stepped in front of Double D to cut off the rest of that sentence. "One more word and I'll be recording your performance of 'Call Me Maybe' and putting it on YouTube."

Double D snapped his mouth shut. "You bargain like the devil, kid. You'd better get to packing. I told Patty if she's not one hundred percent satisfied with your effort, I ain't singin' no song."

"She'll be satisfied," said Fred smugly. "It's a bedroom, isn't it? And they call me Stud, don't they?"

Rachel's eyes widened. Fred had warned her about the raunchy humor of the firehouse. She'd sworn she could handle it. Right now she wasn't so sure.

Laughing, Fred stepped aside as Double D tried to swing a crutch at him. "I won't be much help injured."

"Just get your ass in there and help my wife. And don't forget she's my wife, whether she likes it or not. Seems to go back and forth on that subject lately."

A guy she recognized from the City Lights Grill, the tough-looking one with the broken nose, strolled up, eyeing Rachel with open interest. "Who's this? You look familiar."

Fred took Rachel's arm in a territorial gesture. "This is my cousin, Mulligan. You don't know her. Stay away from her."

Mulligan ignored him and bent a charming smile on Rachel. "Cousin. That your first name?"

"Rachel," she said, putting out her hand. Hopefully he didn't recognize her without the wedding veil, and with her hair in a ponytail instead of all wild. Fred had told her not to worry about Mulligan, but to spend as little time as possible with him. "Rachel Allen."

"Rachel Allen? The dog therapist?" A lovely turquoise-eyed woman shouldered Mulligan aside. Rachel bit her lip, realizing too late that she should have kept her last name to herself. "I've heard a lot about you. You're younger than I thought you'd be."

"You must be Sabina. You're even prettier than I thought you'd be."

Sabina shrugged that off. As gorgeous as she was, Fred said she didn't care much about her looks; they didn't matter on the job, after all. "Luke, my stepson, wants to get a dog. He's been talking about it ever since he and my husband moved here. Do you have any advice on what breed to get? We need a dog who's very patient. One who doesn't bark. Smart. Maybe a dog who likes to field baseballs."

Rachel loved her right away for saying "a dog *who*" instead of "a dog *that*," which happened to be one of her pet peeves. In her eyes, dogs weren't "things," but living beings with feelings.

"We have some very sweet dogs at the San Gabriel Refuge for Injured Wildlife," Rachel told her eagerly. "They're looking for good homes. Why don't you bring your son out sometime?"

Fred jostled her elbow. *Oh crap.* What had she been thinking? If Sabina came to the Refuge, she'd realize Fred was working for Rachel. Then she might wonder why. Then she might start putting things together. Rachel shot Fred a quick look of apology, then stammered, "Maybe in a few weeks. It's a little busy at the moment."

Looking disappointed, Sabina nodded. "Sounds good. How'd you guys figure out you were cousins?"

"Distant cousins," said Vader.

"Distance makes the heart grow fonder," Mulligan intoned.

"Did I just hear an affirmation coming out of Mulligan's mouth?" One of the most handsome men Rachel had ever laid eyes on stopped next to their little circle. He fixed eyes the color of a summer sky on Rachel, who felt her jaw fall open. This must be

Ryan Blake, who'd recently gotten married and was madly in love with his young wife.

"Nope," said Mulligan promptly. "Some simple words of wisdom from times of yore. Affirmations are for pu—"

"So are we going to do this packing thing or what?" Fred interrupted hastily.

"Go ahead, dude," said Mulligan. "Patty's waiting for you in the bedroom. And I'm not even going to mention what she's wearing."

Double D growled, lifting a crutch. "I'm about ready to get spikes installed in these things."

Rachel let out an unexpected spurt of laughter. The sound was so awkward that she clapped her hand over her mouth. Everyone stopped talking and turned toward her. She felt her face slowly heat. She couldn't explain how it felt for someone as sheltered as she was to be plopped into the middle of such a freewheeling, jokey conversation. It was better than the near-brawl at Beer Goggles; better than being taken for a skank at a bowling alley. It was real and fun and she loved it.

"Who offended you?" Double D demanded. "Tell me who, and I'll rip them a new one."

"Classy, D, real classy," Vader chided.

"I'm not offended." Rachel shook her head, dropping her hand so they could all see her wide smile. "You're just all so . . . funny."

"Yeah, funny-looking," said Vader with a wink.

"Funny-smelling," Sabina tossed over her shoulder as she strode away. "Are you guys here to shoot the shit or help out?"

Fred had to hand it to Rachel. She didn't run for her safe zone after meeting the crew, but instead joined right in with the rest of them. Everyone got back to work filling boxes, loading them into a U-Haul, or doing whatever else Patty told them to do. As the slightest, least muscular person on the premises, Rachel volunteered to make sandwiches and hand out drinks. Every time Fred got a glimpse of her, she was chatting and laughing it up with some other firefighter.

Ace, the rookie, spent way too much time talking her ear off. Probably yammering about surfing or all the pranks the guys had pulled on him. Ace was a charmer. He had that Southern accent the girls went crazy over. Since Vader had gotten married, Ace had taken on the role of station player. At the last police versus firefighters softball game, he'd had his own cheering section.

Rachel wouldn't fall for all that, would she?

On his third trip to the yard to grab more empty boxes, Fred decided he'd had enough of Ace's flirting. He headed toward Rachel and the rookie, intending to drag the kid away by force if necessary. Vader stepped in his path.

"Going a little overboard over your 'cousin,' don't you think?" He put his hands on his hips, his massive biceps flexing. Fred tried to peer over Vader's shoulder at Rachel and the rookie, but he couldn't see past the mountain of man in front of him. "How much do we really know about Ace?"

"Are we talking about the same person? The blond one the girls call the Angel in Turnouts? The one who cries into his KFC chicken basket because it reminds him of home?"

"Looks can be deceiving," said Fred darkly.

"No kidding. Look at you. Who figured you for a dog in the manger type?"

"I'm not her dog. I mean, I'm not in her manger."

Fred felt the blood rush to his head. "I mean, we're not . . ."

"Save it, Stud. I see what's going on here. Now that the girls are all over you, you're getting greedy. Protecting your turf. You're like the lion chasing off the other lions. Or maybe Acie's a gazelle and you're about to rip the hide off him. Pull out his guts with your bare teeth."

"Vader, just get out of the way." Fred's vision swam red. Vader had a way of needling him that got under his skin every time.

"Peace, brother, peace." Vader squeezed his shoulder, making him wince. That degree of muscle-power ought to require a weapon license. "I get it, bro. I know what you're going through. Chicks will make you crazy if you let them. And you have to let them, because what choice do you have unless you want to be a sad and lonely lion who isn't getting any gorgeous, fake-cousin pus—"

Fred lunged at him. Vader not only outweighed him by a lot, but he was a dedicated bodybuilder. Fred had seen guys back off at the mere flexing of one of Vader's pecs. It wouldn't take much for Vader to smash his face in. But at that moment, he didn't care. He dove under Vader's arm, yanked his shoulder forward, flipped him over so he spun in the air, then swiped his feet from under him. Vader landed with a thunderous thud on the lawn.

Voices shouted, footsteps pounded across the lawn, but to Fred it was all a vague buzz. He flew through the air, using his momentum to pin Vader's legs to the ground. When Vader tried to swat at him, he caught his arm and bent it backward until Vader swore.

"Holy Mother Mary," said Double D, who was suddenly next to them, staring down. "Freddie took down Vader."

"Damn it, Fred," said Mulligan. "What about my fight club bets? You just blew the whole thing."

"You got some crazy-ass skills, Freddie." Vader struggled to sit up. "What were you doing, saving them for a rainy day? How come you never beat my ass before?" Fred shifted to let him up. He blinked at his captain, the red haze clearing from his vision. What the hell had he just done?

"Sorry, Vader," he muttered. "I don't know what . . . I shouldn't have . . ."

Vader gave a tiny shake of his head, indicating something behind him. Fred looked over his shoulder to see Rachel, wearing a horrified expression, drop to her knees next to him.

"Are you okay, Fred?" Fluttering like an anxious dove, she patted his arms and back.

"Shouldn't you be asking me that?" Wounded, Vader brushed himself off. "I'm the one who got dropped."

"Right. Of course." She switched her gaze ever so briefly to Vader. "Are you okay?" At the same time she reached for Fred's hand and cuddled it in both of hers. The lump in his chest, the tension that had made him explode, dissolved at her touch.

"No, I'm not okay," said Vader. "Your 'cousin' attacked me for no reason."

Rachel turned on him, violet eyes firing sparks in that way Fred knew so well. "Don't be ridiculous. You must have done *something* to deserve it. Everyone knows Fred wouldn't attack someone out of nowhere."

"Sure he would," said Mulligan promptly. "Did it to me once."

Rachel's glare swerved to land on Mulligan. "I'm *sure* you deserved it. You probably always deserve it."

"True, that." Mulligan clapped Fred on the back.

"Freddie, I approve of your cousin. But don't attack me for it," he added quickly. "I know you can beat me."

"That was awesome. How'd you do that?" Ace crouched next to Rachel. *Too* close to Rachel. Fred felt his hackles rise again.

"Keep it up, Acie, and you'll see firsthand." Vader gestured at his position right next to Rachel.

"What?" The kid looked completely confused, as did Rachel. Frowning, she looked from one to the other of them, as if trying to decipher a foreign language. Slowly the truth seemed to dawn, and she yanked her hands away from Fred's.

Vader smirked. "You guys have an interesting family."

"Shut up, Vader," Fred growled. He flipped to his feet in a jujitsu move that had taken two years to master and faced the small crowd of his fellow firefighters. He loved them like brothers, but right now he had to take a stand. Too bad if it caused problems. He could handle problems. But he couldn't handle anyone putting the moves on Rachel.

He raised his voice so everyone could hear. "For the record, Rachel isn't my cousin. But she is *with* me. We're *together.* And that's all either of us is going to say on that subject. Any questions?"

Mulligan raised his hand mockingly. "Just one. Isn't she the one from the City Lights Grill? And the limo?"

Rachel went pale. Fred had been sure Mulligan wouldn't recognize Rachel, since he'd been crushing on her friend Feather. Damn. He had to do something, fast.

"Yes," he said simply, meeting everyone's eyes, one by one. "But now Rachel is under my protection. No one outside of this group needs to know she was ever here. If you're not cool with that, tell me now."

No one said a word. He scanned the familiar faces of Station 1's A shift. Their expressions ranged from curiosity to respect to acceptance. He held Mulligan's glance for a long moment, making sure they understood each other. Mulligan nodded briefly. That's all Fred needed. The man's nod was as good as his bond.

"Say no more. We're cool, Freddie. You need anything, let us know." Double D finally said. Everyone nodded. Fred felt a rush of love for his crew. They always had his back. Always.

"Except my wife is about to blow a gasket," Double D continued. "Think we can get back to business here?"

"Yes." Relieved, Fred let out a quiet whoosh of breath. The firehouse had survived some outrageous scenes, but he'd never been at the center of one before. "Let's do it. Tell Patty I'll be right there."

The crowd dispersed, including Rachel, who huddled with Sabina as they headed into the house. Obviously they were discussing something very serious. He reached a hand down for Vader, who grasped it and hauled himself to his feet.

"I'm sorry, man," he told his captain, low so no one else could hear. "I shouldn't have thrown you. I lost my shit there."

"Yeah you did," Vader said cheerfully. "You proved my point, bro. I hate to say it, Freddie-boy, but you're in love."

Chapter 20

*C*halk up another new experience in Rachel's life; she'd never before had two guys come to blows over her. She still wasn't completely sure if that's what had happened, since Fred had clammed up. After the fight with Vader, he'd stalked into Patty and Double D's bedroom and slammed the door.

Sabina did her best to explain. She took Rachel into the kitchen to help pack up the dishes and flatware. With a morbid sense of humor, someone had draped police crime scene tape around the microwave.

"When Fred first came to the firehouse," Sabina told her as she wrapped glasses in newspaper, "he had a very serious girlfriend. She seemed like a real sweetheart. On his first day she made blueberry pie for the whole crew. It was adorable. The guys teased him because she called him all the time and left little love notes in his lunch. On his first day, Double D overheard her calling him 'you big stud' on the phone, and that's how he got the nickname. Anyway, it turned out she wasn't so sweet after all and she dumped him for someone on the C shift. Someone with more seniority who was about to make captain. So what it comes down to is that he might be a little sensitive about bringing girls around the crew."

"Was that Courtney?" Rachel asked, remembering the girl from the bowling alley. She followed Sabina's lead and picked up a mug, surrounding it with a sheet of newspaper.

"No, this was ages ago. He broke it off with Courtney . . . well, a few weeks ago, I think. Here's the thing about Fred. He's a sweet guy, but push him too far and he pushes back."

"I guess he proved that today."

Sabina laughed. "I know, right? Fred's one of my favorites at the firehouse. He's got a heart the size of California. But he doesn't get the attention he deserves. I've been waiting for the right person to show up, someone who really appreciates Fred."

Rachel couldn't tell if Sabina was welcoming her or warning her. She set the mug in the box and reached for another one. "Fred is . . ." How could she put this without revealing too much? "He takes good care of me." She winced. That made Fred sound like a babysitter. "I mean, I trust him." That wasn't any better; now he sounded like a *trustworthy* babysitter. "I care about him. I . . . we have fun together."

Sabina put up a hand to stop her. "I don't need the details. In fact, I beg you not to share the details. Fred's like a brother to me. But I thought you should know that when his old girlfriend hooked up with that C shift guy, he seemed relieved more than anything. He sure didn't knock anyone around. Something to think about."

Just then Patty hurried into the kitchen like a

hurricane in flip-flops, and the conversation ended. Rachel was dying to ask Sabina more questions but never got a chance. And then they were all draining the last of their beer, saying good-bye, and heading home.

During the entire trip back to her apartment, Fred didn't say a single word.

"Do you miss the station?" Rachel finally asked, just to break the silence. He didn't answer, just frowned at the road ahead. She tried again. "I bet you'll be glad to get back to your real job."

Nothing. Maybe he hadn't even heard her.

The communication blackout continued all the way home. Fred barely said hello to Marsden in the lobby. Once he'd checked the entire apartment and done the usual security check, he took Greta for a walk.

With a sick feeling in her stomach, Rachel used the time to go through the mail she'd been neglecting over the past few days. Her mail went to a post office box, which Marsden emptied twice a week on her behalf. Not that there was anything interesting—mostly solicitations and catalogues. She flipped through a pet care catalogue while she sorted through her thoughts, and especially Sabina's words.

It sure seemed that Sabina was suggesting Fred had feelings for her. More feelings than he'd had for his ex-girlfriend. Strong feelings, the kind that drove a guy to tackle his own captain. But if so, why was he ignoring her now?

She hadn't wanted to think about their feelings for each other, because he wasn't going to be around much longer. Falling for Fred would be a silly thing to do. Her father's testimony would take place any day now, and that would be the end of their arrangement. Fred would go back to his regular life at the firehouse and she'd retreat to her isolated bubble of an existence.

What man would be willing to put up with the kind of constraints she lived under? Once he went back to the firehouse, he'd be the Bachelor Hero again. And if they kept seeing each other, the media might start investigating her, and if they found out who she really was . . .

She shuddered. She couldn't let that happen.

But still . . . Sabina's hints kept stealing into her mind. What if Sabina was right and he was starting to develop real feelings for her?

She rolled the thought around in her mind, testing it to see how it felt. Her hands trembled on the slick pages of the catalogue. To love and be loved by Fred . . . it was something she hadn't really dared to think about. It seemed almost too wonderful to imagine, his warm, sunny strength by her side, forevermore.

But when she tried to figure out how it would work in real life, she ran into a blank wall. How could their lives possibly fit together when he wasn't acting as her bodyguard? What would that look like?

Unfortunately, Fred wasn't talking. He also, for the first time since the night of Cindy's wedding, slept in the guest bed. After his usual careful check of the apartment and testing of the alarms, he gave her a polite good night and disappeared into his room.

Rachel lay awake, cursing her stupidity. *This* was why you shouldn't get involved with your bodyguard. Because if something went wrong between you, he was *right next door*, so close, yet so torturously far.

But what had gone wrong? If only he'd give her some kind of clue. She considered calling Cindy for advice, then remembered she was on her honeymoon. What would Cindy do in this situation? Probably go out and party. Forget her troubles *and* make Bean jealous at the same time. But that wasn't an option for Rachel, not without her bodyguard—the source of her problems. Total catch–22.

The next day, her father called her from his private jet to say he was on his way to Washington and that his testimony was scheduled for shortly after he arrived. Her stomach clenched. This was it. The end, drawing near.

"Isn't that cutting it close?"

"If I'm late, they'll wait," he said with typical arrogance. Only Rob Kessler would make an entire U.S. Senate subcommittee wait for him. In the background, she saw his assistant bring him a glass of water. Lemon-ginger-cucumber, no doubt. Her father had very strict dietary requirements wherever he went. "How's your bodyguard? *Where's* your bodyguard?"

"He's here. He's on the treadmill."

"Marsden says he's working out well."

"I'm alive, aren't I? Still breathing in and out, still exchanging oxygen for carbon dioxide." She couldn't hide her irritation, or explain that it was very likely due to the fact that said bodyguard had slept in his own bed last night.

"You don't sound too happy about that."

"Of course I'm happy. If you're happy, I'm happy."

"Are you going to watch the testimony? It'll be on C-SPAN later in the evening."

"Sure, if you want me to."

"Watch a bunch of politicians make asses of themselves? How could you miss it? Besides, then

it'll be over. As I promised, you can ditch the bodyguard and go back to normal."

She forced a smile. "Yes. That'll be a big relief."

"Thank you for being patient with me, honey.
Means a lot."

"It's all right," she said dully, unable to summon
any particular joy or pride. She knew her safety
meant everything to her father. But sometimes she
wished she had something else to boast about other
than the fact that she was still sentient.

Fred had been walking around in a kind of stupor ever
since Vader had hit him with that "you're in love"
comment. It was just a word, a phrase—"in love"—
what did it even mean? It certainly didn't describe
his feelings for Rachel. No way. He was Rachel's
protector. That's why he'd freaked out about Acie,
not because he was jealous. He was simply protecting her from a Southern-boy charmer. In love? That
would create so many problems, he didn't even
want to think about it. A guy like him falling in love
with someone like Rachel Kessler would be like . . .
asking to get kicked in the head by Vader Brown.

In desperate need of some room to think, away
from her scent, her wide smile, the tumble of her
hair, he took extra care with the safety check, then
closeted himself in his room.

It didn't help. He barely slept. Perhaps the low
point of the night was when he pictured himself
telling Rob Kessler he was in love with his daughter. In his imagination, a SWAT team of Namsaknoi
Yudthagarngams came crashing through the picture windows to take him down. Rachel deserved
the best, someone who could both protect her and
give her the world. Maybe some combination of

Rambo and . . . Prince William. And Bill Gates, for good measure.

Not Fred the Fireman, the only Breen son not serving in the armed forces. The one his brothers loved to tease. It wasn't about the Kessler billions, not really. It was more about . . . worthiness. To win someone like Rachel, there ought to be tests—feats of strength, or daring quests.

The difference between his world and Rachel's had never been clearer than during the evening broadcast of the Congressional Subcommittee on Internet Security's hearings, which had taken place that afternoon. He joined Rachel in the living room, but instead of sitting on the couch with her, he chose the uncomfortable horsehair armchair he'd sat in that very first day. He wasn't sure why; all he knew was that he needed to keep some distance.

Rachel didn't say anything about the seating arrangement. She whistled softly for Greta, who trotted across the room and curled up at her feet. She clicked the remote that controlled the wall panels hiding the big flat-screen, and selected C-SPAN.

As they watched Rob Kessler testify, Fred's heart slowly sank into the region of his toes. The ones in worn tube socks with holes in the heels.

Facing the most powerful men and women in the nation, Rob Kessler made them all look like idiots, the way the guys at the computer store made him feel when his hard drive crashed. Brilliant, articulate, dynamic, even photogenic, he ruled that hearing the way a kindergarten teacher rules recess.

Rob Kessler probably never had holes in his socks.

Fred was frowning at the big plasma screen, searching for similarities to Rachel—same winged eyebrows, same bold cheekbones—when suddenly he found himself staring at a picture of her as a little girl. Her hair was in two braids on either side of her head and she wore a red sweater with a pattern of snowflakes around the neck. There was a gap between her two front teeth.

C-SPAN had taken a break from the testimony while a point of discussion got hashed out in private. To fill the time, they were running a profile of Rob Kessler.

"It was the most notorious kidnapping since the Lindbergh case, the kind of thing we're more used to seeing in Colombia, where the children of the wealthy are under constant threat. Rachel Kessler, eight years old at the time, was snatched off her bicycle and held captive for nearly a month."

Shots of an exclusive neighborhood scrolled across the screen.

"A ransom note was received, but then withdrawn. Two days later another note was delivered. Every communication was sent not only to Rob Kessler, but to the local San Francisco TV station. Experts speculated that the kidnapper was someone with a big grudge against the Kessler family, someone seeking attention, because nothing seemed to satisfy him. Even once the original ransom amount was paid, he demanded more."

They switched to a shot of Rob Kessler, much younger, shoving his way through a crowd of reporters.

"Just when investigators were beginning to despair of a breakthrough, little Rachel Kessler, in an incredible act of bravery, managed to escape. A neighbor in the remote Mojave Desert found her passed out under their trailer, bloodied, bruised, and dehydrated. The kidnapper was never located."

The newscaster, a middle-aged man Fred didn't recognize, paused for drama.

"To this day, Rachel Kessler has never gone public with her story, although she was, of course, questioned extensively by the FBI. Little is known about her current whereabouts, though we have learned that she no longer resides at Cranesbill, the Kessler estate. Wherever she is, it's safe to assume she's under tight security. All requests for comment from the Kessler camp were denied. In the journalistic world, an interview with Rachel Kessler would be considered one of the biggest 'gets' of any reporter's career."

Fred felt sick. The newscaster called Rachel a "get," as if she were some sort of hunting quarry. Maybe that's how the kidnapper had thought of her too. A "get." He glanced over at the couch. Rachel's face had gone completely blank and dead white. Her hands were deep in Greta's fur, gripping so tight her dog gave a soft little whine.

"Rachel," he said sharply, to break the spell she seemed to be under. "Are you okay? That newscaster's a freaking idiot."

She didn't answer. She didn't even look at him. When they'd started watching the broadcast, he'd been lost in his own thoughts, far away from her. Now it was her turn to be distant, and he hated the feeling. Panicking, he launched himself across the room and grabbed her by the shoulders. She didn't resist. It was as if she was somewhere else entirely.

"*Rachel*. Tell me what you're thinking. Tell me what's going on. Please talk to me."

Slowly her eyes seemed to focus, the lost look replaced by something hard and desperate. Her eyebrows drew together, slanting across her forehead. Two spots of pink appeared in her cheeks. "Let's go out," she said abruptly.

"What?"

"Out. I want to go out. We need to celebrate." She jumped to her feet, stumbling a little. He gripped her elbow to steady her. Shaking him off, she dashed in the direction of her bedroom.

He scrambled after her. "Celebrate what?"

"My father's testimony. It's just about done. That means your job is done. He told me I only needed a bodyguard until he testified. Well, he did it. It's done. So you're done. I bet you'll be relieved to get back to your real job, huh? Don't answer that."

He didn't like the manic tone in her voice. There was no doubt in his mind the broadcast had triggered this mood. It must have been terribly unsettling for her to relive her kidnapping via a national news broadcast. "Rachel, maybe it would be better if we stayed home. Maybe you want to talk about it. Or call someone. What about Cindy or Liza or Feather? Or your father?"

"I don't want to talk to my father," she said tightly. "He'll be doing his own celebrating. Caviar sushi or something. I want to get out of here. You can come or not. I don't care. Technically, your job might be already over."

"For crap's sake, Rachel. If you're going, I'm going. I'm not letting you roam around by yourself in this state of mind."

"You don't know anything about my state of mind." She rummaged through her closet, finally emerging with a purple, sparkly dress with a wide zipper up the front. It looked like something Space Barbie might wear. In fact, he was pretty sure Lizzie's old Barbie had that exact same dress.

"What are you doing?"

"Getting dressed to go out. Are you coming?"

Even though it sounded as if she didn't care one way or the other, he repeated, "I said I was."

"Then let's go. It'll be just like the night we went out, except even more fun. We can pull out all the stops because it's your last night as my bodyguard. I'll buy you a drink."

"I don't drink on the job."

"Then I'll buy you a lap dance."

"We're not going anywhere near anyone's lap."

She shot him a furious glare over her shoulder. Bright pink still burned in her cheeks.

"You aren't the boss of me. No one's the boss of me. I'm so. Damn. Tired. Of everyone thinking they can control me."

She whipped off her white T-shirt and shimmied into the dress.

"Who are you talking about? Me? Your father?" He took a deep breath, daring himself to throw out one more possibility. "The kidnapper?"

Thrusting her head deep into her closet, she ignored that question. "I'm leaving in three minutes. Come if you want."

"*I said I'm coming.*"

He had a very, very bad feeling about this.

Chapter 21

Rachel didn't give herself a minute to think about what she was doing. All she knew was that she had to breathe some open air, that she couldn't stay trapped in her apartment with that television one more second. Or was it herself she couldn't bear? Who knew? Didn't matter. The drumbeat of "get out" thundered through her veins and there was no stopping it.

She snagged a little purse made of oyster silk and stuffed her cell phone and some cash into it. She rifled through her wallet, keeping her Rachel Allen driver's license and one credit card and tossing everything else on the bed. If she could have left her identification behind, she would have.

If she could leave herself behind, she would.

Ballerina flats. Loose hair, with an extra bit of spritz for a tousled look. Lip gloss. A quick glance in the mirror to confirm that she looked nothing like that little girl on the television, with her sweet little braids and her innocent grin. What if she hadn't insisted on riding her bike that day? What if she'd stayed home and gone swimming in their own pool? What if she'd run at the sight of the Heating and Cooling Repair van waiting at the corner?

Maybe everything would have been different. Maybe that little girl would have grown up to be the wild, carefree tomboy she was meant to be. Maybe she would have traveled the world, competed in the Olympics, danced on tabletops . . . who knew? All she knew was that girl wanted her moment. For this night, she was going to pretend that girl was alive and well and ready to dance. There must be a table-top out there with her name on it somewhere in San Gabriel.

Marsden jumped to his feet and tossed his news-paper aside as she came barreling out of the eleva-tor. "What's going on?"

She waltzed to his side and planted a kiss on his cheek. "Dancing. That's what going on."

"Dancing?"

"Not the ballet kind. The having fun kind." A frown creased his weathered forehead. She knew she probably sounded kind of crazy and manic, but she couldn't help it.

"I don't like this, Rachel. The timing's bad."

"But that's just it! The timing's perfect. We're cel-ebrating my dad's testimony. He killed it, totally killed it. Didn't you see?"

Marsden started to object again, but Fred spoke up from just over her shoulder. "Don't worry, Mars-den. I got a handle on it. But stay on standby, if you don't mind, in case I need backup." She felt a strong arm come around her. "We'll be careful, right, Rachel?"

She opened her mouth to say she was done with

being careful, but Fred squeezed her shoulder, and she nodded instead. No need to put Marsden on full alert.

As Fred hauled her out of the foyer, she wondered if she was tipsy, and tried to remember if she'd drunk anything alcoholic lately. That led to the memory of sitting on her couch watching the nightmare of her life play out on national TV. She pushed the remembrance aside.

Whatever was causing this light, frenzied, go-go-go feeling, she'd take it. It was better than fear.

She danced into the warmth of the early evening and threw her arms wide. Tilting her head back, she took in the brilliant pinprick stars, the deep comfort of the endless twilight sky. "What does it matter, Fred? One little life in the middle of all this. Why do we get so worried about things? Every time I get upset, I ought to come out here and just look up. That's all. Just look up." Taking a deep inhale, full of wonder at this revelation, she glanced over at Fred.

Fred wasn't looking up; he was looking around, scanning the surrounding area. "Look at the sky, Fred! In case you need directions, it's right over your head."

"Yes. It's nice. Are you done now? I don't know if it occurred to you, but now is not the best time to go out. You haven't changed that much since you were eight. If people were watching the testimony and saw your picture, it might still be fresh in their minds. They might recognize you."

"Up, Fred. Look up," she insisted.

Finally he did so, and she took his hand, swinging it back and forth. A slight breeze whispered against her cheek. A car rumbled past. In this crazy mood, she didn't think about a possible threat inside the car, as she usually would. Instead, she felt sorry for them, trapped inside a car instead of enjoying the unbelievable beauty of a simple evening sky. She filled her lungs with sweet desert air. "Isn't that sky spectacular?"

"Sure." Even though Fred was probably just humoring her—she recognized that tone of voice—she appreciated the gesture. After one more long breath, she squeezed his hand.

"Okay, we can go now."

"Back inside?" he asked hopefully.

"No way. I want to go to a strip club."

"What?" Fred yanked his hand from her clasp and whirled her to face him. "What are you up to, Rachel? What's going on here?"

"I want to dance," she said firmly. "On a tabletop. Or a countertop. On top of something. If I could dance up there, I would." She jerked a thumb toward the sky. "Just dance, that's all. I'm not even going to drink anything. I don't need to. I'm high on the sky right now."

He studied her for a long moment, his jaw working. The amber light spilling from the foyer outlined his solid, well-muscled frame, flickering around him like a halo. She knew he was worried, and she didn't blame him. If only she could share this crazy, transcendent, overflowing feeling with him, maybe he'd relax. She leaned in, puckering her lips slightly, as if she could transfer her mood with a kiss. But he kept his arms rigid, maintaining the distance between them, and she wasn't strong enough to force it.

"Don't do that," he warned her. "I need to think."

She tucked a smile into the corner of her mouth and waited patiently while he debated with himself. The heat of his grip added to her manic restlessness. She wanted him up there on that tabletop too. It would be so much more fun with Fred. Everything was more fun with Fred.

"Okay," he said finally, reluctance dripping from his voice. "I'll take you to a club where occasionally people dance on the bar. It's packed with off-duty firefighters and I know the owners and I know you'll be safe. Deal?"

She cocked her head, thinking it over. "What's it called?"

"Firefly. It's an old converted firehouse. Everyone always has a good time there. Guaranteed."

"Firefly. The little glow bugs that fly around at night, that kids like to catch and put in a jar?"

"I suppose." Two little frown lines appeared between his eyebrows. "So?"

"I'd never, ever do that to a firefly," she told him earnestly. "Never. I'd let them keep flying around as long as they wanted."

A sparkle appeared in the brown depths of his eyes, then the familiar creases fanned from their corners, then his whole face opened into a laugh. A wonderful laugh. A laugh that seemed to capture light from all the stars up above and send it shimmering along her skin.

At that moment, she knew she was in love with Fred.

She didn't do anything with the thought. There was nothing *to* do. It didn't change the fact that he was going back to the firehouse and she was going back to her old life. But it settled into her bones and tissues and fibers as if it had always been there and had no intention of leaving.

He grabbed her hand, and hauled her toward her car, which she'd left parked out front.

"Let's take your truck," she protested. "It's much more fun."

"Your car's safer. Better gas mileage too. But I'm driving."

That was fine. She felt too floaty to drive. With Fred at the steering wheel, she opened the moon roof and sang to the stars. *You twinkle above us . . . we twinkle below.* The air rushing past held a hint of summer, of banked heat ready to be unleashed. In a month it would be summer, and in San Gabriel that meant fire season. Fire season meant Fred would be throwing his precious, beloved self into danger.

Don't think about it. Not tonight.

The Firefly parking lot was jammed; the place must be hopping. They found a spot toward the middle of the lot. She followed Fred as he wound his way between vehicles, toward an old brick building. It had a big garage-type door that must have been where the fire engines used to exit. The glass in the windows had a wavering, watery look; it must be the original, or close to it. Even from halfway across the lot, she saw the old panes rattle from the thump of dance music. Red and orange lights played over the jerking, flowing bodies within.

She stayed close behind Fred as he checked out the parked cars. "I see Mulligan's car," he murmured. "Asshole has an old Mustang my brothers would kill for."

"I liked him," she announced.

"Only because you don't know him," he said darkly. "He has that broken nose for a reason."

"Did you break it?"

"No. It was already broken. He won't say how it happened but everyone's got a theory. He's also got a big ugly scar on his leg and one of his thumbs is crooked. Man likes trouble. Lizzie saw him at a softball game and went all mushy. She says he has that bad boy thing the girls like."

She squeezed past a Corvette with a "Firefighters Can Take the Heat" sticker. That reckless mood seized her again. "You've been ignoring me ever since we saw him and the others."

He frowned over his shoulder, a streetlight picking up hints of gold in his eyes. "No, I haven't. I've been thinking."

"About what?"

"You," he admitted wryly, ushering her ahead of him. "I tried to change the subject, but it didn't work." A melting sensation spread through her, like brandy filtering through her veins. What if Sabina was right, after all?

They'd almost reached the end of the lot, just one more car between them and a triangular stretch of concrete bordered by the street, the lot, and Firefly. She angled her body sideways to inch around the bumper, when suddenly, from somewhere, headlights switched on. Momentarily blinded, she threw up a hand to shield her eyes. Something rammed against her from the side.

Hit by a car, she thought, laughing at the absurdity. In a parking lot. After all her father's crazy security. And then she realized that it wasn't a car. Someone was holding her, roughly. And he smelled strange.

"Hey," she said, pushing at the arm around her middle. It felt like a boa constrictor.

"Shut the fuck up." A harsh voice assaulted her ears. Black panic, thick as smoke, closed in on her.

"Fred!" she screamed desperately, before the man clapped a cloth over her mouth.

Fred had seen the first man and was already airborne when he heard Rachel scream. Two more men emerged from behind the blinding headlights. They

went after him while the other grabbed Rachel. Fred
jammed his elbow into the throat of the man to his
left. A hideous crunch and furious howl told him
he'd connected with the fucker's windpipe.

Good.

The other man wrapped an arm around his neck
and squeezed. Fred didn't waste a second. He half
fell, half dove sideways, making the man lose his
balance. In the split second that his attacker didn't
have control, Fred grabbed on to his arm and
wrenched him sideways. Surprised, the man let
go of Fred's neck and tumbled onto the hood of a
white Toyota. Fred grabbed a fistful of his hair and
slammed his head against the car, once, twice, then
one more time to make sure he was unconscious.
Dark blood seeped onto the white metal, but Fred
didn't linger.

Fred spared one glance for the crushed-windpipe
guy, saw that he was clawing at his throat and wasn't
a threat at the moment. Then Fred launched himself
over the top of the cars that stood between him and
the bastard dragging Rachel toward a black Escalade idling on the street, only a few yards away. He
landed on a white Ford and slid across the hood,
keeping his gaze on Rachel.

Rachel was kicking and clawing at the man who
was dragging her away. Those Krav Maga lessons
must be coming back to her, although fighting in a
real-world situation was completely different. Her
attacker wore a stocking cap and polarized sunglasses and moved like a young man, which meant
it wasn't the same man who'd grabbed her seventeen years ago.

Unless that man had hired these thugs to do his
dirty work.

It didn't matter who was behind this. The only

thing that counted was stopping that man from taking Rachel. The kidnapper was only a few steps away from the Escalade. Fred had maybe half a minute to stop him, if that. He dove through the air, did a somersault across the sidewalk, feeling the concrete scrape his forehead, and whipsawed the guy's feet from under him. He toppled like a tree, pulling Rachel down with him.

"Run, Rachel," yelled Fred. He didn't have time to say anything else, because someone landed on top of him. Someone bulky, someone whose hacking breaths rasped above him. *Crushed Windpipe.* Fred had to give him credit for persistence. He jabbed his elbow backward, making contact with something soft. He didn't really care what, he was focused only on Rachel.

With a deft move, she used the momentum of the man's crashing body to twist out of his grip—mostly. Sprawled across the ground, he still hung onto her with one meaty hand wrapped around her ankle. She yanked hard, but the man kept his hold on her. She was panting, frantic little gasps of fear that went straight to Fred's heart. The man on top of him was raining blows on his head, but he tuned out the distraction and, dragging the man, crawled across the few feet of sidewalk until he reached Rachel's attacker. He used a hard karate chop on the man's forearm. He'd used the blow hundreds, probably thousands of times, to break blocks of wood in half. It was all about finding the right angle, the right amount of force, the right speed.

It worked.

He heard the man's bone crack, and saw his hand fall away from Rachel's ankle. A howl of pain made Fred's ears ring. Or maybe the ringing came from the drumbeat of blows hammering his head. He rolled onto his back to stop the man's attacks. A vicious fist struck the bone above his ear. His vision hazed, went crimson. He blocked out the pain, the way he'd learned in the ring. *Focus, focus. Stop the head jabs.* He needed to stay conscious, at least until he knew Rachel was okay.

Rachel. In her sparkly purple dress, she was dancing around the edge of the action, sidestepping the flailing arms of her former attacker with little hops, even trying to stomp on his hands. To his blurred gaze, she looked like a dancing firefly.

"Fred," she was shouting. "Fred! Help! Someone help!"

Yeah, help would be nice. Where was fucking Mulligan when he needed him? But he couldn't wait for someone to stumble out of Firefly, all buzzed and happy. Gritting his teeth, he dug into his pocket. He grabbed her car keys and slid them across the sidewalk. He overshot, sending them under a Ford pickup, but she immediately crouched to snatch them up.

"Get in your car!" he shouted to her. "Call Marsden." She'd be safe in her car; the thing was more secure than an army tank. And Marsden would know what to do. He'd call the police or Kessler.

"I don't want to leave you," Rachel cried from over by the pickup.

The guy with the broken arm, still writhing on the concrete sidewalk, lunged for her. She gave a little shriek and jumped back.

"Go, Rachel, just go!" Fred scissored his legs behind his assailant's knees, then used the entire force of his body to roll over, then over again, until the two of them landed on top of the man with the broken arm, who let out a yell. Fred had been hurt and had caused pain in countless sparring matches, but this was different. With a ruthlessness that shocked him, he realized he'd inflict all the pain it took to stop them.

Rachel finally turned and ran back toward her car. Fred felt the men scrambling beneath him. Fuck, they were trying to go after her. He couldn't let either of them get free. He needed to buy her some time. He found someone's arm and wrenched it backward, then twisted his legs to immobilize the other guy. This was more like a game of Twister than a bout. The position was horribly awkward, the way it torqued his back, but he needed to hold it only a few seconds, until Rachel was in her car, her headlights on, maybe backing out of the parking lot . . .

Headlights flashed on. Someone shouted from the direction of Firefly's front door. The two men struggled to free themselves, sending lances of pain down Fred's spine as he clamped his arms and legs tighter to keep them in place. An engine started up; he recognized it as Rachel's. Thank God, she was out of there. With enough of a head start, she'd be safe.

Then a tremendous blow caught him on the temple and shards of silver pierced his vision. A black abyss rose up to swallow him. The last thing he heard before he tumbled into the dark was "Forget her, she's gone. Get this fucking asshole in the van."

Chapter 22

*F*red was choking. Something was blocking all the air. And he couldn't see. He was dead. This must be death, this black, suffocating, stuck . . . His hands wouldn't move, or his legs . . . God, was he in a coffin? Was he underground? What the . . . ?

"Stay still, jerkoff."

Obnoxious as it was, the guy's high, wheezy voice calmed him. He must not be dead. Neither heavenly angels nor Satan's minions would use words like "jerkoff," would they?

With a rush his conscious awareness returned and he realized he wasn't six feet under in a coffin somewhere. He was sitting in a chair. His arms and legs were tied to it, and the reason he couldn't see was that he was blindfolded. Some kind of cloth was wrapped around his eyes and mouth. He tested it with his tongue. Rough cotton gauze. That's what was cutting off the oxygen supply. If he calmed his panic and took shallow breaths, he could get enough air.

For a moment he focused on stilling his panic. When his breathing felt close to normal, and his heart was no longer racing, he added more information to what he'd already gathered. He rotated his wrists to test the hold of the bindings. The give of the material told him his arms were tied with the same kind of gauze that blindfolded him. That didn't seem smart. Gauze wasn't enough to hold anyone for long.

Important point of information, he decided. This didn't seem to be a very organized or prepared kidnapper.

Kidnapper.

He'd been kidnapped. He wanted to laugh, but the gag didn't make that possible. Why the hell would anyone kidnap him? Maybe they thought he was Rachel's brother, or even her boyfriend. Someone the Kessler family would rush to ransom. This was all some crazy misunderstanding, and if he could just get this cloth off his face he could straighten it out. He pushed at it with his tongue and waggled his chin back and forth.

Cold metal touched his cheek. He froze. He had no doubt it was a knife.

"It shouldn't need to be mentioned, but only one person is in control of this situation," said the same high, almost boyish voice. Fred had the feeling he was disguising it. "And it isn't you, genius. I'll take your gag off when I want it to come off."

Fred might be temporarily blinded and mute, but he wasn't deaf. And he was pretty good at reading people. His immediate assessment of the man, based on his voice and the way he was tied up—amateur. This kidnapper was in over his head, things hadn't gone as planned, and he was jittery and anxious.

Fred could use that. Maybe he could calm the guy

down, make him think they were on the same side. He wasn't sure how yet, but the first step was to be able to talk.

He nodded, trying to look nonthreatening. Maybe his appearance would help in that regard, since he wasn't a Superman type like Vader.

"You understand that I'm in charge here? You'll do what I tell you to do? I have a knife. And other weapons."

Fred nodded again. A knife was definitely something to fear, especially in the hands of someone who was anxious and trying to prove he was in charge.

Face it, Fred. At the moment he is *in charge.*

"As long as we're on the same page. Me boss, you slave. Think this knife can slice through the gag without nicking you?" He gave a high-pitched laugh. "Because I'm not exactly a knot expert and I did a number on this thing."

Fred braced himself as the chill of metal slid across his cheek. The man sawed at the cloth, and he felt a flick of quicksilver pain. A trickle of blood rolled down his jaw.

"Oops." The kidnapper snickered. "Didn't mean to do *that*. I hope Tree doesn't mind a little blood on his carpet."

Tree? What kind of a name was Tree? Fred had a feeling he'd be better off resolving this situation now, before Tree or other backup arrived. As soon as the cloth fell away from his mouth, he coughed and spat up some cotton fibers. "Water," he croaked. "Please."

"Why should you get water? Do you think the poor wild animals get water? Not during a drought they don't."

Huh? Okay, that was different. Was this guy some

sort of wild animal lover? What did that have to do with Fred? *Information*. He needed more information. Fred had a sudden memory of Rob Kessler in his black sedan, announcing that he was an information addict. *Keep the guy talking*. "Really, they don't?"

"Of course they don't. How could they? That's the meaning of the word 'drought.' "

"Right." Fred tried to clear his throat, but it was so dry. It felt as if he'd been at the dentist getting wads of cotton stuffed in his mouth. "That's a good point."

"Like you care. I know what you are. You're a fireman."

Fred nodded cautiously. He wasn't sure what firefighting had to do with thirsty animals, but the dude was on some kind of crazy mental tangent.

"Do you even care about the animals injured during all those brushfires?" Fred felt the man's restless energy as he paced back and forth. He moved freely in the space, giving Fred the sense that there wasn't much furniture.

"Of course I do."

"But you don't go out there for the animals, do you? It's all about the *people*. And their houses and their ranches and their *property*."

"Is that why I'm here? Because I'm a firefighter?" Was it possible that he'd actually been the target of this weirdo kidnapper?

"Dream on. You're not that important. You're just a bonus. That coward Rachel Kessler's the one who's going to pay."

He knew her real name. Fred tightened his fists in their bonds, but he fought back his fear. He didn't need emotion interfering with his thinking right now.

"Who are you?" He asked. "How do you know Rachel?"

"I know Rachel. I know she hides behind her mother's last name and her father's money. I have no respect for Rachel."

For the first time, Fred felt a real chill run through him. The man's voice vibrated with contempt and even hatred, and from the way he said Rachel's name, clearly he knew her on a personal level. "But how do you know her?" He repeated. "What's your name?"

That question earned him a stinging slap across the face. "Who said you could ask questions?"

"Sorry," Fred muttered, trying to make it sound sincere even though he was seething. Anyone who slapped a bound man had no right to call anyone else a coward. Not that he intended to point that out. "I'm just trying to figure out what's going on here. Maybe I can help. It sounds like you really care about animals. I do too."

He wanted to add that Rachel did too, but figured he'd better steer clear of her name for now, since it seemed to set the man off.

"You're already helping, like it or not. This wasn't the plan, but maybe it'll work out better this way."

"What are you trying to accomplish?" Fred tried to keep his tone of voice curious rather than skeptical, but it was hard. He honestly didn't see how kidnapping Fred Breen would help this guy's cause in any way.

"What we are going to accomplish is simple. And there's no way we can fail. Rachel Kessler might be a coward, but I know her weak points. She's afraid of being trapped, so that was my first choice. That didn't work out, but I think we have a higher power at work here. She likes you. I've seen you two together. I've seen her laughing with you, I've seen how she looks at you when you're not even paying attention. What's it like to have a rich girl like her wrapped around your finger?"

Fred's mind raced, trying to figure out where this man could have seen him and Rachel together. "You've got it all wrong, dude. I'm working for her, that's all."

They'd only gone out that one wild night, and to Cindy's wedding; other than that they'd only been to the Refuge and . . . no. The *Refuge*?

"Wait . . . you work for her too, don't you?"

Shocked silence followed. Fred braced himself for some kind of retribution, but instead he heard a long expulsion of breath. "It's okay," the guy muttered to himself. "It's just a lucky guess. He hasn't seen my face. He's still blindfolded."

The guy was rattled. Fred decided to take advantage. "Look, dude, I'm not out to cause trouble. Like I said, I'm just working for Rachel, so maybe we can help each other out here. Rachel's probably already gone to the cops, or maybe Mr. Kessler has."

"They won't do that. We already left messages for both Mr. Kessler and Rachel. One of them should be calling any minute now. They're probably trying to figure a way out of this, but there is no other way. Not if they give a flying fuck about you."

Fred jumped on that. "That, my friend, is a big fucking 'if' you have there. I'm just an employee. I knew the risks of taking on the job. If you think Kessler's going to pay some sort of ransom for me, you might want to come up with a backup plan. I'd like to think I matter to them, but I sure wouldn't count on it. Like you said, I'm a plain old fireman. Just a working guy. No one will be coughing up any millions to get me back." Since he believed this to be completely true, his voice rang with sincerity.

"This isn't about money, fool. That, right there, is what's wrong with the world today. Doesn't anyone care about what matters anymore?"

The man—Fred had no doubt now that he was on the young side—was circling around the room. It must be a smallish space, because it didn't take him long to return to where he'd started. The sudden blare of a woman's voice made him jump. The television.

Some reality show was playing. Why did he want to watch TV at a time like this? Fred wondered if he had some sort of mental disorder. In fact, he was pretty much convinced of it. Hopefully he wouldn't go into any kind of psychotic meltdown. Fred twisted his wrists back and forth, as he'd been doing for a while, as surreptitiously as he could manage. He couldn't see his kidnapper, but his kidnapper could see him, and that was an unsettling imbalance.

The guy strode toward the TV and began quickly skimming from one channel to another. Fred took advantage and began working his wrist bindings even harder. If he could loosen them enough, he could probably slide them off.

"Fuck it," the guy fumed from near the television set. "She hasn't done it yet. How long could it take?"

"Hasn't done what? Maybe if you explain what you're after, I can help."

"It shouldn't be that hard. She's Rachel Kessler. Protector of freaking animals. This should be a no-brainer."

"What do animals have to do with it? If you work at the Refuge, you know how much Rachel cares about them. She's dedicated her life to helping animals. It sounds like you both agree about that."

"The difference between us is, I'm willing to

put my money where my mouth is. I'm willing to go all out. Risk everything. What does she do but stay closed up in her penthouse apartment and her little . . . Popemobile? Rachel Allen Kessler is chickenshit. She pretends to love animals but she doesn't put it all on the line. We're going to make her. Maybe she'll even thank us for it. She'll kiss my fucking goat-crap-covered Timberlands." He cackled.

Goat crap? Of course. This guy was one of the techs who cleaned out the corrals and the various outbuildings. He took a stab in the dark, remembering the kid with the ponytail.

"Dale?"

A blow across the cheek made his ears ring. "That's not my name, fireman. But you can call me Kale."

Fred wasn't sure he'd heard right. "Kyle?"

"No. *Kale.*"

"Like the vegetable, kale?"

"It's a leafy green, jerkoff. It's packed with iron. Tough and strong. Like me."

Oh yes, he'd definitely tumbled into a weird sort of rabbit hole.

"So what, your parents named you after kale?"

"My parents are carnivores, so of course not. I named myself." He turned back to the TV, manically switching channels. "Come on, Rachel, get a move on."

Fred still had no idea what he was expecting from Rachel, but the fact that Kale worked at the Refuge seemed to provide an opening. "You know, Kale, if you do something to hurt Rachel, the Refuge might have to shut down. That could mean a lot of people out of work, and a lot of animals with no place to go."

"You don't know what you're talking about. The Refuge won't close. It's going to be famous."

"*That's an across-the-board* no." Her father scowled at Rachel from her flat-screen TV. He was in his private jet, on his way back from D.C. after dinner with a few senators, and had just gotten Fred's kidnapper's message. "The money's one thing. It's peanuts to me. The fact that he asked for so little proves what a dope the guy is. I already arranged the ransom. But for the rest of it, he can go fuck himself. We'll offer him more money, that'll have to be enough."

"I don't think it will be. I don't think he cares about the money." Seeing that her father wasn't listening, she turned to Marsden. "Back me up here. You heard the message."

"I heard it," he said grimly.

"Just listen to it again. This man is on a mission." She clicked play on her phone and Fred's kidnapper's voice rang through her living room for the tenth time.

"The time for hiding is over, Rachel Kessler. If you want your friend back, you'll go public with your support for animal rights and your sponsorship of the Refuge. We expect to see your face on TV before the end of tonight, or we'll treat your friend the way the labs treat the mice they use to test mascara." He gave a wheezy laugh. Something about it sounded familiar. "Our group is BEAST, the Brotherhood for Ending Animal Substandard Treatment, and you're going to put us on the map. We shouldn't have to force you to do the right thing, but we will if we have to. This is a matter of life or death."

"Nutty as a Waldorf salad," muttered Marsden.

"Yes, but *he has Fred*. We have to do something. The money's not going to be enough. He sounds like he's on a crusade. I have to do what he says."

Marsden swung his grizzled head back and forth

like a prizefighter scoping out an opponent. "Might be a fake-out. Enough cash might change his mind."

"I already sent double," said her father. "The original amount was almost embarrassing."

"You already sent double the amount?" Rachel put a hand to her head. Her body still ached from her struggle with the would-be kidnappers. Fred had taken even more abuse; she hated to think how he must feel right now. "That proves it. If money was what they wanted, Fred would be free by now!"

"That kid is tougher than he looks," said Marsden. "Military family, great firefighting record, fight training. He might be able to take care of himself just fine."

"Might? *Might?*" Rachel wheeled on him. "He's in danger because he was protecting me. I know what it's like to be totally at some stranger's mercy . . ." Her throat closed up. Ever since she'd watched Fred get bundled into that van, horrible bits of memory had been jumping into her head. The black slime in the corner of the abandoned warehouse. The cockroach family that had scuttled freely across the floor. The sour, gagging stench of the bucket in which she peed.

"Rachel, think rationally for a minute," said her father in his "soothing" voice that he used to talk her into his demands. It made her want to shred glass. "If you go on TV, your privacy will be gone *forever.* You won't ever be able to have a normal life again. People will know what you look like. You'll be a constant target."

"I haven't had a normal life since I was eight, Dad! And we don't know for sure that I'll be a target," she added desperately, even though the picture he painted was basically her worst nightmare. "People have a lot more interesting things to think about than me. It'll be fifteen minutes of fame and then someone else will grab the spotlight. Someone who wants it."

Her father looked like he wanted to jump through the flat-screen and strangle her. "I'm not talking about the media. I'm talking about people who *wish me harm*. Or the people who want my money. Most importantly, I'm talking about the one who already kidnapped you once and promised to do it again. Have you lost all sense, Rachel? Do you think Fred would want you to do something so risky? Of course he wouldn't. That's why he took this job, so you'd be safe."

Of all the arguments her father had made, that one hit home. He was right that Fred wouldn't want her to put herself at risk. But this wasn't Fred's decision to make; it was hers. "I already have insanely tight security, Dad. I'm sure that won't change."

"You're goddamn right it won't. Don't be surprised if it doubles by tomorrow."

"Fine. Double my security. Do whatever you have to do to keep from getting blackmailed. You're not the only wealthy man in the world. Other people have to deal with this. So we'll deal with it. Just like we always have."

She focused on her cell phone, even though her hands were shaking so hard she didn't know how she'd manage to dial. As far as she was concerned, the discussion was over. She'd felt obliged to inform her father of what she intended to do, since it affected his life too. But as soon as she'd heard the message, she'd known what she would do.

"I'm sorry, Dad. But I've made up my mind. I'm going to do whatever it takes to get Fred released."

"If you do that, I'll withdraw all funding from the Refuge." Her father's harsh statement sliced through the room. His face had gone dull red, his eyebrows slashing across it as if they'd been drawn by Sharpies. "I always knew it was a bad idea. Clearly this lunatic group has some connection to that place. We'll be chasing that down, guaranteed. I already have people researching BEAST. I want to know how they found out who Rachel is, and how they got past our screening."

"You will," Marsden said grimly.

Rachel didn't doubt it. But none of that was the point right now. "You want to shut down the Refuge?"

"I want to, yes. I don't think it's safe anymore. But I won't if you agree to let us handle this. I can't permit you to risk your own life for some . . . hired help."

For Rachel, staring at her father's face on the flatscreen, time seemed to stop. Electric fury performed a sort of catalytic conversion inside her, burning away her fear, her obedience, her caution. Once, she'd watched an oak leaf catch fire, until all that was left was a burning skeleton of veins traced in glowing red. That's she felt now.

"That's a shameful, despicable way to try to control me," she said in a low, shaking voice. "This is my decision, Dad. Not yours."

Her father looked past her. "Marsden," he said quietly. "Take care of this."

Rachel swung toward the security guard, who wore a look of deep regret. Would her oldest, most loyal guard, the only one she'd ever truly trusted, try to stand in her way? Would he really do that to her?

She addressed him and her father equally, clutching her cell phone like a lifeline, speaking in low, vibrating tones. "If either of you try to stop me, you're no better than the man who kidnapped me."

"Rachel, listen to me," Marsden said softly, holding up his hands to show he wouldn't use force. "We're tracking down the Escalade. As soon as we get the other two men apprehended, we'll know where the kidnapper is, and we'll go in and put things right so no one gets hurt. There's no need to do something you can't take back."

Despite herself, she wavered. She'd fought so hard for each precious bit of autonomy. Would she have any freedom left once she exposed her identity to the general public?

Marsden pressed his advantage. "Why don't you trust your security team to do our jobs? I'm on your side. I like Fred. Respect him. I don't want to see him hurt any more than you do."

He'd almost convinced her, but then her father spoke up. "We'll make sure Fred gets a bonus when all this is done."

At that, all her determination came flooding back, along with her fury. Money couldn't fix everything. It hadn't gotten her free from her kidnapper, and it wasn't going to free Fred. She snatched up the remote control for the TV and clicked the off button. Her father's image disappeared.

The power of that one simple act registered with a kind of shock. She'd never dared to do that before. He must be going crazy onboard his jet somewhere over the Midwest, where he couldn't control things. Couldn't control her.

With Rob Kessler's overwhelming presence suddenly removed, she and Marsden faced each other. He was a military-trained, battle-tested, mentally superior warrior. They both knew she couldn't best him in a physical fight. It would take a lot more than some Krav Maga lessons to make her equal to him.

She could think of only one way to beat him. "Marsden, you've been guarding me for what, fifteen years now?"

He nodded warily.

"I'm grateful for every moment you've protected me. You know me better than almost anyone. Maybe even my own father. You've kept me safe. You've been the best guardian anyone could have." She reached deep, calling on the bedrock truth of her soul. "But if I don't do something to help Fred, it won't matter how safe I am. Because I won't be able to live with myself. I'm asking you as one human being to another. Let me do this."

After a long, endless moment, he gave a slow nod. When she dialed the phone number she'd already put into her phone, the one that would change everything, he didn't stop her.

Chapter 23

"Now we're talking." Kale said gloatingly, from across the room. "If only you could see all the reporters out there. It's nuts, man. They're going crazy."

"I don't know if that was such a good idea, calling the news. How are you going to get out of here without getting arrested?"

Fred heard quick footsteps, then felt a whack across the side of his head. He'd received quite a few such blows since he'd been captured. But all his martial arts training was standing him in good stead. He knew how to maintain his focus through pain.

"You're a *hostage*," said the guy in that whiny, know-it-all voice that was really starting to grate on Fred. "That's the whole point of taking a hostage. They won't do anything to me while I have you. And you're not just any old hostage. You're one of the Bachelor Firemen. Not just that, but you're everyone's favorite. Fred the Bachelor Hero. I couldn't have planned this better. The media's eating this up. This'll put the pressure on Rachel. Big-time."

Fred ground his teeth. He hated being helpless to correct this ridiculous situation. He didn't mind being tied to this chair, didn't mind the occasional blows, didn't mind the cramps in his legs from being in the same position so long. If the guy hadn't called all the local news stations, he'd be in pretty good spirits.

But knowing that word was getting out, that reporters were gathering, that his family and the crew of the firehouse must be worried—that, he loathed. Just for that, he intended to make this guy suffer.

Unfortunately, Kale had noticed that Fred's wrist bindings were getting loose, and he'd retied them. Fred had to start all over again. And now he felt even more pressure to free himself. Because the kidnapper was right—the more media attention Kale got, the more Rachel would worry about him. He was afraid she was going to do something crazy, like go along with this dickhead's demands. He had to get out of here before she ruined her life on his behalf.

When Kale had refastened his bonds, he'd wrenched Fred's arms together higher up on his back, not noticing that there was a screw protruding from the metal folding chair. If he could just move his arms up and down without the guy noticing, he could snag the bindings on that screw and rip them open.

But now Kale was close by—Fred felt his presence—so he kept still. Kale put a hand on his shoulder, as if they were old friends. The arrival of the reporters had definitely improved his mood.

Kale clicked the TV on again. "Let's see if we're famous yet. Oh yeah. Now that's what I'm talking about."

The sound of Ella Joy's overly dramatic voice penetrated the room. "I'm live tonight outside a dingy little garage apartment where one of our favorite Bachelor Firemen is apparently being held at gunpoint. Firefighter Fred Breen, who's recently been involved in a series of heroic rescues, is apparently inside that little room up there, at the mercy of a deranged and alleged kidnapper who has yet to make any demands. The San Gabriel Fire Department has been notified, but they've received no communication from the mysterious alleged kidnapper. Breen's family, likewise, has heard nothing. For the last two weeks Breen has been on leave for a special assignment. Although we don't like to speculate, it seems this current situation is perhaps related. Unfortunately, no one at Station 1, where Fred Breen works, is talking."

Vader's furious voice came next. "Anyone who would threaten harm to a firefighter or to any other public service officer deserves a special place in hell. That's not a threat, mind you. Just something to think about."

Ella Joy continued. "Reading between the lines, that alleged kidnapper better watch his back. Allegedly."

"I didn't say that," said Vader.

"I said allegedly. Anyway, back to the current crisis. A hostage negotiator has been brought to the scene, but so far no one has been able to contact anyone inside that place of hellish captivity. One must wonder what sort of conditions our Bachelor Hero is enduring. Is he being starved? Beaten? Deprived of water? Members of the Fred's My Hero fan club are arriving on the scene, bringing cookies and flowers and teddy bears and anything else they can think of. And look. A banner. 'Marry Me, Fred!' How cute is that?"

Fred groaned, while the kidnapper laughed like a coyote on meth. "You're media gold, Fred! Pure gold! Seriously, I can't believe how great this is working out! Tree is going to shit himself."

Fred tried again. "Who's Tree? Why isn't he here?" Even though he no longer thought this kidnapping was connected to Rachel's—Kale had his own agenda—he wanted to find out everything he could.

But Kale shushed him as the next interview started, this one with the San Gabriel chief of police. "We don't comment on ongoing hostage situations. You should know that."

"Always worth a try, right?" Only Ella Joy could get away with that jaunty shrug of a response. "I thought you might like to help me get the facts right."

The police chief muttered something along the lines of "hopeless case," but then rallied. "The only fact is that we will not rest until Fred Breen is safe."

"There you have it. Chief Rollins, sending a crystal-clear message to that alleged kidnapper. The only question now is, will it work? We will be here, standing vigil with the rest of San Gabriel as . . . Hang on. My producer is saying something in my earpiece. It's so distracting, I mean honestly . . . oh. We're breaking away for a special interview from Melissa McGuire." She spat out Melissa's name as if it were made of battery acid. Fred still remembered perfectly the time Ella Joy and Melissa had come to dinner at the station. That's when everyone first realized that Melissa and Captain Brody had something going on. Ella Joy and Melissa had been coworkers back then, but now Melissa was an award-winning independent producer.

If Rachel was going to call anyone in the media,

it would be Melissa. His stomach sank. *No, Rachel, don't do it.*

"This is it, Fred." Kale's whiny voice vibrated with excitement. "Special interview. That's got to be it. Yeah, baby! Yeah!"

"Dude, how about you take off my blindfold? You won, right? You're getting your moment of fame. I'd kind of like to see it."

"But then you'll see *me*, bozo."

"Don't you want everyone to know the genius behind this whole plan? What point is fame if no one knows who you are?"

Kale grunted. Fred realized he was too caught up in the TV to pay any attention to him. He put all his energy into working the bindings against the metal screw in the folding chair.

With a sense of despair, he heard Melissa's melodic voice float from the TV set. "Thank you, Ella Joy. I'm here with someone we've all wondered about over the years. Seventeen years ago she went through a horrific kidnapping, and today she's coming forward to tell the rest of her story. Rachel Kessler is here with us in the Channel Six studios. In case you don't remember her case, she's the daughter of Rob Kessler, the founder of Kessler Tech. At the age of eight, she was held for ransom for almost a month. She escaped on her own. A truly extraordinary story, but after that she dropped out of the public eye. It turns out that she's been living right here in San Gabriel for the past seven years. Today she contacted me and expressed the desire to introduce herself to you, her neighbors. Rachel, thanks for being with us here on the Channel Six News."

"Thank you, and thanks for having me."

Fred heard the nervousness in Rachel's soft voice

as she cleared her throat. He imagined how she must look. Did she have that wary look in her violet eyes? Was she smiling at all, or was she hiding that wonderful grin from the public? *Don't do it, Rachel*, he wanted to scream. *This idiot isn't worth it.*

Kale clapped his hands. "There she is," he said gleefully.

Fred's stomach clenched.

"I'm sure the question on most of our San Gabriel viewers' minds is what you've been doing here, of all places you could choose? Why San Gabriel and not Paris or Argentina, or somewhere far more glamorous?"

"To be honest, I'm not a glamorous person at all. I came here to attend San Gabriel College, and I liked the city so much I wanted to stay. For most of my life, I've been devoted to helping animals, and that's what I do here as well. I run the San Gabriel Refuge for Injured Wildlife. We take in wild animals that have been injured and we also work with some pets when people can't afford veterinarian care. Basically if any animal needs help, it's welcome at the Refuge. We're a nonprofit that survives thanks to our generous donors."

"Come on, Rachel, say what I told you to say!" the kidnapper yelled at the TV. "This isn't about you and your fucking Refuge!"

Melissa spoke next. "I assume one of those donors is your father, Rob Kessler?"

"He has been, yes." A hint of hesitation entered her voice. "Along with several other wonderfully generous investors."

What was that all about? Fred didn't have time to wonder. Just then, the cotton around Fred's wrists separated down the middle with a scratchy *rrip*. If the kidnapper hadn't still been shouting at the TV set, he would have noticed. Luckily, the sound was lost amid his furious curses.

"When you called me, you said you had a message you wanted to deliver," said Melissa.

"Yes. I wanted to tell you the story of how I escaped my captivity, and how it has guided the direction of the rest of my life, and why it made me so dedicated to helping animals."

It sounded as if Kale thumped the TV set with his fist. "That's a start. Now mention BEAST. *BEAST.* Just like I told you."

Fred saw his chance. While the kidnapper kept yelling, he ripped the rest of the bindings off his wrists. He spent a precious moment flexing his hands, getting the blood moving again, then inched up his blindfold to check the lay of the land. Kale was bent over the TV set, his back to Fred. Tall and gaunt, wearing a red plaid, long-sleeved shirt, he hunched over the TV, lit by its blue glow. His mud-brown hair was in a short ponytail.

Just as Fred had thought, he was the tech who'd referred to Rachel as "princess" that day at the Refuge. He gave a quick glance around the dim little apartment and located the knife and a gun, both sitting on a card table shoved up against one of the windows. God, this guy was stupid. Still, he might have more weapons on him. Better be as quick as possible.

Fred reached down, maneuvered the bindings off his feet, quietly rubbed his thighs to get the blood moving, then bounded to his feet. He was on top of Kale before the kid knew what hit him. As they crashed to the ground, Fred felt an elbow crush into his ribs. He ignored it.

"It's over, Kale," he growled.

"Get the fuck off me!"

He yanked Kale's head backward and wedged

an elbow around his throat. "I could kill you right now for what you did to Rachel, asshole. But I know she wouldn't want me to. So we're going to get up and go outside and you're going to surrender to the fucking chief of police. Got it?"

"Fuck you." Kale twisted around and tried to bite him, which Fred figured gave him license to knock him out. He did that by banging his head against the floor. Then he hauled himself to his feet, shook his arms and legs out—pins and needles everywhere—and slung Dale over his shoulder in the classic fireman's hold.

On the TV, Rachel was still talking to Melissa, selling herself out for his sake. Goddamn it. Why couldn't she have waited even a few more minutes? He uttered a few more curses. He'd been kidnapped by someone named *Kale*. His brothers would laugh their asses off at him.

He headed for the door of the empty little apartment. On his way out, he grabbed the gun and the knife, just in case someone else popped out of nowhere and tried to stop him. The mysterious Tree, for instance.

"You're such an ass," he muttered to the guy as he manhandled him down the stairs. "You're going to make your stupid animal organization look bad. No one's going to support an idiot who holds a firefighter hostage. Not only that, you made *me* look bad. My brothers are going to eat this up."

As the only nonmilitary Breen, Fred was already their favorite punch line. But now, he felt even more ridiculous, like a mockery of a "hero."

The stairwell was empty. The door at the bottom opened onto a dark garage, which was also empty. Maybe the guys in the Escalade had been smart enough to ditch this operation before it got too stupid. Maybe Kale was acting on his own and had simply hired the thugs who'd attacked them outside Firefly. Maybe there was no Tree, no group called BEAST. The whole thing was unbelievably irritating, and to top it all off, his precious two weeks outside the media spotlight were definitely over.

As he pushed open the side door of the garage, the glare of camera lights flooded his vision. When his eyes adjusted, he caught sight of several police cars, a throng of cameras, and some girls crowded behind a barrier. A couple of them screamed, "It's him! It's Fred!"

He held up his free hand, dropping the knife to the ground to demonstrate he wasn't a threat. Nothing like having a bunch of guns trained on you to make you move very carefully. He caught Chief Rollins's eye and indicated the man slumped over his shoulder. "This is the idiot. What do you want me to do with him?"

Chapter 24

*T*elling her story to Melissa McGuire wasn't quite as horrible as Rachel had feared. For one thing, Melissa was a sympathetic and patient interviewer. She didn't make Rachel feel uncomfortable at all, and didn't push her into areas she wasn't ready to talk about. But as much as she'd already revealed, she knew the kidnapper wasn't going to be satisfied until she mentioned the name of his wacko organization. She was getting to that. Really she was. But she really, really hated being forced into a public declaration that she didn't believe. Not that she didn't believe in animal rights. That was a given. But a quick check on BEAST had revealed that it advocated all sorts of extreme positions that she couldn't agree with. More funding for shelters? Yes. Ban on all consumption of meat products? Um . . . *really*?

Once she announced her support for BEAST, she would be linked to that crazy group. Even if she took it back later and said she'd been acting under duress, her statement would live on, on video, online, in people's memories. It would be impossible to erase.

So she was taking her time getting to that part of the interview. She was just explaining the reason for her love of dogs when she heard raised voices at the other side of the studio.

"He's coming out!" someone called. "We gotta switch over, now."

And all of a sudden the little red light on the camera went off.

Melissa jumped to her feet. "What's going on?"

"Hostage situation's over," answered the cameraman, who was now watching the on-air monitor. "Fireman got out on his own. Best story of the week."

"Way to go, Fred!" Melissa sank back into her seat. "I was really worried," she told Rachel. "But I probably shouldn't have been. Never underestimate a firefighter. We can continue the interview anyway, it will air later."

Continue? Hell, no. Rachel stood, trailing microphone wires. "Is Fred okay?"

"They're taking him to get checked out just in case, but it looks like he's mostly fine," answered the cameraman.

Melissa heaved a sigh. "I'm guessing my big exclusive interview just ended?"

"Sorry," said Rachel, tugging at the little mic keeping her tethered to the set. "I have to get to the hospital."

"That's all right." Melissa helped disentangle her. "Go find your guy. Some things are more important than the news media, as my husband is always telling me."

"He's not exactly my guy."

"Are you so sure of that?" Melissa winked one

forest-green eye at her. "These firemen have a way of sneaking into your heart before you realize it."

Rachel wanted to stay and explain the exact nature of her and Fred's relationship, except that she wasn't entirely sure she could. Besides, the most important thing was to get to Fred. She ran out of the news studio and dashed to her car. Marsden sat in the driver's seat, already turning the key in the ignition.

"Hospital?" he said, barely making a question out of it.

"Have they said anything more?"

"Nope. Just that Fred's fans are going bananas."

As they drove, Rachel's father called in with a report. "They're treating him for some abrasions and a head wound. They were worried about a concussion, but he seems to be fine."

For once, she didn't mind him using his computer superpowers. "Thanks, Dad."

"Don't thank me. Maybe you should worry about the grenade you just detonated smack in the middle of your life. I'm already getting calls. And I ought to fire Marsden."

Rachel hung up. She didn't have room in her mind for that right now. She had to get to Fred.

Good Samaritan Hospital swarmed with visitors and thickets of camera equipment. Marsden shouldered through the crowd as she clung to the back of his jacket. At the reception desk, she hit a snag.

"No, I'm not family, but he was working for me," she explained to the charge nurse. "He was injured because of me. I need to see him."

"Family only." The nurse waved her away. "And don't even try the long-lost sister act. We've had three girls try that already."

"What about . . . but my name is . . . Rachel Kessler," she said. She'd never tried to use her name to get special treatment before, but now that she'd gone public, why not reap the benefits? Turned out, there was no benefit. The nurse didn't even blink.

"You're welcome to wait in those chairs over there."

Just then a dark-haired, frantic girl came flying through the big double doors of the ER. "Where's my brother?" She was gasping for breath. "Frederick Breen. He was brought in a few minutes ago."

"Let me guess. Long-lost sister?" said the much-too-cynical nurse.

"What? No. I mean, yes. I'm Lizzie Breen. The rest of my family's right behind me."

Rachel couldn't help it. She stared at the girl so intently she probably verged on rudeness. Lizzie's long dark hair swung behind her in a ponytail, her lively dark eyes brimming with fear.

"He's okay," Rachel told her. "Head wound but no concussion. Some abrasions."

The charge nurse gave her a hard look. "Who told you that?"

But Lizzie Breen ignored the nurse and grabbed Rachel by the arm. "Are you the girl?"

"What?"

"The girl who's been making him crazy. He won't give us your name but we've all been speculating."

Rachel shook her head, bewildered. "He's been working for me. He was protecting me when he got kidnapped. Those men would have taken me if he hadn't stopped them. I'd really like to see him." Her eyes filled with tears.

"Well, come with us, then."

Lizzie clamped a hand onto her wrist and swept her into a hurricane of rushing, chattering Breens. Besides Lizzie, the group included an older couple and two tough-looking younger men with buzz cuts; they must be two of the military brothers. Rachel was carried along with them like driftwood on a current. She landed next to a bed on which sat Fred, his head bandaged, a scowl on his face. He looked wonderful to her, although the bruise on his jaw made her want to cry.

When he saw her, light blazed in his weary eyes. And then something else. Maybe . . . wariness?

"Hi Fred," she said softly. "How are you—" But she didn't get a chance to finish the question as his family all burst out talking at once.

"I had palpitations when I saw the news, I swear I did!" his mother cried.

"We were already planning a rescue mission," said one of his brothers. "You beat us to it."

"Just had to be the hero, didn't you? When did you become such a camera hog?" asked the other brother.

"Yeah, I hear they're making a movie. *Zero Dark Salad*," said the first. "Get it? Kale, salad?"

Fred's injured face turned a mottled shade of mauve. Rachel felt the urge to chase his brothers out, and wondered just how far her rusty Krav Maga skills would go.

"Leave him alone, Jack, you're going to give him a real concussion with all that noise," said his father.

"Real concussion? What's not real about his concussion?" His mother ran a protective hand Fred's bandaged head.

"I don't—" Fred tried to speak, but didn't get far.

"He doesn't have a concussion," said his father. "That's the whole point."

Fred's mother barreled onward, ignoring her husband. She clutched Fred's hand, and drew one of her other sons against her side. "Do you realize that we have four out of five kids here at this moment? And all it took was a kidnapping to make it happen."

The men laughed, the deep chuckles echoing off the medical equipment. Fred smiled gingerly, then winced.

Lizzie tugged at Rachel's arm and whispered in her ear. "The Breen family has a very weird sense of humor, generally. That's how we deal with deployments and fires and so forth."

"Are you in the military too?"

"No, I'm more in Fred's line. I just finished EMT training, and now I'm working on my pilot's license. Mom, what are you doing?" Lizzie was yanked forward, into the circle of testosterone surrounding Fred's bed.

"I need a picture of this! I don't know when I'll have so many of you together again, especially since you all insist on picking professions guaranteed to give your poor mother a heart attack. Jack, Zee, get over here."

Rachel took a step back, then another. She'd never felt so out of place in her life. "I should go . . ." she said, but no one heard her in the cacophony surrounding Fred. Mrs. Breen had drafted a doctor to take the picture, and the bewildered-looking woman was being directed and repositioned and generally manhandled by the Breen clan.

No one noticed as she slipped out the door. Her last thought, before fleeing down the hospital corridor, was that if it weren't for her, Fred wouldn't even be in that hospital bed. If only she could make it up to him. But she had no idea how.

While he was recovering in the hospital, Fred once again became a sensation. The footage of him emerging from the Carter Street apartment, Kale the kidnapper draped over his back, was replayed over and over again on the national cable news networks. The fact that the kidnapper was a slightly unstable twentysomething who'd only recently become passionate about animal rights didn't take away from the drama. The only other news story that got as much attention was the reappearance of Rachel Kessler.

Her interview was played over and over again. Fred, watching that night, after his mother and the doctor had insisted that he stay overnight in the hospital, noticed with fierce satisfaction that Rachel never mentioned BEAST. Kale and his cohorts hadn't gotten what they really wanted.

But it hardly mattered. Rachel's privacy was completely shattered, judging by the number of times her face appeared on the twenty-four-hour news channel piped into his hospital room.

What would she do now? Her life would never be the same, that was for sure. The news was already showing aerial shots of the Refuge and interviewing her coworkers there. She'd probably need a whole army of bodyguards now; or maybe she'd move somewhere else and adopt a new name and start over again.

The thought tore at his heart. The best thing she could do now was ride out the wave of media attention, then try to regain some sort of privacy. The worst thing for her to do would be to hang out with the so-called Bachelor Hero. Until some of that crap died down, he'd draw even more unwanted attention to her.

For the hundredth time, he relived those moments in Firefly's parking lot. If he were a better bodyguard, maybe he would have noticed the three men before they attacked. Or maybe he should have been quicker to counterattack. He definitely shouldn't have let himself get conked on the head. He'd been so focused on protecting Rachel that it had never occurred to him that he might be a potential target as well.

That oversight had caused this entire mess.

The next morning, he checked himself out of the hospital before any of his family members appeared. It had been great to see everyone yesterday, sort of like getting tossed into a mosh pit. Really fun, but crazy and overwhelming too. And poor Rachel, caught up in the midst of that chaos. As if exposing her identity wasn't traumatic enough, Rachel had been hijacked by his family. It was sort of a one-two punch, and he really had to know if she'd survived.

The get-me-out-of-here look on her face as she'd fled his hospital room didn't give him much hope.

He hailed a cab and gave the driver Rachel's address. On the way, he left a message for his mother and Lizzie. When he pulled up outside the building, he was relieved to see no reporters outside. Either it was too early, or they hadn't located her apartment yet. Something told him it would just be a matter of time.

Inside, he spoke for a few moments with Marsden, who surprised him with a big bear hug. Fred fought his way free.

"I wish people weren't making such a big deal out of it," he told Marsden. "The dude was a few sandwiches short of a picnic."

"Sometimes it's the crazy ones who are the most dangerous," said the security guard gravely. "You can't say he didn't manage to hurt you."

"Nothing to speak of," grumbled Fred, rubbing his jaw, which still throbbed. "Do you have access to what the investigators are learning? Have they run up against anyone named Tree yet? He kept mentioning that name. I think Tree owned the place."

"They all have code names like that, but I don't know which one is Tree. It looks like BEAST recruited Kale about six months after he got the job at the Refuge, which explains how he got past our security check. The three goons they hired don't know much. What are you thinking?"

Fred shrugged. "I don't know. It occurred to me that the group might be a front for Rachel's kidnapper. Tree could be his code name. Kale talked as if Tree was on a higher level than him, but for all I know, he's an imaginary friend. Or his pet caterpillar."

"Might be possible, but this group is pretty young. No one over thirty-five. But it's worth checking out." Marsden clapped him on the shoulder. "We're just glad he didn't do too much damage. And you kept him away from Rachel. You did your job, son."

"Yeah," Fred said despondently, as he headed to Rachel's private elevator. He wished what Marsden said was true, but he didn't believe it. The guy had done damage—to Rachel's life. Fred had kept him away from Rachel physically speaking, but not in the way that counted most. He hadn't prevented Kale from manipulating her into doing the thing she feared the most. As far as doing his job? That was crap. His job was to protect Rachel. Instead he'd exposed her to even greater danger.

He was trying to form the right apology in his mind when the elevator door slid open on the top floor. A blur of pale flesh and dark hair flew toward him.

"Fred! You're here!"

He staggered backward, bracing himself so he wouldn't get bowled over. And then Rachel was in his arms, raining kisses on him, on his neck, on his shoulders, his chin, everywhere she could reach.

"Rachel, sweetheart, what's going on? Are you okay?" He tried to hold her off so he could check her out. He'd never seen her so openly emotional. She usually kept her feelings under close guard, as if she was afraid they'd be used against her. But now she was clinging to him like shrink wrap, not allowing so much as a millimeter of space between them.

He gave in and let her plaster her body against him. It felt good, of course. He didn't mind; he just wanted to make sure she was okay.

"I was so worried about you," she muttered into his neck, when she'd finally gotten all the hugging out of her system, or most of it, anyway. "I hated every second that horrible man had you."

"Are you referring to Kale?"

Even in her weepy state, that got a laugh out of Rachel. "Yes, Kale. I don't care what he calls himself. He stole you and kept you prisoner and I hate him with every cell in my body."

He wrapped his hands around the back of her head, tilting her face toward him, noticing the anxiety tightening the angled lines of her face. Tears stood in her eyes, making them shimmer like a night thunderstorm over the ocean. "I can think of much better things to do with your cells."

And then they were kissing, a joining so electric he was surprised it didn't short out the elevator circuits. He felt as if he held a bolt of lightning in his arms, one turned into flesh and blood by some kind of magic spell. A rush of intoxicating heat flashed through his nervous system and settled in his groin. He sprang into instant, bursting arousal.

"Damn, Rachel. We're in an elevator. What are we doing?" He dragged the words from his throat. In a fever, he ran his hands across her body, then under her ass. He hoisted her up while she twined her legs around his hips.

He nearly came on the spot.

"I want you, Fred." If words could be naked, hers were. Primal and shaking, they acted like an electric prod on his already delirious senses.

"Me too. But here? Now? We're in a freaking elevator. And I know damn well there's a security camera somewhere in here."

She reached over and punched a button. "Nope. Besides, I'm the only one who uses this elevator."

"Marsden—"

"Will figure it out." The rough desperation in her voice scraped across his nerve endings, and made him realize something for the first time.

"You *were* really worried."

"It was so horrible. I guess it was a taste of what my father went through. Honestly, I think I'd rather be the one kidnapped than watch the same thing happen to someone I . . ." She caught herself. " . . . care about."

He wondered what she'd almost said, but the rising drumbeat of arousal kept scattering all his thoughts. Especially because now she was tilting her hips up and down, rubbing her softness against his bursting cock. "Don't do that," he managed to grind out. "I won't last two seconds."

"Then get naked," she urged in a shaky voice. "I want to be with you. I want to touch you everywhere and make sure he didn't hurt you too badly." Her hands were on his fly. She slid free from his embrace and dropped to her knees.

Oh God. Oh God. What was she about to do? His cock pulsed at the erotic sight of her kneeling on the thick bronze carpet of the elevator. She was wearing her black yoga pants and a thin turquoise T-shirt with a picture of an elephant—and no bra. Her nipples strained at the nearly transparent fabric. He groaned, helpless before this vision.

Her quick, eager fingers pulled down his zipper, she shimmied his pants down his hips, and his erection burst free like a bottle rocket. It was so engorged and sensitive he was afraid he'd come before she even touched him.

To distract himself, he glanced aside, at the elevator's elegant cherry-paneled wall. He saw a dim reflection of the two of them, Rachel's head level with his groin, her dark hair a wild halo around her head. The quiet hummed around them; they must be cocooned in soundproofing.

He wanted to say this wasn't smart, that they should go to her bedroom, that she didn't need to put her beautiful lips around him, but the words wouldn't leave his brain. And then it was too late.

The gentle touch of her tongue on the head of his cock made his eyes cross. She seemed to realize that he was so aroused he couldn't take much more stimulation. Instead she gave him a loving touch, sweet strokes of her tongue and mouth, like wine through velvet.

"Sweet Jesus, Rachel," he gasped, tangling his hands in her hair. Even the palms of his hands felt aroused by the feel of her thick curls.

She might have said something, but the words came across as a vibration against the skin of his erection. He sucked in a lungful of climate-controlled air. Was it getting hotter in this elevator, or was he simply combusting under the wet suction of her mouth?

He wanted to be inside her, to plunge into her, spear her on his cock and drive her over the edge, make her fill this silence with wild screams. But one more thought surfaced through his feverish lust.

"I thought small spaces were a problem for you."

She drew back in surprise and looked up at him. His gaze fastened onto her mouth, wet and ripe from his cock. With a slightly puzzled look, she ran her tongue across her lips. He cursed himself for being the world's worst idiot, for interrupting one of the best experiences of his life.

A little pucker appeared between her eyebrows. "They are. But I wasn't thinking of this as a small space. I was thinking of it as the place where you are."

God, I love you. The words blazed across his mind without conscious thought. They almost spilled into the quiet elevator cube, but he managed to keep them to himself by pulling her to her feet, lifting her up, yanking down her leggings, and losing himself inside her.

Chapter 25

Rachel cried out as soon as Fred's hard length touched her core. She felt as if she was being showered with a million sparks. It wasn't an orgasm, at least in the usual sense. It was more of an all-body transformation, as if her ordinary flesh and bones had been changed to something made of fire and stardust.

With her body still wrapped around him, pinned against the wall, Fred yanked up her shirt with his teeth. Every stitch of her clothing felt claustrophobic, an unwelcome barrier between them. When her shirt was out of the way, he consumed her breasts, one, then the other, practically inhaling them into his hot mouth. Excitement screamed through her, a roller coaster off its tracks. She tugged at his shirt, dug her fingers into his hair, writhed against his strong hips. She felt completely out of control, with no memory of what control even felt like.

She wasn't alone; the tendons along Fred's neck

strained tight, his arm muscles bunched hard as iron. His whole body vibrated against hers, the need and power pouring off him. She wanted to eat him alive, every bit of him. She buried her face in his shoulder, glorying in the slick skin over solid muscle. Urging him on, she bit the thick bulge of muscle, not hard, just enough to fill her mouth with his scent and taste. *I want you*, that bite said. *I want you now, forever, again, again . . .*

He responded with thrilling decisiveness. Shifting his grip on her ass, he tilted her just so, spreading her thighs to spear her hard. She cried out again, the sound muffled by the flesh of his shoulder. He took her deeper than she'd ever gone, deeper than she'd ever imagined going.

"Fred, Fred . . ." she heard herself whisper hoarsely. And then she was gone, flying over the rooftops, tumbling end over end in a mind-emptying flood of pure joy.

He came too, one hand still under her rear, the other braced against the elevator wall. She used the strength of her thighs to cling tightly to his hips, so he wasn't bearing the entire burden of her weight. Bent over her, his body shaking with great shudders, his eyes half-shut slits of shining darkness, he rode his orgasm to its world-rocking, bone-shaking end. He was entirely focused on exploding inside her, and the thrill of that gave her another aftershock of pleasure.

Afterward, they both slithered to the ground in a sweaty heap. The tang of sex floated in the still air of the elevator, mingling with the lemon polish the cleaning crew used on the walls. The sound of their pounding heartbeats seemed to echo in the confined space.

At first it felt completely right to sit in silence, as

if both of them needed time to put themselves back together. But then the silence started to feel uncomfortable. Rachel had never let a man take her to such a raw, exposed place before. What did one say after something like that?

Finally Fred broke the ice. "Damn, Rachel, you sure know how to welcome a guy back to work."

She giggled, snuggling her face into his chest. So inappropriate, and yet so perfect. "We try here at Kessler Tech. I can't say that I've ever tried that hard before."

"That's very good to know. Can you move yet? I think I'm back up to about sixty percent functionality."

"What if I don't want to move?" She snuggled deeper. Truth was, she never wanted his arms to leave her.

"You don't have to. I'm the man around here. I got this."

Smothering a laugh, she pointed to his pants, which were still halfway down his thighs. "Like that?"

"Try to get your mind out of the gutter," he said sternly, refastening his pants. "And please cover yourself so I can concentrate."

"Right. Sorry." She pulled down her top, the soft cotton providing a sweet thrill against her still aroused nipples. "Carry on."

He wrapped his arms around her and, bearing her full weight, lurched clumsily to his feet.

She held tight to his shoulders, suddenly anxious. "Isn't this going to hurt you?"

"I'm fine," he gasped, and lurched toward the door. "You know, the first time we met you punched me in the nose. I think things have gone downhill since then."

"Will you ever forget that punch?"

"Nope. Can you get the button? Hands are a little full here."

"Just put me down!" she protested. "You're being crazy."

"Button," he insisted. She leaned down, pressed the button and the door opened. With him still carrying her, they made their way to the couch, where he dumped her, torn between laughing and scolding, onto the plush pillows.

Greta rushed to greet them both with an orgy of licks and tail wags. Fred crouched next to her, petting her and assuring her that he was all right and the world was still spinning. Rachel's heart swelled as she watched the man she loved with her beloved dog. Right at that moment, she was sure she had everything the world could offer her.

When Greta was sufficiently reassured, she turned her attention to chasing down a piece of misbehaving rawhide. Fred rose to his feet and planted his hands on his hips. "Now, Ms. Rachel Kessler, I have a few things I need to say."

Her heart raced. Was he about to tell her he loved her too? She hadn't said the words to him, but he must know. The truth must shine out from every pore.

"First thing is, I need to apologize. I should have seen it coming, that I would be a liability because of the Bachelor Fireman thing. I never thought of myself as anyone someone might kidnap. I thought I was protecting you, but I ended up making things worse."

Apologize? Of all the things he could have said, Rachel never would have imagined that. She scrambled to her knees on the couch so she was eye level with him. "What are you talking about, Fred? None of it was your fault! He was aiming for me, and he nearly got me. If you hadn't been there, it would have been me who got kidnapped."

"And if you had? Same thing would have happened. You would have done the interview and they would have let you go." He shot her a dark, impossible-to-read look, then hesitated.

"What?"

Turning away, he walked to the big picture window, where he shoved his hands in his pockets and ducked his head. Her gaze lingered on his thick glossy pelt of hair, all adorably disheveled at the back. "I'm sorry you did the interview."

"Well . . ." She felt completely at sea in this conversation. "Why are you apologizing? It wasn't your fault some mentally unstable guy decided he needed more publicity. There are some crazy people out there, and sometimes they get what they want." She knew it all too well; she could give a tutorial on the subject.

He didn't answer, didn't acknowledge her point other than with a slight hunching of his shoulders. The distance from the couch to the bank of windows suddenly seemed enormous, even unbridgeable. "What's going on, Fred? Talk to me."

After more silent struggle with himself, he straightened his shoulders and turned to face her, his usual easygoing expression turned mulish. "You shouldn't have done the interview, that's what. I would have gotten away from him sooner or later. I had the situation under control. He was probably the most incompetent kidnapper in history. He made the Shoe Bomber look like a genius. Why didn't you trust me to handle it my way?"

Her hands flew to her stomach, as if she'd just taken a punch. "How was I supposed to know he was incompetent?"

"You got his message. Did he sound like a criminal mastermind to you?"

"But . . . it doesn't matter! Anyone can be dangerous when they've taken control. Even an idiot." The unjustness of this whole line of conversation finally sank in. "I was trying to help you!"

"You didn't let me do my job."

"How can you do your job when you're a prisoner?"

"I had a plan," he insisted, with what seemed to her to be sheer, pointless stubbornness. "It was just taking longer than I wanted. Why didn't you at least give me a chance to make something happen? Instead you rushed ahead and gave him what he wanted. You sold yourself out on national TV. Exactly the sort of thing I was supposed to protect you from."

"That was my choice."

"And you chose not to trust me."

She scrambled off the couch, so she could face him on two feet. Why was he being so obstinate? So unfair? She'd done the interview *for him*. Instead of gratitude, this was her reward? This completely unreasonable accusation? When people were kidnapped, you were supposed to try to rescue them!

She forced herself to stay calm. Fred just didn't understand her side of things.

"It's not that I didn't trust you," she said carefully. "It wasn't that at all. You have no idea what it's like watching someone get grabbed like that. It was horrible, Fred. I watched them heave you into that van like a sack of potatoes. I felt so helpless. I didn't know if you were dead or hurt or what. Can you imagine what that felt like?"

At that, his expression softened a little, making a tendril of hope sneak through her.

"I told you I'd be fine," he reminded her. "I can take care of myself."

"Yes, but that's . . . you know, just something people say. 'I'll be fine.' It doesn't mean anything, because how can you really know it'll be fine? You can't. It's completely meaningless. All I knew was that I didn't want you getting hurt because of me."

"But that's what I signed up for," he pointed out, running a hand over the back of his neck. "To take the bullet. To be the one who stands between you and the bad guy. Like the Secret Service."

"I'm not exactly the president," she snapped. "You were an innocent bystander. Why should I be protected my whole life?"

"And why should I? If my brothers were taken hostage, they wouldn't expect the government to give in to some wacko's demands. They'd take it like a soldier."

"What does this have to do with your brothers? Anyway, you *aren't* a soldier!"

That didn't go over well at all. Fred's expression turned unforgiving as stone. "That's where you're wrong, Rachel. When I'm on the fire lines, I'm a kind of soldier, except I'm fighting fire, not other soldiers. When you hired me as your bodyguard, I became your own personal soldier. Sure, I might not be in the military like my brothers, but that doesn't mean I don't put myself in the line of fire."

This was unfamiliar territory to Rachel. Maybe it was something in the male gender that she just didn't understand. She tried to resurrect every military movie she could think of. "But if your brothers were captured by the enemy, they'd expect to be rescued, right? By the Marines or something. *Zero Dark Thirty* or . . . or . . ."

Fred flung up a hand to stop her. She bit her lip,

suddenly remembering his brother's crack about *Zero Dark Salad*.

"Sure, the Marines would do everything they could to rescue a captured soldier. But that soldier would be prepared for torture or beatings or psychological manipulation or all kinds of crap. But me? I get nabbed by someone named Kale and ranted to about how mean people are to cute, cuddly animals. You know something? The worst part of the whole experience was having to watch you do that interview and know that I'd failed."

Rachel flinched backward as if she'd been slapped. Only the couch against the back of her knees kept her upright. "What kind of thing is that to say? I chose to help someone who matters to me. Why does that bother you so much?"

"I just told you. I feel like an ass."

"You're not an ass! You're a hero!"

"Don't fucking say that!"

She stared at him in utter shock. Never had she expected her kind, sweet-hearted Fred to be swearing at her with that furious look on his face. Especially not after everything that had happened. "Why are you acting like this?"

"You of all people shouldn't call me a hero." His intensity vibrated like a whip across the room. "I was hired to protect you. I was doing my job, until you decided I couldn't handle it."

"That's ridiculous," she cried desperately. "Don't do this, Fred. Is this about the money? Because the money doesn't matter."

He went deadly still. "What money?"

"The . . . the ransom money," she stammered. "I . . . I didn't even have to ask my dad. He paid it right away. He even paid double because the guy didn't want that much. Marsden thought more money would make him back off his demand for me to go public."

"But it didn't, did it?"

She shook her head numbly.

"That's why you don't freakin' give these guys what they want. Fuck!" He pounded a fist into the strip of wood that separated the picture windows. Greta looked anxiously from one to the other of them, ears perking. "I'm going to pay your father back for that money."

"What?" She started across the room. "That's insane. The money was nothing to him. It was just a wire transfer anyway. He can get it back with a few keystrokes."

As soon as she said it, she knew it was the wrong thing. She stopped in the middle of her living room, watching his fury mount.

"*Nothing?* Of course it's nothing to him. Fine, I'll refuse my paycheck. I messed up on the job, I won't accept his money."

"Stop it," she begged him. "You're taking all of this the wrong way. Can't you just see it as people caring about you and not wanting you to get hurt? What's so horrible about that?"

"You don't understand."

"You're right! I don't. I think you're being mean and unfair."

"Then I guess we just disagree," he said stiffly, jamming his hands in his pockets again. "No surprise there."

What was *that* supposed to mean? But Rachel's feelings were too bruised to find out. She didn't think she could take any more. "Maybe you should go. We should talk about this another time, when you're not . . ." *Being ridiculous.* " . . . still injured."

He looked away, the muscles of his jaw working.

"My part in this is done. Your father's testimony is over."

Desolation closed around her, a gray cloak blocking all light.

Somberly, he added, "If there was any way I could get your privacy back, I'd do it. Just know that I'm sorry."

First he was angry at her, now he wanted to apologize? No, he'd apologized first, then unloaded on her, then apologized again. *After* announcing that he was leaving. Rachel felt as if she was jumping from cliff to cliff, with dizzying depths lurking beneath her. None of it made any sense to her.

She stuck out her chin. "I don't accept your apology, as you have nothing to apologize for. I don't accept your accusations either, since I don't think I did anything wrong."

He gave a frustrated shake of his head. "I guess that's it, then."

"I suppose."

He strode across the room, slanting a cryptic look her way as he passed. A flush of heat passed over her, followed by a harsh chill. It felt . . . It felt as if he was trying to memorize her. As if he didn't expect to see her again.

At the door of her apartment, he paused. The elevator door stood open, awaiting him. Rachel had the sudden thought that they never should have left the elevator. They should have stayed there, the two of them, and lavished love and pleasure on each other until there was no room left for anything else.

Fred skirted the elevator as if it held a snake pit, and made an abrupt turn to the left. "I'll take the stairs."

And then he was gone.

Chapter 26

Vader rested his forearms on the captain's desk, a posture that made the muscles of his upper arms bulge like Popeye's. Fred, surveying the stern lines of his captain's rugged features, wondered if he was in trouble for some reason, but couldn't bring himself to care very much. Everything seemed to have gone to shit, and he couldn't quite figure out why.

"Do you need to take another leave?" Vader asked.

"No. I'm fine." The doctors had told him to take a few more days, but Fred was itching to get back to his normal life. "Why?"

"Because Ella Joy, that's why."

"That's not a real sentence." For a pleasant moment, Fred flashed on a fantasy image of Ella Joy and Kale in a cage match from which neither one emerged.

"Oh, sorry, I'll be sure to brush up on my grammar between fielding media requests and evicting your groupies from the hose tower."

Fred winced. "Someone climbed up there?"

"Well, of course they did. How else could they mount the banner? We haven't taken it down yet, so you can enjoy the moment."

He hadn't heard anything about a banner, but something told him it wasn't good news. "What banner?"

"The banner with the phone number of Delta Nu Omega over at San Gabriel College." Vader lowered his voice. "Which, by the way, I could have told you anyway."

Fred saw an opportunity for revenge. "I thought you passed on your phone number collection to Ace. At least that's what Cherie told me."

But Vader couldn't be rattled that easily. "I did pass it on. Cherie knows she's all I want in a woman and always will be. But I dialed that number a lot of times, and some things don't leave your brain just because you get married. But let's get back to your messed-up life. We have a kidnapping, we have a fan club, and then there's Rachel. What's going on there?"

Fred stiffened. "Nothing's going on. My leave is up and I'm ready to come back to work. I heard I missed a few USAR calls. I should have been here."

Vader made a dismissive gesture. "They were handled. You're not the only one who can be a hero, you know."

"I'm not a fucking hero," Fred ground out.

"Really? According to my TV, you are."

Maybe it was the twinkle in Vader's eye, or the sympathy on his rough face, but Fred had just about reached the end of his rope. "Let me ask you something. If you were kidnapped, would you want Cherie to bail you out? You know, pay the ransom or whatever?"

Vader tilted his head thoughtfully. "If I were kidnapped . . . let's say by the entire Taliban, because that's what it would take . . ." Fred rolled his eyes, already regretting that he'd asked the question. "My main concern would be Cherie's feelings. Face it, that's my biggest concern in most situations. I would hate to make her worry. Would I want her to pay the ransom? Sure, if that helped ease her mind. She'd want to do something. You know what gets me, Fred?"

Fred shook his head.

"I know how much Cherie worries when I'm out on a call, but damn if she'll ever let me see it. She puts on that cheery little smile when I head off to work. She doesn't want *me* worrying about *her* worrying. Know what I mean? Women are just as strong as we are, Fred. That means they'll fight like demons for someone they love."

Fred stared at his captain and friend while trying to make sense of his words. Did Rachel *love* him? Was that why she'd done the interview? *I chose to help someone who matters to me*, she'd said. He'd been so wrapped up in his own feelings of failure that he hadn't considered her point of view. Not really.

For the first time, it occurred to him that maybe he'd been too hard on her.

He dropped his head into his hands and groaned. "I think I fucked up, Vader."

"Let it out, dude. Let it out."

If only he could talk about Rachel. But he couldn't, not without betraying her privacy even more. Anyway, he was the problem, not her. "My whole life, I always looked up to my brothers, and guys like Captain Brody. They're heroes, you know? Fuck, I'd put you on that list, and Chief Roman. Now everyone's saying I'm the hero and it just feels *wrong*.

Like I haven't done enough to deserve it. I'm just a fireman, doing the job."

Vader tossed a paperweight from one hand to the other. "Aw, poor baby."

"What?" Fred's head swung up.

Vader pushed his lower lip out, pouting like a two-hundred-fifty-pound infant. "Is a little media circus too much for widdle Fweddie? Are those big meanies giving you a rough time after school? Want me to make those big bad reporters leave you alone? Want me to beat them up for—"

Fred hurled himself across the desk, and suddenly Stan was barking and Vader was on his feet, shoving his face right up against Fred's. "Did you ever think just doing the job is what it's all about?" he growled. "You come in here every shift knowing you might have to do something crazy, like kick open the door on a house that might explode. So does everyone else in this firehouse. You saying they aren't heroes?"

Alerted by the yelling, the rest of the crew was pouring into the office.

"What the hell's going on here?" demanded the new battalion chief. "Breen, is that you? Mind letting go of your captain's jugular?"

Vader stood, brushing Fred's hands away from his neck as if they were cobwebs. He forced a big grin, as if nothing out of the ordinary had just happened. "Firefighter Breen and I were just reenacting his kidnapping. I was playing the part of Kale. How'd I do, Stud?"

Fred took a big step back, clenching and unclenching his fists. Even though Vader's words were still tearing into him like bullets, he knew that his friend had just thrown him a lifeline. The battalion chief would not appreciate a firefighter attacking his captain. "You did awesome, Vader. Might want to keep your day job, though."

"Planning on it. We also agreed that Breen needs a few more days to recover from his injuries. Right, Stud?" Fred nodded meekly.

Then Vader added quietly, "Breen doesn't have anything to prove to me. Or anyone here."

Fred stared at him for a long moment, then wheeled out of the office.

Breen doesn't have anything to prove . . . You saying they aren't heroes? The words kept flashing in his brain like a neon strip-club sign.

Vader, in his in-your-face way, had managed to pound a crazy new idea into Fred's head. Was the big guy right, and it really was all about doing the job? The job he'd been doing all along?

He jogged down the dim corridor that led to the exit. Pushing open the side door that bypassed the apparatus bay, he blinked in the May sunshine.

Maybe he wasn't not-quite-good-enough. Maybe he didn't have anything to prove. Maybe Fred the Fireman didn't have to take a backseat to anyone. Maybe he needed to get rid of the fucking monkey on his back.

Especially if it made him lash out at a wonderful girl who cared so much that she'd tried to rescue *him*. And he'd thrown that gift back in her face. Because he was an idiot. He remembered his crazy ideas about how to win a girl like Rachel. Feats of strength. Quests. Rachel had performed a goddamn feat of strength, and look what it had gotten her. A bunch of crap from him.

Could Rachel ever forgive him? He pulled out his phone to send her a text. *Sorry*, he wanted to say. *I'm a moron.* But that wasn't enough. There was so much more to say. Too much for a text. Or a phone call. He had to see her. Had to tell her . . .

Hot damn. He had to tell her he loved her.

That moment in the elevator, the moment when he'd realized he loved her, came back to him with searing intensity. It was still true. Truer than ever. The whole thing with Kale had messed him up. Messed everything up. He'd acted like such an ass at her apartment. Would she even believe him?

He put a hand to his head, which had begun throbbing dully. The doctor was right; he needed to be back in bed. Putting away his phone, he shielded his eyes from the sun and headed across the parking lot. He had to get this right with Rachel. He'd already screwed things up enough.

Before he got into his car, he took a detour to the backyard to check out the hose tower. A bedsheet— yellow with ruffles, for Chrissake—stretched across the upper exterior portion of the tower. He couldn't tell what ties they'd used, but they were frilly and elastic and resembled garters. In curling letters, traced in purple paint, he read the words, "Call us, Freddie!" along with a giant phone number. He was still mesmerized by this embarrassing work of art when the rumble of an engine made him glance toward the sky.

The Channel Six News chopper hovered overhead. Was that ridiculous banner going to be on the news tonight?

He ran back into the firehouse and went straight to the kitchen. Ace, whose turn it was in the cooking rotation, always included vegetables in his meals. Fred flung open the refrigerator door. Jackpot! A plastic container of ripe tomatoes took up an entire shelf. He snatched it up and dashed back through the firehouse with it, ignoring Ace's outraged yells behind him.

At the base of the tower, he dug his feet into the lawn, loaded up a big, fat, juicy tomato, and let it fly. It landed with a splat right in the middle of the painted 2. The tomato split against the sheet and the juices ran down the fabric. He launched another one, which landed on the F in Freddie. "Call us, reddie!" the banner now read. He could live with that. But he had more tomatoes, so he kept going. Boom, boom, boom. The sheet held up pretty well under the onslaught. Those sorority girls probably bought expensive bedding. He couldn't bring down the banner, but by the time he'd emptied the bowl of tomatoes, not a single digit or letter could be identified.

He heaved a supremely satisfied sigh. Finally, his world felt a little more like it belonged to him.

"You're making dinner tonight," grumbled Ace, who stood to his right, gazing up at the tomato-spangled sheet.

"You can make your damn salad without tomatoes," said Fred. "Nobody eats it anyway."

Ace scratched his blond head, then pretended to have a light bulb moment. "Hey, I know what I'll use instead. *Kale.*"

"Ha ha." Fred gave himself lots of credit for keeping his cool.

"There's a lot you can do with kale, you know? They say it's a very versatile green. Kale soup, kale salad, kale stir-fry . . ."

When Fred refused to react, Ace wandered off. "Kale chili, kale casserole . . ."

Sabina jogged up on his other side. "Good God, Fred. Have you totally lost it? That banner looks like a bad remake of *Carrie.*"

"You ought to know, Scream Queen." Fred realized he must feel better, if he was able to dish it back. Sabina didn't exactly enjoy references to her previous career in the movies.

She gave him a nasty eyebrow-raise. "Joke now, but if that's a news helicopter up there, you're going to have a lot of explaining to do. It looks like a murder scene. I can see the headlines now. 'The Bachelor Hero Massacre. No Tomato Left Alive.'"

Fred felt a smile get started. "Maybe that sorority will take it as a warning."

Mulligan arrived behind him; Fred knew because a hard clap between his shoulder blades made him rock forward. "It's good to have you back, Freddie-boy. I was getting tired of collecting all the panties the ladies were leaving for you. It's hard work, man. You owe me."

His smile gained steam. God, he loved this firehouse. Loved his job, loved his crew.

More of Vader's statements came back to him. *Women will fight like demons for someone they love.*

Rachel hadn't mentioned anything about love, but what if . . . what if . . . ?

His smile suddenly expanded into an all-encompassing, beaming grin.

"You all right, Stud?" Sabina took a wary step away from him. "You look like you just took a hit of something."

"Yeah. Well, sort of. Maybe. Or I will be. Maybe. If what I think might be true is true."

Mulligan and Sabina stared at him in mystified silence for a moment. Then Mulligan threw up his hands. "Aw hell. I recognize that expression. Another one bites the dust. You're in *love*, Freddie. Aren't you?"

Rachel's father arrived without warning, as usual. She couldn't seem to convince him that the fact that he owned the apartment didn't give him carte blanche to barge in whenever he wanted. He whisked her off to dinner at Castles, where they ate surrounded by his security guards.

Rachel tried not to think about the last time she'd been there, for Cindy's wedding, the night she and Fred had finally made love. It had been one of the most amazing nights of her life, and now everything between them was ruined. She still didn't understand how or why, even though she'd been thinking about nothing else.

Inside the restaurant, a few curious glances came their way, but not nearly as many as she'd feared. Maybe the reappearance of a long-ago kidnapping victim wasn't all that fascinating.

"You're not happy," said her father in his abrupt way, after they'd ordered mushrooms en brioche *a la diable* over a saffron-infused risotto—or something along those lines. Fancy food was lost on her. "Why aren't you happy? You got your way. Breen got out. You didn't even have to mention that ridiculous group."

"I'm happy." But even to her ears, she didn't sound happy.

"What's wrong? Something happen I don't know about? How's Breen? Hospital said he walked out on his own."

"I think he's fine."

Her father pounced on that. "You think? Where is he? You give him the night off because we're covered?"

"He . . . um, isn't guarding me anymore. It was only until your testimony, remember?"

He fixed her with that relentless black stare of

his. "He left? Get him back. You need a bodyguard more than ever, thanks to your brilliant move. Breen proved himself."

"He never had to prove himself to anyone," Rachel answered, irritated on his behalf. "Anyway, I can't just 'get him back.' He had a job, and he went back to it."

"So? We'll offer him more money. Double his salary. Quadruple it, who gives a fuck? Enough zeroes and he'll come back."

"Dad, it's not about the money. In fact, he says he doesn't want his paycheck."

Her father tilted his head back and let out his odd, dolphin-squeal laugh. "That's good. I like him. I like him a lot. Tell him we'll double his salary. Hell, what else does he want? A house? A motorcycle? Figure out some kind of signing bonus type thing, and throw that in too."

The brioche dish arrived, fragrant steam pouring from the little vents in the pastry. Rachel pushed it away from her. "You don't get it, Dad. He's done with the bodyguard job." He was also done with her, but she didn't want to mention that. It was still too painful, and her father didn't even know they'd ever been involved. Better to keep it that way.

"I'll talk to him," he said, arrogance pouring off him the way the steam rose from the brioche. "Don't worry about it. You watch, I'll have him back at work in no time."

"What are you going to do, Dad, kidnap him? I told you, he's *not interested*."

"I won't have to kidnap him. I have other ways." He tucked into his brioche, his eyes flickering shut for a moment as the flavors hit him. Rob Kessler loved his food, though he was notoriously particular. He'd probably only have one or two bites. He went for a brief dose of flavor, then moved on to the next dish. He'd once explained to Rachel that he liked to be in control of the food and not allow its savoriness to defeat his own willpower.

Her father's willpower was a force of nature.

As she watched him consume his few bites of brioche, Rachel imagined her father marching into Fred's firehouse, or maybe his little house in the suburbs, prepared to use all his weapons to bend Fred to his will. Bribery would come first. Then a threat of some kind. Maybe he'd try to make Fred feel worthless, as if he needed to be in the Kessler orbit to have any future. Maybe he'd play on Fred's fear of not being as important as his brothers. When her father wanted something, he was relentless. The only time he'd failed was during negotiations with her kidnapper.

She rose to her feet, rattling the plates and drawing attention from nearby tables. She didn't care. Her message to her father was too important to deliver sitting down. "Dad, listen to me very carefully. Manipulating me is one thing. I let you because I love you and I don't want to hurt you. But you cannot, *absolutely cannot*, bother Fred."

Her father blinked once, then put down his fork, and waved for a waiter to remove his plate. "I manipulate you? And you 'let me'? I don't know what you're getting at, but you're out of line."

"You know exactly what I'm saying. If you mess with Fred, I won't go along with your rules anymore. I'll leave that apartment. I'll walk around without protection. I'll do whatever I want."

"You'd do that?" A low, dangerous hum vibrated in her father's voice.

Even though her hands were sweating so much she had to grip them together behind her back, she held her father's snake-charmer gaze. She couldn't back down. Not now. If she gave so much as an inch, he'd take it. "I would. I don't want to, because I know how much you'd worry. I know how hard it was when the kidnapper had me. But I can't let you bother Fred Breen. It's not fair to him. I don't have a lot of leverage here, but I'll use what I have."

"Rachel, I appreciate your concern for Breen." He paused as the waiter set another plate before him, some sort of baked fish, its dead eyeball staring up at the two of them. "But I think you're bluffing. You've lived under my protection your whole life. You've never lacked for anything. You don't know how to survive on your own. Why would you want to? Yes, you're bluffing."

"I'm not. I'm not bluffing." But she *was* shaking. She willed herself to stop, so that her father didn't think she was afraid. She'd never stood up to her father in such a decisive way. She'd fought to go to a regular college, she'd fought to start the Refuge. But each time the final decision had been up to him.

This time, it wasn't up to him. She couldn't let it be.

"How do I know you're not bluffing?" Her father dug a fork in the breading that encased the fish. Juice leaked onto the plate. He tilted his head at her, as if she was providing welcome entertainment, almost as good as the fish.

"Do you love me, Dad?" she asked suddenly.

"Of course." His black eyes flashed with outrage. "How can you ask that?"

"Then why aren't you listening to me?" She heard the helplessness in her voice, fought against it. More than anything, she hated feeling helpless. That's how she'd felt in the kidnapper's cage. And she'd felt that way, to some degree, every day *since* her kidnapping. Every day that she'd allowed her life to be dictated by someone else.

"I think I've been fairly patient." There was her father's "soothing" voice again. "*You* did that interview. Now you need more security. Breen proved he's willing to take a bullet for you. When it comes to the issue of your safety, *I* have the final say."

Rachel dragged in a deep breath, calling on all the grit she knew was in there somewhere, the grit that had gotten her out of that warehouse. "Well then, I'm calling your bluff. Keep the apartment. Keep your security guards."

The red tinge creeping up her father's neck told her exactly what was coming next. She held up a preemptive hand. "In case you're about to threaten to withdraw funding from the Refuge, there's no need. I reject any further donations from Kessler Tech. I'm going to handle things myself from now on."

Chapter 27

*S*ince Rachel wanted only to make a clear break, not give her father a coronary, she informed him she planned to stay at the Refuge until she found her own place. She also reminded him that her mother had left her some money, and even though she'd spent most of it on the Refuge, a small amount remained in her bank account. She wasn't going to be destitute.

The shell-shocked look on her father's face haunted her as she drove to her apartment building to pick up Greta and a few personal items. She hated making him worry, but how else could she get him to understand she needed a say in her own life?

In the foyer, she briefed Marsden on what had happened.

"I'll come with you," he said promptly. "You shouldn't be on your own."

"Of course I should be. I'm twenty-five. Everyone should be on their own at some point in their life, don't you think?" She spread her arms wide and spun in a circle, as if testing her freedom. "I can't pay you, Marsden, so you'd better stick with the billionaire who can."

"You know he won't let you wander around unprotected," Marsden pointed out. "He's probably already setting up a security team to tail you."

Rachel glanced over her shoulder, into the darkness beyond the glass doors. "He might be. But you know something? He can do whatever he wants. I'm going to do what I have to do."

"And that is?"

"I'm not exactly sure yet. It's like jumping into a lake. You just close your eyes and go." She leaned toward her longtime guard, wondering how much a hug would freak him out. Then she stopped worrying and threw her arms around him. His familiar scent of cigar smoke and detergent made her tear up. "Thank you for everything, Marsden. You'll never know how much it meant to me that you were always nearby."

He held her in a long embrace. "You have my cell number. Use it if you need me. I'll come, no matter what."

"I know you would. Thank you."

After collecting Greta, her leash, some dog food, her toothbrush, and a bag of extra clothes, she rode her elevator one last time. As she left, she gave the foyer, with its gilt mirror and elegant orchid arrangements, one last sweeping, bittersweet glance, then walked out into the murmuring, starry San Gabriel night.

Here she was. Rachel Allen Kessler. Alone at last.

She glanced down at herself, barely remembering what she'd put on her body for dinner with her father. Skinny black pants, a silky patterned tunic top with a print of gold-stitched tulips. Comfortable black flats with a kitten heel. Most importantly, her biggest purse, a black leather satchel that contained her journal, her wallet, her cell phone, her phone charger, her e-reader, her iPad, dog treats, a first aid kit tailored to animals, a packet of hair ties, and a book of matches that she'd grabbed on her way out of Castles.

She intended to hang on to that matchbook to remind her of this momentous day in her life. Something told her it was going to rank right up there with that other big day, when she'd taken her life into her own hands and run out of that cage.

Once, her therapist, Dr. Stacy, had asked her how she made the decision to escape—what had made her think it was worth the risk. She'd answered that Inga had bitten the guard's leg and she'd seized the opportunity. At eight, she hadn't calculated the risks. But now, standing there in the warm May night, with the breeze kissing her face like hope itself, she knew there was a different answer.

Sometimes you just can't do it anymore—whatever *it* is. Sometimes you reach that point where the unknown is the only choice you can make, because the known is no longer bearable.

So now what? It was almost midnight. She could find a hotel. She could roam the streets, reveling in her freedom. She could call Cindy and Liza and Feather, let them know about this seismic shift in her existence. More than anything, she wanted to talk to Fred, but she didn't want to bother him in the middle of the night.

She looked down at Greta, who was surveying the lamplit street, ears perking this way and that, clearly fascinated by this unexpected change in routine. "Let's go check out our new digs, shall we, Greta?"

The security guard on duty at the Refuge, Tony, looked shocked to see her. "Everything okay, miss?"

"Perfect. Greta and I will be in my office."

"Very good. Oh, a police officer stopped by earlier. He questioned the staff and he wants to talk to you too."

She sighed. "Thanks, I'll call him back tomorrow."

As soon as the outer gate slid shut with a firm click, and the night sounds of the Refuge—the soft whistles of the mockingbirds, the snuffling of dreaming animals, wind playing in the treetops— surrounded her, a sense of peace descended on her soul. She and Greta spent the night curled up on the loveseat, moonlight slanting through the windows.

She didn't sleep much; too many thoughts kept running through her head. The Refuge staff was probably wondering what was going on, especially if they'd seen her interview and heard about Dale/ Kale. They wouldn't ask, of course. They were used to keeping their distance and doing what they were told. She rarely interacted with the staff, being more occupied with her dog therapy practice. For three years she'd floated in and out of their sphere, with them, and yet apart from them. And she'd never really questioned it before now.

But this place was her creation, her baby. Shouldn't she start acting like she was in charge, not just some distant, untouchable figurehead?

The next morning, after all the workers had arrived, she called a staff meeting. The guards, she noticed, had reported for work as usual. Maybe they hadn't gotten the message that Kessler Tech was no longer involved with the Refuge. Everyone gathered under the big oak tree in the front yard, three security guards and five staffmembers, whom she barely knew.

With Greta at her side for moral support, she faced the small group.

"Hi," she said, clearing her throat awkwardly. The faces before her showed no expression other than wariness. "As you all know by now, one of our techs, Dale, has been arrested for kidnapping. You've probably already been questioned by the police or maybe interviewed by the media, so I thank you for your cooperation."

From the corral, a goat bleated. *Out with it, Rachel.*

"Also, I . . . um, in case you missed my interview on Channel Six, I'm actually Rachel Kessler, not Rachel Allen. I apologize for the deception."

No response from the group. Maybe they didn't care what last name she used. Maybe they already knew. Maybe she was making a big deal about nothing.

"Now that the word is out, it's quite likely things will change around here. Actually, scratch that. Things are definitely going to change."

Finally, a reaction. One of the techs, a young woman with her hair in two braids—Becky?—raised her hand. "Rumor has it you'll be closing the Refuge."

"Who said that?"

She shifted back on her heels, hands in her back pockets. "There was an e-mail from Kessler Tech that got people talking."

"We're not closing down. It's true that Kessler Tech will no longer be one of our donors. But we don't need them. We have plenty of other means of raising money."

Tolliver, a leathery-skinned older man who was as good with birds as she was with dogs, spat into the dirt. "Be straight with us. Without Kessler's dough, you can't guarantee our paychecks, can you?"

Paychecks. Rachel pulled the skin of her lower lip between her teeth. Of course the staff wanted to know how they were going to get paid. Since she'd never drawn a paycheck herself, she hadn't even thought about that detail. "I can't give you a firm answer until I see where our finances are," she admitted.

A groan rose from the group, and Tolliver turned away with a gesture of disgust. "Then what are we even doing here? Why are you wasting our time?"

"Wait! Wait, don't leave yet. Please." Rachel dug her heels into the dirt. She'd worked so hard to build this place. Now she'd have to work even harder to keep it going. Anchored by the solid ground beneath her, she said, "Here's what I can promise you. We have other donors, and I'll be working with all of them to make sure they stay on board." Well, maybe with the exception of Bradford Maddox IV. "Right away, while the media is still interested in my story, I'll be doing a major media outreach myself."

Was anyone listening anymore? They were looking this way and that, at their feet, at each other. Maybe they were already mentally updating their résumés.

"Please give me your attention for just a little longer." That didn't work either. Becky was checking the messages on her phone. Tolliver stuffed another wad of gum in his cheek and looked at the sky above.

Momentum was definitely not going her way. *Crap.* If the staff members left, the animals would be put at risk and the whole place would degenerate before she could hire anyone else. And she liked this crew; they did a good job. She couldn't let them abandon the Refuge. She had to be . . . She looked down at Greta, who sat patiently by her side, the way Rachel had trained her to. Why? Because she, Rachel, was the leader of their little pack of two. People were social animals, just like dogs, she reminded herself. They responded to strength, to decisiveness, to leadership.

"Let me make this perfectly clear," she said, with enough crisp command to capture everyone's lagging attention. "I'm Rachel Kessler. There isn't a media outlet in this country—maybe the world—that doesn't want to talk to me. I can get us more media exposure than any nonprofit could ever dream of. And once those camera crews come in here and show Becky setting a splint on an injured dog's leg, or Tolliver making friends with a baby raptor, hell, we'll have so much money pouring in we can . . . build the Taj Mahal here. And populate it with elephants. The sky will be the limit. I might not have the money right now, but I promise you I will put everything I have and everything I am into securing the future of this Refuge. It means everything to me."

The passion in her voice echoed through the yard. Even the animals in the outbuildings seemed to be listening. Surely she was getting through to the staff members. She scanned their faces, meeting each of their gazes. Mick, the big security guard, offered a nod of approval.

"The animals do, you mean," said Tolliver in a grumpy voice.

"Excuse me?"

"The animals mean everything to you. No one doubts that. But what about us?"

Her mouth dropped open from surprise. The people? Of course the people were important. They took care of the animals, after all. Hearing that thought echo in her mind, as if listening to her words played back on tape, her cheeks went hot. Oh my God. Had she really been that neglectful of the people who worked here? Yes, she really had. She wasn't even entirely sure of all their names. These were people who put their hearts and souls into this place, just as she did. And yet she'd allowed an invisible barrier to come down between them.

That's what happened when you let fear guide you.

"I see your point," she told him. "You guys are all dedicated, skilled, and wonderful. I'm very grateful to you. Well, everyone except Dale."

A smattering of laughter gave her hope that she was on the right track. "I'm going to be really busy for the next couple of weeks working on raising money. But after that, I'd like to get to know you all better. And I want you to get to know me. Because if you stay on, you're investing your time and energy in me, Rachel Kessler. So what I want you all to know, right now, is this. I can be very hardheaded and willful. When something really matters to me, I fight for it. And I fight hard. Even if it means I crawl out of a cage on my hands and knees over broken glass. Even if it means I get kicked in the head so hard I couldn't speak for weeks."

She certainly had everyone's attention now. The only sound to be heard was the oblivious twittering of the sparrows overhead. She hadn't told Melissa McGuire, Fred, or even her friends the extent of the damage she'd suffered. The memories were too harsh.

"I fought to escape that kidnapper, and after I was home, I had to survive the aftermath. It took nearly a year to get back to where I had been, developmentally speaking. I had a lot of help from my father and all the doctors and physical therapists. But mostly it was sheer, pigheaded determination. I intend to fight for this Refuge just as hard. If you stay, you're taking a bet on me. Rachel Kessler. Not my father, and not my trust fund, because there's not much left there. I don't know how long it will take to get the financial situation stable, but your paychecks will be my top priority."

She looked from one to the other, letting them scrutinize her, giving them time to assess her seriousness and her sincerity.

"So . . ." she said finally. "Who's with me?"

No one left. It was, without a doubt, the most gratifying moment of her life.

After a busy day of setting up interviews with board members and media outlets, she drove to the South Desert Plaza Mall, where she picked up some clothes and a few other basics. She didn't want the staff members to figure out that she was staying at the Refuge. She felt safe there—at night it was impossible to get in without the security codes—but didn't want the word to get out.

From the mall she headed to Fred's neighborhood. She longed to see him. So many things kept running through her mind, things she wanted to say to him, apologies, explanations. She wanted him to know that the interview with Melissa hadn't ruined her life; instead it opened her up to new possibilities. What would he think of her decision to do an all-out media blitz? What would he think of her speech to the Refuge staff? What would he think of her break with her father? There was so much to tell him! And that wasn't even the most important thing. There was something much deeper, something she couldn't keep to herself any longer. Something private, that couldn't be shared with . . .

The kids from next door.

The three boisterous boys were bouncing around the front yard like rubber balls, careening off one another, pushing one another over, somersaulting across the grass, and generally creating mayhem. Fred was nowhere to be seen. When the boys caught sight of her emerging from her car, they sorted themselves out and scurried to the sidewalk.

The smallest one, Kip, she recalled, grabbed the handle of her door and opened it with a deep bow. Apparently he was still on doorman duty.

"Thank you, kind sir," she told him with a princesslike nod. Greta rushed past her, running to each boy in turn to sniff and make friends.

"Welcome to the 'hood," said one of the twins. "We been practicing our routine. Want to see?"

"I'd love to, but I'm looking for Fred—"

"What you want with him?" The second twin sidled closer to her. "He's no fun anymore. We wanted to spar but he kicked us out, said we had to play by ourselves for a while. I don't know if he's gonna want to see you."

Rachel didn't know either, but she figured she had to take her chances. "So he's here?"

"He's inside with his sister," said the kid. "Talk about no fun! She babysat us for two weeks and we had to do our homework every day. Every *day*. You know how hard that is? Every *day*!"

"Sounds completely inhumane."

"And you know what? I know that word, 'inhumane,' because she made us spell it. *Spell* it. What's the point of studying spelling when everyone's got spell-check? Even my cheap-ass phone got spell-check." The boy's righteous indignation made her laugh.

"It sounds like she took good care of you."

"And no Froot Loops either," piped up their little brother.

"Yeah, she made us eat muesli. That's what she called it. Meeeyoooslee. What kind of food's named muesli? Sounds like a damn Pokemon."

Rachel burst into laughter, which made the boys look even more disgruntled. The front door opened, and Fred stepped out, with Lizzie right behind him. The sight of him sparked tremors all the way to her core. He looked so yummy, barefoot, in a white T-shirt and black sparring pants, his dark hair just a little rumpled, his square-jawed face lit with a big smile just for her. Even though he looked tired and bruised, the eager light in his shining dark eyes still pulled her like a beacon.

That horrible, distant, hurt look he'd had during their fight was completely gone. Her heart jumped. Maybe there was hope for her. For them.

The boys were still talking but she no longer paid any attention. She took a step forward, toward the man who truly was the light of her life. Everything would be okay between them, it had to be. Once she'd explained that she'd acted out of love, he'd understand. He'd kiss her and hold her and make love to her and . . .

When a small hand grabbed her pants leg, she stumbled.

"Let me go," she said to whoever was keeping her from Fred. "What are you doing?" When the tugging didn't stop, she finally looked down. The smallest boy held a handful of her black pants. He gestured toward her car.

"Why you have a bumper sticker on your door?"

"I don't have any bumper stickers," she said, turning back to Fred.

"Yeah, you do. It sure is a funky one," said one of the twins. "Says . . . To Be . . ."

She swung around, nearly sending the youngest

brother flying. A bumper sticker was plastered on the passenger door of her car, at an angle, as if someone had just flung it there in passing. But it wasn't a mistake. Oh no. Not with that message.

To be continued.

Shock fizzed from her head to her fingertips. The kidnapper was here. Or he'd been near her. He knew her car. Who knew what he was planning? Whatever it was, she couldn't put these little boys in danger. She needed to get away from here. Now. *Get out. Get out.*

Waving at Fred, Lizzie, and the boys, she called, in as normal a voice as she could manage, "I forgot I'm supposed to be somewhere. Greta, come." Looking a bit confused, Greta trotted to the car and jumped in. "I'll call you later, Fred, okay? Bye, guys. Bye, Lizzie. Have a nice night."

She managed to buckle herself in without giving away her panic. Barely daring a last precious glance at Fred, who was staring after her with a puzzled frown, she started up the car and pulled away from the curb.

Chapter 28

"What was that about?" Lizzie peered after the taillights of Rachel's reinforced Saab.

Fred shook his head slowly. "Maybe the boys said something to upset her. Or maybe she wasn't ready to see me yet. I was an asshole the last time I saw her."

"Yeah, but she drove all the way over here. Why would she turn and run as soon as she saw you? I mean, that bruise is bad, but not flee-at-the-sight-of-you bad. Not even puke-at-the-sight—"

"I get it. I look like hammered shit."

"See, I never understood that one. Who hammers shit? Why? Why would anyone—"

"Lizzie, don't you have somewhere to be? I really don't need this twenty-four-hour guard service." His family had refused to give him a moment's peace. They called it keeping an eye on him in case he showed symptoms of concussion. He was starting to call it harassment. He hadn't even had a chance to see Rachel, even though he'd been thinking about her nonstop; now she'd disappeared right before his eyes.

"A soldier never leaves his or her post," said Lizzie with a mock salute. "Especially a Breen."

"Hey boys," Fred called across the yard. "Come here, would you?"

"Oh, so now you want to talk to us?" Jackson crossed his arms over his chest. One of his feet was planted on the back of his brother Tremaine, who sprawled facedown on the grass. Judging by Tremaine's out-of-breath, profanity-laced mutterings, Jackson had just flipped him. "I don't think so. You can't kick a brother out of your house and then pretend like everything's cool."

"Stop messing around. I'm serious. I need to know what Rachel said before she took off."

"Dude, you heard her. She didn't say nothin'. 'Bye, kids,' or some shit like that. Oh yeah, and 'Fred, I'll call you later!' " He mimed a sultry female voice that sounded nothing like Rachel's.

"Before all that. What happened to send her running? Did you say something? Swear at her? Make one of your age-inappropriate jokes?"

"You're saying it's all our fault? Tremaine, get your butt up. We got a problem here." He lifted his foot and hauled his twin upright. "We're facing some unjust accusations."

Fred stalked forward and grabbed both brothers by the scruff of their necks. "You don't need to go all Amistad on me. I just want to know what you were talking about right before she left."

"Nothing. The bumper sticker."

"Bumper sticker? She doesn't have any bumper stickers."

"No, she *thought* she didn't have any bumper stickers."

But before Fred could sort that out, their mother hollered from across the street. "Dinner, kids. Mac and cheese, while it's hot. Fred, you hungry?"

"No, thanks, Jasmine. Next time, for sure."

She gave him a friendly wave, then opened her arms to the little boys hurtling across the street.

"Bumper sticker?" Lizzie frowned, biting at her thumbnail. "Maybe she got upset because someone put a bumper sticker on her car that she didn't like. Like a Papa John's or something. Or a political candidate."

"Yeah." It still didn't seem like enough of an explanation. Something strange had just happened; he just didn't know what, exactly. He pulled out his phone and dialed her number. He got no answer, other than her soft, husky voice on her outgoing message. "Leave a number." No name, no promise to call back.

Irritated, he clicked off without leaving his number; she knew it and if she wanted to call back, she would.

"You should go back to bed," Lizzie declared. "How's your head?"

His head felt horrible, as if someone was taking a ball-peen hammer to it, striking the same spot over and over again. As if someone was trying to wake him up from *inside* his skull. "If I didn't need it so much, I'd get rid of it."

"That bad, huh? Aw, Freddie." Lizzie took his arm and bundled him toward the front door. "You'd better be okay. You're the only one of my brothers I can stand."

He let her guide him through his house toward his bed, where he'd spent much of the day. Those rumpled, messy sheets looked like heaven right now. "You know that's not true. You love us all equally."

"No, Mom loves you all equally. I love *you* best. Of course I love them too, but you're my favorite."

"If you say it's because I'm such a nice guy—"

"Don't be ridiculous. You know something, Fred? I'm a Breen too, and I know how hard it was to stick up for what you wanted to do, even though Trent and the others teased you. You inspired me. If not for you, I probably wouldn't be getting my pilot's license. I kept thinking, 'If Fred can tough it out, I can.'"

He squinted at her, lowering himself onto his bed. "Tough? You think I'm tough?"

"I think you're all kinds of tough. The *best* kind of tough. I know you, Fred. You're just as fierce as Trent and Jack and Zee. You're a warrior, like them, but you wanted to help people in your own way. And you did. You *still* do. I'm proud to be your sister. And I'm tired of you downplaying yourself."

Maybe it was due to his weakened state, but a sort of warm, fuzzy sensation was spreading through him. He'd never seen Lizzie so fired up—and all on his account. He smiled at her tenderly. "Is that what I do?"

"Yes. You act like everyone else is a hero except you. But you've always been my hero. And you don't treat me like a silly child. Even when I am a silly child, like with Trevor. And Brendan."

"And Chase." He winked at her. If she kept up with the mushy talk, he might really embarrass himself.

"Don't mention Chase. I'm not ready." She hovered over him, trying to settle him into his bed but managing to poke him in the ribs instead.

"Jesus, Lizzie, I'm not an invalid. It's a minor head

wound. And there's no need to get all sentimental. I'm not going to die."

She gave a soft snort, but her usual sparkling smile did nothing more than haunt one corner of her mouth. "Just . . . just let me, okay? You're always there for me, now I want to be there for you."

Fred wanted to ask if "being there" had to mean poking him in the ribs, but instead he stayed quiet and let her pull the covers over him. Mercifully, she left him alone after that, announcing that she was going to make some grape Jell-O, their mother's surefire comfort food.

Alone at last, he bunched up his pillow to make it more comfortable. *Lizzie.* What a pistol, cheerleading for him like that. The funny thing was, before he met Rachel, he would have thought Lizzie's lecture was ridiculous, trying to convince him of his heroic qualities. But now . . . now . . . after everything that had happened, something had changed inside him. It didn't matter if he wasn't Rambo, or his brother Trent, or even Captain Brody. He didn't need to be Prince William or Bill Gates either.

He was Fred, he was a firefighter, and he was the man who loved Rachel Kessler with his whole being.

And he was cool with that.

A short sleep, then he'd try Rachel again. And maybe Marsden for good measure. Marsden always knew what was going on. He'd know if someone had defaced Rachel's car, or if the kids had imagined the bumper sticker and it was really a bumper *car*, and he'd bumped Rachel too hard against the side wall and sparks were flying everywhere, like thousands of fireflies released from a jar, and the light was so beautiful it was terrifying, and Rachel was cowering away from it, shielding her face with her arm, but it was no use, because . . .

He jerked awake. Something was wrong. Rachel was in trouble. He knew it. He didn't know how or where, but he knew it.

Even though Rachel knew she'd be giving some control back to her father, she had to let him know about the bumper sticker. As soon as she left Fred's house, she called Marsden.

"You're sure it says, 'To be continued'?"

"Of course I'm sure," she snapped, not in the mood for silly questions. "But I don't know how long it's been there. I didn't notice it until someone else pointed it out."

"Do we need to check on that someone?"

"No! I don't think an eight-year-old kid could be my long-lost kidnapper. Look, you know I hate to say this, but I need you. I don't even have my gun. I left it in the apartment. Are you there right now?"

"No, your father switched up the security teams since you're not living in the apartment anymore. I'm halfway to Marin, but I'm turning around right now."

"No, no, that's okay. Is there anyone still in San Gabriel? Oh, of course! The security guards at the Refuge. Do you know who's on tonight?"

"I believe it's Mick. He's been with us for a while. Very competent. Want me to give him a call?"

"Yes. Tell him I'll meet him at the Refuge. Thank you, Marsden, that makes me feel a little better. Maybe I'll stop at the apartment and grab my gun. Two is better than one."

"No, Rachel. Don't stop that car until you get to Mick. He can take you back to your place. The building isn't under guard right now, and whoever left that bumper sticker could be waiting for you there."

"Crap, you're right, you're right." Rachel pressed

the heel of her hand to her forehead. That bumper sticker had freaked her out so much, her thoughts were all scrambled. The sight of that message had made her realize that at some point, she'd stopped believing the kidnapper was still interested in her. Now she felt as if the world had shifted into a kind of doomsday scenario nightmare. "I'll go straight to the Refuge. Will you call my father and let him know what's happening? He's probably still mad at me, but he'll want to know about this."

"You bet I will. He'll definitely want to know. Tell you the truth, I think he's still in shock that you haven't called begging for his help yet."

"I hope he doesn't think that I'm begging for his help now. I don't want his money, just a trustworthy guard for the night."

"Don't worry. Your dad will probably have security pouring back into town within a couple of hours. You'll be all right. Lock your doors, keep driving, and don't stop for any reason until you reach the Refuge. I'm beeping Mick right now."

Relief flooded through her. "Thank you, Marsden. I feel better already."

"Good. But don't relax. Be smart."

"I promise."

After she ended the call, she saw that Fred had called. He was probably wondering why she'd been so rude. Should she call him and let him know what was happening? Absolutely not, she decided. He was injured, and she didn't want him to jump into rescue mode. She could call him and try to explain away her weird behavior, but she doubted she could pull it off. Not when she was this rattled.

Instead, she sent him a quick text. *Call you later.*

Later, when she'd found Mick and gotten the situation under control.

Fred didn't answer back. Despite her determination not to involve him while he was injured, she longed to hear his voice. What if she never got a chance to hear his voice again? What if she never got a chance to tell him she loved him?

Stop that, she ordered herself. *No need for panic. Focus on getting your ass to the Refuge.*

Dusk was creeping in by the time she reached the big iron-work gates of the Refuge. Even though San Gabriel was a smallish city, it had rush hour traffic like anywhere else. Never had the crawl across town been so torturous. She couldn't help sneaking glances at the people in the cars next to her, wondering if anyone was going to try to cut her off and ram into her or drop a construction crane on her. But she saw nothing more than the occasional rude gesture in an intersection.

For once, she welcomed the sight of the ugly cement block walls topped with barbed wire that surrounded the Refuge. She pressed the button to alert the security guard, and turned her face toward the video camera. Unlike most video cameras, this one was her friend. This camera wouldn't allow any unwelcome visitors to enter her Refuge. When the gate had opened all the way, she drove in, more quickly than usual, checking her rearview mirror to make sure no one snuck in after her.

All clear.

She heaved a huge sigh of relief as she made her way down the driveway. Maybe it had all been a false alarm. Maybe someone from BEAST had unearthed the "To be continued" tidbit, even though it had never been released to the media. Maybe they were trying to spook her because they hadn't gotten what they wanted out of her interview with Melissa.

She caught sight of someone leaving the security shack and making his way toward her car. Must be Mick, who had the kind of physique she found very reassuring at the moment. Wide, brawny shoulders, a bit of a paunch to his belly, a no-nonsense stride. The kind of man you wanted on your side in a situation like this. After pulling into her usual parking spot, she jumped out. Not wanting to take the time to put Greta on her leash, she signaled her to stay put inside the Saab, and closed the door.

"Hi Mick. I'm really glad you're still here. Did Marsden call you? We have a potential emergency on our hands."

"Mick's checking the perimeter," the man answered. "I'm Officer Lee with the San Gabriel PD. I was here earlier, left my card."

Embarrassed, she peered at him. Of course it wasn't Mick; Mick had a good thirty pounds on this policeman. "Oh. Right. Sorry, I was going to call you back, but—"

"Mick called me in, said you had an emergency."

"Yes, um . . ." Rachel hesitated. The man wore a San Gabriel PD uniform, but should she ask to see a badge anyway? Before she could do so, he handed it to her.

"You should always ask," he told her. "Lots of crazies out there."

It was definitely a real SGPD badge. Relieved, she handed it back. "Thank you. And I'm glad you're here. I need someone to check out this bumper sticker on my car. Maybe dust it for fingerprints. It would be great if we could figure out where it came from."

He came closer, playing his flashlight over the door of the car. "Funny thing for a bumper sticker to say. Sounds like a comic book."

"Yeah, well, it would have to be one of those scary comic books where people die gruesomely."

"Why's that?"

"Oh, you don't need to know the whole story. It's basically a warning. A warning I intend to take very seriously. Did Mick secure the grounds?"

"He did."

"Whew. I don't mind saying I was a little scared out there. I almost didn't get back in my car."

"That would have been smart."

"What?" She peered at him, confused. "You mean it wouldn't have been?"

He said nothing, walking around the car as if looking for something else unusual. Kneeling down, he plucked a small black object from the undercarriage.

"Oh my God." Without him saying a word, she knew what the object must be. A tracking device. Panic fluttered in her chest like a trapped bird.

"They know I'm here. I mean he. I assume it's a he, but I don't really know anything for sure. Except we're not safe here. You're right, I shouldn't have gotten back in my car. If they could put a bumper sticker on it, why not a tracking device?"

She was babbling, damn it.

"Relax. I'm not worried," Officer Lee told her. He lifted the tracking device high overhead and smashed it to the ground, then crunched it under his foot. The sudden violence of the act made Rachel shy away. "No one can get in here, I made sure of that."

She couldn't drag her gaze away from the shattered object on the ground. "Don't you think we should save that tracker as evidence?"

He shrugged, his wide shoulders shifting in the shadows. It was nearly full dark by now, the blackness of the night concentrated under the trees just outside the fence, then graduating to a deep violet overhead. "No need."

"But . . . why not? There could have been finger-prints on it."

"Probably were."

Confusion flashed through her, following by a sense of horror, the threat of knowledge her mind re-fused to accept. She was missing something. Some-thing so obvious. And yet she was rooted to the ground. Unable to move, unable to react. "What . . ." She stopped. *Unable to speak.*

Officer Lee produced something that might have been a smile, she couldn't tell in the dimness. "The fingerprints wouldn't survive anyway."

"Oh." She put a hand to her head. There was something surreal about the moment, the quickly falling darkness, Officer Lee's eerie calmness, his odd statements. She felt thickheaded, the way she had after the kidnapping. Back then, it had been such a challenge to put everything together, to make sense out of things. Words hadn't gone with objects, objects shifted, words kept disappearing or chang-ing their meaning. It had felt like pinning a million butterflies to a wall and making them stay put.

Watching the policeman calmly circle her car, she had that same feeling, that nothing was adding up. She had to do what she'd done back then. Pin a but-terfly to the wall. One step at a time.

Very carefully, she asked, "Officer, I'm not com-pletely understanding you. Why wouldn't the fin-gerprints survive? Because of the surface material of the tracker? Or because you already touched it when you took it off the car?"

He gave a long, quiet laugh. It would have been reassuring if dread hadn't been flickering up and down her spine. "No. Nothing like that." Then his voice deepened, the way things happen in dreams, one thing seamlessly shifting into another.

And the familiar tones of this new voice made bile rise in her throat.

"The fingerprints won't survive, Miss Rachel Allen Kessler, because this entire place is going to get burned to the ground. Nothing's going to survive. Except me. I always survive."

Chapter 29

"Who are you?" Rachel's heartbeat drummed in her ears.

Officer Lee smirked. "Surprise." He lowered his voice, until it sounded exactly like the one she'd never managed to forget. "I still have the hair I chopped off your head."

"Why?" Now that the kidnapper of her nightmares was standing right in front of her, the fear that had shadowed her all these years felt different. Her heart raced and adrenaline flooded her body, but her head was clear. She was entirely focused on this moment, on him. Seventeen years had changed him, added bulk and a hunch to his shoulders. She'd never seen his face, and in the darkness still couldn't make out his features.

He kept playing the flashlight across her face, as if looking for her fear. She didn't give it to him.

"Why are you doing this?" she demanded. "Who are you? Where's Mick?"

"Mick got sick," he said succinctly. "I sent him home. I'm the man who's been waiting for this moment for seventeen years. Knew if I joined the local heat I'd get my shot. Couldn't have planned it better, with that nut job going after you."

"You were behind that?"

"No. As if I cared about animals. I want you here. With your damn animals."

His words flashed back to her. *This entire place is going to get burned to the ground.* "The animals?" she whispered. *Greta.* Everything in her wanted to check her car, make sure Greta was okay. But she didn't want him to know her dog was so close, so she forced her gaze to stay fixed on him.

"There it is." He looked at her greedily, shining the light on her face. "I knew that would hit you where it counted."

"Why do you have to hurt the animals?" She had to force the words through her frozen throat. "Why? Why not just hurt me?"

"Oh, I will. But first I want you to watch your precious creatures get burned to a crisp."

"But *why*?" She couldn't keep her horror from showing. Part of her knew she was in the presence of something she could never really comprehend. Someone so damaged and twisted her mind wouldn't be able to grasp his motives. The other part of her wanted, needed, to know *why*?

"KZ Ventures," the officer said succinctly.

"What? That old partnership?" Before Kessler Tech, there had been KZ Ventures. But there'd been a split, and her father had gone on to create an empire. "That was forever ago. My dad and . . ." She drew a blank on the name.

The earned her a sudden blow across her cheek from Lee's flashlight. She wheeled around, remembering almost automatically how to take his punches. You fell away as they struck, going with the momentum of his fist rather than fighting it.

"Zander," he said tightly. "Paul Zander. My father. I use my mother's name."

With a hand to her cheek, stopping the flow of blood from the slash he'd left, she stared at him, still not understanding. "They were friends. Paul Zander was my dad's professor. Then they went their separate ways." It had all happened before she was born, so she knew only what her father had relayed.

"Separate is one way to put it. Kessler became a billionaire. My father became a suicide."

"I . . . I'm sorry." The night shadows were drawing in closer. The only light came from Lee's flashlight, which was moving restlessly from her face to the grounds beyond, and the guard shack at the far end of the corral. Her eyes dropped to the pistol at his hip. Her gun lay in the bottom drawer of her office desk. He held the advantage in every way.

"Sorry for what? For driving my father to put a rope around his neck? Stealing my childhood?"

"Then we're even. You stole mine."

He bared his teeth in a flash of white. She tried to remember his hair color. He might have close-cropped sandy-brown hair, or he might not, she couldn't say for sure. He must have worked hard to fade into the background. "That month was the best time of my life," he said in a thick voice that made her sick. "Knowing how much Kessler was suffering. Knowing all the control belonged to me. When you left"—the words seemed to leave a bitter taste in his mouth—"I knew this day would happen eventually. When you'd be under my thumb again."

As she watched the flashlight trace an arc of light through the air, some of the familiar Krav Maga sayings ran through her mind. *Switch from defensive to offensive as quickly as possible. Improvise. Use anything available.* There had to be something she could do to fight back. An idea came to her. A risky one, and probably painful, but at least it was something. If she could get him to go after her with that flashlight again . . .

"Mr. Lee, I had nothing to do with what happened to your father. And these animals definitely didn't. Forget them. What satisfaction will you get out of hurting a bunch of goats and turtles?"

"You forgot the dogs," he said grimly.

Her breath stalled in her throat. Did he have a grudge against dogs, because one had helped her escape? "The dogs?"

"I hate dogs." He lifted the flashlight and she winced, turning her face away. But instead of hitting her, he simply brandished the flashlight at her. She gave it as close a scrutiny as she could. It was one of those heavy-duty ones, the kind the guards carried. The side of her face still burned from where he'd struck her.

"Whatever. Whatever I call you, you're still a coward if you hurt innocent animals. You should really get help, you know. Have you ever tried talking to a therapist?"

"Shut the fuck up. Just for that, I'm going to make you pour the gasoline. I got two cans' worth, and if it's not enough, you probably have extra in that hundred-mile-an-hour eco-mobile."

He reached for her wrist but she danced backward. Letting him get his hands on her was not part of her plan.

"There's nowhere for you to go, Kessler-bitch.

You're trapped here. You got no options except to do what I say."

"You wish that were true. But there are always options. I just learned that recently, as a matter of fact. You have options too. You could consider pursuing something other than pointless revenge. I really think if you talked to a qualified counselor you could make real progress with your issues of abandonment and loss of control." She'd had enough counseling herself to throw some valid-sounding terms around. "I'm a dog therapist, you know. But it probably wouldn't be too much of a stretch to work with you. Tell you what, I won't even charge you." She inhaled a deep breath, praying this next bit would send him over the edge. "It would hardly be fair to charge you when my father ended up with all the money and yours got nothing. What's it like to grow up with no father and no money? I can't even imagine, but I guess I just got lucky. And know what? I still have a father and lots of money. Life just isn't fair, is it?"

And here it came, just as she'd hoped. The flashlight sliced through the air with vicious force. Anticipating its trajectory, she slanted her face away, her hands flying up to meet the attack. It all happened at once, and so fast. The agony of the heavy metal object hitting her already injured cheek, the sudden pain of one of her fingers getting bent backward by the flashlight. Her primitive grunt as she flung her body away from him, using the momentum of the flashlight to wrest it from his hands. He lost his balance and took a few stumbling steps past her.

She was so shocked that her plan had actually worked that she bobbled the flashlight and nearly dropped it. Hearing him come at her, she clamped her hands around on the slippery metal and aimed the bulb directly into his eyes. He reared back, stumbling again. Then she switched the light off and, in the sudden darkness, ran as fast as she could toward the corral.

The thought of conking him on the head with the weighty flashlight was tempting, but she couldn't risk him grabbing it back. Instead, she stuck it in the back of her pants, where it bumped awkwardly against her butt as she ran.

Finally, all of Mr. Eli's lessons had paid off.

She undid the latch of the corral and swung open the gate, to the confused bleating of an alpaca and a mountain goat. Maybe the goats and other animals would provide a distraction. If he did set the place on fire, at least they'd have a fighting chance instead of being penned up. If all she could give them was a slight chance, she would.

If only she had time to free the birds in the aviary and the injured dogs in the kennel. *And Greta.* But she had to get her gun before anything else. From the front yard, she heard his angry voice and heavy footsteps as he stomped toward the guard shack.

"This isn't going to work, Kessler-bitch," he yelled. "One flashlight isn't going to save you. I still got the gun and all that gas."

A horrible thought struck her. What if he just shot the animals instead of setting a fire? The goats had begun wandering out of the gate, tempted by new grass they hadn't tasted yet. They were such easy targets. She bit down hard on her lip, so sure a gunshot would be next that she could practically hear the retort.

But he didn't shoot. Maybe he realized it was a waste of bullets and would just make a big mess. Besides, it was completely dark everywhere except the guard shack. He might risk a stampede if he started firing his gun.

She pictured her gun, a tidy Smith & Wesson .357 Magnum nestled into the bottom drawer of her turn-of-the-century mahogany desk, the one she'd inherited from her mother. The challenge was how to get to her office. By now his eyes had probably adjusted to the darkness and if she crossed the open yard, he might spot her. She waited an agonizing few moments until a few goats had ventured into the front yard. Then she went onto her hands and knees. Maybe in the dark she'd look roughly like a goat. Or maybe he'd be looking higher up, for a human shape, and wouldn't notice her. Barely daring to breathe, she crawled across the open, grassy area to her office.

For every second of that crossing, she expected a bullet to zing past her. It had happened just that way, back then. She'd been half crawling, half running, her legs weak from terror and disuse, her head ringing from the guard's kick. Gunshots, one after the other, rat-a-tat-tat, had struck the dirt and a clump of dry grass near her. But she'd kept going.

This time, no bullets came as she crawled to the back door of the office. She slipped inside, keeping to her hands and knees, and scrambled to her desk. Her revolver, black and solid, nearly leaped into her hands.

As soon as she held it, the seriousness of the situation seemed to increase a thousand-fold. Could she shoot Lee? Of course she could. When she'd been held captive, she'd kept fighting even when it meant more pain. If she'd had a weapon, she would have used it. What scared her more was the knowledge that she sucked with a gun. What if she missed and hit one of the goats? Or what if she just nicked him and made him angry? Her gun had only six bullets in it. She'd have one chance, maybe two. No, only one, because the retort always threw her off and she never managed to get the second shot anywhere close to the target.

She'd always done a lot better with Krav Maga than with a handgun. But she'd just have to do her best.

She crawled to the window and peered out. It took her a moment to spot him. Then she saw him at the edge of the wooden fence that enclosed the large corral. He held a large, squarish object that he shook slightly as he walked.

Oh my God. It was a gasoline can. He was pouring gas around the corral. With the dry grass, the whole place would light up. They'd all get incinerated, she and the animals. Greta, still shut up in her car. Her hands shook as she pried open a window. She had to shoot him before he set a match to the gas. Even though she'd never hit a target at that distance, she'd have to try.

He was nearing the guard's bungalow, which was at the farthest point from the office, and then he'd start curving in closer. She decided to wait until he passed the shack and she could get a clear shot.

The slight reprieve gave her a chance to line up her shot. She crouched at the window, her forearms resting on the sill for extra stability, and watched his steady progress along the fence.

Evil. The man was evil. Or so fucked up he was beyond help. In other circumstances, she might feel sympathy for him. But not if he was going to deliberately set a fire aimed at destroying animals. No. *He deserves to die*, she told herself fiercely. Hurting the innocent was just fucked up.

The vibration of her phone in her pocket startled her so much she let out a tiny shriek. Luckily, the bleating of the goats milling through the yard masked the sound.

Cell phone. God, what was wrong with her? She'd been so focused on getting away from him and grabbing her gun that she hadn't thought to call for help. Keeping the gun aimed past the guard shack with one hand, she dug in her pocket with the other.

Fred was texting her. *Thinking about you. Can we talk?*

Fred. *Fred.* She longed for him, craved him with the sudden intensity of a newborn craving air. If only Fred were here, his open, wonderful, square-jawed smile pouring sunshine into the room.

She quickly texted back. *Call 911. Refuge. Kidnapper setting fire. Come quick. I love you.* If she never got a chance to tell him in person, at least she'd said it.

Hang tight. Love you. On my way.

She shoved the phone back in her pocket. Did he mean "love you" the way she meant it, or in a generic, calm-down sort of way? That made one more thing the evil kidnapper had stolen—a precious moment between her and the man she loved, one that should have taken place in person, not over a text message.

The man had a *lot* to answer for.

She resumed her position, arms braced on the windowsill, gun pointed to the right of the bungalow. He must be behind it now, because she couldn't see him, or any movement from that end of the property. Closer to her, a few goats wandered across the lawn, chomping and occasionally bleating softly. The goats usually slept at night, but this change in their routine must have thrown them for a loop.

If we get out of this, sweet clover for all, she silently told the goats. Maybe some sugar cubes and alfalfa and . . .

A weird rumbling noise interrupted her thoughts. Somebody gave her a violent shake. Somebody enormous, like the world itself. Then everything was jerking this way and that, the walls, the floor, the windowsill. Utterly confused, she pulled the trigger, saw something go winging out the window toward the treetops. She fell back onto the ground, the gun dropping from her fingers. Books were leaping out of the bookcases like rats deserting a sinking ship. The noise was horrendous, as if a freight train was hurtling through the office.

Door. She should get to the door. Or hide under her desk or something. The desk was closer than the door, so she crawled across the floor on her hands and knees. It kept tilting back and forth, making her slide this way and that. She grabbed onto the nearest leg of the desk and hauled herself toward it. Or maybe it was careening toward her, she couldn't tell. It was like some kind of weird shipwreck with no water. Just flashing lights and rumbling and furniture going free range.

How could it still be going on? It seemed as if she'd been jolting around forever. Using all the arm strength she possessed, she swung herself under the desk, suppressing her automatic panic at sticking her head in such a small space. Now was not the time for a phobia. She glanced cautiously above her. *Pretend that's sky overhead, not the underside of a mahogany desk.* As sharp and heavy things rained onto her legs, she tried to curl into a ball small enough to fit under the desk. Then everything went black.

Chapter 30

The earthquake struck while Fred was driving helter-skelter toward the Refuge. He pulled over, leaving his lights flashing so other cars would do the same. He set the parking brake and held on through the violent jarring. Out on the road, a few other cars slowed down, one crashed into a telephone pole, but most followed his lead and pulled over. His instinct was to run outside and direct everyone, but it would be stupid to get out of the car before the shaking had stopped. He counted the seconds. Thirty . . . thirty-one . . . finally, after thirty-two seconds of bone-jolting, stomach-churning destruction, the earth settled down and lay flat.

He knew the stillness wouldn't last for long. Aftershocks could be just as dangerous as the earthquake itself. Quickly, he sent Rachel a text. *Are you okay?* When she didn't answer, he tried calling; when that didn't work either, he turned on the car radio. The news announcer sounded just as shaken as the rest of San Gabriel. "Preliminary reports say this was a 6.3 on the Richter scale, centered just to the north of San Gabriel. This is the biggest earthquake San Gabriel has experienced since 1942, when a 6.5 struck at four-thirty in the morning on Easter Sunday. Damage reports are just starting to come in, but we know that several neighborhoods have been hit hard, especially on the north side of town."

The Refuge was on the north side of town. He had to get to Rachel, *now*.

Fred turned the key in his ignition and pulled back into the road. All around him, drivers were getting out of their cars, turning to their neighbors. The streetlights had blinked off; power must be out across the city. The only light came from headlights and the peaceful, unworried stars overhead. Fred rolled down his window and cruised along the street, quickly scanning passersby for injuries. If someone needed help, he'd be in a real bind, since every second away from Rachel felt like an hour.

Everyone seemed shaken up, but unharmed. "Drive slowly and carefully," he warned people as he sped up. "Watch for obstacles in the road. Keep your radios on."

"Is it safe to drive?" someone yelled.

"Stay away from overpasses, ramps, anything that might have been damaged," he called back. "Keep to surface streets and take it slow and careful. But yes, go ahead and drive home. Traffic lights are out, so stop at every intersection."

No one questioned his instructions. He'd noticed before that in emergency situations, people seemed to naturally respond if someone stepped up and provided guidance. As he drove, he dialed the number for the station. No one answered. Even though there was nothing on the radio about fires so far, earthquakes always triggered them. The crew could be at a fire, or helping evacuate damaged buildings, or extracting victims from crushed cars. He'd be right there with them—head wound be damned—as soon as he made sure that Rachel was okay.

He contacted the USAR team next and told them he was headed to the north side of town. "I've got an unfolding situation there, but once that's dealt with, I'm all yours."

"What's the situation?" In the background, Fred could hear the tactical channel, people shouting instructions, the controlled madness of an emergency situation. He knew where they were; all hunkered into the bunker behind the station house, with the emergency backup generators going and communications lines being set up. The entire infrastructure of San Gabriel's emergency response was swinging into action. If it weren't for Rachel, he'd be doing the same.

But right now, all he could think about was Rachel alone with a lunatic trying to set fire to the Refuge.

"I have a possible arson and assault out at the San Gabriel Refuge for Injured Wildlife on Mountain Way. I may need backup."

"That could be tough, Breen. I have two collapsed overpasses and a fire at a shoe factory. And that's two minutes into this thing."

"Got it." He was on his own. "Where do you want me after this?"

"Hey. I didn't say no. You check it out and see how bad it is. You got your gear?"

"Enough." He had work gloves and steel-toed boots, and that would have to do.

"Good luck." And the man clicked off.

He drove on. Every block brought a new vista of destruction. Downed power lines, a few automobile collisions, a tree that had fallen onto a house. While he wanted to stop and help, his growing panic wouldn't let him. One-handed, he tried texting Rachel again, but again got nothing.

His eye lingered on her last message. *I love you.* Even though it was just a text, he could picture her saying the words. Her eyes would be wide and serious, her heart shining through. Rachel didn't let many people get close. But once someone won her trust and made their way past her shields, the most tender, passionate, softhearted, fierce-willed person awaited. *I'm coming, Rachel. Hang on.*

He also knew she must have been very, very frightened, or she wouldn't have put "I love you" in a text. That's what scared him the most.

Incendiary fury made every muscle clench. He was going to take that man apart. Just please, God, let him have the chance.

As he approached the Refuge, he saw the orange flicker of fire between the cypress trees. Sweet Jesus, the man had already started a fire. The Refuge verged on wilderness, and if this blaze really got going, it could build into a brushfire threatening scores of homes in the area. As horrified as he was, Fred forced himself to stay calm and remember his training. One thing at a time. First step: GYST. Get yourself together. Think, plan, then act. Size up the situation, make an action plan based on strategy and tactics, *keep your fucking head.*

The gate was open, and animals were pouring out in a melee of milling, bleating beasts. He spotted a few goats and an alpaca. Their panicky cries mingled with the determined crackle of flames eating through dry vegetation. Had Rachel left the gate open when she came in? Or managed to open it later? Or maybe the kidnapper had opened it to make his own escape after fucking over everyone else.

As he rattled up the drive, he saw that the usual security lights were off, and the only illumination came from the flames licking along the fence that surrounded the corral. At this point it could still be contained, but he needed to get some retardant on it, fast. Scanning the rest of the compound, it looked as if two of the compound's older buildings had collapsed, Rachel's office and the guard shack. If Rachel was in one of those . . .

He didn't see any people at all. The absence of human activity was not only eerie, but terrifying.

He stopped next to the corral fence. If Rachel's attacker was still here, wouldn't he have appeared at the sight of Fred's truck? Or would he shoot at Fred from the bushes?

Whatever the risks, he had to find Rachel.

"Rachel," he shouted out the window.

No answer.

He jumped out of his truck, then grabbed the fire extinguisher from the backseat. After pulling on some work gloves, he stuck a flashlight in his back pocket. He wished he had a gun, but this would have to do. He glanced around again, scanning for signs of life . . . or ambush.

He tried again. "Rachel! If you can hear me, make some kind of sound."

Nothing.

Sick dread filled him. He checked his phone, realized he had no service out here. The nearest tower must be out. Damn damn damn. With no idea where Rachel was, he didn't know where to start. Put out the fire or check her office? Her last text hadn't said, but his gut told him she'd been in her office. But what if he was wrong, and she'd holed herself up in the guard's building, with the flames beginning to feed on themselves, dance and roar and . . .

Shoving that thought aside, he ran to the fence line and activated the fire extinguisher. He sprayed the foam until the canister was empty, then kicked dirt on the remaining flames. The stench of gasoline prickled his nose. The asshole had poured accelerant around the property, the sick bastard. Why had he stopped? Where had he gone? Had the earthquake interrupted him?

When he reached the bungalow, he stopped cursing the man, because what was left of him lay splayed next to the building's shattered wall. His neck was bent at a repulsive angle, his face set in lines of horror, one side smashed to a pulp, the other intact. A chunk of roof tile lay next to him, and crumbled bits of plaster covered him like gruesome confetti. A spark had caught the lower part of his pants leg, which smoldered and released a gagging, burnt-flesh stench.

Fred kicked a big rooster tail of dirt over him to put out the fire. He knelt next to the man and felt his pulse. Definitely dead, though his skin was still warm, either from the fire he'd started, or from the dying embers of his life's breath.

"You had it coming," Fred muttered. "I'm just sorry I didn't get a chance to kick your ass first. I will take your jacket, though." He rolled the man onto his stomach and removed his jacket, then used it to smother the rest of the flames eating at the fence. He peered inside the darkness of the partially collapsed structure.

"Rachel?" he shouted into the void. Maybe she'd been with the kidnapper as he poured the gasoline. Maybe he'd shut her inside the bungalow, knowing how much she hated small spaces. The man was insane, Fred wouldn't put anything past him. He took a cautious step forward, eyeing the damaged wall. It didn't look too precarious, but without any way to shore up the concrete, he shouldn't go inside. On the other hand, if Rachel was in there, he didn't have a choice. He turned on his flashlight and took another step forward.

And then, amid the increasingly distant bleating of the goats, he caught a sharp yip. He stilled and listened again. Sirens in the distance, the rumbling of an aftershock racing across the terrain . . . and there it was. Greta's bark.

He swung the beam of his flashlight in the direction of the barking. It caught a slight gleam from something metallic . . . he squinted through the darkness. Rachel's rear bumper! Was Greta somewhere over there? Was she with Rachel? He ran across the yard to the Saab. The border collie was inside, scrabbling at the window. When he opened the back door, the dog launched herself at him, jumping up and clawing at his chest. "Hey, girl. Where's Rachel? How'd you get stuck in the car?"

Greta whined loudly, then took off like a shot toward Rachel's office.

As he started to go after her, an aftershock hit. He dropped to his hands and knees to ride it out. As soon as the shaking stopped, he raced across the yard, running faster than he ever had in his life. Greta was barking like crazy, but when he got close to her, his stomach dropped with a sickening plunge. The front of the guesthouse had sustained the worst damage. The roof had caved in, crushing the walls. Plaster dust floated in the air; he wished he had a face mask or even a bandanna. Greta was sniffing at a pile of splintered wood and plaster that looked as if a giant had stomped on his toys in a tantrum. How could anyone survive under all that?

But Rachel must be alive, because Greta was trembling and letting out sharp, excited barks, just like a real rescue dog. Fred knelt next to her and gripped a roof tile that perched atop the rubble like a jaunty beret. He gently rolled it down the slope of the debris pile, keeping control of its movement so it didn't trigger an avalanche.

The removal of that block opened up an air hole through which sound would travel better. "Rachel," he called. "Are you in there? It's Fred. And Greta."

He shushed Greta and waited for any sound from under the wreckage. It would help to know where she was. If he made a wrong move, the entire pile could collapse in an unwanted direction.

"Rachel," he called again, urgently. "Sweetheart, it's Fred. Wake up. I need your help. I can get you out of here, but I need your help. Come on, my sweet love. I need you. Please, Rachel. Say something. Anything."

He aimed his flashlight directly into the gap between jagged pieces of plaster. Maybe the light would wake her up if his voice didn't. Greta gave a few more eardrum-shattering barks right next to his cheek.

"Ow," he told her. "No need to deafen me."

But then the softest breath of sound caught his attention. "Shhh," he told Greta, wishing he had her toy with him, the one that rewarded her for finding a victim. When her barking subsided, he bent his ear to the hole.

"Fred?" A hoarse voice floated from deep inside the pile.

"Rachel! Are you okay?"

A pause. "Uh . . . sort of? Been worse?" The upward,

almost comical lilt at the end of each sentence made him want to cry from relief. But he kept a tight grip on his emotions. He had to keep his cool. She'd be following his guidance, and he needed her to keep calm.

"That's what I like to hear. Listen, Rachel, don't make any sudden movements, but can you move at all, or are you completely pinned?"

"I . . . I can move a little. My arms. I crawled under the desk."

"You're brilliant." He remembered exactly where the desk was situated. Now to get the rest of her office off her back. He wondered if she was getting claustrophobic, but decided it was better not to ask. Best to keep her focused on each moment and what needed to be done.

"Fred," she called urgently. "There's a man, Officer Lee, and he's the one who—"

"He's dead," Fred said bluntly. "Very very dead."

"I—I didn't shoot him, did I? I was going to, but I'm not a good shot, and I wasn't even ready to shoot, but then the earthquake hit and I didn't know what was happening and the gun went off and—"

"Shhh, sweetie, it wasn't you. I saw his body and there was no bullet wound. No blood at all. His neck was broken by a flying chunk of stucco. And if that hadn't killed him, he probably would have burned to death. Earthquakes are not the best time to commit arson. Things have a way of getting out of control."

"What about the fire? The animals?"

"Fire's out. And there's a whole gang of goats heading for the highway." He propped his flashlight on the pile so he could work faster, plucking more chunks of plaster from the pile.

"They got out? Was the gate open?"

"Yes. I'm guessing that Lee guy opened it so he

could make a quick getaway after he torched the fence."

"What a jerk," she said, with a touch of bemusement. "Then the earthquake hit. I can't believe it. Why now? In the middle of all this?"

"Earthquakes happen when they happen. We get them all the time, but this is a big one."

Greta bumped his arm, scrabbling at a hunk of metal—a light fixture? "Greta, your job is done. I got this." But the dog refused to stay still. Instead she danced around him, digging at the debris until her paws bled, leaving streaks on the broken sheet-rock. "You sure have heart, girl," Fred murmured as he helped her with a stubborn piece of two-by-four. "You'd make an awesome search and rescue dog."

"What?" Rachel asked, her voice sounding just a little clearer, as if he was unearthing it with each piece of rubble he discarded.

"I was telling Greta she has heart."

"You know what I was thinking about, down here?"

"What's that?" *Keep her talking.* The more she spoke, the easier it would be for him to follow her voice.

"I was thinking that all this time, there's something I overlooked about dogs. I've been working with them, training them, helping them, interpreting their body language and their behavior. And I did a good job. I really can connect with dogs. But that whole time, I should have been acting more like a dog."

"How? Have a bigger appetite? Get more excited about walks?"

She gave a wheezy laugh, which made him nervous. Why was she wheezing? Was something resting on her chest? Was she starting to lose her cool?

Talk about a confined space. It didn't get much worse than being under a desk piled high with rubble. Even though his shoulders and chest were burning from the effort of shifting the heavy joists and sheets of ripped plaster, he picked up the pace.

"No, no," she continued. "The thing about dogs is, they always bring their whole selves to whatever they're doing. Have you noticed that? They try their best, every time. They love completely, even if it's just a silly little chew toy. They're a hundred percent alive, every moment, until they die. And you know, Fred—"

Through his shock at that word, "die," Fred heard the telltale rumble of another oncoming aftershock. "Hold on tight, honey. Here comes another one." He reached for the trembling Greta, huddling his body around her, and braced himself.

The earth shook again. Fist-size pieces of debris tumbled toward him. Dust rose in a choking blur. When it cleared, and he called again for Rachel, he got no answer.

Chapter 31

Rachel was in the middle of saying something very important when everything started shaking again and she passed out. When she came to, her mouth was full of plaster dust. At least she hoped that's what it was. To keep a lid on her simmering panic, she refused to think about other possibilities. After the horrible jolting stopped, she spent a few minutes unclogging her throat and spitting out the nasty stuff.

She heard lots of noise from overhead. Greta's barking, the sound of a helicopter's blades, strange voices shouting. She heard Fred saying, "Rachel! Rachel!" over and over again, and though she tried with all her might to make sounds come out of her mouth, it was too dry and she was too out of breath to manage more than a dull groan. It felt like one of those nightmares in which she was trying to run and scream, but no matter how hard she worked, she was stuck in the same place, unable to make a peep.

Carefully, keeping her mouth tightly sealed, she turned her head to look up at the spot of light—not so much light as a slightly paler gray. Fred must be doing something else with the flashlight. When he'd first aimed it down the hole he'd made, it had shone like a ray of heavenly light, a shaft of hope lifting her heart. Now she couldn't see much at all. Maybe the aftershock had shifted the debris and blocked her air hole.

And just like that, she was back in that place where all her nightmares began. Back in the cage inside that windowless warehouse, where the only light came from a door propped open during the day. At night, her prison went completely black. Her hearing would get super sharp at night, when everything was quiet. The only sounds were made by Inga, the stray dog who skulked around the warehouse. She knew when he was curling up to sleep, when he was gnawing at the fleas on his rump, when he was slurping water from a tin can.

At night, in the blackness, she would dream. She'd dream of her mother, who had just died the year before. Of the way she smelled, like the rosemary she grew in big planters on the terrace. The way she smiled, wide, so her mouth stretched all the way across her face. Of the way she scolded when Rachel was too wild, which was often. Of the fairy houses she used to build in the stand of redwoods at Cranesbill. Of the crumbling cliff that looked over the Pacific, and the gazebo where she blew bubbles. Of how she'd watch to see how far out to sea they'd float before popping. Of her favorite blue Schwinn, and the freedom she felt racing down the road to the beach.

Inga the dog had helped her escape. But before then, her dreams had saved her. No one could take those away. Not the mean man with the mask, not the stupid guards, not even her own fear. Because at night, the dreams would come and she'd feel strong and free and invincible.

Now, buried under rubble, a different dream shimmered across her vision. There was a man out there who loved her. A man so true and kind and strong that nothing in this world was going to keep her from him.

Ignoring the pain, she maneuvered her hand to her face and clawed the rest of the gunk out of her mouth. "Fred," she croaked. The sound barely penetrated the dense silence under the desk. Desperately she worked up more saliva and spit out more dust. "*Fred*," she said, louder.

"Rachel?" From the wild hope in his voice, she knew he'd heard her. "Are you all right?"

"Yes." She spat again, feeling as if she were spewing out years of blockage. This time, her voice came out more strongly. "I was about to tell you that I love you so much and I don't think we should let anything get between us. It doesn't matter whose daughter I am or how much money he has. I don't care about any of that stuff. And I'm sorry I didn't leave it up to you to rescue yourself from Kale. I should have known you'd think of something . . ."

"No, Rachel, I was wrong. I was completely wrong!" He broke in, as if he couldn't hold back another moment. "I had my head up my ass. I was too worried about myself, and trying to prove something. I shouldn't have gotten mad, I should have been grateful, and I hope you can forgive—"

"Stop it, Fred! This is my time to babble! You know I have to babble when I'm feeling claustrophobic. You can talk when I'm done."

She became aware of a loud mechanical noise

nearby. But she still had so much to say, so she just raised her voice and talked over it.

"What I'm saying is, I don't regret doing the interview, I'd do that again in a heartbeat. It worked out for the best anyway. The part I'm sorry about is the money, because it's my dad's money and I'm used to money solving everything, but sometimes it makes things worse. And then I tried to protect you again when I saw the bumper sticker at your house, but I should have just told you and you probably would have thought of something, instead, now look at us . . . what *is* that sound?"

"I've been trying to tell you. It's a compressor. We're going to inflate a couple of air bags to create some space. The helitack team choppered them in."

"Air bags?"

"The air bags will lift the pile enough so I can crawl in and dig you out. Here we go with the first air bag."

She heard a short drone, then a slender crack of light appeared. Bright light; there must be more flashlights out there, or maybe spotlights. A sudden thought struck her. Was she getting special treatment, once again? "Doesn't the fire department have a lot more urgent problems than me?"

"You're trapped, Rachel. That's urgent. We have crews out all over San Gabriel, but this area was hit the hardest."

"My father didn't have anything to do with this?"

"No, this is the San Gabriel Fire Department doing its job." She heard the pride in Fred's voice. "But your father is on his way."

"That's good." She wanted to see him. No matter how suffocating his eccentric ways, her father loved her, and she loved him. With her whole heart—like a dog.

"We're deploying another air bag."

The crack grew bigger, until artificial white light was filtering in. The space grew wider, almost as wide as her body. Surely she could just crawl through.

"I'm coming out," she called to Fred.

"No. Don't move. It's safer if I come in and get you. I'm handing in a helmet. Put it on if you can. There might be more loose pieces and we don't want you getting hit on the head."

About to protest, she snapped her mouth shut. Hell no, she didn't want more brain trauma. She had too much to say, too much to do. There was the Refuge to rebuild, fund-raisers to plan, investors to woo. And most of all, Fred to love.

An object blocked the light, passing haltingly through the crack, which was now as wide as the heating vents at Cranesbill. It must be the helmet Fred was pushing toward her. When it was close enough, she painfully stretched out an arm and snagged it. By dint of much careful twisting and maneuvering, she managed to get it on her head, but the effort exhausted her.

"I'm coming in," Fred announced. She didn't protest this time, knowing she needed his help. Now that she could see the outside, taste the night air on her tongue, the craving for freedom nearly made her lose her cool. *Out, out, she wanted out.* A dark lump blocked a large portion of the light, and she knew it was Fred. Strong, true-blue Fred, coming to her rescue.

"What should I do next?" she asked him.

"How badly do you think your legs are pinned?"

She tried to move her legs, and managed about two inches. "I can move them a tiny bit. I just don't have any room."

"I'm going to dig you out then. Hopefully there's enough loose stuff to get you some space." A light was now shining directly in her eyes. She squeezed them shut. The sounds of grunting and digging kept her company. When she opened her eyes again, Fred was there, his dear, wonderful, smudged, exhausted face so close to hers that tears began flowing down her cheeks.

"You're here," she said weakly.

"Yup." His cheerful tone left no room for the hysteria that threatened to burst free. "I missed you. Thought I'd drop in for a visit."

"Don't make me cry too much," she warned. "Because if I start I won't stop."

"Please don't do that, the last thing we need down here is mud."

She smiled, making cracks in the dust that coated her face.

"I want you to hold this flashlight for me," he told her. In one hand, he held a slim flashlight and a hand shovel. "Can you do that?"

"Of course." Mildly insulted, she took the flashlight into her trembling grip, then used both hands to steady it.

"You're lucky your father buys such expensive office furniture," Fred said, eyeing the cracked mahogany overhead.

"He didn't. This desk belonged to my mother." That reminder made more warm tears trickle down the sides of her face. Her mother's desk had saved her life. So had Inga. So had Fred. So had her father, and Marsden. So much had conspired to save her; never again would she waste a single moment being anything less than fully alive.

"Hey. No crying. It looks like there's plenty of soft stuff around your legs. I'm going to pull myself forward so I can dig at it. Keep the flashlight aimed at your feet and keep trying to pull your legs free. As soon as you can, we're headed out. Got it?"

"Got it."

He inched forward, his body pressing against hers. Maybe it ought to make her feel even more claustrophobic, since the two of them were wedged together in an incredibly slim slice of space. But it didn't. "Fred?"

"Yeah?"

With her voice roughened by plaster dust—or deepest truth—she whispered, "There's no one else in the world I'd want to be in a confined space with. Only you."

At first he didn't answer. When he did, the words seemed to be ripped straight from his heart. "Well, that settles it, then. You'd better marry me."

"What?" Little shockwaves of elation traveled from her heart through every bruised limb of her body. "You want me to marry you?"

"More than anything." He gave a little cough, as if trying to clear dust from his throat. "Funny how I can barely see a foot in front of me, but everything else is perfectly clear. I love you, Rachel, and I'd rather stay under this desk with you than be anywhere else without you."

Her throat closed up over a swell of emotion. She couldn't speak, couldn't answer.

Fred filled the silence. "I'm even on my knees. How many guys propose while they're flat on their stomachs under four feet of rubble?" He inched further forward, so his lower ribs were pressed against her face. She tilted her head so she could breathe and, more importantly, not miss a single word that he said. "I probably should have picked a different moment. Like with flowers instead of a shovel."

Grunting with effort, he moved his arms above his head to jab at the debris with the shovel.

"No." She felt his body flinch. "I mean, no, it's the perfect moment."

"Your face is shoved into my stomach. How can it be the perfect moment?"

"Because we might not have another one." She hurried past that possibility. She and Fred were going to have lots of moments. Her headstrong side would make sure of it. "And because the answer is yes. Yes, I want to marry you. As soon as possible." She rubbed her face against his belly. "How's it going down there? Are my limbs intact? I'd really like to be able to walk down the aisle at my wedding."

"Already planning the wedding, huh?" He grunted with the strain of digging with no leverage. "Women."

"Hey, I've got to think about something while I'm lying here like a sardine in a can."

"Try thinking about moving your legs."

She tugged her right leg toward her chest. It came free easily, but more debris tumbled down to fill the space. Wincing, she felt some of it collide with her other leg. "Better keep digging unless you want a one-legged bride."

"I'll take you however I can get you," he told her between grunts. "But you're not losing a leg on my watch. Your dad would kick my ass. He might refuse to let me marry you."

"Oh no. Dad has nothing to do with this. Did you know that I told him I'm not taking his money anymore? I'm no longer a rich girl. I'm on my own. I really think I can make the Refuge work and pay myself a salary. It might take me a little while, but I know I can do it."

"Of course you can. Anyway, I can support us.

And if we live at my house, the Sinclair kids can take care of security." She giggled, thinking that sounded like pure heaven. Fred loosened some of the debris still pinning her left leg. His body felt so good against hers, so alive and warm and *breathing*.

Starting to feel a little faint, she took as deep a breath as she could manage. She wasn't sure what was happening, why she was so dizzy, but she wasn't going to take any chances. "I love you and I want to marry you. Don't forget. Whatever happens, don't forget."

And then a black river was sweeping her away in its fast, swirling current.

After Rachel fell silent, the flashlight dropping to an un-helpful angle, Fred worked as quickly as he could. He could feel the shallow rise of her chest against his torso, which was enormously reassuring. He dug away as much of the debris as he could, then wormed his way back toward the opening, enough so he could drag her right leg out of its confinement. He had to tug hard, but finally she was free.

"I'm going to pull you out now," he whispered. "Hang on, my sweet girl."

He arranged her arms over her head, took hold of her wrists, and began working his way backward past the inflated, Teflon-coated air bags, pulling her along, slowly but surely. Behind him, at the entrance of this narrow, makeshift tunnel, the rest of the crew stood waiting to grab his feet and pull him free. Before him, gripped tightly in his hands, he held his future. Nothing, not the sprays of dust that kept cascading onto him, not the aftershock that sent his heart into his mouth, not the scrape of exposed nails against his forearms, would stop him from bringing Rachel out safely. Four more feet . . . three more feet . . . two more feet . . . Sweat dripped down his neck from pulling both himself and Rachel. His muscles screamed for relief. His vision wavered, going sparkly around the edges.

Then strong hands were gripping his ankles. He was being gently but firmly pulled along the narrow passage. *Hold on to Rachel*, he told himself. *That's all you have to do. Hold on. They'll do the rest. You can trust them with your life . . . with her life . . . our life . . .*

The fresh open air greeted him like a blast from a water hose. Noise surrounded him. People yelling, a medevac chopper coming in for a landing, Greta's excited barking.

"Hey!" A shout as the dog broke free. A cold nose nuzzled him, then a warm, eager tongue swiped his cheek, over and over again.

"Greta, girl," he said, with an attempt at a laugh that came out more as a bleat. "I'm okay. I'm okay." Satisfied, Greta moved on to Rachel, just emerging from the rubble. She draped her warm, wiggly body across her beloved owner's chest. Fred let go of Rachel's hands and tried to pull himself onto his knees, only to groan from the pain.

"Someone grab the dog," he called. Rachel needed medical assessment before any more doggie love.

"You reopened your head wound," came the rough voice of Mulligan. He was kneeling next to Fred, doing a quick check of his injuries. "It's always something with you and that girl."

"Mulligan? What are you doing here?" He stared, bewildered, at the rugged, broken-nose face of the newest member of Station 1. Behind Mulligan, he could see the USAR crew extracting the air bags, and two San Gabriel police officers.

"Vader sent me. Every firefighter in town called

in so we have hands to spare. So you got mine, baby. The USAR crew has to take off, but I'm staying."

The paramedic at Rachel's side gave a thumbs-up. "Your girl's pulse is thready but she's okay, Freddie."

Rachel made a soft sound. Fred, forgetting the pain in his knees, scrambled to her side, followed by Mulligan.

"Sweetie? Did you say something? Are you awake?"

"Fi . . ." She mumbled.

Fred, completely mystified, looked at Mulligan. "Can you understand what she's saying?"

"I heard an F and an S. French fries? Are you hungry, Kessler? Did you work up an appetite under all that rubble?"

Rachel pushed the EMT's hand from her throat and sat up. "I said," she said, coughing. "I'm not just his girl. I'm his fiancée." Fred put his arm around her, supporting her while she hacked up more dust.

"Okay then. Fiancée. Good work, Freddie-boy." Mulligan slapped him on the back, making him cough too. "You work fast, bro. Not everyone crawls into a collapsed building and comes out engaged. No wonder they call you the Bachelor Hero."

"Shut up, Mulligan." Fred kept his focus on Rachel, tenderly smoothing the hair from her face, brushing mortar crumbs from her cheeks. In the harsh light of the spotlight the crew had set up, her eyes glimmered with a glorious, mysterious violet sheen.

"Or what? You'll beat my ass?" One look from Fred had Mulligan backing down. "Right. You will. You can. But you won't, since I just saved *your* ass, and I think that earns me a spot in the wedding party and . . ."

But Fred didn't hear the rest, because Rachel had

taken his face between her hands and was kissing him so deep and hard, he forgot where he was. He could have been back under the rubble, in Rachel's elevator, or in a bumper car, for all he knew. The only thing that mattered was he was with Rachel, she was alive, and they could hold each other and love each other until the sun rose and set and rose again.

Chapter 32

San Gabriel was hit hard by the quake, which the United States Geological Survey named the Los Feliz Earthquake, after the neighborhood of its epicenter. Dozens of people were injured, a hundred homes damaged beyond repair. Two overpasses collapsed and much of the city lost power for up to twenty-four hours. But thanks to the dogged efforts of the city's first responders and emergency workers, no lives were lost. Stories would be told for decades about the neonatal intensive care unit nurses, who carried each tiny patient to safety after a gas leak was discovered at Good Samaritan. Grocery stores handed out food and water, restaurants brewed endless pots of coffee, residents brought blankets and snacks to the overcrowded shelters.

Rachel had never loved her adopted city more.

After making sure she was in good medical hands, Fred reported to duty with the USAR team and spent the next long hours going from one hard-hit neighborhood to another, helping trapped victims and putting out fires.

As soon as Rachel was released from the emergency room, she went straight to the makeshift pet shelter to tend to the panicked animals rescue workers kept bringing in. A news crew showed up, shooting a story for their twenty-four-hour coverage of the earthquake. Recognizing her, the reporter made a beeline in her direction.

Facing the camera, Rachel took a deep breath and embraced her new existence, that of a public person with a meaningful mission. She explained how she was helping the animals and what people should do if they were missing a pet. She offered a list of supplies the shelter needed. When the reporter asked her to spell her name for the camera, she didn't hesitate.

Rachel Kessler, she told him. *San Gabriel resident.*

Her father arrived soon after. Since the shelter was a madhouse and terribly stinky, she met him outside, where he leaned against his black sedan. At the haunted look on his face, she burst into tears. He strode toward her, enfolded her into a long, hard hug, and poured out a stream of apologies.

"Stop it, Dad," she said, finally pulling away and wiping the tears off her cheeks. "It wasn't your fault."

"We investigated the Zander family seventeen years ago, but everyone checked out. We should have run a report on the entire police department when you came here. Sneaky rat-weasel."

"It wouldn't have made a difference. I bet he joined later, after I decided to stay."

"Smart girl." And he hugged her again. "You're tougher than he is, you proved it. Twice now. Don't mess with a Kessler. Look at you, safe and sound."

"Fred deserves a little credit for that too. It's not every day your office falls on top of you."

"Sure." He gave an expansive gesture to include the entire town. "I figured a donation to the San Gabriel Fire Department should do the trick."

Rachel put her hands on her hips and shook her head at her father. "I had a different idea. I'm going to marry him."

"*Marry* him?" The black wings of his eyebrows pulled together in a frown. "That's going a little far, don't you think? Marry a fireman?"

"Marry *Fred* the Fireman," she corrected. "The fireman I'm in love with. He's no ordinary guy, you know."

"I know." The frown cleared from his face. "At this point, I'm not sure I'd trust anyone else in the world with my daughter. I just hope he knows what he's getting into." He winked.

"What's that supposed to mean?"

"You're on the willful side. Hardheaded. When you were little, you never did as you were told. Always tearing about the place like a little wild thing. Never could keep you in one place. But I realized something." He took her by both shoulders and fixed her with that intense, unblinking stare.

"What?"

"I never should have tried." He shifted his feet, looking nothing like the powerful visionary who'd faced down Congress. "I let you down once, letting you get taken. I didn't want to fail my daughter again."

"Oh Dad." She curled her hand around his forearm, savoring his familiarity, the citrusy scent of his aftershave, the nervous energy he always radiated. "You never failed me. I just need more—"

"You need to live. I see that. You need to reach

for the stars and follow your passion and fall in love and whatever the hell else you think of. You're going to do great things, Rachel, all on your own. Without your paranoid parent. I suppose you're keeping the fireman around. So be it. Where is he, by the way? I want to thank him personally."

"He's . . ." She gestured at South Harlow Street, which was still eerily empty compared to the usual bustle of midday. "Out rescuing someone or putting out a fire. Being a hero. That's what he is, even though it's hard for him to admit it."

"Hmm."

"I love you, Dad."

"Me too, honey. Me too."

Before they set a wedding date, Fred insisted on one more thing. One night about two weeks after the earthquake, he dragged her to Lucio's Ristorante Autentico Italiano, the restaurant owned by former fire chief Rick Roman. At an intimate cushioned booth, by the light of a wall sconce adorned with plastic grapevines, sat four women. Baskets of garlic bread and glasses of red wine cluttered the table. The only woman she recognized was Melissa, who stood up and ushered her into the booth.

"We'll take it from here, Fred," Melissa told him. "You can go."

"What's going on?" Rachel asked, slightly panicked to see Fred back away from the booth, leaving her with a bunch of unfamiliar women who seemed to mean business. He gave a quick wave and disappeared. The dark-haired girl next to her smiled and pushed a glass of red wine toward her. Rachel took a long sip, peering around at the group.

"Fred wants us to make sure you know the

down-and-dirty truth about being married to a fireman before you take the ultimate step," explained
Melissa, sliding next to her. "That's Katie Blake next
to you, she's married to Ryan, who used to be at the
1's before he started the new academy."

Petite and dark-eyed, with inky black eyebrows,
Katie looked like a live wire, someone who would
be really fun to have around. She gave Rachel a
jaunty little two-fingered salute of greeting.

Melissa turned to the lovely, lush-figured woman
right across from her. She had pink-streaked blond
hair piled on her head. "This is Cherie, she's married to Vader, the captain on the engine company."

Cherie offered up a friendly smile and said, with
a slight down-South accent, "Pleasure to meet the
girl who won our Freddie's heart."

"Sabina wanted to be here, since she can offer
a unique perspective, being a firefighter *and* married to a firefighter, or at least a former one. But the
crew's kind of busy, so she couldn't make it. Next to
Cherie, we have Dr. Lara Nelson, Psycho's wife, who
took a break from helping out at the rescue shelters.
She drove all the way from Nevada to volunteer her
medical skills."

A gorgeous amber-eyed, blond woman, Lara
leaned forward and patted her on the hand. "Sorry
to ambush you like this. But none of us can turn
down Fred. You know how it is."

"Fred dragged you into this?"

"Yes," answered Melissa. "My friend Nita Moreno,
who's married to Jeb Stone, wanted to come too, but
she's busy at the mayor's office dealing with the press.
Thor's wife Maribel isn't getting in until tonight. She's
flying in from Alaska just to lend a hand."

Rachel counted up all the women who'd been
mentioned. Melissa, Katie, Cherie, Lara, Sabina, Ma-

ribel, and Nita. "So all of you are married to firemen and you're supposed to tell me why it's a bad idea? Talk me out of it or something?"

The women exchanged a cautious look. "There are probably certain things you should be aware of," said Lara. "For instance, during wildfire season, I worry all the time."

"It's almost like sending your husband off to war every other day," agreed Cherie. "And the annoying thing is, they love it. If you're thinking you'll get him to quit, forget about it."

"I'm not—"

"They think it's their job to save the whole world," interrupted Melissa. "It makes them overprotective and maybe . . . dare I say, bossy?"

The other women murmured their agreement. Katie raised her hand. "Getting married to a firefighter is like marrying into a whole new set of brothers. And I already have enough brothers, let me tell you. The firehouse is like a frat house sometimes."

"Other girls will flirt with him," threw in Cherie. "Hose chasers, some people call them. If you're the jealous type, you might have a problem."

If she could handle Fred's fan club, she could handle anything. "I'm really not—"

"You have to be okay with being alone," added Melissa. "They work overnight shifts at least two nights a week. With the baby and Danielle, sometimes that's tough."

"I'm very used to being—" But they were on a roll now and Rachel couldn't get a word in edgewise.

"But then their shift is over and they're home for four days, practically bouncing off the walls. So you have to like that too," said Cherie.

"That doesn't sound so—"

"If they catch a bad call, it stays with them for a long time. And each firefighter handles it differently," said Melissa. "Sometimes I wish I could be out there in the middle of it all, instead of home worrying."

"They're adrenaline junkies. Type A personalities. Alpha males," said Lara thoughtfully. "And they're never really off the job."

Katie nodded in agreement. "If you're at a restaurant and someone starts choking, boom, there goes your guy."

"Right. It's not just fires. If someone's robbing the 7–Eleven, they'll charge right in like it's their personal business," said Cherie. "And if it's something medical, they think they know it all."

And then they started in for real, talking over each other, while Rachel took refuge in her wine.

" . . . knot in your stomach whenever you hear the siren going by . . ."

" . . . has anyone mentioned the smell? Sweat and retardant and . . ."

" . . . better get along with the other fire wives . . ."

" . . . right, because there goes the rest of your social life . . ."

" . . . I check the news a lot more often . . ."

" . . . they miss birthdays and anniversaries . . ."

" . . . constant laundry."

The women took a collective pause for breath.

"Then again," said Katie thoughtfully. "When Ryan comes home, I'm so happy he's okay, I can't get enough of him. So I guess there's a silver lining."

"Oh yes, it's like makeup sex *every* time Vader comes home from a shift," agreed Cherie.

"Really? Then it's not just me and Brody?" asked Melissa.

"Oh no. Hot sex. *Very* hot sex," Lara said, with a sound almost like a purr. "You know what they say about danger enhancing the libido. I think it's scientifically proven."

Rachel was pretty sure her face had turned as red as the vinyl booth.

"And their hearts are in the right place," said Katie. "They're good men, they really are."

"The absolute best," said Melissa.

"No argument there," murmured Cherie. "You can count on them to your last breath. I wouldn't want anyone else as the father of my future child."

"What? You're pregnant?" Katie gave an exuberant squeal, and all the women turned to Cherie with delight.

"Figured I'd better explain why I passed on that wine. Y'all know I've never done that before."

"I didn't want to say anything, but of course I noticed," said Melissa.

"You and your evil reporter ways," Cherie teased.

"So." Lara turned laughing eyes on Rachel. "Did we talk you out of it?"

Rachel opened her mouth, closed it again, fighting the smile that threatened to split her face wide open. "I think I get the picture."

"More wine?" Katie refilled her glass. "Because now we have some questions for you."

By the time Rachel stumbled out of Lucio's into the fresh, starlit night, she had a pretty good buzz on. Fred was leaning against his truck, waiting for her. He looked a little worried, so she skipped across the sidewalk and threw herself into his embrace. Even though he had no warning, he caught her.

"What did they tell you?" He wrapped his strong arms around her.

"The truth, the whole truth, and nothing but the truth," she intoned drunkenly.

"Oh no, they gave you wine. I should have warned them about that."

"They're beautiful. *You're* beautiful. I love you. With my heart, my whole heart, and nothing but my heart." Rising on tiptoe, she scattered kisses along his jaw. "Okay, my body too."

"So we're still getting married?"

"If you were trying to talk me out of it, you'll have to try harder than that."

"It's not that I was trying—"

"No, no, I get it. You wanted to do the honorable thing, because you're Fred and that's how you are. Strong and true and kind and honorable. I never even dreamed of a man like you. But here you are." She blinked. "You're still here." Blinked again. "Still here."

"Just how buzzed are you?"

"Buzzed enough to know we belong together. Same as when I'm not buzzed." She snuggled even closer and threw her whole heart and soul into the smile she aimed up at him. "You know what I wish we could do? I wish you'd take me home so we can have hot makeup sex even though we haven't exactly had a fight, but maybe we could have that other fight again, the one about Kale and the kidnapping, and *then* we could have hot makeup sex and—*oof.*"

He swooped her into his arms and swung open the door of his truck.

"What are you doing?"

"Speeding things up." He plopped her onto the seat and jogged to the driver's side. When he slid inside and closed the door, his presence seemed to fill the cab of his workaday truck with enchanted starlight.

"Where are you taking me?"

"Where you belong. With me."

She sighed deeply and scooted closer to him. "Good answer."